FINDING VERITY

Jenny Loudon

○○○ WHITE MOTH PUBLISHING ○○○

Published in 2017 by White Moth Publishing, United Kingdom.

ISBN: 978-1-9998630-0-5 (paperback)

ISBN: 978-1-9998630-1-2 (e-book)

For my beautiful family, Oaks, Laura, Ollie, Ellen, Hux,

Rosie and Jack,

and last but not least, for Sparrows, my rock

'Tell me, what is it you plan to do with your
one wild and precious life?'

Mary Oliver

1

Verity danced, body rippling, arms raised. The room swam and she laughed. Stopping abruptly, she squinted at a cluster of people gathered at the dark edge of the basement, attempting to spot her new boyfriend, wanting to wave him over to dance with her. He was nowhere to be seen. Picking up the rhythm again, Verity twirled, holding her arms out. Another lusty laugh rose from inside her. The music lurched and stopped. Someone fumbled to change a cassette. Others who were dancing groaned. Verity stood still but the room spun on, a blur of dusty concrete floor littered with cigarette butts, a sea of other people's bodies. Someone bumped into her, making her stagger as she pushed her fingers back through sweaty tendrils of hair. She needed air.

'Allow me,' a voice said.

The music began again, a raunchy, soulful tune. The energy in the basement became languorous. An arm snaked around her back.

'I love Annie Lennox,' she murmured, more to herself than to the man. The stranger held her firmly, and she leant into his embrace; not something she would normally do. She was a tall woman, but the man was taller and broad-shouldered. Her cheek brushed against a leather jacket; it smelt divinely of wood smoke and a faint scent that conjured foreign places. The stranger's dark eyes dazzled her before he lowered his gaze, and pulled her closer. He danced

1

wonderfully, in time with the music. Verity loosened her grip on the leather jacket, and began to enjoy herself.

'What's your name?' she shouted above the volume of music.

'Edward.'

'Posh name, Edward.'

Edward raised an eyebrow, a small smile curling at the corners of his mouth.

'Can I call you Ed or Eddie?'

'I'd rather you didn't.'

'Surely not Ted? That's even posher.'

'Edward. Just Edward.'

'You're American?'

'Yes.'

'That explains it.'

'Explains what?'

'Everything!' Verity peeled away from the man, gyrating, her arms outspread, long hair lifting as she whirled. She wondered if Matt watched her. Was he the type to mind her dancing with another man? She had not known him long enough to judge.

'Lost someone?' Edward's hands pressed either side of her waist.

'Aren't you hot in this thing?' She plucked at the leather jacket.

'I'm not sure I've ever been hot in England.'

'What are you doing here, anyway? Are you one of Alison's friends? You look like you might be.'

'Alison invited me here, yes.'

'Are you one of her flashy new work colleagues?'

'No.'

'Oh.'

'You ask a lot of questions.'

'Just want to know who I'm dancing with.'

'Don't talk, just dance. You're very good at it.' His spread hand warmed the small of her back through her thin top.

'Were you watching me?'

'I was.'

'That's weird.'

Edward took a swift step back and held up his hands. Without his body as ballast, Verity swayed. She narrowed her eyes, and reached for him. He stood back, arms folded, and studied her quietly. 'Half the room was looking at you,' he remarked steadily.

2

'Okay, sorry. I need some air.'

'Come this way.' Edward's fingers curled protectively around hers as he led the way to a door at the far end of the basement. He walked quickly and she stumbled.

'Are you okay?'

'Yes.' In the garish light beside the door, Verity took in the full sight of his smooth brown skin, shaggy dark hair, and the healthy shine in his eyes. There was something bear-like about him, definitely foreign. Heat rose in her cheeks.

'Those are some shoes.' He looked down.

'Thank you.' She tried to smile, but felt queasy.

'Come on, you need to get outside.'

They climbed a set of stone steps and reached a long narrow stretch of overgrown grass, setting off down it, away from the party and the noise. At the point where illumination from the house dispersed and the garden became shadowy, there was a wooden bench, blackened with damp and patchy with lichen. A full moon shone down. Verity broke free of Edward's hold, dropped abruptly onto the bench and put her head in her hands. He followed and sat close beside her. She lifted her chin to the night air, and took a few deep, clarifying breaths. He rested his forearms on his thighs and clasped his hands together. They sat for a few moments in blessed silence while Edward studied the night sky and the higgledy-piggledy rear facade of neighbouring houses, and Verity tried to ignore the ringing in her ears and the nausea in her stomach. Eventually she stood up and wobbled across the bumpy, ill-cut grass on her ridiculous heels. Beyond a couple of shrubs, the garden fell into pitch darkness, and after scanning the area to make sure no-one could see her, she unzipped her jeans and squatted down.

'Are you peeing behind there?' Edward's voice, soft in the darkness.

'Maybe.'

His quiet laughter rolled out across the dark garden, and the sound of it made Verity smile. Having relieved herself and hauled up her jeans, she stumbled back and sat down beside him, and he shrugged off his jacket, and put it around her shoulders.

'Thanks. Don't you need it?'

'No, I'm fine. You need it more.'

'So, tell me, how *do* you know Alison?'

3

'I met her in a bar.'

'Alison likes handsome men in bars.'

'You're saying I'm handsome?'

'I'm saying that Alison would find you handsome.'

'Ha, you don't give much away, do you?' A smile played around his lips.

'Edward, are you married?'

'God, you're nosey.'

'I'm protecting my friend. There's a pale band of skin where a wedding band might go, right there on your hand.'

'I'm divorcing.'

'Sorry. Must be very recent.'

'No worries. It is.'

He took a deep breath, and Verity stared at her own hands before tucking them into her armpits. 'Apologies if I touched a nerve. I sometimes open my mouth before I think.'

'No big deal.' Edward flicked a bit of lichen off the arm of the bench.

'What brings you to London then?'

'The weather.' He laughed quietly, his shoulders shaking.

'Ha, ha.'

'Stop asking me questions.'

'I'm making conversation!'

'Well shush then, and listen.' He pointed a finger upwards, and raised his chin. Verity observed his profile, noted how the moonlight lit his jawline, how the shape of it was so clean and strong she would paint it with one swipe of her brush.

'There's the music from the party. And listen…' Edward leaned in, his face so close to hers that she inhaled the clean scent of his skin as she heard a plaintive mew.

'Yes!' she whispered, suddenly inexplicably excited. A cat appeared from the darkness, and wound itself around her legs. Its fur was damp with dew, and cat hairs stuck to her fingers. 'Aw, hello, sweetie,' she murmured, exchanging a glance with Edward. He smiled at her, a very nice, lazy smile, the sort of smile she could live with.

'Better,' Edward remarked. 'Who are you?' he added, suddenly, gently.

'Who am I?'

'Yes. I mean, what is your name?'

'My name is Verity.'

'Pretty name. You have beautiful hair.' He touched a long dark curl that reached halfway down her back.

'Thanks. And you, what are you *actually* doing here in London?'

'I came to visit my brother, but he isn't in town. On reflection, it might have been better to tell him I was coming.'

'Ah, yes, probably.'

'Are you feeling a bit better?'

'Yes. I drank too much. I'm not used to it.'

'Special occasion?'

'No reason. I just wanted to cut loose for a bit. Do you ever get that feeling?'

'Yes, I do.'

Verity ran her fingers back through her hair, conscious of him studying her. When their eyes met, their gaze held. Her attention was drawn to his lips, before she turned away and stared up at the night sky. 'How long have you been here?'

'Since yesterday. I'm only here for two nights. I'm off to Berlin in the morning.'

'Why Berlin?'

'I'm a journalist, and there's a lot of civil unrest there, big changes afoot.'

Verity nestled into the leather jacket, and leant back against the bench. The cat, having finished fastidiously washing itself, tiptoed away across the grass. Between scrawny, scudding clouds, the moon reappeared, its luminescence temporarily bathing the garden in white light.

'I bet you have a good way with people. I bet you can get them talking.'

'That's what I do. I tell their stories. I roam and I write. And I'll never stop doing either.'

'How very wonderful.' Verity squeezed Edward's hand where it rested on the bench. He rubbed his thumb over her fingers, and then traced her arm with his fingertips before drawing her towards him. Their lips touched. He is the one, she thought absurdly; he is the one.

'Verity?' Matt's voice, his heavy footfall on the basement steps. She pulled back, and snatched her arm from around Edward.

'What's going on here then?' Matt asked, squinting into the darkness. He was unsteady on his feet, quite drunk, Verity noticed. She stood up, and wobbled over the bumpy grass toward him.

'Matt, this is Edward. Edward, Matt – my boyfriend.'

'Ah,' Edward murmured, and gave her a significant look. 'Your boyfriend.'

'Yes.'

'How do you do?' Matt reached towards Edward, who ignored the proffered hand and nodded. 'Aren't you the chap our charming hostess dragged in from the pub? She's looking for you.'

Matt's relaxed drawl suggested that he had not actually seen her kissing the stranger, and Verity's tension uncurled a little. 'He is. Alison found him in a bar,' she answered for Edward.

'I'd like to be going,' Matt said, glancing at the leather jacket with a questioning look.

'I wasn't feeling too good. I couldn't find you. Edward here has been looking after me.' Verity shrugged off the jacket and offered it back to Edward. As he took it, their fingers touched and the night air chilled her shoulders, making her shiver. She folded her arms, and carefully studied the matted grass at her feet, longing to grab the garment back.

'Thanks,' she said.

'You're welcome,' Edward murmured, adding, 'any time.' Their eyes met and their gaze lingered. Verity shook her head. She should never drink so much.

'Come on then,' Matt insisted amiably, unaware of the emotion that thickened the air.

'I guess it's goodbye then.' Edward's words drilled into her. Goodbye was not right, not yet, not now.

'Yes.' She frowned, and her throat tightened as she imagined Edward disappearing to Berlin or wherever, never to be seen again. She glanced at him once more. He observed her coolly, waiting, but she wrenched herself away, striding out over the garden, leaning on Matt, and leaving so much unsaid that she thought she might explode. She had a new boyfriend who was kind, caring, and decent; she was not the type who messed people around, she told herself. Edward was merely a test, and she would not let her head be turned by any handsome man who crossed her path.

6

In the taxi back to Matt's flat, she reminded herself that if in doubt, it was always best to do the right thing, and the right thing in this case was to go home with Matt. Despite her determination, a rogue voice in her head shrieked that she was being utterly stupid and making the biggest mistake of her life.

As Matt fumbled to open the door to his neat little flat, Verity was filled with the urge to run, and imagined dashing back through inky streets to Edward, to his scent and the knowing look in his eyes. But Matt stepped aside and politely gestured for her to enter the flat before him, and she did. When Matt made love to her that night – gently, sweetly, thoughtfully – Verity imagined Edward; and in the morning, after a dead sleep brought on by exhaustion and alcohol, she woke early. The dull grey light of an autumnal dawn seeped around flimsy bedroom curtains, and the street outside was quiet. Matt lay fast asleep, arm flung out across the bed, mouth open. Verity slid carefully from under the duvet, wriggled noiselessly into her jeans and tugged on some Converse boots, roughly tying the laces. In the cramped hallway, she pulled a coat over the t-shirt she had slept in. Once out of the flat, she fled. She didn't even take the key Matt had recently given her or pause to brush her hair or teeth; she simply ran, and carried on running the mile or so through the Sunday morning streets back to Alison's basement flat. Her mouth dried, her throat grew sore, and her lungs ached with the effort. She did not care if Edward had stayed with Alison. Alison slept with everyone, it hardly mattered. All she knew was that she wanted to be with him again. She *had* to see him. She had never been more certain of anything in her whole life.

'He went,' Alison said, looking blankly at her. 'He didn't stay. He left.'

2

It was in the midst of the pre-wedding frenzy that Edward Farrell returned to London, on a blustery day towards the end of March 1990 when showers squalled and blackened the London streets, and an icy wind snaked through the city.

'How did you find me?'

'I went back to the place where the party was, and begged your friend.'

'Ah.'

Verity noticed Edward's attention drift towards the gleaming ring that hung heavily on her finger. He blinked slowly before his eyes sought hers.

'You're married?'

'Engaged. The wedding is in July.'

'Quick.'

'Five months actually. Matt proposed to me after five months. It's not as quick as all that. And Matt wants it this way. I mean, we both want it this way. And if I'm going to do it, it might as well be sooner rather than later, right? No point in waiting,' Verity gabbled, unravelling at the sight of Edward in his jeans and leather jacket, a scarf wrapped casually around his sensational, stubbled jawline. His eyes glittered and his mouth formed a stubborn line while his long hair blew in the city wind. If she had a stick of charcoal, she would sketch him rapidly, to capture his magnificent defiance.

'And yet you agreed to meet me?'

Verity frowned, and tucked a stray lock of hair behind one ear. 'Surely we're allowed to have lunch?'

'Lunch. Of course. Why not?'

They wandered down a crowded street, jostled and separated by a throng of office workers heading in the opposite direction, all in a hurry. Verity did not know where they should go to eat or what she was doing, really. Her heart had leapt so high at the sound of Edward's voice on her office telephone less than an hour before that she had simply said 'Yes' to his request immediately, before reason had entered her head.

'Here, let's get off this thoroughfare,' Edward muttered, and took her hand as if it was his to take, leading her into a quieter side street. 'That's better.'

They ate lunch in a little Italian restaurant and shared a bottle of wine. Verity used the restaurant phone to call her office, saying she was going home with a headache. After lunch, they walked in Hyde Park, eventually sitting down on a bench. She turned up the collar of her coat, and Edward put his arm around her, and drew her to him as if it was the most natural gesture in the world. He tried to warm her hands with his. After a short time, they agreed it was foolish to sit still on such a frigid afternoon, and hired a rowing boat on the Serpentine. They splashed each other playfully with arcs of icy droplets that sparkled in the sunshine, and Verity sang 'Row Your Boat' raucously. It struck her that she rarely laughed and messed around in such a way with Matt; but she blanked out *that* disloyal thought as soon as it arose.

The sun sank behind buildings and a chilly wind whipped ever more busily between the parkland trees. Verity hugged herself as they lingered beside the edge of the lake after climbing out of the rowing boat. In a gesture that brought home the memory of their first meeting, Edward — who it seemed barely registered temperature — draped his jacket over the top of her thin coat. It was the same leather jacket, imbued with its alluring scents of wood smoke and spice and foreign lands. Some deeply-buried desire for adventure blazed inside Verity as she inhaled its exotic fragrance, and she suddenly longed to be out of the city and in a forest or a mountain range instead, somewhere wild and beautiful. Edward's handsome face and dishevelled dark hair aroused her creative

9

energy too, making it swell and spill over the edges of her mind so that she longed to express her emotion on a glorious, huge canvas.

As they walked through Hyde Park, Edward, perhaps not so impervious to the weather as Verity had imagined, hunched his shoulders against the cold.

'Take it back. You're freezing!' She wriggled out of the jacket and handed it to him.

'I'm a man. I can cope.' He shared a rich, lazy laugh.

He had told her earlier that he was staying in a hotel in Bayswater. 'Let's go to your hotel now. Warm up,' she suggested.

'But –'

'Let's just go.'

Edward inclined his head, and studied her silently for a moment before he took her hand again. They walked slowly at first. He stopped and kissed her beneath a plane tree, still bare-limbed after winter, its naked arms reaching for the sky. At the touch of their lips, fire burned in Verity's belly so fiercely that her knees weakened. She stretched up on her tiptoes and curved her arm around Edward's neck, pressing her mouth against his.

'Come on!' he murmured.

'Let's run!' she cried, and they raced hand-in-hand out of the park.

They were forced to stop and wait at a crossing, and Verity panted for breath. Edward's cheeks had turned pink. His eyes shone.

'How much further?'

'Not far, just over there.'

In the hotel room, Edward swept clothes and books off a rumpled bed cover, and turned to her; and as he did so, she was assaulted by a deep sense of wrongdoing.

'Are you sure?' Edward sensed her hesitation.

She held her breath, and spread her hand on her chest, frozen, as reality trickled through her body like iced water. 'I can't. Edward, I'm so sorry, I shouldn't be here. I can't.'

Edward stayed in London for a total of twenty days. They met again. The hotel room incident was not the way Verity wanted to leave things, at least that was what she told herself, and so after Edward had accompanied her back down to the hotel lobby, she had agreed to join him for a coffee a couple of days later. The coffee ended with a plan for lunch before the end of the week, and so it went on – a series of snatched and inexplicable moments that threaded through Verity's otherwise tedious life like a beautiful, multi-coloured ribbon. Edward did not once mention her refusal in his room, nor did he make her feel bad about it. They kept a small physical distance between them at all times, and chatted, sometimes for hours, about the unfolding political scene in Berlin, or the habits of dolphins, the architecture in Morocco, or the size of the sun in Africa – and Edward's stories of a world she could only imagine created vivid, enticing pictures in her mind. He told her about his brother Jay, recently returned from abroad and refurbishing a house in Putney, with whom he would stay in future – suggesting there was some kind of future for them. If Verity ever pondered the fact that while Edward made her spirits soar, Matt kept her focus firmly on the ground and the practicalities of their wedding plans, or if she once stopped to consider which relationship might in fact be best for her, she did not linger on the question for long because she always reached the same conclusion: after the childhood she'd had, she was now a person who valued stability. She prided herself in honouring her word and making rational decisions. Matt was stable and secure and decent – everything she needed, and he would not desert her in the way her father had deserted her mother. As for all the meetings with Edward, there was a simple explanation. He was her friend, and as she was not actually married yet and she was not sleeping with or (any more) kissing Edward, her 'secret' time with him was nobody's business. Edward had blown back into her life so unexpectedly, fragrant with foreign adventure, eyes glinting with worldly knowledge, that of course it was exciting; but while his presence thrilled her, it also made her wary. Edward would never settle. During their brief time together, she had noted the faraway look in his eyes, the constant fidgeting, the way a spark of information or a request from his agency had him contemplating instant flight, and she was not as adventurous – a part of her longed to be, but fear always held her back.

The day before Edward left for Europe again, they arranged to meet in a café in Covent Garden. As she approached the café, he came around a corner towards her, all smiles in the chilly street, and something about the enhanced red of his lips and his loose, lazy walk told her that he had been with another woman. As he bent to kiss her on the cheek, he smelt of sex. Inside the café, Verity excused herself and hid, appalled, in the women's toilets. She gripped a washbasin as emotions of every colour washed over her. Eventually, she stood upright, smoothed the palms of her hands over her face, and stared at her own reflection for some time. She told herself firmly that her hypocrisy was ridiculous.

'I thought you'd climbed out of a back window and done a runner,' Edward joked when she finally made it back to the table. 'Are you okay?'

What could she say? She hardly knew herself these days.

After his departure, her life settled as a steady work routine and evenings spent with Matt unrolled like a favourite old rug beneath her feet. There was much wedding talk in the air, and a heady sense of shared anticipation about their future together. Verity adored the fact that with each new day, she discovered more hidden tenderness beneath her future husband's handsome looks. Matt was attentive and delightful company; but as April became May, and just when the outside world brightened with the promise of better weather, Verity became inexplicably despondent. She pined to be anywhere but the dusty city, longed to escape to the countryside of her childhood, and eventually decided to take a weekend away by herself with her oldest and best friend, Stella.

As she drove along a road which curved down from the Chiltern Hills, the vastness of the Oxford plain came into view and almost took her breath away. Verity loved the great plain that stretched out before her eyes. It was a place where she had once been happy as a child, and the sight of it brought comfort flooding through her veins.

In her cottage kitchen, Stella busied around cooking spaghetti bolognaise. Her husband was in the village pub, and her baby was asleep upstairs. With her newfound responsibility, Stella struck Verity as suddenly very grown-up and capable, and after two glasses of wine, Verity found herself confessing to her own confusion and depression, and admitting how she missed the clandestine meetings with Edward.

'Since he went away, I miss him,' she stated, eyes blinking in bewilderment.

'Verity MacLeod, you dark horse. And Matt hasn't caught on that something's up?' Stella chewed a mouthful of spaghetti with gusto.

'No, why would he?'

'Well, that's true. Matt Westwood wouldn't notice emotion if it jumped up and hit him in the face.'

'What's that supposed to mean?'

'Oh, come on, Vet.'

'What d'you mean?'

'Well, he's not exactly a warm person, is he?'

'Of course he is.'

Stella let this trail of conversation go, and asked instead to hear more about Edward. Verity confessed there was nothing more to tell, as she hadn't heard a word from him since he had left.

'It's not too late to jump ship, you know,' Stella offered. 'If you're not sure about this wedding –'

'Stella, how can you even say that? As if I would!'

'Just saying… I never had you down for this posh London wedding scene, I must say,' Stella mused. 'I always thought you'd run away somewhere and wed romantically, in secret.'

'Matt doesn't want that.'

'No, I don't suppose he does.'

'And I'm just not bothered. I want to do what's right for both of us.'

'Oh well, here, have some sticky toffee pudding. I bought it from the Co-op, and I picked up some of that divine tinned custard too. Then we're going to finish off this wine, and I'm going to send you up to bed for an early night. You look like you need it, and I know I do.'

Whether it was the wine or the country air or simply the relief of sharing her secret, after guzzling the pudding, Verity's shoulders fell and she relaxed. She curled up on the sofa and listened to Stella's news while the baby slept on and Stella's husband still did not return from the pub; and a little later she snuggled under a duvet in her friend's tiny spare room and had the best night's sleep she'd had in weeks.

Throughout June, the weather in London was colder than average. Verity reprimanded herself for her low spirits and hoped word from Edward might cheer her up, but as time went by and he did not get in touch, she consoled herself that he was probably not the friend she had imagined. The wedding plans progressed smoothly under the steely guidance of her future mother-in-law and added yet more weight to the belief that everything in her life was

13

as it should be and her despondency was simply a case of pre-wedding nerves.

On the afternoon of Saturday, 14th July 1990, Verity approached the church of St Michael in Highgate, with its terrifying pointy-fingered spire, on the arm of her mother's brother, a man whom she barely knew. As they approached the church door, she allowed herself to think of her lost father for a moment before hastily shutting down the emotions such memories always inspired. Inside the church, Verity's mother Fiona MacLeod, Stella and her husband, and a scattering of Verity's friends from work were among the few people she recognised. Most of the pews were filled with banks of Matt's relatives whom she had never met. As she stood beside Matt, and the wedding ceremony marched swiftly on, her breathing became rapid. The rogue voice in her head lamented that marriage vows were so absolute and urged her to reconsider before it was too late. It would be a dreadful thing, but she could still run. She shook her head at such an appalling notion, and heeding her own sense of decency, took a deep breath, and whispered 'I do' to Matt.

Verity stripped the spare bedroom of their new flat in Islington, set up her easel and bought a cupboard from a junk shop to house her art materials. She painted vast brightly-coloured canvases of people and landscapes. Matt complained about the smell of her oil paints and the mess she made. There were, he complained, finger-prints and splatters of paint on their mugs and plates, Verity frequently had paint smudges in her hair which he really did not find attractive, and she had been late to meet him too – more than once – because she was painting. The regular disapproval in Matt's beautiful china blue eyes eventually began to spoil her studio time. Verity found that she watched the clock so that she would never be late again, and tried not to get paint on herself or their crockery. She was reminded of the days when her father would let her mother and her down in some way because of a painting he was working on, and how frustrating it had been for them. Verity might share the same passion for art as her father but she would deal with it in a better way. She would limit her artwork, and prioritise her marriage (unlike her father) because it was the fair thing to do.

One night, sitting on a kitchen stool with a mug of hot chocolate cradled in her hands, alone and unable to sleep, Verity listened to the night sounds of Islington – a siren's wail, the hiss of wet tyres on tarmac, distant roadworks. She had asked Matt about when they might move out to the countryside, as they had always planned. She longed to spend weekends outdoors with her easel and to find a job somewhere local so that one day they could start a family and raise their children in a village, the way they had always dreamed. Matt had replied that he was not ready for a commute 'just yet'. Verity reflected on how quickly they had established a dynamic on this particular touchy subject – one where she nagged and he became instantly defensive.

On occasion, Matt arrived at the flat with flowers, and literally swept her off her feet with his embrace. He would insist they made love, there and then, on the rug in the tiny sitting room, and Verity would laugh, delighted by her husband's spontaneity. At parties, he would watch her dance, and applaud her with a big grin on his face. At times like these, and usually after plenty of wine had been drunk, Matt told Verity she was beautiful and meant the world to him. He confided that his friends fancied her, and his chest swelled as he reflected on his good luck. Verity was grateful and appreciative of her lovely new husband, and all the insecurities of her past began to rise like butterflies off a summer meadow and flutter away.

1990 drew to a close. Verity decorated the rest of the flat and planned their first Christmas together, but as December progressed, it became apparent that they were expected at her in-law's house on Christmas Day, and Matt refused to listen to her objections, insisting this was the way his family always spent Christmas. When the great day arrived, Verity felt nauseous and exhausted. She put it down to her annoyance, but as she tried to pull on a skirt, she noticed the waistband appeared tight. She vowed to diet, but then on Boxing Day morning, was sick in the toilet. When the surgery reopened after the holiday, a doctor confirmed that she was pregnant.

At the beginning of March 1991, Edward landed in London and called Verity at her office. They met in the café in Covent Garden. His skin was tanned and he was unshaven. His dark hair was shaggy and bleached chestnut at the ends. He had just arrived in the country and had come straight to see her, he said, and then he noticed her tiny swollen belly as she peeled off her coat. His features froze and he swallowed hard. Though not a word was spoken, Verity knew instinctively that her pregnancy marked some kind of ending for Edward. He reared his head like a startled animal and took a step backward. His eyes met hers, shot through with confusion, and he gestured to the café door.

'I just have to…' he stammered.

He strode out without looking back, turning left abruptly outside the café door and disappearing from view. Verity ordered coffee, and sat and waited to see whether he would return, her heart flattened with a bleak, indefinable emotion, her swollen belly tense. She sat in front of the two full mugs until the drinks turned cold.

3

Fulham, 2013

'I want to talk with you, Matt. We agreed we would move to Oxfordshire when Tills started university, but you've been avoiding the issue.' Verity kept her voice calm and measured, and spread her slender fingers flat on the table either side of her dinner plate. The pendant kitchen lamp, a feature of their newly remodelled kitchen, cast a pool of elegant light over a smart birch dining table. Verity held her husband's gaze steadily although the reproach in his china blue eyes threatened to disarm her, as always.

'But babes, look around you, this is fabulous.'

'Not to me, it's not.'

'But you designed it – it's a testament to your genius.'

'Designing places like this is my job. You know I don't actually like to live with this stuff; it's simply what sells.'

'Oh, V, are you sure you don't love it, just a little bit? I do.'

'Matt, come on. We didn't spend all this money as a luxury for ourselves; we made a calculated investment.'

'I think it's really stylish.'

'It's grossly opulent. Give me a cottage kitchen with a treasured Aga, mismatched cupboards and a scrubbed wooden table any day.'

'I thought you'd grown out of all that hippy stuff.'

'Look, we've been through all this before. This house is ready now, and we agreed that as soon as it was we'd sell it, but for some reason I'm not very clear about you're digging your heels in.'

'It's a risk.'

'No, it isn't.' Verity tucked a strand of hair behind her ear and clasped the table edge. 'You know as well as I do that we'll make enough profit here to cushion us financially until I can start to make some money from selling my paintings.'

'Oh, I don't know.' His chin lowered, pleating the skin on his neck.

'Matt, I need to make this move – you know I do. I promised myself. I've been hanging on for this moment for years.'

'It's just such a lunatic idea. I love the city. I don't want to go and live in some cow field and have to commute every day.'

'But ever since we had the girls I've wanted to live in the countryside and work as an artist, and we put it off because you promised me that when Tills started university, we'd move. And you've watched me spend the past year getting the house in shape, on top of working flat-out with my business. I've worked bloody hard to make this happen.'

'If it's just about your painting, you've managed a couple of exhibitions over the years and you can do more now the girls are grown up. We can stay here, enjoy the fun and entertainment in the city, and you can run your business, and you'll have spare time to paint.'

'You are not listening to me. If I give it my best effort, I still have time to begin a second career, Matt. I don't want to dabble! I can't possibly run my business and put the hours into painting as well. Now the girls have both left home and we're in a strong financial position, I want to try.'

'Can't you do it here, without us selling the house? There must be a less drastic alternative.' Matt washed his food down with a loud gulp of beer.

'We couldn't afford to live here if I sold my business! And anyway, I hate city life and always have done – and you know that. I've only lived here all these years because you wanted to. I only did it for you, or are you forgetting that?'

'But babes, you've been such a success. Om Interiors is thriving! Everyone loves your designs.' The familiar rakish smile stretched across his face.

'Don't turn the charm on me, Matt, because it won't work. I can't believe you're trying to back out of this!' Verity glared. 'Look, the market has picked up. There's a huge demand for these houses. We'll make a fortune selling it now.'

'I'm just not ready.'

'But we *agreed*!' She leant forward. 'We agreed,' she repeated.

'I never thought you'd actually want to go through with it.'

Verity's fists curled. 'That's not true! At one point, you were as excited as I was.'

'I never was, not really.'

Verity closed her eyes and shook her head. 'Okay, well even if you have changed your mind, you have to change it back again and do this for me. I want to live in a place where I can get outdoors to paint whenever the light is right, a place where there is inspiration all around me, a house that is mortgage-free, that we can afford on your salary. I need, want, *have* to paint landscapes, *en plein air*. I've stuck by you and lived in this bloody city for years, and it's my turn now.'

'Well, we'll see. Tills only left this morning, and you're being very emotional – and way too fast off the starting blocks. There's no rush.'

'This is going to happen!' Verity thumped the table. 'I'm getting the estate agent round to value the place this week. I'm beginning the process.'

'Don't do that, V.' Matt shook his head, leant back in his chair, and folded his arms across his belly, handsome jaw jutting forward.

'Yes, I am doing it.' Verity's eyes flashed, and the strand of hair slipped back across her cheek.

'I can't do this,' he murmured suddenly, his gaze searching her face.

Verity glared back. 'Living here is making me ill, you know. I'm getting all these odd symptoms and the doctor says I need to relax and do more things that I enjoy.'

'What sort of symptoms?'

'Panic attacks caused by constant worrying.'

'That's just your age. My mother was the same.'

'It is not "just my age"! How dare you!' She got to her feet, and paced across the kitchen. 'I'm absolutely worn out by working twelve-hour days, and frustrated by you. I've known all summer that you were avoiding this discussion but I told myself you wouldn't let me down, and that everything would be fine. How wrong I was.'

19

Matt rubbed his forefinger over a patch of the table.

'What is it? What is it you're not telling me? There's something you're not letting on. I know that look.'

'Nothing,' he said. 'It's nothing.'

Verity leant against the new kitchen worktop with her arms folded, and frowned at the patch of thinning sand-coloured hair on the crown of her husband's bent head. He continued to pick at the table edge with his thumb nail, and her temples began to throb. Emotion washed over her in waves, and she swallowed hard. She studied the empty seat where their youngest daughter Tills had sat only that morning, chattering about her friends, and airing her opinions a bit nervously before her big day of leaving home for university.

'God, I miss her already,' Verity sighed.

'She'll be fine.' Matt looked up.

'I'm not convinced she will be fine. She's still very young for her age, and easily influenced. Don't you think that?'

'No.'

'No,' Verity echoed quietly.

'You think too much.'

Verity sat down again and fumbled for her wine glass. 'Matt,' she began again, calmly, 'before your obvious cold feet this summer, you'd always told me that I deserved a chance to do what I wanted. You even joked about joining that golf club outside Oxford, and how we'd have weekend house parties in the country for all your friends.'

'That was before.'

'Before what?'

'Oh, I don't know. Before now.'

'Matt, what is going on?'

'I don't know. It's just not right, now the time has actually come.' He rubbed the end of his nose and sniffed.

Verity's eyes narrowed in suspicion.

'What?' he asked, rounding his eyes at her and raising his palms to the ceiling.

'This is not a game. You're being really unfair, you know that? Because for once I am insisting that my needs take priority in this marriage, and your reaction is to just think about yourself. A marriage is a partnership, and for twenty-three years you have had pretty much everything going your way. That has to change.'

He looked away then, and with a down-turned mouth and slight shake of the head, pushed his chair back, abruptly. Verity watched her husband as he tidied away his supper plate. It was not something he normally did, and he stacked the plate the wrong way around in the dishwasher before closing the machine's door, and checking his watch.

'I'm going out for a pint.'

It was Sunday evening, and every Sunday evening forever, Matt had met a couple of friends for a pint in the local pub. He was a creature of habit; Verity knew exactly when he would be back too, could set her clock by it. He did not peck her on the cheek before he left the way he usually did though, and Verity did not say goodbye to him either. She let him leave in a silence that stretched to snapping point.

The house fell still. Since the renovations, it was no longer a home. There was nowhere to curl up and relax, none of Verity's photographs or books to comfort her, and few of her paintings still hung on the walls. It was like living in a department store showroom; but it would sell at a good price like this, she knew. She owned an interior design business, and regularly dressed houses for sale, so it stood to reason that she had done an excellent job on her own property. She sighed, put some music on, and began to tidy the kitchen, pausing to look at a black-and-white wedding photograph placed on an otherwise empty shelf, purely with a view to the sale. One tasteful photograph of wedded bliss was right up there with freshly cut flowers and the smell of coffee when it came to making a sale, clichéd thought it was. In today's Matt, she could sometimes still see a glimpse of the man she had married that day. He was just as gregarious and charming, and had kept his good looks. He could still manage a smile that lit up his face so that Verity usually had no choice but to smile back at him. In recent months, though, something had shifted; he had begun to hold back from her in some way. It was nothing that she could put a finger on exactly, but there was something in the way he rubbed his chin or stared out of a window or ran his fingers through his hair. All her instincts were alerted. Something was up – she sensed it.

21

With the kitchen tidied, Verity climbed the stairs to her tiny box-room studio at the front of the house, and examined a painting she had begun that summer but never found time to finish. Taken from a photograph and worked on in poor indoor light in the cramped room, it would never be brilliant, or quite what she aspired to, although it was, she supposed, a decent enough attempt. Yet if there was anything these past years of trying to paint had taught her, it was that she worked best outdoors, and she needed a proper large and well-lit space in which to complete her work. She favoured big canvases and liked to step back and view her pieces from all angles as she layered on the colours. The paintings which had been chosen for exhibitions over the years were all landscapes she had done while on holiday in Italy or France. It was hopeless trying to do anything in this confined space where her elbow hit the wall and her canvases, of necessity, were small. The years had flown by and she felt the pressure of time now too. She could not put off her dream any longer.

Realising she had forgotten to let the dog out, she went downstairs again. She straightened three cushions with quick flicks of her wrist, and tidied a magazine to a pile beneath a glass coffee table. The table, turquoise sofa with mustard-coloured cushions, and a restored leather armchair were the only pieces of furniture left in the room. Everything else Verity had put into storage. A polished wooden floor, white walls, and a tall mirror over the fireplace created stillness and simplicity. Certainly, Verity could have sold the house as it was a year ago – a comfy family home full of clutter – but every penny counted. She stood a moment, convincing herself, her head cocked on one side and her lips pursed, double-checking that she had not neglected anything, and then she bent down to stroke her old dog.

'Come on, Charlie, let's take you out in the garden,' she murmured. She slid a tall glass door open to let the dog out, and watched him totter around the small patch of grass on his short arthritic legs. The night air was cold and filled with siren and traffic noise from the Fulham Palace Road, sounds that drained her spirit, and judging from the sigh on his return, Charlie's too.

Verity collected her wine glass, topped it up, and headed back up the polished wooden staircase with the dog. Her bedroom had freshly-painted pale walls. The throw on the bed was a soothing purple shade which reminded her of Scottish heather, a long-lost association from her early childhood days. Verity kicked off her shoes and sat back against a pile of crisp white pillows while Charlie settled in his basket in the corner of the room. She had always hated Sunday evenings. Her thoughts inevitably turned to the week ahead, to the million things she had to do, and did not for the most part want to do. She picked at a cuticle, with her phone cradled on her shoulder.

'Hi Stella, how are you?' She pressed the phone to her ear, and ran her fingers back through her hair.

'What's the matter?'

'Ha, is it that obvious?'

'You know me. I can read your mind.'

'Well, nothing really, but Tills went today.' She sniffed.

'Of course, she did! Sorry, I forgot. How did she get off?'

'She was fine. Matt took her in the end because I had to give my mother a lift to see one of her friends who's in a hospice. I miss her already!' She swiped a tear from her cheek.

'Aw, she'll be back before you know it, Vet.'

'I'm not convinced she's ready. She'd have been much better taking a gap year, but you know how it is, she wouldn't listen to me. And I'm really happy for her in spite of everything, if that makes sense.'

'Yeah, it does. It's always a bittersweet experience when they go.'

'It feels so final. It wasn't so bad when Livia left, somehow,'

'Yes, well, Tills is your baby. Of course you'll be upset.'

There was a pause while Verity blew her nose on a tissue. Then, 'Matt's really bugging me,' she admitted. 'He's digging his heels in about us selling the house.'

'I told you he would! He'll get over it. He just hates change, and believes deep in his bones that men rule the world and get to make all the decisions. That posh education did for him.'

'I know, I know.' Verity was no stranger to Stella's feelings about Matt. 'I kind of saw this coming. I'm just not sure what to do about it.'

'Where is he now?'

'In the Blue Anchor. It's Sunday.'

'Of course he is, silly me. Why don't you go and join him, sit down in a corner, just the pair of you, and talk it through.'

'I could, but I don't think it would get me anywhere.'

'So, what are you going to do?'

'I don't know,' she said again. 'Matt has never understood my painting, has he? He just pushes it aside or gives me a pep talk telling me I can do it all, like I'm some kind of superwoman.'

'Truth is, it would cramp his style to live out in the country, that's what's at the root of it. A much smaller audience. Very few people to impress. Not much to do, either. He's a city boy, through and through.'

'Am I being unfair to him, Stell?'

'Definitely not! If I was cynical – which of course I'm not – I would say it suits Matt very well to keep you stuck in London, working away as usual: Verity, the high-earning superwoman, always there to be relied on. You're his rock.'

'D'you think so?'

'He often sulks when he doesn't get his way, does your Matt,' Stella observed. 'Oh, Christ! It's Tom, hang on!'

Verity heard the wail of Stella's small grandson in the background, and while her friend thundered upstairs, she sipped her wine and studied her neglected fingernails.

'I'm back.' Stella exhaled.

'Everything all right?'

'He'd woken up and got his duvet in a tangle.'

'Aw, he's so cute. The thing is, getting back to Matt, if I leave it much longer to move, I'll be drawing a pension not a landscape.'

'Ha, ha. Gawd, don't say that.'

'Be honest with me. Do you think I should just count my blessings, and knuckle down and get on with Om Interiors? I mean, it is kind of precious of me to want to 'be an artist'. How do I know I can even do it well enough?'

'Oh, my dear Vet, you listen to me. Of course, you're bloody good enough – and of course you should follow your dreams! What the hell is life about if you don't? And it's not like you're acting on a whim – you've waited for years and you've thought it all through.'

'Really? You're not just saying that?'

'Really. I will be bloody furious with you if you *don't* do it.'

'But I don't see you doing anything mad like this.'

'I don't want to. I'm happy where I am with my kids and little Tom here. We're not the same that way. Besides, you made a lot of

24

lifestyle changes when you married Matt. I think you've got to do what you want now.'

'Did I?'

'Yes! He didn't like your friends so you had to go around with his posh group. You stopped painting for ages when he complained about the mess.'

'That's true, I did. There's something else bothering me too.'

'What?'

'Well, look what Dad's artistic career did to our family – it ripped us apart!'

'That wasn't his creativity; that was his lust for a girl half his age.'

'It was his need to live an artist's life; that's what he always said.'

'Yeah, well, I beg to differ, and this is not the same. Look, don't go there. The past is in the past; stay positive. This is your life, not your dad's. Come on.'

'But...'

'What?'

'Something about Matt's behaviour isn't right either, Stell. I can't put my finger on it. He's not looking me in the eye and he keeps sucking in his cheeks.'

'Surely not sucking in his cheeks?' Stella laughed lustily.

'You may laugh, but after twenty-three years of marriage, I can tell you that is not a good sign.'

'Have another glass of wine, Vet – you're stressed. Matt is throwing his toys out of the pram, that's all. It'll all be fine.'

When the phone call ended, Verity got ready for bed and then wandered into Tills' silent bedroom, folded a sweatshirt and a pair of leggings discarded from the luggage at the last minute, and held a pillow to her face, breathing in the sweet smell of her younger child. Another tear trickled feebly down her cheek and she brushed it away. She prayed she had done a good enough job of raising her daughter. When she thought of Tills, worry often niggled away inside her. Livia, her elder daughter, was capable and solid, had graduated with a good degree from Manchester University without any fuss and had gone on to find a job in the same city, where she now lived with her dependable boyfriend, Josh. Livia had never caused Verity much bother even as a child, but Tills was different. She presented a strong front but beneath the surface could be vulnerable, and school had not always been a good experience.

Returning to her phone, Verity sent Tills a message, and then settled down to read for a while in the hope that she might get one back. She must have nodded off because she awoke some time later to the rustle of the bedcover as Matt inched in beside her, his cold legs weaving around hers.

'What are you doing? What time is it?'

'Your light was on. Come here.' She felt Matt's hand creep under her camisole top; the coldness of his fingers making her flinch.

'Matt, it's late. I have a lot to do tomorrow.'

'Don't care, come here,' his voice slurred, gentle but insistent.

Verity turned out the glaring bedside light and stared at the bedroom ceiling, now softly lit by streetlight. Matt burrowed beneath the duvet and roughly attempted to pull her pyjama bottoms down. She tried to feel excited, grateful even (it had been a while), and vaguely stroked Matt's head as he kissed her stomach. She willed herself to wake up and respond, but felt nothing.

'Matt,' she murmured. 'I'm half asleep.'

Matt did not seem to notice, pushed up her camisole top so that it wedged in her armpits, and kissed her breasts, a low moan of pleasure escaping from his lips. In a series of tugs, he yanked the pyjamas down to her ankles, and nudged her legs apart with his knee.

'No!' Verity shouted, sitting up suddenly. Could he not tell that she wasn't ready? Her heart thumped in the horrible way it so often did of late. Matt rolled off and lay beside her, a waft of his beer breath clouding her face.

'I love you, V, but you are getting very boring,' he gasped, before swinging his legs out of her bed, collecting his trousers off the floor and retreating to his own attic bedroom.

4

Verity was awoken by the squeak and slam of the front door – a noise which signified Matt leaving for work and the fact she had overslept. She swung her legs out of bed, and sat with her head in her hands, struggling to rouse herself and cursing Matt for not waking her. When Livia had left for university four years previously, they had agreed that Matt would move into Livia's attic bedroom as he snored loudly and Verity talked in her sleep, and they had both reached the point where they were really fed up with each other. These days, it was only when Livia came home that Matt shared Verity's bed, and the encounter the night before was the first time he had shown any interest in her for months. She had wanted to respond but as he had come to her fuelled by beer while she was asleep, how else could she have reacted? She stood, brushed her hair furiously and slammed the brush down on a chest of drawers. Her brain was horribly foggy and her head throbbed.

'You look nice – new dress?' Mel, her assistant asked, as Verity hung up her coat.

'Yes, it is. Thanks.'

'I wish I was as slim as you. I'd look like an old matron if I wore a loose dress like that. You are lucky to be so tall. And how's my favourite little doggy today?' Mel bent to scratch Charlie's ears.

Verity took a deep breath. 'In your bed, Charlie. So, did that rep bring the new swatches?'

'Yes.'

'And how's it going with chasing the unpaid invoices?'

27

'I'm on it. Are you okay? You seem a little stressed.'

'Sorry, I overslept and Matt is getting on my nerves.'

'Tell you what, I'll make us both a coffee.'

'You're an angel. Sorry, I don't know why I'm so ratty.'

Charlie eyed her warily from his basket beside the radiator, and Verity bent to pat him before sitting down at her desk. She ran her fingers back through her hair, and still in a defiant mood, picked up her phone and made an appointment for an estate agent to value the house.

'Here you go.' Mel put a mug of black coffee down on the desk.

Verity and Mel worked from a studio tucked behind Verity's interiors shop in Hammersmith. They undertook interior design projects, in private or rental homes, mostly in central London. Much of the work came by word of mouth or through customers who visited the shop.

'Mornings just seem to get worse, especially Mondays,' Verity moaned.

'Know what you mean. I was going to take this lot down to the post office in a bit,' Mel suggested, pointing to a pile of envelopes and small parcels, 'get them out of the way, if that's okay with you.'

'Good idea. Shall we run through the week first?'

Verity and Mel went through the diary together while sipping their coffees, and then Mel left with a full bag for the post office. While she had a private moment, Verity pushed her work aside and began to gather some of the papers she would need to sell her business, as advised by Francesca her accountant. Until Verity knew the facts, she would not tell any of her staff about her plans. She had a twinge of conscience about Mel in particular, but there was no other way to deal with things until she had a more definite idea of the value of Om Interiors, and how long it might take to sell.

Around mid-morning, Mel left the studio again to do an inventory at the storage unit where they kept furniture for sale or rental for special occasions, and alone again, Verity saw the mountain of work she had to do. Everywhere she looked, jobs demanded her attention, jobs that she resented. Her heart started to race and her pulse grew loud in her ears. Striding quickly to the small washroom, she bent over the basin, thinking she might be sick. Her heartbeat continued to be rapid and she felt dizzy. Her legs weakened and she dropped to a kneeling position on the floor, grasping the toilet basin to steady herself, trying to take deep breaths. Slowly the frightening symptoms subsided. After several minutes, she stood again cautiously, gripping the door handle to steady herself. She stumbled back to her desk, sat down gingerly, dialled her doctor, and asked for an emergency appointment.

A vast sky dwarfed a cluster of cottages that huddled beside the narrow country lane. The spires of Oxford were visible from some parts of the village on a clear day, and the river Thames snaked lazily through the adjoining landscape, just across the nearby meadows. Stella still lived in the ancient timbered house she had inherited from her parents, not long after the demise of her marriage. With mildewed white walls bordering the quiet lane, and in need of a new thatch, her friend's home retained the spirit of their shared childhood, and Verity loved to visit. Sitting neatly at the foot of a sloping garden dotted with ancient apple trees, it was a place where time seemed to stand still.

As Verity pulled her Mini onto a patch of weed-strewn gravel beside the front door, her spirits lifted at the prospect of the weekend ahead. Her doctor – who had ordered blood tests and listened to her heart but not seemed at all concerned by her latest 'funny turn' – had told her to rest, and Verity had figured there was no better way to do so than to spend a weekend with her closest friend. From the back seat of the car, Charlie whimpered with excitement, recognising their destination. Verity noted the sky overhead was a boundless dome of cobalt blue and the air was sweet with the scent of cut grass. This was just what she needed – the sights and smells of the English countryside to restore her energy. She took a deep breath and wriggled her shoulders to loosen them a little.

Stella came out to greet her. Her pale curly hair formed a nest for a pair of bright pink reading glasses. The two friends hugged, and the handful of estate agents' brochures that Verity had impulsively collected on her way through the neighbouring town were crumpled in the crush. After a cup of tea and some delicious shortbread, they walked Stella's grandson Tom in his buggy, along with an energised Charlie who tugged at his lead, to the village playground. Earthy aromas of damp soil and fallen leaves – so absent in the city — lingered in the air, and made Verity nostalgic and happy.

'I remember when I used to bring my girls here for the weekend when they were little.'

'Yep. We played here, our kids played here, and now Tom plays here. Three generations — who'd have thought it?'

Verity looked over at her dear friend, and felt a surge of happiness. Stella bent stiffly and pulled her glasses down onto her nose to inspect a possible graze on Tom's tiny hand. Life had not been easy for her. She had been a single mother to her own two children for most of their childhood, and then Mandy, her daughter, had given birth to a little boy, when she was only seventeen. These days Stella was often left with Tom while Mandy worked.

'So how are you doing?' Verity asked.

'Not bad, all things considered.'

'I'm going to treat us this weekend. You can put your feet up, and I'll cook for us and we'll drink wine!'

'You're supposed to be resting.'

'Pah! I don't have a little person to look after like you do. You know, this is what I miss,' Verity sighed. 'The sky, the smells, the feeling of nature all around, and the peace. The beautiful silence. You don't get any of this in London. D'you remember how we used to play in the little woods over there, the hours we spent messing around and building dens, the things we'd collect for the nature tables in our bedrooms?'

'God, yes! Nature tables — I'd forgotten about them.' Stella pushed her glasses back into her hair with one hand, and set Tom's swing moving forward again with another.

'I only ever meant to live in London for a short time. I can't believe I've spent quarter of a century there,' Verity mused. Charlie nosed around in a patch of long grass outside the enclosed play area, and Verity sat on a bench, closed her eyes and put her face up to the weak sun. 'I wish I'd been able to bring up my girls here in the village like you did your two.'

'Don't kid yourself about that, Vet. Miles left straight for London as soon as he could, and Mandy, well, we all know what happened to her. She'd love to be living in London or anywhere with a bit more life to it, but she can't afford it, not yet.'

'But you still love it?'

'I wouldn't live anywhere else.'

'I envy you. I want something like this, like you've got.'

'I'm not sure you'd love the reality. You were always more of an adventurer than me.'

'I've calmed down a lot. I'm older – and wiser.' Verity sighed. 'Sometimes I get the feeling time is running out and I don't want to waste one moment.'

'Don't say that! You've got years left in you yet!'

'I'm feeling my age! I'm getting hot sweats and panic attacks. I'm turning into an old woman.'

'You and me both with the sweats – horrendous, isn't it? So, what did the doctor say, exactly?'

'Stress and hormones. Well, "stress-induced depression" was what she actually called it, and she wrote me a prescription for anti-depressants which I already told her I'm never going to take. And she gave me stronger pills for the panic attacks because I've been having them for a while but they seem to be getting worse. She seems to think it's fairly normal for someone to have them regularly. "The stress of modern living," she called it. Personally, I don't think it's normal at all. It's horrible. That last one was horrendous. I honestly thought something terrible was going to happen to me, but the doctor insists the attacks won't kill me, and what I need to do is to exercise and enjoy myself more. Fat chance with my life the way it is at the moment.'

'Vet, you have to look after yourself better, sweetie. You're running on empty.'

'I know, I know – and I'm trying, but it's not easy.'

'No-one ever warns you what it's going to be like at our age, do they?'

'I wouldn't have listened if they did; but I'd hate to go to my grave knowing I'd never tried to do the things I really want to do, or that I'd never bothered to make any time for myself or listened to what was in my heart. I am so fed up with what I'm doing, I hate it. When the girls were young, I could see the point. But now? Now I wake up each morning and wonder what on earth life is all about.'

'But what are you talking about? You're doing so well.'

'Not really. I'm so bored. I know it's ungrateful, but the business doesn't make me happy. Most of my clients want what's in this month's Home and Garden magazine, and they want to play safe all the time, copying their friends, basically. Just walking into my studio raises my blood pressure. And my old London friends are driving me mad! All they ever want to do is drink wine or go shopping and I'm fed up with all that so I've been keeping my distance from them, and feeling a bit lonely and sorry for myself.'

'Drinking wine and shopping sounds good to me.'

'Oh, I know. But I want more. And I get so tired!'

'Are you definitely going to sell the business, then?'

'Yes, I'm just getting all the paperwork sorted so we can put a value on it – but I haven't told anyone except you, yet.'

'What about Matt?'

'He knows what I want to do, obviously, but he's trying to pretend it's never going to happen, so I haven't told him anything for now.'

'Typical Matt.' Stella picked up baby Tom from the swing. 'You've got your father's blood in your veins, Vet. You always were a brilliant painter. I'm sure you could earn some good money from it.'

'The smell of oil paints, a dusty studio, lapsang souchong tea and rags soaked in white spirit are the only things that make me feel at home. They're like nothing else.'

'You are funny.'

The heat from the Aga warmed one end of the low-ceilinged kitchen, and the chill of an autumn evening seeping around a draughty door cooled the other. Charlie curled up on a folded blanket beside the stove, and fell asleep. Verity skimmed through the brochures of houses for sale that she had picked up on the way there while Stella folded baby clothes and Tom dozed in his pushchair.

'You know what you were saying earlier about the money? You mustn't worry about it so much, you know,' Stella advised. 'You've always worried about money but you have plenty; you'll be fine.'

'I know, but with what happened to Mum and then ever since Matt ran up all those debts, it's all I can think about sometimes.'

'Well, they were both a long time ago.'

'They were, but I can't let go of it.'

'Maybe we don't ever really get over something like that. I remember when you had to move house – that was awful – and Livia had to change schools and it upset her. You had terrible nightmares. I remember coming around to your place, and thinking how amazing it all was with expensive new furniture, and televisions in the kids' bedrooms, and computers, and then you found out he couldn't actually afford any of it and it was all on those bloody credit cards.'

'Yes, and for me the distress wasn't just about the money, it was the *lies*. He always told me everything was fine – which is what he always says, I've now learnt.'

'For me, it would have been about the money, make no mistake. And you did your best with it all. I don't know how you forgave him. He shouldn't have bloody done it.'

'Exactly.' Verity took a slug of wine that burned the back of her throat. She winced. 'He never ever apologised, you know – not once.'

'Well, it's behind you now – and that's what I was trying to say: you're still worrying when you don't need to. All that is in your past.'

'I hope you're right. Anyway, enough of Matt,' Verity went on. 'I'm here to have a break from him. Changing the subject, I've got lots of old sample books for you, for your patchwork, and I've been clearing out my storage unit so there are a few bits and small pieces of furniture that you might like for the cottage or to keep for Mandy when she moves on. Anything you don't want, you can just give away. The samples are all out in the car and I'll send you some photos of the other stuff so you can see if you want it.'

'Aw, thanks. And listen, you really do deserve this, you know, this change of career so you can paint. Don't let anyone ever tell you otherwise.'

Very early on Sunday morning while Stella, Mandy and Tom were still asleep, and the flat rays of dawn had only just begun to disperse the shadowy night, Verity tiptoed out of the cottage and collected her easel, canvas and satchel of paints from the boot of her car. With Charlie at her heels, she headed out over the fields behind the house and climbed a nearby hill. Finding a good sheltered spot, she set up her easel, and worked rapidly, spreading paint onto canvas, as the sun began to creep over the Chiltern Hills in the far distance. She created a vision of a vast lemon-and-tangerine-streaked sky illuminating curves and sweeps of brown and purple hills. She struggled, hastily mixing colours on her palette, to get the right shades of paint to convey the majesty of the quietly spectacular daybreak. The light shifted rapidly, the colours of the natural world mutated before her eyes, and Verity was simply not fast enough or skilled enough with her paints and brushes to capture what she saw. The finished product was disappointing – dowdy and flat. The colours were wrong, there was no sparkle to what she had created. It was not good enough.

'I'm sorry if I've been a pig,' Matt apologised. 'You look lovely, darling. The break did you good.' He pecked her on the cheek, and Verity felt a rush of irritation at the whiff of a new, no doubt expensive, aftershave.

'I'm instructing the agent to put the house on the market tomorrow,' she snapped.

'Christ, you never give up, do you?' Matt replied bitterly. 'You need to listen to me sometimes.'

'I listened to you the other day when you said you'd like muesli without nuts in,' she retorted, 'and I bought some. When you said that you missed having people in the house two weeks ago, I invited the Smiths and the Shearers to dinner even though I was knackered and don't especially like the Smiths or the Shearers. You looked tired last week, so I cooked lasagne because I know you love it. I am constantly listening to you and considering you! But when did you last listen to me? When did you last do something for me?'

'You don't understand.' The softness in her husband's eyes vanished, and his tone became heavily weighted. 'I won't sign the house over. I'll tell the estate agent you're doing it against my will, and he'll run a mile.' A muscle in his jawline twitched.

'You can't do that.'

'Oh yes, I can.'

Verity grabbed a mug off the work top and hurled it across the room, Matt ducked and the mug smashed against a cupboard.

'You want a fight? Then you'll get one!' Verity screamed.

Matt threw his car keys up in the air, caught them and widened his eyes. 'I'm out of here. Don't wait up,' he said.

5

Verity leant closer to the mirror, pressed the tips of her index fingers into her cheek bones, and drew her skin back towards her hair line. The fine creases that ran from her nose to her mouth disappeared like magic. It was a much better look. She took her fingers away, and the creases returned. She sighed. Who am I? she wondered. I'm not young, I'm not old. I don't know who I am anymore. Unable to hide in the toilet any longer, she took a final look in the mirror, pushed her hair up at the back to make it look less flattened, and unbolted the cloakroom door, plastering a smile on her face as she followed a housekeeper across a pristine hallway and prepared to meet her client.

Earlier that week, Verity and her accountant Francesca had decided upon a likely valuation for Om Interiors based on premises, profits and the loyal client list. Verity had researched where to advertise, and in addition there were a couple of interior design businesses in London that might be interested. The prospect filled her with a mix of excitement and anxiety. After escaping the client's smart and stifling house, she walked quickly down Sloane Gardens towards the tube station with her head full of plans for the future. A sudden squall of rain drenched her, and she ducked into the station entrance, pushing tendrils of wet hair from her face. Squinting in the fluorescent light with the polluted dust of the city filling her lungs and people jostling all around her, change could not come soon enough. After Livia was born, Verity had made the 'sensible' decision to channel her artistic talent into profit, firstly via textile design and then her interior design business; but neither of these things had ever given her the same sense of vitality as creating a beautiful picture from nothing. Her body rocked with the movement of the tube train as it hurtled through tunnels. Matt and Verity had agreed on re-locating to Oxfordshire so that she would have the magnificent skies over the Oxford plain, the delights of the River Thames, and the swollen beauty of the Chiltern Hills to work with while Matt would still have a manageable commute. So, what *had* happened to change Matt's mind? Verity frowned and chewed the corner of her fingernail.

In the Courtauld Gallery, she wandered slowly past an array of Impressionist and Post-Impressionist paintings, occasionally pausing to study the depiction of a landscape, her head tilted on one side as she tried to figure out exactly how each artist had achieved their final image. Cezanne's work fascinated her. She squinted and leant forward to study his *Montagne Sainte-Victoire with Large Pine*, marvelling at each tiny brush stroke. Cezanne's technique looked deceptively simple, but how had he decided on that particular shade or angle of his brush? Or had he not decided at all but worked on instinct alone? Verity peered at the canvas, analysing the artist's technique, the apparently effortless way he achieved light falling on fields and mountainside, and the proportions of the entire piece. Goosebumps broke out all over her body and she shivered. How *had* Cezanne done it? Could Verity ever hope to get remotely close to this standard of work? This particular mountain landscape took her back to her early childhood, before the years in Oxfordshire, to the time when her family had lived in Provence, in a village to the north-east of the Montagne Sainte-Victoire. Living in that region of France, even as a young child, she had sensed the wealth of natural environment available for her father to paint and the extraordinary light that created deeply-hued shadows and atmosphere. She had always understood her father's passion for the place.

Verity hugged her laptop bag to her body and moved to scrutinize the next painting in the gallery. Oxfordshire would provide her with a good amount of material too, she hoped, and she intended to make trips to Scotland, Cornwall and the Lake District for inspiration. She had lots of ideas but fretted about how she would make them happen – and whether she would ever be good enough.

Matt was working late, and Verity picked up a tuna salad for one on her way home. As she took her first mouthful of the salad, her phone rang and she saw it was Tills calling.

'Hello love!'

'Hi, Mum.'

'How are you?'

'Fine, fine.'

'How was fresher's week? What have you been up to?' Verity felt stupidly eager for news.

'We had our first lecture today, and I met my tutor. I've made loads of new friends, it's so much fun. Listen Mum, I can't chat, I'm going out. I just didn't want you to think I was ignoring your texts so this is a very quick call to stop you worrying. I'm really sorry, I promise I'll call you for a proper talk soon.'

'No worries, but I'd love to hear what the halls are like and how you're settling in.'

'Can I call you at the weekend?' Tills sounded rushed, and Verity bit back her own longing.

'Okay, of course you can. I love you.'

'I love you too, Mum.'

Tills ended the call. Verity put her phone down, covered her face with her hands, and burst into tears. It was so silly, she knew, but she ached to give Tills a hug, to see the dimples in her young cheeks, and the sparkle in her blue eyes, so like Matt's. Verity stared at the barely-touched tuna salad, and her appetite failed. She blew her nose on a paper tissue, poured a large glass of white wine, took a deep breath, and reminded herself that Tills was happy – and that was the most important thing. To compensate, she rang Livia, but there was no answer. She left a message, desperately trying not to sound as lonely as she felt. This was the way it was going to be now, she told herself firmly. For over twenty years, if she had reached out for company or a chat, her daughters had been there – hormonal tantrums permitting admittedly – but they had been around. And now they had both moved on, which was natural progression and she was so proud of them, even if it did hurt and was so very hard to accept.

Verity changed into her yoga gear, and headed out to her class, reminding herself these were her doctor's orders. It was the last thing she felt like doing, and she wished she had not drunk the glass of wine. Her feet dragged as she headed off down the street. The doctor had insisted that taking more exercise would give Verity more energy, which seemed totally illogical, but who was she to argue? And she certainly needed energy! She could easily have played truant from yoga, crawled upstairs, lain down on her bed, and not woken up until morning.

Since the row in the kitchen when she had hurled the mug at Matt, the two of them had skirted around each other, neither one mentioning the house sale again.

'How was yoga?' He pecked her on the cheek when she returned home.

'Good. Relaxing. So relaxing that I fell asleep when we did shavasana.'

'When you did what?'

'The Corpse Pose. Shavasana. You lie flat on your back on the floor.'

'All right for some.'

'You could come.'

'Oh yeah, right.'

'Some men do.'

'Hmm, and no doubt they're all called Tristan and are vegan.'

'You'd be surprised. Not all men are as old-fashioned as you.' Verity bent to stroke Charlie who had got up out of his basket to greet her. She scratched the dog behind his ears and he leaned against her leg in appreciation. 'I'm going to take him up the road.'

'Sure. Listen, before I forget, can you sign these papers?'

'Yep, what am I signing?'

'Insurance. New policy.'

'Okay. Where?'

'Here, thanks. All ready for next week then?' Matt asked.

'What?'

'France,' he reminded her.

'Oh God, I'd completely forgotten.'

Matt rounded his eyes at her, and Verity rapidly recalled that a long weekend was planned with one of Matt's colleagues and his wife, as a thank you for some favour Matt had done for the man.

'I'm so busy!' Verity ran her fingers through her hair. She had never met the couple but even so, how had she managed to completely forget a weekend away?

38

'How can you forget a long weekend away in the South of France?' Matt said, as though reading her thoughts.

'I don't know, but I did. Don't worry, I'll rearrange some stuff. Come on, Charlie.' She picked up the dog's lead.

'You will come, won't you? We're flying out on Thursday, and you'll need time off.'

'Yes, yes. Of course, I'll come.' Verity headed out onto the quiet residential street with Charlie. Chilly night air circled her head making her ears ache. Steam curled from her mouth as she sauntered beside her arthritic little dog. The street where they lived was so benign. Leafy plane trees, easy street parking, and quiet neighbours made for a safe haven in the mad dash of London. This street had been her home for almost fifteen years. Was she mad to want to leave it? She was astonished that she had forgotten about the weekend away. How could she have? She felt an all-too-familiar ripple of nerves at the prospect of flying. In her younger days, she had hopped on and off aeroplanes without a second thought, but something in her had changed and now the thought terrified her. She took a deep breath of damp air, and told herself to get a grip. Recalling the Cezanne she had studied at the Courtauld, she consoled herself with the promise of the beautiful landscapes of the Côte d'Azur, and almost convinced herself to feel happy.

Verity put the lid on her laptop down, rubbed the back of her neck, and stretched out her arms. Reports had come from Francesca detailing her tax liability in a way that made her head spin. She was fretting about Mel, Julie and Annie who helped run Om Interiors, and what the sale might mean for their futures as it was not a great economic climate and jobs could be hard to find; she was still not sure when would be the best time to tell them. The estate agent had given a brilliant valuation for the house but she had not yet managed to admit to Matt that she had had the man round. With a throbbing head, she bent and rifled in her handbag for a paracetamol, shoving the leaflet on depression and accompanying prescription to the bottom of her bag. What a load of rubbish that diagnosis was, she tutted to herself. She was not the depressive type. She swallowed a painkiller, and checked her watch.

'Come on, Charlie!' she called to the dog who nestled in his basket beside her desk.

After forty minutes in her car, crawling through London traffic, Verity finally found a parking space in Bushy Park. She let Charlie out, and dawdled beside him, taking in a sweep of gentle grey sky. She cleared up Charlie's mess, and stood beside him as he tottered in a circle on the grass, his grey whiskered nose held aloft to the air, the arthritis tempering his instinct to explore. She pulled her coat collar up against a snappy breeze and, mindful of the vet's instructions to only walk the dog for ten minutes, led him slowly back to the car. She lifted him onto his blanket where he curled up gratefully, his soulful brown eyes catching hers before the lids closed and he sighed into sleep. Watching Charlie grow old saddened Verity, and she recalled all the years the little dog had kept her company, right back to the days when her daughters were young. They had been through a lot together, Charlie and Verity. She locked the car and strode out across the park alone, noting the pleasing shapes of clustered antlers on a herd of deer and the muted fawns and tans of their varying hides against autumnal horse chestnut trees and long, yellowing grass. The air smelt damp and fungal, and all the leaves were beginning to turn.

Later, Charlie pulled at his lead as they approached the familiar red-painted door to Fiona MacLeod's house. Verity stood and waited for her mother to answer her knock with the sense that time was collapsing around her. She fought off the usual awful memory of the first time she and her mother had trudged up to this very door during the heatwave in the summer of 1976. The heat and stench of melting tarmac had stifled Verity's youthful and outraged sensibility and she had thought she might explode with fury. Fresh from the Oxfordshire countryside and a childhood lived outdoors, she had been utterly naïve and unable to believe that people actually lived so squashed together in a hideous street where the invigorating greens and browns of the earth were covered so entirely by depressing buildings and tarmac.

'Welcome to your new home,' Fiona had announced on that day, as she had inserted a new key into the lock, and pushed open the door to the stuffy, unlived-in house.

'Is this some kind of joke?' Verity had retorted, full of spiteful pre-teen gusto – a response that shamed her to this day. Her mother's thin shoulders had turned rigid as she had snapped at her not to behave like a spoilt brat.

Fiona MacLeod now opened the same red front door, and warmly welcomed her daughter inside. While Verity sat down and settled Charlie on a rug in front of the fire, her mother went into the back kitchen to make tea for them both. Fiona was a woman of few words, and she remained silent as she poured tea through a steel sieve into a bone china cup. The tired front room was a hangover from a different life. Fiona had never 'made over' the house, regarding the whole notion as beneath her and a frivolous waste of money. Over the years, she had listened aghast, genuinely horrified by Verity's clients and their demands, dismissing them all as "nouveau riche" or having "more money than sense". Fiona's house still had a front room, a rear dining room (hardly ever entered, the door kept closed for half the year to reduce heating costs), and a narrow, dingy hall that led down to a tiny sliver of kitchen and a miniscule rectangular bathroom beyond. Converting upstairs rooms to bathrooms or knocking down walls to enable more living space were unnecessary expenses – although Fiona did occasionally refresh the walls herself using discounted paint from the hardware store "to keep the place looking decent". The Laura Ashley curtains sewn from a roll of seconds fabric in that sweltering summer of 1976 still hung at the windows and were carefully cleaned each spring. The corner of a curtain where a mouse had once nibbled was still visible if Verity squinted hard enough. The sight of the enduring curtains made her nostalgic, and she was strangely proud of her mother's frugality. She ran her fingers through her hair and sighed.

'So, I'll be in a taxi on Thursday, Mum. I won't be able to stop, I'll just drop Charlie and his things off, and then leave.'

'He's a poppet. I'm looking forward to having him again.' For such a practical woman, Fiona was surprisingly fond of dogs. 'You don't seem very excited about your trip.' Her mother's perception was sharp as ever, and she had never been one to mince her words.

Verity sighed. 'No, I'm not. Not looking forward to the flight. Don't know the people,' she muttered, feeling like a child again.

'You know what they say; it's safer on a plane–'

'–than driving a car, I know, I know.'

'Well then.'

'I'm hoping to get some inspiration from the French countryside. I thought I'd start painting again,' Verity deflected, vaguely. She had not yet told her mother of her plans to sell up and move, fearing that she would unsettle her, bring unwelcome warnings from her about financial insecurity, and possibly even another harking back to her father and his irresponsible ways.

'Well, that is nice and I'm pleased you're taking a break. You work too hard, Verity. You look worn out; you have black rings under your eyes. Life's not all about work.'

Verity ignored her mother's remark and studied one of her father's paintings which hung over the fireplace, as it had since that landmark summer of 1976. At the time, Verity had accused her mother of being mad when she had hung the picture there, after everything her father had done, and all the pain they had both suffered. 'You simply don't understand,' her mother had retorted on the sweaty summer's day, muttering through thin lips that were pressed together, holding the second nail for a picture hook while she hammered in the first.

Verity looked at the painting now, and longed to ask her mother what it was still doing there, after all the years and everything that had happened. She recalled the sickening day they had arrived in Portugal, earlier that same year. Her mother had remained married to Ralph MacLeod despite their separation, and she had been required to fly to Portugal after his accident. She had also wanted desperately to go. Verity had been nearly twelve years old, and had not understood her mother's decision at all. Her sundress had been too tight under the arm-pits, and she had her period, and felt flushed and weak. It was only her second period ever, she had not really learnt how to handle the monthly inconvenience of it yet, and her mother had been scant with the details. Her hair had been greasy as they had left England in a hurry with no time to wash or prepare. Verity had stood beside Fiona in a tiled hotel lobby, somewhere on the Algarve. Her mother's back had stiffened as a young woman had approached them.

Lucy Wilson was her name. She had introduced herself confidently in an accent softly rounded by her comfortable upbringing. Lucy Wilson was all wrong, was the only way Verity had been able to assess her at the time. But then again, no-one would ever have been right. This person, this Lucy who her father had abandoned them for, was not even a proper grown-up woman like her mother – but neither was she still a girl. It had been disgusting but fascinating, coming face-to-face with her. Lucy was a bit like one of the prefects at school – mature, powerful and intimidating – and beautiful too, had been Verity's immediate, appallingly disloyal thought. She had amazing turquoise eyes, a steady gaze, and high breasts that swelled beneath a tight t-shirt. Verity had felt grubby and colourless, faced with her. It was no wonder her father had gone and left them; there was no happy comparison between the plump firmness of Lucy and the way she crossed the foyer confidently on long coltish legs with her chin up, and her mother's bowed, taut form. After the initial rush of disloyal observation though, Verity had soon accumulated hatred for this Other Woman.

After the initial handshake with her mother and a nod at Verity, Lucy had convulsed into messy sobs and flung her arms around and just hung onto her mother's narrow, stooped shoulders, clinging, wailing and snorting for what had felt like forever. It was not what one did with Fiona MacLeod, even at the worst of times.

Verity had folded her arms across her chest and sucked in her cheeks. Her mother's arms had hung at her sides, the pink fingers stretched straight in alarm, until eventually she had patted Lucy lightly and scantly on the back, taken her firmly but gently by both shoulders, and set her apart, establishing a boundary. The two women had stood and regarded each other. Lucy's hair had been mussed, and her mascara blotched. On closer inspection, Verity had noted bitterly that Lucy wore a beaded ankle bracelet; she could have stepped right out of Cosmopolitan magazine. This was the person her daddy had died for. This was the person whom he had leapt into the sea to rescue, managing to swim with her back to their boat and hand her up to safety before the same rip-tide that had threatened her and all her perfection, had dragged him, a weakened and not-so-young or beautiful middle-aged man, to his death.

At the thought, Verity had stepped forward and slapped Lucy Wilson's tanned cheek. The action was over in a flash; she barely knew that she had done it except that her hand stung, Lucy gasped dramatically, and Fiona gripped Verity's forearm with a strength that belied her skinny form.

'I hate you,' Verity had spat.

Fiona had cried out Verity's name, and turned livid red eyes on her.

43

Verity had retreated, appalled that her mother had sided with Lucy at this time, of all times, and reeling from the shocking absence of a hug when she most needed one. Turning on her heel, she had stalked out of the hotel lobby and into the bright heat of the miserable afternoon.

'Where are you going?' her mother had barked after her.

'To buy some sanitary towels,' Verity had yelled, delighted by her own vulgarity.

They had moved from the Oxfordshire countryside not long after that trip, selling the expansive but dilapidated cottage that Verity had loved so much, and moving to this little box in Teddington so that her mother could "get a proper job" and "put food on the table". The whole episode had been appalling and had made a shackle around Verity's heart, so tight that it still hurt sometimes. She regarded her father's painting again, standing up to take a closer look. It occurred to her that the painting was exceptionally good – an evening landscape imbued with light so yellow, so dense and yet so transparent that she could almost hear lazy insects buzzing around her head, and smell the earth and long grass, as she looked at it.

'He was good, wasn't he?' she murmured.

'Oh, he was brilliant.'

'Yes,' Verity nodded, a deeper understanding slotting into place somewhere inside her.

Fiona raised an eyebrow at Verity before taking another sip of her tea. 'You're very skittish today.'

Verity sat back down, and fought off a hot flush that made her want to run out into the street to cool down. She loosened the collar of her blouse, and fanned her face with her hand. 'I'm fine,' she managed, defensively.

'Have you got a temperature?'

'I'm just a bit hot. I don't think it's that.'

'Ah.' Fiona nodded, knowingly.

Verity recalled the brick-and-flint cottage in Oxfordshire where they had lived when she was a child – the sagging roof, the unmown lawn, the studio in the garden where her father had worked, with its long windows that faced north-west, white paint peeling from the frames. She remembered summers when butterflies and moths flitted above the meadow grass, swallows dived through the evening air, and pollen made her eyes itch. She recalled the big old Aga, the gassy smell of the primus stove which took its place in a hot summer, the washing line slung from a hook on the side of the house to the apple tree in the lawn. Why had her mother really moved them from there to here? Surely, she could have taken a job locally or got in a lodger? How had she coped with the loss?

'I'd better go, Mum. I've just realised how late it is. I've got so much to do, and I don't want to hit the rush-hour traffic. Thanks for agreeing to have Charlie at such short notice.'

'Oh, it will be my pleasure.' Fiona smiled, a rare smile.

Verity's car inched forward in the queue of traffic as she headed back to Fulham with Charlie curled up on the back seat. How would her mother fare if she moved back to Oxfordshire? Fiona did not drive, was not getting any younger. Would she take her mother with her? Tears sprung in Verity's eyes; from nowhere, it seemed as if some invisible weight threatened to squash her spirit altogether. She looked around at the leaden grey afternoon, the crowded suburban street, and the closed faces of the people walking by, and fought a huge impulse to jump out of her car, abandon it in the bloody awful rush-hour traffic, and run far, far away.

Run, run, run. Just like her father had done.

After shrugging her shoulders into her trench coat, Verity grabbed her door keys and an umbrella. On leaving the house, she wrenched the sticky front door to get it shut properly, reminding herself for the hundredth time that she must get it fixed before she put the house on the market. She strode out down Rannoch Road, registering a trace of diesel fumes lingering in the drizzle.

Test results had shown that she was not anaemic and there was nothing physically wrong with her, but the doctor had repeated that she must get outdoors every day and do more exercise. 'I do some yoga,' she had countered defensively, but the doctor had replied flatly that Verity should do more.

Embracing this advice, she had developed a new routine and begun to take regular morning walks by herself, as Charlie was so slow, and to treat herself to coffee somewhere, with her phone turned off, in an effort to relax. One of the few joys of owning her own business was that she could occasionally structure her own time, and she had vowed to make the most of it. As she walked

45

now, she tilted her umbrella to stop a fine drizzle falling on her face. It was hard to believe it was still only October. A long winter of cloud and cold lay ahead, and Verity dreaded the prospect of being stuck in the city in the bad weather. She dodged a puddle which nestled in a broken paving stone before crossing the junction at the top of her street. Forcing herself to think brightly, she admired the yellow leaves on the plane trees and noted how beautifully they contrasted with the grey sky. Despite the cheery observation, she still tasted the cloying city air in her mouth, and the muscles across her chest remained stiflingly tight.

In the café, Verity put her umbrella in a stand beside the door before queuing at the counter for a latte. She found a small table and shrugged off her coat, folding it neatly over the back of her chair before sitting down and dabbing her nose with a tissue. The latte was hot and scalded her mouth. She tried to look out at people walking past on the street but the café windows were misted with condensation. Around her, people chatted, a small child squirmed and squealed, chairs scraped, and a mug clattered down on a table top. Verity watched a drowsy young woman breastfeed a tiny baby, felt a wave of nostalgia and then realised she might be staring so looked away. She observed a middle-aged man who read a newspaper through half-moon reading glasses and kept looking up when the door opened, as if he was expecting someone. The air in the café was stifling and damp from everyone's wet clothing, and her head swam a little as she fought off a feeling of claustrophobia. She focussed on the door, debating whether to abandon the latte and leave, but decided to try to sit fast instead. She fought the rising sense of panic by focusing on the curled shape of her hands and taking slow breaths.

For no apparent reason, an image of Tills kneeling on a sandy beach in Dorset, building a complex sandcastle with a moat and shells for decoration, came into Verity's mind and tears welled in her eyes as it struck her that all those days with young children really were gone for good. One day there would be no more bangs of the stubborn front door either, no damp towels strewn on the white wicker chair in the bathroom, no comings and goings, or girly chatter, or shampoo smells, or the regular bleep of texts arriving. Already, the house was eerily tidy and the shopping list had shrunk to virtual insignificance – a good thing in some ways, she supposed,

46

but so saddening too. She swiped unwelcome tears from her eyes, hoping no-one had noticed them, and sipped the latte. She hated the way emotions ambushed her as if she were a teenager again, and promised herself she would get up early one morning on the long weekend away in France, and spend some time painting to relax a little.

A man walked by outside and she narrowed her eyes at the foggy window. The shape of his head was the same, as was his gait. Her heart leapt into her throat. Surely not? After all this time? The café door opened, and Verity held her breath, but as the man entered, she realised it was not him. It was not Edward, it was nothing like him. Her shoulders drooped. She had not done that for a long time – mistaken someone for him – and thought she had got over the habit, long ago. The man bent to kiss a woman at another table, and pulled up a chair. The couple exchanged warm glances, and Verity recalled the time when she and Matt had fallen in love, and he had made her laugh and steadily earned her trust by the little things he did; giving her a bunch of daffodils on a spring day, squeezing her hand when she needed reassurance, listening to her when she needed to talk. She recalled the admiration that used to shine from his eyes when he looked at her and the way his gaze lit up something inside her. He had been a part of her life for over twenty-three years now, and every memory she had of this time was threaded through with him, for better or worse. Inevitably perhaps, things had shifted as the years had passed, the joy they had once shared in small, simple things had worn thin, and their passion for each other had dwindled. It had been a long time since he had shown her any warmth, and these days, even the memories were turning bitter sweet.

Nerves and sadness rippled unbidden through Verity's body again. The table in front of her swam, she felt suddenly overwhelmed, and fought back more tears. She stood up, scraping her chair noisily on the tiled floor, grabbed her coat, and tried to shut out the crashing noises of cutlery scraping plates, cups rattling in saucers, and children shouting. Her fingers fumbled with her coat buttons. She told herself to calm down, attributing her nervous panic to the prospect of the flight the next day, and telling herself it would pass if she breathed steadily. The long weekend would help her relax, it would be fun, she told herself. She could take her camera and a few paints and her yoga mat away with her. Everything would be fine.

She stepped shakily back out into the street, noting that the rain had stopped. Immediately she started to feel calmer and walked briskly home. She was shoving her shoulder painfully against the stuck front door when she realised she had left her umbrella in the café.

'Oh crap,' she thought. Another thing lost.

Verity had almost finished packing her suitcase when the phone rang. Matt's mother, Marjorie Westwood, made no introduction but shouted a garbled tale to Verity who stood, listening and startled beside the folded clothes piled neatly on her bed, and with her hand spread on her chest.

'Leave it with me!' Verity exclaimed. 'We'll be there as soon as we can.'

She tried to ring Matt, but as Marjorie had shrieked, his phone was turned off. In a panic, she phoned his office, and spoke to someone who was working late. Then she pulled on her coat, snatched up her bag, and wrenched the awkward front door shut behind her before running off down the street.

She arrived at The Blue Anchor, where the colleague had said Matt was, panting and with hair stuck to her sweaty face. She spotted him before he noticed her, sitting at a round wooden table with a woman who had her back to the door. Verity made to move toward him but froze as she witnessed her husband lean forward and rest his hand on the woman's knee. The woman's back was slender and curved in at the waist beneath a tight black top, and she laughed at something Matt said. Verity's first instinct was to turn and bolt but as she hesitated, Matt saw her. He hastily withdrew his hand. Verity mustered her courage, and strode over to him.

'Your father has had a heart attack,' she stated, brutally.

'God, is he all right?'

'He's at the Royal Free in Hampstead.'

'Christ.'

Verity examined the woman. She was maybe in her late-thirties. After initially looking up at Verity and flashing a nervous smile which revealed dimples in her cheeks, she blushed and looked away. Verity could see highlights growing out on the crown of her head,

48

noted the droplet earring threaded carefully through an ear lobe, and the crossover-style top that emphasised her breasts.

'I'm Matt's wife,' Verity announced.

The woman made no attempt to reply.

'Verity, this is Ellie Stansbury, from our Content Creation team,' Matt interjected.

'Your phone is off. Where's your car?' Verity demanded.

'Round the back. Look, I'm sorry,' he said to the woman, and touched her lightly on the shoulder as he rose. 'I'll have to go.'

The woman gave a little shrug.

Outside, Verity barked, 'Who is she?'

'No-one. A colleague.'

Verity slid into the passenger seat of Matt's shiny Mercedes. She hardly ever travelled in his car, and it felt alien – his territory, not hers. As the Mercedes lurched through the streets, she noticed a sandwich wrapper in the door pocket. Crayfish and rocket. Matt was allergic to shellfish.

'Your mother has been trying to call you.'

'My phone was off.'

'I know. Why is it always off, Matt?'

'So that I can forget about work.'

'Well, I can see you were certainly doing that.'

'Can we focus on my father?'

Verity sniffed, pushed her hair back off her face, and opened the glove locker to search for a tissue. A tube of lipstick lay in the little space.

'Matt, what is this?'

'God knows. Ellie must have left it there.'

'Ellie?'

'You just met her. Ellie Stansbury. I expect she left it in my car.'

'She left a lipstick in your car? Why would she do that?'

'You tell me. You're a woman. Women do these things – beats me why.'

'You were touching her knee.'

'What?'

'When I arrived at the pub, you were touching her knee.'

'No, I wasn't.'

'You were. Matt, what's going on?'

49

'Nothing, there's nothing going on! You're not going to go jealous on me now, are you? Can we just concentrate on my father, please? Call my mother.'

Verity reined in her desire to interrogate. 'Okay, I'll try but her phone will be off in the hospital. She told me she'd call you when she could. Where's your mobile, let me turn it on again. She might be trying to get you.' Matt retrieved his phone from his jacket pocket and handed it to her. She switched the phone on, and put it down in her lap. 'It doesn't make any sense your father having a heart attack. He's not overweight, he's always playing golf.'

'I know, I know,' Matt agreed, watching a set of traffic lights, and tapping his fingers on the steering wheel.

A text arrived with a bleep on Matt's phone, and Verity picked it up and read it.

'"Hope your Dad is ok, so sorry Matt. I'm around this weekend if you need me. Call me, E x."' Verity read out loud.

'Give me that!' Matt reached for his phone.

Verity folded her arms. 'Why has she finished the text with a kiss?'

'Women do that. I expect you do it yourself.'

'So, you holding her knee and meeting her in a pub in the evening has nothing to do with her putting kisses on her text to you? I thought she was supposed to be a colleague!'

'Don't be like that, V! Don't you put kisses on your texts to your colleagues?'

'Yes, but that's different. There was something not right about her, Matt. She was smirking. And she had funny eyes.'

'One of her pupils is dilated. She had meningitis when she was a baby. Give me a break.' Matt was driving through the busy streets as fast as he could, and Verity grasped the dashboard to steady herself as he swung the Mercedes around a corner at speed.

'You'll get a ticket.'

'I don't care. Try my mother again.'

Verity rang. Marjorie's phone was still switched off.

'How many times have you met her?'

'I meet her all the time. I work with her.'

'Something is very wrong here.'

Matt's chin jutted out and he pressed his lips together in silence. His nostrils flared and his jaw muscle tensed. After almost quarter of a century of spending time with the man, Verity knew these were not good signs.

At the hospital, they parked the car, and jogged to the entrance. Matt grabbed Verity's arm, and stopped her before they went in.

'I'm not sure I can do this.' His eyes were lit with fear.

'Of course you can, come on.'

The lights in the hospital were dazzling, and Verity squinted. When they found Marjorie, Matt stood rigid and distant while Verity stepped forward and hugged her. She looked at Jim, her normally strong father-in-law, prostrate on a hospital bed. His cheeks were slackened and pouched as he apparently slept, his skin was grey, and his hand curled on the hospital bedsheet, a cannula taped to his skin. A man who was never quiet or still appeared drained of all his noise and energy. How fragile he looked, she thought.

'They think he's going to be alright,' Marjorie murmured, her face awash with relief, a trickle of mascara filling the creases at the corner of her eye. 'It was just a little one. They've given him something to calm him down a bit – you know what he's like. He wanted to go straight home again.'

When they got back to Rannoch Road in the small hours of the morning, Matt poured himself a large Scotch, and Verity rested her hand on his shoulder and said, 'It'll be okay, you know.'

Matt stepped away from her, and did not reply. Later, after Verity had got into bed, there was a quiet knock on the bedroom door, and he poked his head into the room.

'Mummy just rang. They will be keeping Dad in for observations and tests but we can still go to France tomorrow. She wants us to go, carry on as normal.'

'Great,' Verity replied brightly.

6

It had been a while since he had been here, and looking around, Edward Farrell recalled why he avoided the place whenever he could. The cold air outside was unpleasantly thick and cloying, reeking of diesel fumes and nicotine from a cluster of smokers on the sidewalk. People appeared grey-skinned, and a chain of cars hustled impatiently for what little parking space there was. A fizz of human activity assaulted him as he entered the terminal building, and pressed forward through it. He was familiar with the airport, of course – he was familiar with airports everywhere, and each time he found himself in one of these big, ugly temples to modern travel, he hankered after the dusty landing strips in remoter parts of the world where a small plane would set him down without ceremony, and his passport was checked in little more than a shed, if it was checked at all.

Edward halted, and tried to recall the exact location of the coffee bar where he had arranged to meet his brother. A shaven-headed man shoved past, jolting him, and not pausing to apologise. Pain shot through his strained shoulder and he gritted his teeth, loathing the crudeness of urban life and the inconsiderate way so many people behaved. He was feeling crotchety, he knew. Lack of sleep at the hotel, the sore muscle aggravated by the weight of his suitcase, and work worries, were the culprits.

As he queued to order coffee, he stretched out an arm to check his watch. He had about fifteen minutes before he was due to meet Jay, which was just about perfect. The queue inched forwards, and

Edward shoved his suitcase along with his foot. He recalled how in the past he had paid large sums of money to upgrade his flight and capture a bit of peace, buying himself a quiet lounge to wait in or a seat where he could lie flat and catch a good night's sleep on a long flight. These small things made a world of difference, and with the amount of travelling he did, he could sometimes justify the extravagance; but he also wondered if he wasn't getting old and a bit too long in the tooth for the constant globetrotting.

Part of the reason he felt so cranky and out of sorts was also, he knew, the date: October 10th. Would Jay remember? He rarely saw his brother these days, and did not know whether Jay would acknowledge the anniversary of their father's death or not. Dick Farrell had passed away a staggering thirty-six years ago, and as Jay never remembered birthdays it was possible he would not recall this anniversary either. Edward would certainly not mention it unless Jay did; Jay's life had been tough enough recently. Edward pondered his brother as he queued for his coffee. They were so very different; Jay was sociable whereas Edward was a loner. As a child, Edward had been content to sit on a rug and play with his toys while Jay was always hankering to be outside with the neighbour's kids, or so their mother had always said. Edward conjured memories of the warm, woody atmosphere of their modest cedar shingle home, the way the dirt felt gritty in his sandals as he walked up the track through the redwood forest on their side of the canyon. As they grew older, he had not minded when Jay went off with the older boys and left him alone. The stillness of a day without wind, when the sun blazed on the little patch of dry grass beside the house was forever imprinted in his memory. He recalled the sweat running in his eyes when he played ball games with their dogs, the cries of circling red-tailed hawks, and Jerusalem crickets chirruping in the long grass at the back of the house. These things had been enough.

He placed his order for an espresso and biscotti, and paid with a handful of loose change. As he waited for the order to be made up, he recalled his father. If he had to choose one word to describe the man, he would say he was a rock. Edward had never known quite how his father was feeling, but he had always known what was expected of him – hard work, the truth, and decent behaviour. There were few hugs, few affectionate words spoken, and only the occasional pat on the back after a race won in college or a pile of logs stacked neatly in the yard; and yet despite the lack of words, Edward had loved his father, and knew he was loved in return. From a young age, they had gone out running along tracks on nearby Mount Tamalpais. He could still recall the fragrance of early morning air, heavy with scents from the forest floor as the mist rose up through the redwood trees. He could still hear the patter of their separate footfall and the rush of their breaths as they ran. This was the defining memory of his childhood, the one around which all other memories circled – the image of running in the Californian woods with his father, an unspoken bond between them, and the calm, meditative state which running induced. Dick Farrell had done everything right in life – kept fit, eaten modestly, not smoked – and had been far too young to die at fifty-three, not far off the age Edward was now. The doctor had said his passing was caused by an aneurism and could happen to anyone at any time, but there had been little comfort in that.

In the airport café, the hiss of the coffee machine intruded into his thoughts, and Edward became aware of his curled fist. He released his fingers and stretched them into a star shape. He took the packet biscotti the server gave him and put it in his jacket pocket, collected his espresso, heaved his case up off the floor, and found a seat at a counter close to the entrance where he could easily look out for his brother.

His flight today was a short one to Nice, France, and for once it was not work-related, although Edward would still need to make some phone calls somehow. There would be no mobile phone reception or internet at the place they were staying in the Massif des Maures, which meant he would be out of touch with his contacts in Yangon for the best part of three days. Anticipating this, he had worked into the small hours of the morning in his hotel room. The story he was working on showed signs of reaching a critical hiatus and he feared the worst for the man, a fellow journalist, who was its subject. As he sipped his coffee, Edward fretted. What had seemed like a great idea the week before when he had spoken to Jay on the phone, was starting to feel like an error of judgement. What if something did happen to the fellow journalist, currently imprisoned in Yangon's notorious Insein prison, while Edward was sunning himself in the South of France? Although he tried not to, he tended to take these things personally, and hoped that by telling

54

the man's story, he would draw enough attention to his case that human rights agencies would pressurise the Burmese authorities to release him. It sounded like a naïve idea but it sometimes worked. Edward stared hard at the stained surface of the coffee counter, reminding himself that Jay had been through a big health scare, and it was important to see him too – crucial, in fact, that he showed his brother some support.

He unwrapped the biscotti, and took a bite. It tasted stale. A woman watched him from the other side of the coffee bar, and when he returned her stare, looked away. The woman reminded him of a girlfriend he had once had; same long brown hair and serious, academic look. He scanned the collage of faces massed around the café area but still could not spot his brother. Anxiety stirred like a snake in his mind. It might be possible to keep up with developments in Yangon if the house had its own phone, and he could always make a trip to somewhere with better communications. Jay would understand. He wondered if he could re-structure his story and try to sell it as it was, and make his upcoming visit to Yangon a follow-up article, but he was not convinced he had enough material or time. He rubbed his fingertips along his jawline, lost in thought.

'Eduardo!'

A hand slapped his back and he was crushed in his brother's clumsy embrace. After hastily steadying his espresso cup, he turned and hugged his brother back, then greeted Caro, Jay's wife, by kissing each of her cheeks in turn.

'And this is Matt Westwood,' Jay beamed, introducing a man who stood coolly on the edge of their small family reunion. Edward shook hands with the newcomer, noting his expensive jacket, thinning hair, and the shadows beneath a pair of interesting blue eyes. He thought he had seen him somewhere before, but then he met so many people, it was hard to be sure.

'Pleased to meet you,' Matt said.

Jay grinned at them all, and took a deep breath. 'Well, no sign of your wife yet, then?' he addressed Matt brightly.

'She's taken our dog to her mother's and may be stuck in traffic,' Matt apologised. 'I suggest we carry on and find somewhere more comfortable to park ourselves. She'll catch up with us.'

'Are you sure we should move on without her?' Caro asked. 'It's not a problem to wait here for a while. We have plenty of time.'

'No,' Matt countered. 'Punctuality is not her strong point. Let's get through security and find somewhere nicer to grab a drink, and wait for her there. I'll text her, and let her know where we are.'

'Matt's a bit of a law unto himself at times, but he's a good bloke,' Jay mouthed to Edward as they queued at the check-in machines. 'I think you'll like him. I owe him one, big time. I've never met the wife.'

The brothers grinned at each other.

'You're looking good,' Edward remarked.

'So are you, bro, so are you.'

The group progressed through security, stopped for a coffee, and a bit later when they were called, walked the distance to a departure lounge – and still there was no sign of Matt's wife, a fact that Edward found disturbing. Matt had left another message for her, but she had not replied. By the time that the group reached the queue to board the plane, they were stressed and distracted by her absence and wondering what to do. Edward sensed that there was more to the story than her simply being late. He had noted the way Matt's eyes shifted when he spoke, and figured that if his wife was not even answering her phone at this stage of events, there must be something quite wrong.

'It's a great house we're staying in,' Jay began, in an effort to lighten the atmosphere. The queue was not moving yet and there was still time before a decision had to be made. 'It sits high up above the Côte d'Azur, surrounded by miles of forest. Right up your street. Edward.'

'Sounds great.'

'It belongs to the ancient mother of a chap from work who only lets it out to people the family know. The location is quite spectacular, apparently. Peace and privacy, and with great food available in some fancy coastal towns, only a car ride away.'

Edward could take or leave the fancy coastal towns and the fine food, but he felt a spark of interest at the promise of forested hills. 'We could take a hike together, like we used to,' he suggested.

'I'd like that,' Jay grinned.

'Can you see your wife anywhere?' Caro asked Matt anxiously.

'No. I can't.'

'We'd better step to one side to wait for her. The queue has begun to move.'

'I agree. We can't board without her. I do hope she's all right,' Jay said.

'I'll try to call her again.'

Edward looked out through the lounge window at the grey English sky, and felt mildly exasperated. His own phone rang from his jacket pocket. 'Sorry,' he mouthed to Jay.

Jay smiled a little too brightly. 'Sure, go ahead.'

Edward lifted his phone to his ear, watching as Matt glared at his still-unanswered phone. Some weekend this was going to be.

7

Verity was out of breath and slightly dizzy as the dread of getting on a plane loomed larger with each step she took through the terminal building. It was impossible to concentrate and she had to re-read all the airport signs which swam before her eyes and re-check her flight number repeatedly. Horrific premonitions of being trapped in a plane high up in the sky and panicking, with no possibility of escape or relief, dogged her every move. On top of that, she was running late because Julie, one of the shop assistants, had called in sick. Mel would now close the studio and open the shop but this had meant cancelling a client whom Mel was due to meet, and the client had been hard to reach. Her phone rang again in her bag but having glanced and seen it was Matt, she ignored it. The unresolved issue of the woman in the black top made her seethe and she feared losing her temper, despite knowing that after Jim's heart attack, it was not a good time. That morning, she had left the house with Charlie before Matt was awake, having judged it best to avoid her husband until she had more time to compose herself. All through the night, she had tried to tell herself to forget the woman and get some sleep but it had been hopeless. When a raw morning light had finally dawned, she had felt less susceptible to her own wild imaginings but her hurt and annoyance had grown to bursting point. She had no idea how she was going to get through the weekend ahead.

On reaching the boarding lounge, Verity purposefully averted her eyes from the massive plane parked just outside the window. She would not admit to anyone how frightened she was; it was so stupid to be afraid of flying at her age. Chin in the air, she managed to keep on walking across the endless grey-tiled floor. Eventually, she spotted Matt, and wove her way toward him, whispering 'excuse me' to people waiting in the queue. Matt shook his head in disbelief when she stepped up to him. He introduced her to Jay and Caro, and Verity shook hands with the couple. He explained that Jay's brother was with them too, and gestured to a man with broad shoulders who stood with his back to the group, and talked intensely into a mobile phone. Something about the man looked familiar but she was too distracted to work out what.

'Was there a problem?' Matt asked her.

'I'm so sorry, problems at work and then the traffic,' Verity addressed Jay and Caro to offer her explanation. 'It was nose-to-tail today, choked.'

'We're just glad you made it. We were beginning to worry.' Jay smiled politely.

'I probably should have left more time.'

'Well, it's impossible to judge these things sometimes. I'm glad you made it. You must be shattered. I personally hate to rush,' Caro added kindly.

Out of the corner of her eye, Verity could see the plane's huge gleaming form through the plate glass window. They shuffled forward in the queue, and Caro and Jay stepped ahead.

'I thought you might not come,' Matt muttered.

'Of course I'd come. I said I'd come.'

'Yes, but you left the house at the crack of dawn and then you were late, and you didn't answer your phone. Did you not see me calling?'

'It's been a tough morning, Matt.'

'Was it your mother then, or the dog?' Matt asked her, staring at the floor.

Verity rubbed her hand along her arm. 'Mum was fine. Charlie was fine,' she replied distractedly. '*They* are not the problem. How's your father this morning?'

'Okay,' Matt shrugged. 'They're doing a few tests and talking about sending him home.'

'Already? That's a bit quick.'

'He's in good hands. They know what they're doing.'

59

'I did speak to your mother again, late last night. I offered to drive over to be with her but she wouldn't hear of it. She's a tough old bird.'

'I knew you were looking for a way out of this weekend.'

'I was not! I was thinking of Marjorie. Tell me, do you ever actually miss Livia and Tills?'

'What an odd question. Of course, I miss them.'

'They were the only thing that made any sense,' Verity blurted.

Matt adjusted his grip on his hand luggage and stared at the floor. Verity rubbed her neck to try to ease her tension, and turned away from her husband. She was too cross and disappointed and fragile to speak to him. The queue started to move again. Matt moved ahead to talk to Jay, and Verity found herself behind Jay's brother who had re-joined the queue while she and Matt had been talking. Something about the soothing tone of his voice as he spoke on his phone was familiar but Verity could not think where she had heard it before. The hand which held her passport and boarding card grew sweaty. She really did not want to be at the airport. The last thing she needed was to be stuck in the South of France with a trio of total strangers and her extremely frustrating husband. She longed for some time to herself, and some space and peace, away from the stresses of her life. She could still make excuses. It was not too late. The back of Jay's brother's neck was only inches from her face now as people jostled in the queue behind her. His grey-streaked hair was cut neatly, the ends of it touching clean tanned skin above his collar. She studied the weave in the dense linen fabric of his jacket, noting all the shades of cream and the tiny bumps in the threads. He finished his call, slipped his phone into his pocket and after a prompt from Jay, turned around in the confined space to introduce himself.

'Hi, I'm Edward.'

'I'm Verity.' Her mouth fell open and her eyes widened. They gripped each other's fingers. Her heart made one of its familiar flips. His eyes shone, black as coal. He was broader, not as tall as she remembered. She could smell his skin – the exotic fragrance of vetiver – it was the same smell, his smell. Her senses reeled. A thousand tiny sparkling impressions tumbled about her as they stood, squashed so close, her nose almost touching his chest and her gaze resting on his pale, clean shirt as she remembered to

60

breathe. He was, and yet was not, what she had always expected. She took a step back, bumped into someone, apologised vaguely and searched Edward's rugged face. Greedily, she noted the soft curve of his mouth, the whiteness of his teeth, and that jaw line – the one she would paint with one swipe of a brush.

'We're on holiday now. You can leave your work behind, you know,' she muttered – a stupid, blustering thing to say. She leaned away from him and smiled awkwardly, raising her eyebrows, willing him to say something back to her, anything. For some reason, she could not exclaim, 'I never thought I would see you again!' She could not manage it, did not dare. So much time had passed since they had last seen each other, it had been a different life. Edward paused for a second, studying her with his dark, dark eyes, and Verity absorbed his gaze for what felt like forever.

'Glad you could join us, at last,' he murmured, and something about the glimmer in his eyes and way he uttered the words, his shoulders falling, told Verity that he knew it was her, he recognised her, of course he did. But still, neither of them mentioned their past. Jay tapped Edward on the shoulder, and he turned away from her. They had reached the departure gate.

After they had found their seats on the plane, Matt glanced awkwardly at Verity and gave her a tight smile, and she felt a twinge of her old guilt. Matt had never known a thing about Edward or the clandestine meetings. The plane lurched upwards, roaring into the air.

'Ugh,' she murmured, feeling her stomach churn.

'Nobody enjoys this part of a flight,' Matt declared.

'How do you know that? The pilot probably loves it,' she muttered, bracing herself. Her stomach tightened and, not normally a believer, she prayed fervently for everyone's safety, tucking her hands between her thighs, curling her shoulders and squeezing her eyes shut. The roar of the engines amplified in her head, loud and threatening. Verity experienced a flash of panic as she realised she was locked into the cabin now, stuck high up above the earth, and unable to get out. She fought to dampen her fear by locking her fingers and squeezing them together until they hurt. It would soon be over and then she would be on the ground again, she repeated to herself.

'Are you all right?' Matt asked gruffly, leaning toward her.

'Fine,' Verity replied snappily, but of course she was not. She longed for the type of husband who would hold and reassure her in her distress, and for the woman in the black top not to exist, and she was thrown and baffled by the twist of fate that had cast her and Edward together again after almost a quarter of a century's separation.

As the plane settled at a chosen altitude and passengers started to shuffle in their seats and chat again, Verity felt suddenly, overwhelmingly drained as if she was breathing in treacle instead of air. She turned to look beyond the couple beside her, who sat quietly reading, to see a brilliant circle of blue sky glowing through the thick glass of the porthole. She pulled out an in-flight magazine from the pouch in front of her and flicked disconsolately through the pages. On the other side of the aisle, Matt closed his eyes and leant his head back against the headrest. In the seat in front of him, Edward took out his laptop and typed rapidly. The air was filled with the whining thrum of the aeroplane's engines, and Verity sat, willing the time to pass. After a while, Caro got up from her seat, and came and stood beside her. She had a neat blonde bob, clear skin and a warm smile. She crouched down beside Verity, nodding back at Matt's sleeping figure.

'Your husband has been a real tonic to Jay, you know. I'm very grateful to him and I'm looking forward to this weekend with you both.'

'Thanks. Matt told me Jay's a brave man. It's very kind of you to invite us away like this.'

Caro softened. 'Not at all, and yes, we hope he is over the worst now. I've never been to this part of France before, have you?'

'Not since I was a child. When I was younger, we lived in an area a couple of hours west of Nice for several years.'

'Goodness, you'll know it well then. I think we're in for a bit of rain during this trip but I still plan to shop while the men hang out together. Perhaps you can show me round a few places?'

'A shopping trip sounds good, although it's a long time since I've been here and I'm not sure how much I'll remember.'

'Jay is really looking forward to catching up with his brother. He was only able to join us at the last minute. I hope you don't mind.'

'Of course not!' Verity replied, wondering whether to admit she already knew Edward but deciding against it. Why had she not said to Edward earlier, 'It's you'? Why had Edward not said anything to her? The whole situation seemed so unreal and so unlikely, it was hard to know where to begin.

'Both Edward and Jay are American but Jay has been in England so long that his accent has almost completely gone,' Caro explained. 'Jay hardly ever gets to see Edward as he's a complete workaholic, always flying all over the world writing about people and rescuing them.'

'Edward rescues people?'

'He's a journalist, but in his spare time he works for a charity which helps people who've been unfairly imprisoned – prisoners of conscience, that type of thing. We hardly ever see him from one year to the next as he's nomadic and impossible to contact. He lives out of a suitcase, travelling from one job to the next, and has done for years, so you can see how special it is to have his company now, and we've kind of seized the chance. Jay didn't think you guys would mind.'

'Of course we don't, not at all,' Verity murmured. She was trying to imagine Edward living out of a suitcase, the image striking her as both sad and yet defiant and wonderful.

'I can't imagine not having a home, by choice,' she mused, and glanced at Edward who sat with his head bent over his laptop, lost in his work. 'Does he really not have a home?'

'No, nowhere. Not anymore. Anyway, it's nice to meet you. I must go to the loo.'

Why, Verity wondered, would a person choose to be homeless? She studied the back of Edward's head. The urge to draw him sprang within her again, after all the years. The shape of his head and his thick dark hair, now peppered with grey, always reminded her of a mountain bear. He leant toward Jay, quietly muttered something, and the power of his smile took her by surprise. She had forgotten how magical it was.

'What are you working on these days?' she heard Jay ask.

'A story about a Burmese journalist. He reminds me of a younger version of myself,' he replied.

'Got under your skin, has he?'

'Yes, you could say that.'

'So, tell me his story. I love to hear your stories.'

'I read a translation of some of his work where he exposed the corruption and abuse of human rights in the Burmese Army. It didn't go down very well with the military rulers in Burma, as you can imagine, and he was arrested and sentenced to fifty-nine years in prison for "public order offences". In prison, his health has deteriorated rapidly as he's asthmatic. He isn't getting the medication he needs as it gets stolen before it reaches him. In the past week, I heard reports that he's become quite frail, and so I'm seeing what I can do to get medicine to him. I just picked up some more news before we boarded, and it's not great. A doctor has visited him and reported that he's seriously ill. He left medication but it's generally felt that the prison guards will take it as soon as the doctor's back is turned. The good news is there's a local military official who might help in return for certain favours.' Edward chewed his lip thoughtfully. 'The military official could be the difference between life and death for the journalist but these officials are rarely honest.' He shook his head. 'It's a risk.'

'Every man out for himself?'

'You said it. The negotiators have mailed me asking for my assistance as I'm possibly the person who is most up-to-date on the whole situation. It's important to establish that the military official has the power and intention to deliver the medicines. Experience has taught us that an ill-chosen official will take the bribe money and run, and what's worse, they can turn in the contact to the authorities in the process.'

'You need to deal with this pretty quickly?'

'Yep, bro, I do. And when this is done, I'm all yours.'

'Ha! I've heard that one before!'

As they neared the end of the flight, Verity walked to the back of the plane to queue for the toilet. Her nerves were beginning to get the better of her again at the thought of the plane landing. She had become a little breathless and dizzy, and focused her attention on the floral blouse of the woman in front of her in the queue, in an attempt to calm down. A voice behind her whispered, 'Hi', and she turned, but before she could reply, the plane lurched appallingly, and she staggered and was forced to reach out for support. Edward caught her forearm and steadied her, seeming to balance effortlessly himself.

'Turbulence,' he remarked, the corners of his mouth curling upwards. The plane dropped dramatically, Verity's feet almost lifted off the floor, and a few passengers exclaimed. Edward held on to her forearm, and she gripped his jacket sleeve. The plane fell again, and her face plunged into his chest, her teeth knocking shut as her chin hit his body. She pulled back but the plane took yet another sudden dive and her forehead hit his chest again, cushioned by the soft fabric of his shirt and the warm flesh beneath it. It was a moment before she managed to straighten up and find her balance.

'Crikey,' she muttered in disbelief, nerves ripping through her. Edward moved his hands and firmly held the top of her arms.

'It's okay,' he reassured, dark eyes seeking hers.

She stood up tall, laughed nervously, and he smiled steadily back at her. Her hair had fallen over her face and she pushed it back as he loosened his grip on her. She swallowed hard and took a deep breath to speak but once again the plane lurched, and they were frozen in a strange, fractured dance as he grabbed her again, and the years peeled away, and she was back in Alison's basement, head swimming, young again, lost.

After a few moments, the plane steadied, and Verity heard the ping of a warning bell in the cabin followed by a steward's announcement asking everyone to return to their seats and fasten their seatbelts. The queue for the toilet had to be abandoned.

'Sorry.' She let go of Edward's jacket sleeve, and clutched the edge of a seat.

'Are you okay?'

'Fine.'

'It's just turbulence, nothing to worry about. Happens all the time.' Edward turned, leaving everything unspoken between them, and led the way back to their seats. The plane lurched again as they walked, and his strong hand flew backwards, found her forearm and gripped it, steadying her. She grasped the fabric of his jacket at the back, to avoid bumping into him. Something about his protective gesture, the instinctive nature of it, made the heat rise in her cheeks. With Edward close, her fears fell away and peace washed over her like warm water. She laughed as the plane shook in the air, imagining a dog shaking rain from its coat. She looked down at Edward's strong, blunt fingers curled around her forearm, and knew instinctively that whatever happened, she was meant to be in this plane, here, now. The plane lunged for the umpteenth time, an engine thrummed, someone screamed and a woman burst into tears. Edward drew her hands around his waist and she leant against his back, grateful for his solid, sturdy body which cushioned her. Held in this position while the plane juddered, and passengers exclaimed and murmured all around her, she felt as if life itself gripped her, shook her and reassured her, all at once.

Eventually the plane steadied again, and Edward let go of her hands. They managed to stagger the few steps back to their seats as the plane jolted less dramatically. As she sat, Verity caught Edward's eye and returned his gaze for a moment. His eyes were so dark it was impossible to tell what he thought. Something about Edward was wild and knew few boundaries, she realised, and suddenly understood her choice all those years before. If Edward was the ocean, Matt had been her harbour.

The pilot made an announcement, apologising for any inconvenience. He reassured passengers that they would be landing shortly, and informed them that a big storm was expected to reach the region that evening.

8

When Edward took his seat again, he snapped the belt shut over his lap, ran his hand back across his head, and struggled to figure out what exactly had just happened. During the spell of turbulence, Verity had looked so bewildered, it had shocked him. As she had fallen against him, a head full of dark curls crushing his chest, she had stirred his instinct to protect her. She had looked embarrassed and apologised for her nerves, but his intuition had already come alive. When they had met in the queue at the airport, he had been stunned; it had taken him one long dawning moment to recognise her, and then he had simply been lost for words. She still had the same great hair – thick, brown, and a little crazy-looking – although it was cut shorter now. He had forgotten how tall she was, almost matching him in height. She had tucked a loose strand behind her ear when they spoke, and the familiar gesture had sent his emotions reeling. She had appeared vulnerable then, even before the turbulence, her features pinched with exhaustion. He had stood to one side to allow her to enter the plane before him, and she had swallowed hard, gingerly extending one foot over the threshold, and it had dawned on him then that she was afraid of flying. He had wanted to offer her reassurance but she had taken off down the central aisle at a determined pace. The woman he saw now was not the same Verity he had once known, or imagined over the years. He wondered how her brazen confidence had been lost as he had only ever recalled the wild beauty of her dancing, her radiant smile and brilliantly light approach to life.

He continued to observe her as they walked through Nice airport. She strode purposefully and quickly, paying no attention to her husband and not talking to anyone as she queued for passport control – a tall, lonely figure in the crowd, the sort of character Edward identified with only too well. In the baggage reclamation area, she muttered something to her husband, and left their group to seek out the toilets, re-joining them a few minutes later.

'Am I the only one who checked in luggage?' she asked on her return, looking around the group.

'You and my dear brother,' Jay replied.

'Ah well, that makes me feel better.' She gave Jay a quick, nervous smile. The group waited, chatting amiably as the carousel lurched into action and a line of luggage crawled like a lumpy caterpillar from behind a screen of plastic flaps.

'What does your case look like?' Jay asked Verity.

'Sort of big. And red,' she answered.

'Not a light packer then?' Jay teased, and Edward smiled at the familiar pattern of his brother's humour.

Verity tipped her head on one side, a smile playing around her lips too. 'I don't do this 'travel light' thing,' she shrugged. 'It's unnecessary. I have a couple of books, some paints, a yoga mat, a raincoat – which you may laugh at now, but I did read the forecast.'

'A yoga mat?' Matt interjected. He had an accent that sounded like his mouth was full of pebbles, and tucked his chin into his neck as he spoke.

'Yes. A yoga mat,' Verity began firmly, and caught Edward's eye.

Edward recognised his own suitcase on the luggage carousel. 'Excuse me,' he said, and stepped through the small group. He pulled his large, battered leather case off the carousel, and set it on the floor.

'Well, and I thought I'd packed a lot,' Verity remarked.

Edward smiled. 'Ah, but my whole life is in this case.'

'A very small life,' she replied, before seeming to falter. 'Sorry, I didn't mean it like that,' she apologised hastily.

'Oh, I think we all have small lives,' Edward found himself replying, steadily.

'I'm sorry, what I said about your small life. I didn't mean it that way,' she repeated, as they walked through the customs hall, forced together by a swarm of people who funnelled towards the exit.

'It's a fair point, actually.'

'Well, I didn't mean it like that.'

'I know you didn't.'

When they regrouped at the car hire desk, they realised that the vehicle they had booked only seated four people, as no-one had known at the time that Edward would be joining them. A discussion ensued about what they should do as the company's larger models were taken, and eventually they all agreed to squash into the smaller car. Edward glanced at Verity striding out ahead of him towards it, dragging her red case on its wheels. She wore flat shoes, and her skirt was loose and moved with a swing. As they loaded luggage into the boot, Edward considered the group. Caro looked sophisticated and unruffled in her pale trouser suit, even after the cramped plane journey. Jay wore a pink-striped shirt and his face shone with pleasure, but the tension around his eyes remained as a subtle indicator of the previous year's ill-health. Matt issued commands and cracked loud jokes bullishly with Jay.

As Jay drove them away from the airport, the city of Nice flashed past at dizzying speed, out at sea clouds hung thick and low, and a wind whipped the fronds of palm trees bordering the roadside.

'I think that storm is coming,' Verity remarked.

'It'll probably stay out at sea. They often do,' Matt countered.

'Is that so?' she murmured, obviously disagreeing. 'Would someone mind opening a window?'

'The air conditioning is on,' Matt reassured her.

Edward let the window on his side of the car down a little. 'Let me know if you'd like it open further.'

'Thank you,' she replied, and closed her eyes as a delicate sea breeze swept into the vehicle.

As they travelled out of the suburbs and into the hills, it became impossible for Edward to ignore her shoulder brushing against his. She had opened her eyes again and appeared absorbed by a cluster of jagged hills which pierced the azure sky with their huge, unkempt silhouette.

Eventually, after an hour and a half's travelling, Jay steered the car off the main highway and onto a narrow road with much less traffic which wound between craggy, wild hills that rose above a dazzling coastline. The terrain was blanketed in cork oak, pine and mimosa, and was largely uninhabited. At one point, a broad sweep of chestnut-coloured earth with a downy growth of saplings and scrub came into view.

'What's happened there?' Verity asked.

'A landslide, I should imagine,' Jay replied. 'Apparently, they have quite a few in this region if they get lots of rain after a dry summer. They can take out whole stretches of forest like this.'

'The power of nature.'

'Yes indeed.'

They travelled on a while in silence, turning eventually onto a single-track road, and journeying up a steep hillside for several miles until, up ahead, just before the road was about to disintegrate into a rutted track, there appeared a modest stone gateway to a gravel drive flanked with mimosa and a cluster of swaying pine and oak trees.

'We're here,' Caro announced, with obvious satisfaction. 'Look, there's the sign. The house is called Les Chênes.'

Jay parked on an area of gravel, close to the front door of the house and beside a small Renault. 'I guess that's the maid's car,' he said.

The architecture was typically Provençal, Edward thought as he studied the low terracotta roof, blue-painted window shutters, and the light-coloured stone of the buildings. He strolled across the drive to stretch his legs. The house stood behind a wide lawn, tucked up against a cliffside to the rear. The entire property was cut out of the swell of a hill, and almost at the top of a ridge where a straggle of windblown trees grew. The location, he presumed, protected the house from the worst of the mistral. Below the property, a series of lower hills rolled and dropped, down and down, until in the far distance the land eventually plunged into the sea. A steady wind blew from the west, gusting already. It came like a blast of relief after the confines of the day, and sensing its freshness, Edward immediately relaxed. He stood on the lawn with his hands shoved into his pockets, and considered the scene before him. The wind carried with it the threat of the approaching storm that was not far away, judging by the bank of cloud slung low over the sea in the distance. He tasted the salt in the air, smelled the impending rain, and felt the liveliness of the breeze. Looking out at the wild beauty of the uninhabited landscape before him, he felt glad he had come. He walked back to the car, retrieved his suitcase from the boot, and followed the others into the house.

The vast entrance hall seemed to double as a typically French salon with a massive stone fireplace midway down one side. A high ceiling was supported by thick beams, each the size of a tree trunk. A couple of large, comfortable-looking sofas and a low table were grouped beside the fireplace, and a piano and more bits and pieces of furniture stood beyond them. A stairway curled up from the left-hand side of the space, and cut into the far wall were a row of tall glazed windows and a pair of doors that led out onto a covered veranda. The group stood just inside this space with an excitable maid who gabbled rapidly in French. Matt stood slightly apart, inspecting the cover of a guide book on a side table, and jangling the coins in his pocket. Jay listened to the maid with his head on one side, and wore a sympathetic expression but seemed at a loss to understand what was being said, while Verity asked the maid, in perfect French, to speak a little more slowly. She nodded and frowned as the maid continued her outpouring. Edward, who was fluent in French, put down his case on the stone floor, and listened in to learn what all the fuss was about.

The maid was telling Verity that a huge storm was forecast, and she needed to collect her son from the nursery in their village, some distance away. She did not want to get trapped on the mountain road if the storm came, and neither did she want her son to get stuck at his nursery. In this region, these things happened, she insisted. She had cleaned through the house but had not had time to make the beds. She wanted to leave immediately and suggested that the group might want to consider staying down in the town themselves where it was safer, as when storms hit these hills, it was dangerous. There were landslides, and the power lines went down easily. The maid jerked her forearm from a vertical position to horizontal, to emphasise her point.

Verity touched the woman's arm, and explained that she would translate for the others. While she did, the maid fidgeted impatiently with a clasp on her handbag, already slung over her shoulder.

'Well, surely there's no panic, the skies are still blue, she can make up the beds before she goes,' Matt objected from the side of the room.

Jay blinked at his friend before countering, 'I think she should just go, she's so worried, poor thing.'

'Bien sûr, vous devez aller,' Verity decided firmly but the maid glanced at Matt. 'Don't you worry about him,' Verity reassured her in confident French. 'He's my husband.' The maid nodded and raised an assessing eyebrow.

Matt bit his lip. 'Ask her where we can go for a beer this evening,' he instructed, 'and find some decent steaks to eat.'

The maid recommended a restaurant beside a harbour, some eight or nine kilometres away, but added that she had put some simple provisions and wine in the fridge. If they insisted on staying here, they would have plenty for the evening and by morning the storm would hopefully pass. They did not want to be stuck in a car in these hills in bad weather, she repeated, adding an emphatic, 'c'est traître!' Verity translated this advice for the others before ushering the maid out to her car.

There was an awkward moment while the four of them who remained stood in the large salon, uncertain about what to do next. Caro looked around her and said brightly, 'What a lovely room, so full of character.' Matt moved to stare out of the far windows, still jangling the coins in his pocket.

Jay added, 'I love old buildings. And the biddy who owns this place is obviously not short of a bob or two. Look at that piano.'

Matt turned suddenly. 'It's a great place, Jay,' he enthused, rubbing his hands together.

Edward heard the little Renault start up and drive off across the gravel, and then Verity reappeared in the doorway. 'She's off, poor soul – she's so worried.'

'How splendid that you speak such good French, Verity. You got us out of a sticky spot there,' Jay enthused. 'What a clever wife you have, Matt.'

Verity murmured, 'Oh, it was nothing,' walked into the centre of the space, and looked around.

A discussion ensued about what they should do next, with Matt favouring a trip to the coast, Verity suggesting they take the maid's advice and stay at the house, and Jay intervening with a compromise, suggesting a quick excursion to buy steaks to cook at the house, and if they were lucky, a drink in a bar before the storm arrived. Edward's heart sank at the thought of having to get back into the car and besides, he had his own plans.

'I tell you what,' he offered, 'you guys go. I'm going to spend a little time winding down here.'

'You're going to work, aren't you?' Jay nudged his brother playfully.

'Perhaps, but there's no signal here, so I won't be working for long,' Edward nudged him back good-humouredly. 'I've had a few long days, Jay. Let me get out there and take a run through the forest, and I'll be in a much better shape to enjoy the evening with you all.'

'That settles it, then.' Matt ran his hand back over his hair. 'Let the party begin!'

Verity moved to the piano and ran her fingers silently over the piano keys. 'Do you know, I think I'll leave you all to it too,' she announced. 'I still feel a little queasy after the journey up here, and as I'm the one who dismissed the maid, I'll make up the beds.'

'Don't you even think about it! We can all do that later,' Caro insisted.

'Yes, no bed-making allowed. Get out that yoga mat of yours or pour yourself a glass of wine – you must promise us!' Jay agreed.

'I'm not making any promises,' Verity laughed.

As he drove off, Jay skidded the car on the gravel for Edward's benefit and roared with laughter through the open car window. Edward laughed gently and shook his head. The sound of the car engine receded, and he stood quietly for a moment. Although the sky was still blue, the pines beside the driveway flattened in a stiff breeze that whipped across the vast lawn and swirled around the side of the house.

'So, they've gone,' Edward began, as he stepped back into the house. He felt awkward, not quite knowing what to say or where to begin.

Verity murmured, 'Yes.' She moved to the far side of the big, shadowy room, hugging herself as she walked. Edward wanted to say something but paused and ran his fingers along the top of a sofa back, staring hard at the piece of furniture.

'I can't believe we've met again, like this,' she said.

'Me neither. It's been a very long time.'

'It *was* – a lifetime ago. Did you know I'd be here this weekend?'

'No, you?'

'No, no, of course not.'

'Fate, then.'

'Yes. Or coincidence. What will we say to the others? I feel awkward.'

'Oh, I don't know. Is Matt the same guy you married? I can't recall what he looked like.'

'Yes, yes. Same person.'

'Ah,' he paused. 'Well, it's good to see you again.'

'Thanks, yes. It's astonishing to see you!' Verity laughed, and then folded her arms. 'It's very isolated here.'

'It has that feeling, but civilisation isn't far away.'

'True.'

Edward took a decisive breath. 'Well, look, I hope you don't mind but I'm going to find myself a room, get changed and take a run in the forest before dusk falls or the weather changes, whichever comes first. Would you excuse me?' He grabbed the familiar handle of his suitcase.

'You go ahead. It sounds like a very good plan.'

Sunlight cast shadows on her slender body. She had grown thinner, looked more brittle, he thought sadly, hauling his case towards the stairwell. The polished staircase doubled back on itself and led Edward to a wide landing with an arched window at the far end which overlooked the driveway and the forest beyond. He figured he would take the smallest bedroom, and after opening a couple of doors, located it at the front of the house. As he set his suitcase on the bed and opened it out in a well-practised gesture, it struck him that he might have been too dismissive with Verity – there was so much news for the two of them to share, potentially; but he yearned to get out into the forest, put the long day behind him and clear his head of work stress and worry, and they would surely have time together over the weekend. He jogged back downstairs wearing trainers, shorts and a running vest.

'See you in a while,' he called out to her.

'Yes, see you,' she replied hesitantly from the kitchen.

As he headed out of the door, Edward considered what she might do while he was gone. He hoped she would curl up in a comfortable chair, and maybe take a nap. Her beautiful grey eyes glittered with stress and her skin was unnaturally pale. As he stretched his muscles

74

out on the gravel before his run, he questioned again what her life had been like during the years since they had last met, and what on earth she was still doing with her cocky husband. Many years ago, he would have argued vehemently that he knew her well, loved her even, but with hindsight he could see there was a part of her he had never understood, and that included her loyalty to Matt. He took a deep breath of the earth-scented air that blew gently over the wild hillside, before jogging down the driveway. At the gate, he turned left and ran up what remained of the mountain road. The tarmac soon gave way to a rough track which wound along the side of the hill before plunging into the forest.

As soon as Edward was surrounded by trees, he started to feel better. His shoulder muscle loosened and stopped aching for the first time that day. His footfall was muffled by a fresh carpet of oak leaves that even now spiralled from the trees around him as branches swayed in the mounting wind. It was a release to be out in the wildness, to let go of the hustle of a manmade world, and to put some of his concerns out of his mind. As he ran, he focused on the subtle sounds of his own breath flowing steadily in and out of his body, distinguishing it from the broader rush of a wind that played tag through the trees. The track was wide and clear, probably designed for the use of forestry and fire trucks, and there were not too many ruts underfoot. He swiped the first beads of sweat from his forehead and increased his pace. As he ran on, to his right, he caught glimpses of the spectacular forest canopy that covered the hills down to the coast. Jay had been right about the location being special. This was better than he could have hoped for. It came to him that there was one more phone call he could make – to the editor of a newspaper which had long campaigned for freedom of the press in Burma. The editor had a good knowledge of local officials and might be able to offer some advice. Spurred on by a sudden sense of urgency, Edward turned and increased his pace back to the house.

9

After everyone had left, Verity took a deep breath, raised her chin, and said, 'Yes!' out loud in the cavernous space. All day long she had yearned for some time alone. She wandered around noting the comfortable furnishings, and fingering the keys of the piano, peppering the air with a few light notes before moving on and approaching the glass doors at the far end of the room. She turned a key in a lock, and stepped out onto a wide veranda which had a cobweb-infested tiled roof, and ran along the length of the back of the house. Bougainvillea climbed pillared supports, and handfuls of dried leaves curled comfortably in dusty corners. Shallow steps led down to a huge empty lawn. Apart from the piercing cry of a buzzard and the rush of the wind, it was wonderfully quiet. Verity studied a picturesque clump of tall trees which stood close to the back of the house. A deserted table and chairs beneath their canopy suggested a shady spot to eat on a hot day. She inhaled the warm and salty air. How beautiful it all was compared to London where droning aeroplanes, the stench of diesel, and the sound of wailing sirens were relentless.

She walked away from the house, out across the lawn, and gasped at the view that unfolded. A canopy of azure sky arched above the distant ribbon of storm cloud. Beyond the trimmed lawn was a stretch of scrubby grass where straggling wild plants grew alongside scattered creamy rocks, and in the far distance folds of forested hills rolled out towards a sliver of sparkling grey sea. The landscape and smells were so familiar and dear to Verity from her childhood that her emotions welled and tears sprung in her eyes. The pale-yellow hue of the boulders, the scents of the nameless flowers and fungi, the quality of the afternoon light as it fell on the hillside – her heart knew all of it, and standing at the edge of the lawn, she felt as if a part of her had come home again. She wiped tears from her cheeks, and wished she had brought her camera outside, but could not tear herself away to go and fetch it. As she breathed in the dear, familiar air, her heart ached and more tears rolled unashamedly down her face. It was almost too much. She had not expected this, had no idea that such a reaction had been buried deep inside her, waiting to be released.

There was so much space! Walking through the rough grass, she looked around, and everything was vast and simple – sky, lawn, forest, sea; big swathes of each confronted her, and no fussy detail of bricks or awkward angles of buildings clouded her view. She felt a thousand beautiful miles away from her normal life.

She considered Edward, and folded her arms against a sea breeze. What did it mean, Edward reappearing out of nowhere like this? A sudden gust of wind nudged her forward, encouraging her to walk on through scrubland to the very edge of the property until she reached the point where the land suddenly dropped away in a wild tumble of rocks and tatty plants. Fingers of breeze lifted her hair and cooled her neck, and Verity turned her face to the sky, opened her arms wide, and twirled slowly around. Once, twice. She brought to mind the pressures in her life – the arguments about moving, frustrations at work, her father-in-law's health, the hurt of seeing Matt touch that awful woman's knee, her anxiety attacks, the constant tearfulness that she kept shoving back down inside her, and a nagging, unspoken worry about Tills – and then imagined all of them being blown away over the hillside, across the forest canopy and out to sea, far away. Feeling lighter, striding back toward the house, she studied the curved terracotta roof tiles and faded cornflower-blue shutters either side of each window, and thought how picturesque and welcoming it looked. As she reached the veranda door however, she stretched to pull it closed behind her and a fierce gust of wind snatched it from her grip, smashing it violently against the house wall. She gasped, fearful that a pane would shatter, and the small incident rattled her nerves. Her hand trembled as she grabbed the handle firmly and pulled the door properly shut. Hugging herself and hunching her shoulders, she walked to the kitchen to find a teabag and a mug, and looking out of the window as she waited for the kettle to boil, she saw that the vast bank of cloud appeared to have moved closer to the shore.

After drinking the tea, she headed up the wide wooden staircase, looked in all the rooms, and decided that Jay and Caro should have the master bedroom overlooking the beautiful lawn. She made up their bed, and left towels in their room. When she was done, she went back downstairs and fetched her own suitcase. The bedroom she chose for herself and Matt was a small double room at the top of the stairs. The windows, which were set into a sloping ceiling, looked out into the cluster of tall trees at the back of the house. The decor was simple and rustic – a bed, a chest of drawers and a wardrobe, all painted in soft grey and white, and an ancient kilim rug over a wooden floor. The walls were palest grey and the curtains made of plain white linen. It was a classic French look, and Verity liked it. She was not, however, looking forward to sharing the room with Matt. She had got used to sleeping alone without his hot restless body and loud snoring, and that was before the spectre of the woman in the pub and all the suspicions that now wriggled in her mind.

In Edward's bedroom, Verity felt awkward and keenly aware of the battered suitcase and neatly discarded clothes. As she moved the case to the floor to make the bed, it felt like an intrusion but she reasoned that the maid would have done the same thing and she could hardly exclude him and leave his bed unmade.

With everything done, she ran a bath in the little room that led off from her bedroom, and added some geranium essential oil she had brought from home. She sniffed a new tablet of soap from beside the bath, inhaling its strong, clean lavender scent. The bath itself was narrow and deep, and quite old-fashioned – rusty marks ran down the enamel beneath each tap – but Verity stripped off her travelling clothes with a feeling of relief, and lowered herself into the deep warm water, with a sigh of pleasure. She reclined for a while, looking out of a tall window to the cliff behind the house and a strip of pale blue sky above it. Crows made a racket in the tall trees, just out of sight. After a night with little rest and the long, emotional day, the warm water made her sleepy and she fought to stay awake. A short while later, she started when she heard a distant thud as the front door shut followed by footsteps on the stairs. Edward, she decided, returning from his run. She could not bring herself to stir from the heavenly bath and submerged herself totally in the soothing water before sitting up and slowly shampooing her hair.

She heard Edward enter an adjacent bathroom, and turn on a shower. The situation felt unreal, like a dream. For many, many years, she had believed that Edward had been an opportunity lost, a small tragedy, and she had railed against a fate that had made her choose between two men. And then enough time had passed, and her memory of him had faded – but she had never forgotten him or completely let go of him, always saving some small part of herself for him alone. As the water cooled around her, she climbed out of the little bath, and towelled herself dry.

Downstairs, she found Edward bent over the main fireplace tending a tepee of balled newspaper, kindling and logs. His wet hair was combed back, and he set a lit match to the newspaper, just as she approached a sofa and sat down.

'Thanks for making up my bed. You didn't need to do that.'

'No problem.'

'I figured I'd light us a fire to take the chill off the place. It's cooling down outside already, and the wind is getting up a little.'

'Great idea,' Verity agreed, impressed at the way Edward adjusted a log to catch the flame perfectly. 'You've done that before.'

'Oh, yes, many times.' He kept his attention on the fire, and Verity studied the curve of his broad back, longing again to grab a stick of charcoal and sketch him, crouched in the mouth of the cavernous fireplace.

'By the way, the old lady who owns the house called while you were upstairs, and gave me a list of instructions about which shutters to close, where candles are kept, where gas cylinders and logs are stored, you name it. Apparently, the power comes and goes at the slightest hint of a storm, and she's heard a forecast and is worried for us. It sounds like she has the whole place stocked up for every kind of emergency. She didn't spare me any detail.'

'Your brother did say she might call and fuss,' Verity recalled. 'And there was I thinking we'd be sitting on warm sandy beaches this weekend, catching a bit of autumn sun. Rain is not what you think of when you imagine the Côte d'Azur.'

'Yeah, it may yet come to that. These things can blow over.'

Outside a gust of wind wailed, and upstairs a shutter banged. 'You were saying?' Verity laughed.

'She warned me about that shutter.' Edward raised his eyebrows. 'I'd better go and secure it.'

He left her and swiftly headed up the stairs, taking them two at a time. The fire began to crackle in the grate, and Verity watched new flames curl around the seasoned logs. When he came back downstairs, he excused himself again, saying he needed to make a phone call, and disappeared through a doorway to the right of the fireplace, closing the door quietly behind him. Verity sat neatly on the sofa, her legs crossed, and one foot wiggling up and down. Flames lapped against the blackened stone fireplace and wood crackled. The house was so quiet she could hear the rush of the wind outside and Edward's low, indistinct voice. She stood up and wandered around. An oil painting depicting a bowl of graceful, etiolated red tulips hung on one wall. There was a closed door to the left-hand side of the fireplace, and on opening it, she discovered a small sitting room with a television, a box of toys, an indoor football table and shelves full of English books. Another door led to a little lobby full of coats and boots and bits and pieces, and an exterior door that led to the gravelled yard at the side of the house, edged by a wall on one side and a row of outbuildings opposite. Verity considered the woman who owned the house and wondered what her story was, imagining what it must be like to have such a wonderful bolthole to stay in. If Verity owned a house like this, she might never go back to London again.

As the shadows outside lengthened, she felt uneasy, finding it strange and disconcerting to have nothing to do. Normally at this time of day she would be listing all the things she had to attend to after work − walk Charlie, shop for supper, do housework, and so on. She was not used to having time on her hands. Taking a seat on the sofa again, she watched flames leap in the fireplace. From where she sat she could not help overhearing Edward − his voice had risen and his words, spoken in some unfathomable language, were laboured, as if perhaps the line was bad. She sensed his patience with whoever he talked to. Who was Edward now? she mused. Who had he become since they had last met?

'What language were you speaking?' she asked when he returned.

He paused beside the fireplace, and bent to adjust a log. 'My own poorly-rendered version of Burmese.'

'That's very impressive.'

'Not if you're a Burmese person, I can assure you. The poor man barely understood a word I said.' Edward stood up and rested his elbow on the mantle-piece.

'Do you mind me asking what you were talking about?'

'There's a journalist in Burma who has been unfairly imprisoned. He suffers from asthma, and I'm trying to get some medicine into the prison for him.'

'Can you do that?'

'It's a long shot, but I'm trying.'

Silence fell between them. The fire crackled.

'I still can't believe we've bumped into each other again like this,' Verity muttered.

'Strange, isn't it?'

She imagined a chain of unspoken words circling them both but did not know where to begin. Edward perched on the arm of the sofa opposite her, his broad shoulders relaxing. 'I used the house phone to speak to my brother earlier after I got in from running. They were in a bar. The barman had told them that the storm was forecast to just sweep along the coast. It would be the boats in the harbour that got the brunt of the damage, he reckoned. He told Jay that up in the hills, it would be quiet. They have bought the steaks for supper and will be back soon.'

'That figures about the storm, I guess. I don't know much about these things.'

Edward stood and walked towards the tall windows. 'From the signs that I saw while out running, I'm not so sure that barman was right. The wind was gusting, and there were branches down in the forest already. I told Jay that, but when you get my brother into a bar, it's hard to get him out. He'll be inflicting his few words of French on any local who'll care to listen, and loving every minute of it!' Edward turned and smiled, his gaze lingering on her before he looked away again. 'I need to get in a supply of logs. Shall we take a look outside?'

'Okay,' Verity agreed.

'You might want to put something warm on; it's cooling down out there.'

She paused, surprised that Edward considered her comfort. Matt would never think of such a thing.

Outside, the light was beginning to fade. The colours of the landscape had softened, and were bathed in translucent yellow. Verity's hair was still not dry from the bath, and damp tendrils whipped around her face, making her shiver.

'Have you seen the view from the lawn?' she asked Edward.

'Not all of it.'

'Come, it's spectacular.' She stepped onto the lawn, arms folded as she walked away from the house, drawn back towards the dramatic view. The horizon was now obscured by a curling mass of bruised, dirty yellow and grey cloud, and a fresh breeze blew in her face. 'Oh, my goodness, look at that storm coming in! Those clouds weren't here earlier,' she exclaimed.

'The storm isn't far from the coast,' Edward remarked, 'and judging from the wind direction, it *is* headed our way.'

'It's quite exciting.'

Edward turned silently, and studied the house and the clump of mature oaks. Some of their branches lifted in the wind, making them look like dancers.

'I can smell the sea,' she said, closing her eyes, as the wind blew her skirt into the contours of her thighs.

'Shall we go and get those logs then?' Edward suggested. She opened her eyes and saw Edward watching her with dark observant eyes. His face was brown and the skin still taut although it had roughened a little with age, and he appeared like a rock in the landscape with the swirling mass of cloud behind him. They walked back across the lawn and wide gravel parking area at the front of the house to the small courtyard at the far side. It felt curiously still and silent in the yard, surrounded by the garden wall and outbuildings. Behind a wide, bolted door they found a stack of split wood exactly where the old lady had told Edward it would be. He fetched a barrow, and they loaded it with logs.

'I love the smell of seasoned wood.' Verity held a split log to her nose and inhaled.

Edward smiled at her. He pushed the overloaded barrow back to the house with little effort, walking fluidly and steadily like a big cat. They stacked the logs neatly to one side of the door, under the eaves.

'Shall we take a stroll down the hill a little way before darkness falls?' he suggested. 'The others will have to drive up that way — they might give us a lift back up.'

'Sure, I love it out here.'

'I have some field glasses upstairs. I'll run and fetch them.'

As she stepped away from the relative shelter of the house and garden and out onto the hillside road, the force of the wind hit Verity like a body blow. 'My God!' she squealed, bending into it.

'D'you want to take my arm?' Edward offered his elbow.

'Yes!' She laughed and her hair blew into her face. She steadied herself, twisted her hair and tucked it down inside her coat collar before linking her arm through Edward's.

'Well, look at that,' Edward murmured. The bank of cloud in the distance had turned the colour of black denim and now filled the sky, spilling over the hills, and tipping out sheets of rain over the landscape, while above Verity and Edward the evening sky remained innocently pale and quiet, a wash of lemons and greys.

'It looks like a Bierstadt painting,' Verity remarked quietly.

'We have time to walk to the passing point down there, and back. We might be able to see the state of the road and warn the others. There's going to be a lot of mud and debris where the rain is falling so heavily.'

She let go of Edward's arm and they walked briskly down the road, side by side. A cool wind whipped around her bare legs and made a buffeting noise in her ears. A beautiful yet frightening streak of lightning flashed over the forest. They reached the passing point in the road — a lay-by edged with boulders at the top of a high cliff. Edward focussed his field glasses on the hills below them. 'I can see bits of the road,' he reported, his voice barely audible above the cracking wind. 'No sign of any vehicles. Want to look?' he offered, stepping back towards her. She edged forward and looked through the binoculars. Her vision swooped to tracts of rain-sodden cork oaks and glimpses of empty road already running with rusty-coloured mud.

'The road is a river of dirt,' she shouted.

'They simply aren't built for rainstorms. There's still no signal on my phone here either but I'll try to call Jay from the house when we get back, to warn him.'

'It's fascinating, a bit scary,' she admitted, and handed the binoculars back.

'I had hoped to see more. I hadn't reckoned on such poor visibility so soon.'

The wild wind whipped Verity's hair into her face and made her skirt ride up her thighs as she walked back to the house. By the time they reached the front door, Edward's brown-skinned cheeks had turned pink. A splatter of rain hit the gravel.

'We just got back in time,' she gasped.

'Looking out there, I'm not sure you'll get to sit on a beach, after all.' Edward raised his eyebrows, and she was surprised by his good humour. Matt would be furious about the weather by now.

Edward tried to call Jay but the house phone had gone dead. Neither of their mobiles had service. 'I hope he'll seek advice before driving up here,' he said, bending to put another log on the fire and spreading his hands to warm them in front of the flames. 'I wish we had a way of contacting him.'

'You're concerned?'

'I've seen one too many storms perhaps, developed a healthy respect for Mother Nature. That's a monster headed our way.'

'Matt will insist they drive back. He likes an adventure. I'm sure they'll be here safely before we know it.' She ran her fingers through her tangled hair. 'I'm going to make a salad ready for when they arrive with the steaks. Caro was hungry, even before they left.'

'Sounds good. I'll come and help,' Edward offered, peeling off his sweater.

While Verity washed a lettuce, and tore leaves into a bowl, Edward sliced tomatoes and avocado. He crumbled feta over the salad leaves while she found an empty jam jar and tipped in olive oil, lemon juice and crushed garlic, seasoning it liberally.

'That maid did a great job with the shopping,' she remarked.

'Do you like to cook?'

'Sometimes. You?'

'I don't often have the opportunity.'

She unwrapped two large baguettes and set them on a board with a knife in the centre of the kitchen table. 'Now, let's hope they are not much longer. I'm hungry,' she said. A sudden deluge of rain splattered against the kitchen window, making her jump. She spread a hand on her chest, and laughed nervously.

84

Edward held her gaze, and nodded towards the window. 'Well, I reckon the storm has arrived, even if the steaks haven't,' he said lightly. 'Let's take a drink and sit by the fire. There's wine in the fridge, and you like rosé, if I remember?'

'I did, I do – thank you.'

Settling on the sofas either side of a low table in front of the fire, each raised a toast before tasting the wine.

'So, you never came back to the coffee shop that day?' Verity quizzed him.

'Nope.'

'I always hoped you might return at some point.'

'And your child? What did you have?'

'A daughter. She's twenty-two now. And I had another daughter, three years later. She's eighteen, just started university.'

'What a blessing.'

'Yes, I think so too.'

'It would never have worked, me coming back that day, you know.'

'I know. But it would have been good to hear from you.'

'Honestly? You really think so?'

'I would have liked to know how you were, what you were doing.'

'It was best left, as I recall it.'

'Do you remember the very first time we met, at that party?'

'Of course. The music was extremely loud and the air stank with cigarette smoke. Your friend had dragged me there protesting. And then I watched a crazy woman dancing like a dervish.' Edward laughed. 'Wearing extraordinary shoes.'

'I'd forgotten about those shoes!'

'It was a miracle you managed to stay upright on them, a bit touch and go at times.'

'I'd drunk too much.'

'You were amazing.'

'It feels like a lifetime ago.'

'It sure does.'

'So, tell me about you,' Verity challenged. 'What have you been doing all these years?'

'I still work wherever there are problems or conflict.'

'Do you just go anywhere?'

'Yes. I work for a couple of agencies, freelance.'

'Where's your favourite place?'

'Wherever I am right now.'

'Ha, ha, very philosophical.'

'It's true.'

'Not always, I'm sure.'

'Okay, perhaps not always. The Far East. I love The Far East, Burma in particular. It's a place undergoing massive transition right now.'

'Don't you ever want to go somewhere where it's peaceful and everyone is happy?'

'Oh, like the Côte d'Azur for a weekend break with my brother?'

'Yes, somewhere like that.' Verity smiled.

'Well, that would be nice, certainly. How about you? Do you travel much?'

'Mostly on the tube around London.'

'Nice. Grubby, I seem to recall.'

'Very.' Verity took a sip of wine, and leant back on the sofa. 'So, is your life really all in that suitcase?'

'Kind of.'

'You never married, settled down?'

'I'd divorced before we met.'

'I remember. You never married again?'

'Nope.'

'Sorry, I'm very nosey!'

'You are,' he laughed. 'You always were, now I come to think of it. No, relationships are way too complicated for me. I'm very happy the way I am. Changing the subject, you speak pretty good French.'

'I lived here when I was a child. Did I never tell you that?'

'Maybe. I vaguely recall it, now you mention it.'

'We lived an hour or two from here, actually, inland a way, in a village called Rians. My father came here for his work. He was a great admirer of Cezanne. I went to school here for a number of years.'

'Do you ever miss it?'

'It's funny, I didn't think I did, but standing out on the lawn earlier, the air smelled so fragrant and familiar, and then I noticed the light on the rocks, and it made me massively nostalgic.' Verity got up and wandered over to the piano, sat down on the stool, and rested her fingers on the keys, hesitantly.

'Go ahead, play us something,' Edward encouraged.

'It's been a long time,' she apologised.

'Don't mind me. You could make a hundred mistakes and I wouldn't notice.'

Verity closed her eyes and attempted to pull the memory of a Chopin nocturne back through the years. She began and faltered but then found the tune. She had been reasonably good as a child, had eventually taken all her grades, but it had been a long time since she had played. When she finished, Edward clapped quietly and she jumped, having forgotten where she was for a moment. Covering up her confusion, she pushed back the piano stool, and smiling, took a small bow in his direction.

'That was beautiful, thank you.'

Her cheeks burned; all this niceness – she was not used to it. She walked over to the coffee table, picked up her glass, and downed the rest of the wine in one. 'The others must surely be back soon,' she said.

Edward rose and turned on a couple of lamps. 'I'm not too convinced about that. Shall we go ahead and eat that bread and salad? I'm starving.'

In the kitchen, rain lashed the night-blackened windows, and the growing storm pressed in. Verity took some ham and the remains of the bottle of rosé from the fridge. Edward put on his reading glasses, pressed a button on a CD player, and some melodic gypsy jazz filled the kitchen. He returned his spectacles to his shirt pocket in a practiced gesture which made Verity reflect on just how long it was since they had seen each other and how they had both aged. In some ways, it still felt like yesterday, as if time was playing tricks on them. Edward lit a pair of candles on the table which were already part-burnt by a previous occupant. They raised a toast before they ate.

'Bon appetit.'

'To a happy weekend,' Verity replied. 'I hope the others are all right. I checked my phone earlier, and there was no message from Matt.'

Edward began to eat in a slow, measured way, so unlike Matt who bolted his food.

'I do wish I'd admitted to Caro on the plane that we already knew each other. It feels awkward. I don't know why I didn't.'

'Well, it would be equally awkward if you had, and then it came to light that we were meeting up while you were engaged and then again after you had married, and your husband never knew about it.'

'True. I never thought of it like that though. It didn't feel like I was doing anything wrong at the time.'

'I know, I know. But we were always more than just friends, you and I. That was the trouble.'

Verity ate on in silence for a moment. 'So, exactly how long have you lived out of that suitcase?'

'Sometimes I've based myself in one city for a while and rented a place, but I've never really found a place to call home. With my work the way it is, it's pretty easy and logical to just keep moving around, living my "small life".'

Verity winced. 'I'm so sorry about that,' she muttered.

'No problem. I'm a tough man, and I'm teasing you.' He chuckled before asking what she had done in the intervening years, and listening thoughtfully to her reply. 'What would you paint?'

'The sea; I'd like to paint the sea and the landscape, the points where land meets sea or even where the sky meets the sea. Confluence interests me, the place where two different elements touch, the moods and the colours.'

'Not much sea in London.'

'That is very true.' A flash of lightning brightened the room, and was followed by a loud crack of thunder which made Verity duck involuntarily. 'It's so peculiar, sitting here with you in this storm,' she said.

'It does *not* feel like quarter of a century since we last ate together.' He picked up the wine bottle to refill their glasses, and the kitchen lights flickered. 'Uh-oh,' he muttered, setting the bottle back down on the table.

Without any fuss, the music ceased, the kitchen slipped into darkness, and the humming fridge fell silent; the candles on the table became the only source of light and the room filled with flickering shadows.

'It might be a blip,' Verity suggested. The storm seemed to press in closer, as if it was wrapping the house in its fury. As they sat a moment, waiting to see what would happen, she laughed – partly out of nerves, and partly at the absurdity. Edward smiled too, his cheekbones highlighted by the soft candlelight. He looked down and shook his head in disbelief. 'The old lady said this would happen.'

'A great holiday this is!'

'Yes, actually it is,' Edward replied emphatically. 'We are warm and dry. We have food and wine, and each other for company. Let's find some more candles and sit by the fire.'

She watched his broad, shadowy back as he got up and crossed the kitchen.

Flames flickered in the fireplace, and shadows danced in the cavernous salon. Edward set down a couple of candles on the low table, and fetched his sweater off the back of a chair, pulling it on over his head, so that his hair was left ruffled. The place felt chilly, and Verity rubbed her arms for warmth. She returned to the kitchen, found a torch in a drawer, and climbed the stairs to her bedroom. The old house felt reassuringly solid against the wind that howled outside and her room smelled comfortingly of beeswax. She balanced the torch on a chest of drawers and rifled through her suitcase to find a cardigan, yawning after the meal and wine, and the lack of sleep the night before. She wondered fleetingly where Matt was, but recalled his hand on the knee of the woman in black and the tawdry fact of the lipstick in the glove compartment, and wrapped her soft cardigan around her. She hoped that he was safe but she did not miss his company this evening.

Downstairs, she perched on the sofa arm closest to the fire, and rubbed her hands together, warming them. The wind and the thrashing rain were less obvious in the salon, kept at bay by the room's central position in the house. The fire hissed and crackled. Verity felt as if she had washed up on an island, a million miles away from her life in London.

'You look like you belong here,' she remarked to Edward, who sat comfortably opposite her, his head turned to watch the flames of the fire.

'Ah,' he spoke lazily. 'I learned a long time ago to make myself at home wherever I stay.'

'Sounds very sensible.'

'Born of necessity, yes – and it's easy once you make your mind up.'

'I'll take your word for it. I'm not good with change.'

89

'You're probably better at it than you realise. The whole notion of constancy is a complete fiction. Everything is always changing. Even if you live in the same house for many years, things are still changing.'

'Oh, yes?'

'Yes. People come and go, the contents of your home get worn out and replaced, some days the house is warm, others cold. The lives of the people who live in your home or who visit are evolving, too. It may feel the same, but there are constant subtle shifts, and sometimes huge, more noticeable ones.' His dark eyes shone in the firelight.

'That's a bit nit-picky.'

'It is, I know. But I've come to believe "home" is a place in our minds rather than an actual location. It's like a stillness inside that we carry with us, which helps us cope with change. If you feel full of peace, you are at home wherever you are. You don't have to be tied to one place.'

'Most people would disagree with you.'

'You're right, and I'm being way too philosophical!' He laughed and rested his head back on the sofa. 'Just tell me to be quiet.'

'My home is the place where I raised my daughters. It's the four walls where I sleep, bathe, cook my food, and retreat from the world, not some place inside my head.'

'Ah, but when you move house – as you say you want to?'

'Then I will make another home.'

'Exactly. And if you moved again?'

'I would make another home again, I guess.'

'And if you kept on moving every few days, or every week or month?'

Verity laughed, and threw open her hands. 'Okay, okay, point taken – you win. I'd end up making myself at home wherever I was and being quite relaxed about it, just like you!'

'There's a difference between a house and a home. Home is a frame of mind, you can take it anywhere. A house is just a building.'

'I do kind of see what you mean.'

'I've had many years to work it out, believe me.'

'I'm not sure many people would cope with your lifestyle.'

'Oh, anyone can cope if they want to. There are many nomadic people all over the world. Eventually, given enough practice, I'm sure you'd start feel at home anywhere – even in this draughty French farmhouse on this stormy night – and you'd probably find yourself living easily with just one large, battered suitcase, enjoying your very small life.' Edward's dark eyes twinkled.

'I wish you'd stop reminding me of that remark.' Verity shook her head.

He smiled lazily. 'I won't mention it again.'

Verity fell silent for a moment and then said, 'My husband doesn't want us to move. Maybe I'll employ some of your logic with him,' before pausing and adding, 'Tell me, don't you ever get lonely?'

'Sure. But don't you?'

She stalled. 'I do, actually, yes.'

'Well, there you go then.' He looked away.

She imagined what it would be like to live a life like Edward's with no cupboards to fill, no furniture to dust or carpets to hoover, no attic full of junk or garden to tend, nothing but a few precious and practical things in one suitcase. It would be a lot less work, for one thing, she mused. 'I can't believe you don't long for a place to call your own.'

'Oh...' Edward stretched out his legs and clasped his hands behind his head. 'I long for a world where all of us are truly equal and valued. That is what I long for. A house is pretty far down my list.'

Verity raised her eyebrows, not knowing what to say.

'Your turn,' he challenged, his eyes sharp. 'What do you long for?'

'Nothing so grand, I'm afraid. I long simply to paint. To be out in nature and to paint. It's a very small thing really. I don't know why it seems so impossible.'

Edward leant forward, picked up his wine glass, and raised it slowly. 'To Verity the artist, and to a good night's sleep tonight.'

'I'll drink to that too.' She sipped the cool wine. 'Can I ask you a personal question?'

'Ah, here we go.' He laughed quietly.

'Do you mind?'

'Depends on the question.'

'Has there been anyone special for you, Edward?'

He had one arm stretched along the top of the sofa, and his eyes did not leave hers. 'Well, there was my ex-wife Marie – you know about her – and there was someone else, years later in Sweden.' He moved, squatted in front of the fire, and gently shoved a log into the centre of the grate, offering nothing more. A little smoke blew back from the soot-stained fireplace, and as he looked upward to inspect the chimney, Verity studied the line of his cheekbone and the profile of his lips, so beautifully lit by firelight, and recalled how he had always been a man of many secrets.

'I'm going to make a hot drink. Would you like one?' she offered.

'Sure, that'd be nice. Whatever you chose, I don't mind.' He left the fireplace, followed her to the kitchen, and lingered in the doorway. He took a deep breath as if he was about to speak but then looked away. Verity stared out at the black night. Rain streaked the window panes which glistened in the candlelight.

'What if they did set out and something has happened?' she fretted.

'There are three of them, all fit and able. They would work something out.'

'But it's really blowing a gale out there.'

'It certainly is. But they will be fine.'

The kettle whistled, and Verity poured water onto mint-flavoured teabags. She picked up a mug, handed it to Edward and their fingers touched for a moment, making the heat rush to her cheeks. Back in the salon, the fire spat a stream of red sparks into the soft darkness and candles flickered in a draught. The wind flung itself against the row of tall windows making them rattle. What did them being here in France together really mean? Was fate playing some kind of hand?

A loud crash made her jump up and spill hot tea down her front. She brushed it off furiously. Edward leapt up and turned. The front door gaped open, swinging wide and knocking over a tall pot of umbrellas and walking sticks, scattering them across the tiled floor.

'Is it them?' Verity gasped. She followed Edward, and squinted into the black mouth of the open doorway. Edward roughly pulled on his boots and jogged out into the rain.

'Hello? Anyone there?' he called out.

She watched him search the front of the house and the driveway, and rain ran down her face and soaked her cardigan. It drenched the door mat and made a puddle on the limestone floor.

'There's no-one here!' Edward shouted, before running back inside and stamping his boots on the sodden mat. 'Just a gust of wind.' He stood beside her, and they scanned the garden for a moment longer, looking for signs of life. His hair was flattened and dripping went, and raindrops ran down his cheeks. He wrestled the door shut and turned the key so that it would not blow open again.

'What if the others come, and they can't get in?'

'They can ring the bell,' he stated firmly. He moved back to the fire, pulled off his jumper and hung it up to dry in the warmth of the fire.

'You're soaked,' she whispered, and reached out and touched his hair.

'You too,' he replied, lightly running his hand over her shoulder. They both stilled, and Edward withdrew his hand awkwardly, studying her with an inscrutable look on his face that she knew of old, his gaze curious but his feelings buried deep. His bronzed damp skin glistened in the firelight.

'I'm going to head to bed,' she muttered, tearing her attention away. As she spoke, the past swept in to the room like a ghost, and an unbidden sense of longing – hard to believe, after all the years – flooded her body. Flustered, she turned away from him. 'Good night then,' she murmured.

'Good night,' he replied quietly. 'Sleep well.'

The bedroom was chilly and Verity strode about to keep warm. Tired, and having drunk more wine than she was used to, she could not be bothered to unpack anything and rooted around in her suitcase for a t-shirt and pyjama bottoms, letting the suitcase lid fall shut on everything else. She changed hastily, and quickly brushed her teeth, spitting the cold water into the basin with force. Outside, thunder rumbled and banged so loudly that she jumped. As she lay down between cold bedsheets, thoughts churned in her head as her concern for Matt's safety mixed with the lingering anger she still felt towards him. She pulled the duvet around her and tried to shut out her worries. Outside, a shutter rattled sporadically. She leaned over to blow out the candle and drifted off to sleep.

10

Edward was not ready to sleep. He sauntered over to a cupboard and found what he thought he might – a few opened bottles of spirits and some glassware. He poured himself a Scotch, and took it back to the sofa. On the way, he caught sight of the others' hand luggage, still at the bottom of the stairs, and checked his instincts; his gut feeling was that they were okay, and in any case, there was nothing he could do about it. Outside the thunder cracked its whip. He swirled his drink around in the tumbler and contemplated the strange reality of finding himself stuck for the night, alone in this place with Verity, of all people. He reminded himself that he needed to keep his life the way it was – no possessions, no attachments. Feeling the muscles tighten around his forehead, he took another large swig of Scotch. It would be simple enough despite this chance encounter to continue the way he always had, so why did he feel so unsettled? He sighed, threw another log on the fire, and perused a bookshelf in the hope of finding something to read. He picked out a copy of Murakami's *Wild Sheep Chase*, took out his reading glasses, and settled back on the sofa, grateful to have found a good distraction.

A sudden crash tore his attention from the book. He snatched at his glasses, dropping them on the table as a cacophony of breaking tiles, shattering glass, and a series of heavy thuds caused the floor under his feet to vibrate. He grabbed the torch and raced towards the ear-splitting noise.

'Verity!' he yelled, shoving open her bedroom door. She stood shuddering in the middle of a wrecked room, her head turning blindly in the direction of his voice. The torch's beam lit tunnels of vision through dusty air. It was hard to figure out the full extent of the damage but a hole was torn in the sloping ceiling of the bedroom, and a tree limb reached through the gape, its twisted arm propped on the floor beside Verity's bed. Clearly this one limb supported a whole tree and might give way at any moment. Verity stood inches from it, in her nightwear, dripping wet, her hair matted and hands reaching out like a sleepwalker. Debris littered the floor, and the noise of the storm filled the room; billowing, cracking and wild. The bedroom door slammed shut behind him.

'Edward!' A gritty-looking powder covered her face, making her look spectral.

'Let's get you out of here,' he called, reaching for her.

'I can't open my eyes – dust, or something.'

He grasped her hand. 'Mind your feet, step gently.'

'What happened?' She shivered, and he squeezed her hand to reassure her.

'It looks like a tree has come down, and broken through the roof.' He put an arm around her icy shoulder, and held her firmly. 'You're going to be fine,' he spoke forcefully, close to her ear as the noise of the storm was deafening. 'I have a torch – I'll guide you out. There's debris all over the floor.'

'Okay.' She leaned against him, gingerly picking her way across the littered carpet, as he led her toward the door.

'Stop here now. Take a big step. There's a chunk of plasterboard or something on the floor. Can you feel the top of it with your foot? That's the way. Now step down the other side of it. Well done. Nearly there. I'm going to need both hands to open the door. Okay?'

'Yes.'

Cracking thunder split the air and lightening lit up the room. Bullying wind and biting rain rushed in through the hole in the ceiling. 'Walk towards my voice, two or three steps. I'm having to hold the door open with my foot. That's it, keep coming, you're doing fine.'

She found and gripped his fingers. Something creaked alarmingly. 'What was that?' she squealed.

'I don't know, and we're not going to hang around to find out. Come!' Edward drew her forward, and she stumbled out through the door on to the upstairs landing. She shivered and rubbed her arms while he pulled the door firmly shut, and shone the torch around to assess the state of the ceiling above the landing where they stood. The beam roamed over Verity, showing her covered with clumps of gritty powder – plaster dust, he guessed – and looking pitifully fragile. Edward circled her slender body with his arms and cradled her gently. 'You're safe. You're fine,' he murmured.

'My eyes,' she said.

'I'll take you to the bathroom along the landing here, and we'll have a look. Don't worry.'

'What about the broken roof, the danger?'

'It's just that corner of the house, I think. This place is built like a fortress. We'll be okay here. You're safe,' he repeated, urging her to believe him. He pulled back from her but kept a reassuring hand on her shoulder. 'Come.' He guided her slowly along the landing. 'You're soaking wet. You must be freezing.' He led her to the bathroom he had used earlier, and propped his Maglite on a shelf, pointing its beam at the bath, so there was some light to work in. 'I'm going to wash the dust and grime off your face, and then I'll bathe your eyes. Lean forward over the bath here,' he led her to the bath edge. 'Prop your hands on your legs to support yourself, and turn your face towards me.' He took the shower attachment from its holder and tested the temperature of the water. 'I'm going to hold your hair back, and first of all wash off all the dirt from your face, okay? Keep your eyes closed for now.'

'Okay,' she faltered. He realised she was shaking, grabbed a towel off a rail and put it around her shoulders in an attempt to warm her up. It pained him to see her so vulnerable. Her hair was tousled, and her long body was covered from neck to ankle in clinging wet nightwear. She must be frozen, but Edward knew the priority had to be cleaning her eyes.

'This will soon be done,' he reassured her. He took her matted hair in his hand, held it back, and ran the spray from the shower attachment gently over her face. Rivulets of dirty water appeared on her cheeks and ran down her chin and after a moment or two the water ran clear, revealing the skin on her face as pink but undamaged. While he cleaned her face, Edward considered the ramifications of the damage in her bedroom, running his mind back to their walk around the garden earlier that evening. He recalled the stand of mature oaks, still in full leaf, close to the back of the house, and concluded that one of them must have come down.

'How are you doing?' he asked, squeezing her shoulder gently.

'Okay,' she muttered.

'The water is running clear now. Keep your eyes closed and wait while I set up the basin.' He touched her arm to reassure her before running a tap. 'Here,' he said, and gently placed her hand on the basin rim. She leant forwards, cupping the tepid water in her palms to flush out her eyes. Her dark lashes stuck to the fine skin but the clotted dust began to wash away. When he asked her to, she opened her eyes, and he rinsed away the last of the grit with fresh water. He could see how sore they were, but she laughed with relief.

'I'm fine,' she said and turned to look at him. 'I can see you.'

The whites of her eyes were bloodshot, the irises a beautiful warm grey. 'That's great,' Edward said, with relief. 'Why don't you take a shower with whatever hot water is left. I'll fetch you some clothes. Your hair would look good for a Halloween party,' he joked.

'Thanks a lot.' She laughed weakly.

Edward left one of his t-shirts, some clean pyjama trousers, and a sweatshirt in a pile beside the bathroom door before returning downstairs. When Verity came down and sat on the rug beside the fire, she looked pale. She ran her fingers through her hair, now clean and shiny, fanning it out in an attempt to dry it, and her slender shoulders bowed beneath his large sweatshirt.

'You must be cold,' he whispered. 'Here, I made us both a hot toddy. It'll help us sleep.'

'What happened up there? Do you think the house is safe?' Verity took the mug from him.

'Yes, I'm sure this central part is fine. It's solidly built.'

'I want to sleep down here, on the sofa, beside the fire.'

'Good idea. I'll bring some bedding down.'

'Will you stay down here with me?'

'Of course.'

'I don't want to be alone. I'm sorry.'

'Don't apologise.'

The stories Edward reported meant he often witnessed human suffering, survivors struggling to understand a terrible accident or natural disaster, and the shock after a near miss. He noted familiar signs of shock in Verity as her fingers quivered, her shoulders were hunched and rigid, and she gazed uneasily about the room. He brought bedding down, set up a bed for her on one sofa and made up his own on the one opposite. She had finished her drink, her hair was drying, and she sat staring into the flames of the fire.

'Come on,' he suggested. 'Get into your bed here, keep yourself warm.' She did as she was told, giving him a fleeting smile of thanks. He held the duvet for her, and tucked her in as he would a child. 'I'm going to play you some music,' he said, nodding to the piano. 'Help you relax.'

'You didn't tell me you played.'

'You didn't ask.'

She managed a watery smile. He sat down at the piano, and fingered the keys, making just enough music to push the billowing noise of the storm out of the vast room. Though his intention was to soothe Verity's frayed nerves, he played for himself too, and soon became lost in the gentle jazz he loved so much.

'If you had a home, you could put a piano in it,' Verity remarked sleepily, sometime later.

'But I like things the way they are.'

'How many people have you helped like you just helped me? It's not the first time.'

His playing faltered just for a second, and then he resumed concentration. 'A few. It's not often just me though. There are others who help too – other journalists who get caught up in the lives of the people they are writing about, or local people, aid workers and the like.'

'It was just you tonight.'

'You were doing fine without me,' he insisted quietly. 'You'd have got yourself out of there.'

'Do you keep in touch with any of those people you write about?'

'Not usually.'

'So, what happens, after you've told their story?'

'I move on.'

In the morning when he awoke, the fire had gone out and Edward did not want to start a new one for fear of waking Verity. The pungent smell of wood ash lingered in the room and he noticed a new crack in the wall above the mantelpiece and a fine layer of fresh dust on a side table. Outside the storm raged around the building fiendishly, and a series of lightning flashes lit up the lawn. Over on the sofa, Verity stirred and opened her eyes.

'Good morning,' she muttered.

'Hi, how are you feeling?'

'Fine, fine.'

'Would you like some coffee?'

'Please, yes.' She ran her fingers back through her hair before sitting and pushing the duvet aside. Noticing that she wore Edward's clothes, she frowned as if she had temporarily forgotten what had happened. Edward wore his creased cotton dressing gown. He poured coffee from a jug on the low table, set a mug down for her, and rubbed his fingers over the stubble peppering his chin.

'What time is it?' she asked.

'Ten-ish.'

'Ha,' she laughed feebly. 'I haven't slept so late in years. The storm is still with us then.'

'It's wild. The thunder and lightning has been going on for hours.'

'You've been up a while?'

'Yes. I couldn't sleep. How are your eyes?'

'Fine, a bit sore, but fine.'

'Good. I think they'll soon recover.'

Verity walked to the row of tall windows, and rubbed the back of her neck before peering cautiously out. Lightning forked the air, scratching the earth with long fingernails.

'My God! There's so much damage!'

'It's contained to that corner of the building – I've had a look. I retrieved your case and your handbag too. They're at the bottom of the stairs.'

'Thank you. What's it like up there?'

'Messy. There's a great big hole in the roof. The tree hasn't moved anymore which is good news. The small sitting room below has damp coming through the ceiling already though, and I've moved what I can out of there to the lobby at the side of the house. There's a new crack across the ceiling over the stairwell so we should avoid going upstairs unless we have to.'

'Crikey.' She grimaced.

'It's just a precaution.'

A roof tile fell and shattered on the veranda steps outside the window, and she backed away.

'How's about some breakfast?' he asked. 'There are some eggs.'

'That sounds good.'

As she sat down at the kitchen table, a smile played around her lips. 'What is it about men and their dressing gowns?' she asked. 'You live out of a suitcase with so few possessions, and yet you still have space for a dressing gown? This fact baffles me.'

'It's a very useful item of clothing! You can use it in all sorts of situations. The robe (as we call it where I come from) is an extremely versatile garment. And I would like to point out that if we're going to discuss eccentric luggage choices, you packed a yoga mat for a weekend trip.'

'Fair point,' she conceded, tucking in to the plate of scrambled eggs. Another flash of lightning lit up the gloom of the kitchen. 'I never know what to do in lightning. Is it, stand under a tree or don't stand under a tree?' she asked, in between mouthfuls.

'Don't. When it's like this, stay indoors. If you get caught out in a lightning storm, crouch down like a frog.'

'Crouch down like a frog?' she laughed. 'Really, is that true?'

He nodded.

'I shall try to remember that. You know a lot of things.' The colour was returning to her cheeks, and her eyes, although still pink, were brighter.

'I used to read Tom Browne when I was younger. Survival stuff. I loved it.'

'I used to be a Girl Guide but the only thing I can remember is how to tie a reef knot!'

After breakfast, Edward retreated to the study to change while Verity washed and dressed in a small cloakroom beside the kitchen. She returned the folded pile of his clothes to him before sitting down abruptly on the edge of a sofa.

Edward swivelled round to look at her. 'Okay?'

'Dizzy.'

'It's the shock. It really knocks you for six. You must rest today.'

'Oh, and there was I thinking we might head out to an art gallery or down to the beach for a swim.' She smiled weakly.

'Put your feet up, lie back on the cushions,' he ordered, quietly. He moved the crumpled duvet out of the way, and patted the sofa.

'You're very bossy.'

He patted the sofa again, and she relented and lay down. 'You need to rest,' he insisted and quietly left her. He returned to the study, sat down in a wing-backed chair, closed his eyes, and put his hands in a mudra to meditate. His breath was rapid but by silently repeating a mantra, he began to slow his thoughts, breathe more deeply, and relax. Outside, the thunder and lightning passed, and in its place came torrential rain, so dense and aggressive that he imagined it drilling holes in the earth, ripping leaves from trees, and creating streams that would rush muddily down the hillside road. Something scudded across the gravel outside and banged against the front wall of the house. Water spluttered from a choking gutter, and squalled against the windows. Gradually, Edward let the sounds and thoughts of the storm go and found the place of stillness and peace, deep inside his body.

He emerged from his meditation, calm and back in line with life. Moving quietly from the study, he returned to the salon where Verity smiled sleepily at him from her bed on the sofa. She sat up and smoothed her hair down.

'I bet you were looking forward to taking out your paints or visiting an exhibition this weekend,' he began, reclaiming his place on the sofa. 'This region is so famous for its art.'

'I was hoping to take some photographs, and perhaps manage a quick sketch or a painting. I love to take my easel out to a hillside or the coast, and paint directly from nature. My passion for it began when I was a little girl and my father used to take me out painting with him. Many times, we spent whole days out in the hills in the region just north of here. My mother would pack the two of us a picnic, and if it didn't get too hot or rainy, my father and I would stay out all day long.'

'And so, this is what you're going to do again – paint straight from nature?'

'Yes, I hope so. I really don't want to turn into some middle-aged lady who *dabbles*. I have to... I *want* to produce beautiful, worthwhile art that pays the bills.'

101

'You'll do it!' Edward encouraged.

They found partially defrosted fish and sweetcorn in the freezer and ate it at the kitchen table for lunch.

'Can I ask you a question?' Verity asked between mouthfuls.

'You'd make a great journalist,' Edward deflected.

'Did something happen to you? Why did you abandon the conventional way of life?'

Edward took a deep breath. 'I didn't so much choose my lifestyle, as it chose me, and I went along with it,' he replied, cautiously.

'I always assumed my life would follow a certain plan too,' she mused, 'but now I realise that so much is out of our control.'

'Life happens *in spite of* the plans, not as a result of them,' he agreed.

'Did you really never think about returning to London?' she asked and looked down at the table.

He studied the crown of her head with its mass of dark tousled hair. 'We were a train crash waiting to happen,' he answered quietly. 'We were this close to having an affair.' He held his thumb and finger up, an inch apart.

'I know,' she admitted, looking up.

'Not meant to be.'

A small, sad frown flashed across her face, and Edward struggled, wanting to say more, but for once, unable to find words.

11

'The lightning stopped a while back. Perhaps we should venture out?' she suggested. 'It would be good to get some fresh air.'

'It's still fierce out there. Don't be deceived.'

'We can wrap up, be careful. I'm going to try it anyway.'

Seeing her determination, he relented. 'We could do with bringing some more logs over from the barn.'

While Verity retrieved her raincoat, tied her hair back in a ponytail, and tucked her trousers into a pair of somebody else's boots found in the front cloakroom, Edward shook out a down-filled jacket, and put it on. He zipped it up and bent over to lace up his boots.

'Is that climbing gear?' she asked.

'Yep,' he replied, efficiently tying his laces.

'You climb mountains?'

'If I get a chance. I hike in the mountains more often than I climb them.'

Verity shook her head. Spending time with Edward really brought to light the sad limitations of her own life; she was nearly fifty years old and had never hiked in any mountains – and yet she would love to! Why had she not done so many things she wanted to do? What had she done with the past quarter of a century?

He stood up, and grinned at her. 'Ready?'

As they stepped out into lashing rain, Verity ducked her head, squealed, and linked her arm instinctively through his. He cupped a hand over hers, protectively.

'I'm not sure this is wise,' he shouted.

'I need it,' she insisted, compelled to be out in the wild air, breathing in its reviving, salty odour and blowing away the cobwebs of fear from the night before.

'Let's keep clear of the trees – there's debris everywhere.'

Verity's eyes watered and the wind rammed up against her thighs making each step forward an effort. She clasped the collar of her coat under her chin, and felt her cheeks burn in the wind. A sudden rush of rain hit her full in the face, streaking her vision, and she staggered. A couple of small trees had fallen and blocked the driveway. 'Look!' she exclaimed, and pointed at them. Edward nodded silently, as if making some kind of assessment. The rain streamed off his flattened hair and ran down his face. The discomfort did not bother him; he looked around calmly, taking everything in.

As they stepped from the gravelled area in front of the house onto the lawn, and were exposed to the full might of the wind, Verity stumbled and gripped Edward's arm, and even Edward bent forward into the force of it. The wind's playthings, they were like small mice for a cat; but she was not afraid. Wild delight surged through her body and her laughter was whisked straight away and thrown up to the sky.

'This is far enough,' Edward cautioned, and covered her hand, as if she might suddenly fly away. He swayed a little before anchoring his feet and standing fast, and she closed her eyes, and stood still and firm beside him.

'Let's turn!' she shouted.

He nodded, and by consent they shuffled around to face the house. It was immediately easier to breathe with their backs to the wind as the air was no longer being rammed down their throats. Another squall of rain slapped her uncovered head. Wisps of hair tore loose from her ponytail, and whipped around her face.

'Oh, my goodness, look at it!' she shouted, letting go of her collar and pointing at the huge oak which leant precariously against the house. One of its major limbs had torn a gash in the roof, and other huge limbs flexed unnaturally. The tree's root ball reached into the air like a splayed hand. Rubble was strewn everywhere and the end of the veranda roof had collapsed. Behind the oak, another tree had fallen into the courtyard wall, demolishing part of it. A few remaining leafy stems flew in the wind like tattered clothing on a washing line. High above on the ridge above the house, trees cowered away from the cliff's edge.

'I can't bear to look at it,' Verity shouted. 'That poor woman – the house owner!'

Edward squeezed her hand. The tip of his nose had turned pink and his dark hair flattened and parted to reveal a line of tanned skin on his scalp. The wind dropped a fraction and he lifted his head to it in acknowledgement. 'Come on then!' he shouted. 'Let's make the most of it while we're out here.' He grinned as they staggered to the far edge of the lawn. Verity sensed danger but she did not care. 'Okay, this is far enough.'

Her eyes ran with tears, and she squinted in an effort to follow the line of the road, noticing that many electricity poles had fallen, and others leant at odd angles, supported only by their wires.

Edward scanned the area. 'Look over there,' he said, his mouth close to her ear. He pointed to the hillside beyond the far edge of the garden where, the evening before, there had been cork oaks, rocks and pines. Now all that remained was a giant brown scar of bare soil studded with a chaotic jumble of broken trees and boulders. It looked like the skin had been ripped off the earth. A landscape that had seemed as old and inevitable as time had disappeared, destroyed overnight. Verity swallowed hard. The hillside terrain had been thrown around as if it were no more than a toy, and only a short distance from where they had slept. She finally understood the storm's power, and felt sickened. Everything was so fragile; nothing lasted.

They turned their backs on the devastation, struggled across the lawn and around the corner of the house to the front drive. Large puddles covered much of the gravel, each grey and choppy, like a miniature lake. Edward released her hand, insisting – despite her protests – that she return to the house while he fetched a barrow of logs from the barn to see them through the night ahead. She did not want to go back inside, and stood and watched Edward stride over the gravel with the barrow. He struggled with the rusty bolt of the barn door but it suddenly freed, and instantly a vicious wind flung the door wide open. Verity exclaimed with horror as the door smashed Edward on the jaw, knocking him to the ground. He rolled on the gravel, and the wind regrouped and hurled the door at him a second time, jamming it over his foot and pinning him to the ground. She shouted, and ran to help him.

'Get back!' he yelled at her, breathing heavily. 'The door is going to fly any minute! Move clear!' Blood stained his boot already where the door had wedged over his foot. He attempted to free himself, and Verity crouched to help him. 'Get out of here!' he yelled again.

'No, I won't. Let me help you.' She reached forward but the storm did not wait for her. The barn door was ripped back off Edward's foot with a force that made him curse out loud, and slammed back against the building where part of it splintered. As soon as he was freed, Edward scuttled backwards like a crab, pulling her with him and out of further danger, as sure enough, the door swung open again, this time ripping clean off its hinges and flying across the courtyard into a clump of pines. Verity watched the door warily, and looked back at the barn to make sure there were no more hazards coming their way. When she turned back to Edward, she saw that a fat splinter of wood remained stuck through the tongue of his boot and into his flesh. He stood up and tested his foot. It barely took his weight.

'Your face is bleeding,' she said, and he put his hand to his jaw; his fingers came away covered in blood. 'Your foot – can you walk?'

'Yes, if you can give me a hand.'

'Lean on me.' She nudged her shoulder under his armpit, and put her arm around his waist. He limped back towards the house through dirty rain puddles. When they were both inside Verity shoved the door firmly closed behind them and locked it; the noise levels dropped and the air felt still again. Rainwater dripped from their clothing, making small pools on the limestone floor. They shed their coats, and hobbled to a sofa where Verity helped Edward sit down.

'That was the stupidest thing I've done in a while,' he shook his head.

'It was an accident,' she countered, trying to figure out how to undo the boot laces around the chunk of wood. The sight of blood seeping through the Gore-tex made her stomach turn, and she was wary of hurting him, but figured that getting the boot off was a priority. His face looked strained and pale beneath his tan. His jaw was cut, and the skin around the cut was already turning blue and swelling with a bruise. He rubbed his fingers along it.

'Here, let me,' he said, and leaned forward to pick at the laces.

'I'll get some scissors.' She ran to the kitchen, and searched through some drawers. 'You do it,' she said, handing him a pair. He snipped the laces, and freed the boot, and, at his suggestion, she hurried to the study and located the first-aid kit in his suitcase. It occurred to her to fetch a bowl of water and a cloth to clean the wound, and a large salad bowl was the cleanest vessel she could find. She took a fresh dishcloth from a packet under the sink, and grabbed a couple of clean tea towels from a drawer. A splinter of dirty wood the size of a small kitchen knife penetrated his skin at a low angle. She began to clean around the wound. 'We need disinfectant. There must be some here somewhere,' she muttered.

'Water is all we need. I'm going to pull the splinter out, and then I need you to put pressure on the wound with that tea towel,' Edward instructed. His face contorted as he pulled the piece of wood out of his foot. Blood spurted from the gash, and Verity covered it quickly, pressing down as firmly as she dared.

'That's not what I should have done but I didn't have much of an option, and I think it went in more sideways than deep,' he declared. 'Let's take a look. I want to make sure there are no splinters left in there.' Blood trickled down his foot, but the flow slowed after the initial gush. 'The bleeding will help clear out germs. We need better light,' he said, and Verity handed him the torch that lay on the table from the night before. She poured clean water over the wound while he held his foot over the salad bowl. He winced. Water splashed over the rug, and Verity fetched kitchen towels to soak it up. They repeated the action a couple of times using fresh water each time. Finally, she folded a clean tea towel on top of a cushion placed on the coffee table for Edward to rest his foot on.

Verity tried not to think of the wound as Edward's skin, while she taped it up using Steri-Strips, but as a tear in fabric. That way, it was not unlike the sewing work that she was used to, and getting the two 'seams' to match up was not too hard. By the time she finished, she was quite pleased with the result. She bagged up the remains of a tray of ice from the freezer, wrapped it in a tea towel, and placed the bundle on Edward's swollen foot.

'Why don't I make us both some tea and see if I can find some biscuits?'

'What a very English thing to suggest,' Edward smiled, but his eyes blazed with pain.

After a mug of hot tea and a couple of madeleine cakes from a packet found in the back of a cupboard, they sat a while in weary silence, and Verity felt guilty for having suggested they go out. If they had stayed inside, the accident would not have happened. The fire crackled in the soot-stained fireplace while the rain still thrashed against the windows and spilled through holes in the veranda roof, splattering noisily. Surely the storm had to clear soon, she thought wearily. She wondered about Matt and the others, and took reassurance in the fact they were together and would look after each other. Edward fell asleep on the sofa opposite her. Even in repose, his face was taut with pain, and she suspected the injury was worse than he was letting on. Overwhelmed with exhaustion, she laid her head back on a cushion, and closed her eyes too.

When she awoke, the light in the salon had faded, and the fire had burned low so that only a glowing pile of red embers remained. Her neck was stiff and she felt chilled and groggy. Edward was still asleep, his head nodded forward, arms folded across his chest, the injured foot still propped up on the coffee table. Verity placed a couple of logs on the embers and raided the candle supply in the kitchen before setting a trio of lit nightlights down on the low table. She rifled through her case in the cloakroom, and changed out of her crumpled clothes and into a comfortable dress and a cardigan, smoothing the dress to rid it of any creases, and brushing her hair in an attempt to feel brighter. When she walked back into the salon, Edward was not there. She turned in time to see him appear from the study, having changed his clothes too. He wore a fresh pair of trousers, a pale shirt, and was barefoot. He had combed his hair. Verity paused and appraised him. He held his injured foot off the ground and leaned on two walking sticks, taken from the pot by the front door. His cheek was cut and swollen but the sparkling energy in his eyes took her breath away.

'That sleep did you good,' she muttered.

'I like your dress.'

'Thanks.' She studied his broad back and strong shoulders as he limped to the piano, and then fetched them a glass of wine each, placing his on top of the piano. As she watched his strong fingers rest on the keys, warmth blazed in her belly. He bent his head as he began to play, and his thick hair shone in the candlelight. It was such a delight to be with him, she realised. No matter what happened, there was no tension, everything was simple, and he was remarkably resilient – she remembered that about him now. He did not linger on the fact of his accident earlier, was already moving on. He had always lived for the moment, she thought; he was so wise. He played light gypsy jazz, and the atmosphere in the house transformed as music filled each gloomy corner of the salon. The tune spoke to Verity of summer parties outdoors, late nights, and good times. As she sat and listened, allowing the sound to wash over her, she rubbed her neck absent-mindedly, and her shoulders dropped. She stretched out her legs, crossing her ankles and allowing her head to rest on the back of the sofa. Her tension washed away. After a time, she got up and slowly put together the ingredients of a basic supper while Edward played on. She found a tin of tuna in a cupboard and freshened up the leftover salad from the night before with some olives from a packet, the remains of the feta cheese and a big tomato, sliced thin. There was some baguette left too; it was dry but she warmed it in the gas oven.

It grew dark outside, and candles flickered in their holders around the kitchen. Edward stopped playing and limped to join her. Feeling suddenly warm, Verity slipped off her cardigan, and put it on the chair beside her, fanning herself as a wave of heat swept through her body, as it so regularly did these days. She sat down at the table and Edward leaned the walking sticks against the wall and sank down opposite her.

'What would you do, if you could do anything in the world?' she asked.

12

'Wow, that is a big question.' He smiled. He fingered his wine glass and studied Verity, noting that her eyes had recovered from the night before and now shone with amusement. What *would* he do if he could do anything? It might be tempting to stop work, he thought, but then again, he loved his work. Would he buy the boat he often dreamed of, and sail to places he had not yet seen? He glanced across the table, admired the beautiful curves of Verity's long neck and slender shoulders. As the combination of wine and painkillers weakened his resolve, he mused that if he could do anything, he would take Verity's hand, lead her to the rug in front of the fire, and lie down with her, finally.

'You're not giving me an answer,' she prompted.

'I'm debating.'

'Surely it's not that hard.'

'You'd be surprised. It's a mighty big question.'

'Off the top of your head, gut instinct.'

'What would *you* do?' he batted the question back at her.

'I asked first.'

'Well, as I'm obviously stuck for an answer, perhaps you'd help us out here.'

'Okay, I'd fly. I'd grow wings, and I'd fly like a big human bird over rivers and seas and mountains, swooping through the air, gliding in the breeze, free.'

'Wow.'

'Don't you think that would be brilliant? The best thing?'

Edward laughed. 'Yes, it would be brilliant.'

'Imagine the feeling of flight. No heavy, weighty human body keeping you tethered. Imagine if you could just lift off, take to the air, and leave your troubles behind on the ground. It would be magical.' She swept her hand in an arc as she spoke and her beautiful mouth curved into a wide smile.

'It would be magical,' he agreed.

'Are you teasing me?'

'No.'

'You're teasing me!'

'I'm not.' He laughed.

'At least I could think of something!'

'Oh, I thought of something.'

'What?'

'I can't tell you.'

'Why not?'

'Just because...'

'Would I laugh?'

'I don't think so.'

'What then?'

'It's a secret.'

'Oh, for heaven's sake. It's just a game.' She laughed and shook her head.

Edward could not answer that.

She took another sip of wine before spearing a fork full of salad. 'How do the French get their vegetables to taste so good?' she asked.

'Beats me.'

'This is so tasty, isn't it? Or is it just me?'

'No, it's delicious. Would you like some more?' He offered her the salad bowl.

'I'm fine, thanks. You finish it off.'

He tipped the remains of the salad onto his plate, and ate it slowly before putting his fork down and leaning back in his chair. Her dress had a wide neckline, and her dark curls rested on the pale skin of her shoulders. He smiled and she smiled brilliantly back, a dazzling exchange. He suggested they open another bottle of wine, and after retiring to sit beside the fire, they fell into easy conversation, sharing stories from their past while outside the wind

111

still howled like a wild dog, and on the low table more candles flickered. Eventually, Verity held up her palm and absent-mindedly rubbed the underside of her wrist as if something irritated her, her long fingers stroking the pale skin.

'It would be nice to have some more music,' she said. She stood up, and ran her hand down her thigh, smoothing the material of her dress.

'There's an iPod dock in the study that might have batteries, and I have music on my phone,' Edward offered.

'Sounds good. I'll go and have a look.'

While she went to the study, he took more painkillers, washing them down with wine.

Verity returned. 'The dock is working and I brought your phone.'

'Great. This summer playlist is mellow,' he suggested, as Cuban guitar music filled the air. He propped his bare foot up on the coffee table, wincing as he did so.

'It needs a splint,' she told him, and fetched a book from her suitcase. She sat down on the coffee table, carefully placed his foot in her lap and fitted the slender volume to the sole. 'Perfect! I didn't want to read it anyway!' She laughed, and wound the bandage in a figure of eight around his foot and ankle. He studied her face while she concentrated. Despite the fine lines around her radiant eyes, her skin was soft and clear, and she had aged beautifully and with dignity. Once the bandage was secured with a safety pin she sat back down opposite him, and tucked her feet beneath her.

'Tell me about you,' he prompted.

'Not much to tell. Ordinary woman, ordinary life.'

'Oh, I don't think so. You're not getting away with that.'

'Oh?'

'I knew you, remember. You were wild and full of joy, and your dancing was divine. Ordinary didn't come into it.'

She shrugged. 'I grew up.'

He shook his head. 'Sorry, I can't accept that. There's more you're not telling me.'

'No, there isn't. That's the thing. I did grow up. I got sensible. I married, had kids, worked, kept house. That's it.'

'What happened to my dancing woman who was so full of her passion for life? You used to talk for hours about all the things you wanted to do and the places you wanted to go.'

112

'Honestly? I don't know.'

He frowned.

She went on, her tone flattening. 'The Verity who danced and dreamed and laughed, and met you for indulgent lunches and long walks through the city and those beautiful parks, quietened right down after she married, knuckled down to real life, faced up to her responsibilities – all those things.'

'So, you no longer go dancing?'

'Nope. Haven't danced for years.'

'That's a little sad.'

'Oh, there's nothing to be sad about.'

'But you loved to dance; it showed in every inch of you.'

Verity let out a ripple of quiet laughter and shook her head, as if remembering. 'I did, that's true.'

He watched her humour die. 'Are you okay?'

'Yes.' She paused. 'All this talk of the past makes me nostalgic, that's all.' She rubbed the top of her arm.

'I'm sorry, I didn't mean to pry.'

'Oh, I don't mind. It's natural; we want to find out more about each other. And what else is there to do?' She opened her hands to the air, and shrugged again. A log crackled in the grate, firing a plume of tiny sparkles up into the fireplace. 'Do you ever think what might have happened if I hadn't got into that taxi at that precise moment after Alison's party? Or if my conscience hadn't kicked in, in that hotel room in Bayswater? I know the timing was all wrong for you too, but...' She left the question hanging.

Edward looked away, and into the fire.

'A part of me always believed I'd made a mistake, losing you,' she confessed.

'I knew how you felt.'

'You did?'

'Yes.' His mind lit with memories and remembered passion. 'Because I felt the same,' he admitted. 'When I walked away from you that last day, I knew I had missed something special, lost my chance. The timing was never right for us.'

'I know, I know.' Verity shook her head. 'Yet here we are again.'

'What were the chances?'

Silence stretched between them until Edward was struck by an idea. 'Shall we dance?' he offered.

She looked up, her eyebrows raised in surprise. 'Can you dance?'

'With this splint, I'm sure I can, slowly.' He limped to a clear space in the semi-darkness of the salon and held out a hand to her. As she moved towards him, her eyes lowered. Her features softened and her hair shone in the candlelight, a twist of silver threading its way through the dark curls beside her face.

The first touch of their fingers was electric. They were hesitant and careful with each other, not like that first time when he had barely been able to contain her in his arms. This time, the music was slow and mellow, an old favourite by the Buena Vista Social Club. Verity rested her hand lightly on his shoulder, and he curved his arm around her waist, gently pulling her close. After a song or two, she rested her cheek on his chest, and he scooped her body even closer, spreading his hand in the small of her back, feeling the dip of her spine beneath the soft fabric of her dress. Her arms wrapped loosely around his neck, his lips brushed her hair, and her back was one long curve as she leant against him. Their closeness was startling and yet utterly natural – like rain on grass, or wind on sand, or a hot morning sun on damp brown earth. Dancing with Verity made him realise how much was missing from his life, and how he had always longed for a moment like this without even knowing it. The years melted away, and it was as if someone had simply changed the music and there had been no interval between their first dance and this one. Colour seeped back into his life, his pulse slowed and his body warmed. His mind swam with peace, and yet he was the most alive and alert he had ever been, registering every touch – the soft pads of her fingertips at the very top of his spine, the heat of her breath on his neck, and the slow strong movement of her thigh brushing his.

A crash ripped through the air. They halted before leaping apart.

'What was that?' she cried.

'I don't know.' He hobbled to grab the torch. 'Something shifted upstairs.'

'I'll look,' she insisted, holding out her hand for the torch. 'You can't climb up there.'

He hesitated. 'Okay, but be careful. Don't go up all the way up. Just shine a light and check what's happening.'

She climbed quickly to the turn in the stairway, aimed the beam up into the darkness, and squinted. Something groaned. 'My bedroom door has blown open. I'm going to try to secure it,' she called down.

'Check the ceiling first. My guess is that the tree on the roof is shifting.'

'The ceiling is cracked but it looks fine,' she said, shining the torch beam around. As she peered into the bedroom, there was a rush of falling debris. Edward began to climb the stairs but the pain from his foot made him gasp. He saw Verity step warily over the threshold of the bedroom.

'The room is ruined. It's drenched with rain from where the ceiling is ripped open. The tree is still lodged in the hole. It's horrific.' She backed out hastily, and stuck the torch between her teeth while she felt around to retrieve a big key from the inner lock. She heaved the door closed, shoved the key shakily into the keyhole, and managed to twist it. Taking the torch in her hand again, she hurriedly scanned the wide upstairs landing for further damage. Something creaked in the darkness. 'It sounds like there might be a problem elsewhere, maybe over the bathrooms.'

'Are you okay? Shall I come up?' Edward called.

'No, you stay there. I'm coming down,' she called back, her voice trembling.

'Well done,' he whispered as they reached the ground floor again. 'Hey, come here.' At the foot of the stairs, he hugged her, gently rubbing her back. 'It's going to be okay, you know.'

'Is it?'

'Yes,' he insisted gently.

They stood together for some moments, taking strength and comfort from each other. 'I want you,' she murmured, her voice not much more than a whisper, her fingers seeking his.

'I want you too, but...' He gazed at her, seeing the lost look in her soft grey eyes, the way she appealed to him silently, yet sensing his own deep inability to respond. He pulled away, took a lit candle, and limping, retreated to the study.

Chilled air penetrated his thin shirt and the single flame from the candle in front of him leapt, creating restless shadows on the walls. The relentless wind outside still harboured so much energy, it left Edward feeling hollowed out and empty. He bent to grab a sweater from his suitcase, and pain shot up his leg. Anger obliterated his normal steady thought processes as he pulled it on, and limped to the window where he grasped either side of the tall frame, and leant there, staring out into the shiny blackness of the night to watch wave after wave of rain rattling down onto the gravel driveway. He tightened his bruised jaw, and tried to control the swell of his emotion, focussing on the pitifully thin pane of glass that separated him from the monstrous weather. He pressed his forehead against its chilling hardness, and took measured deep breaths before closing his eyes. Dancing with Verity had unleashed emotions he thought he had buried, and he wanted nothing more than to pack his bag and escape, to run far away. He registered the musty scents of old books, polished wooden furniture, and the ever-pervading damp stone. Straightening, he stared down at the dim, chipped paint of the sill, and shook his head.

Two days previously, he had been at peace with life. He did not have any roots or feel a part of any culture and was content to be nomadic, existing as his own small tribe of one. He had friends here and there, dotted around the globe – people he could visit and places where he could share food and laughter, and feel comfortable. It had not been easy, getting this far and rebuilding his life this way, and now he had done it, he valued his achievement. He thrived on the fact he had put tragedy behind him, and was a free man who could travel the earth without a backward glance, living only for the moment, and bound only by his sense of purpose – telling the stories of people's lives in an attempt to bring help to them; telling other people's tragedies, perhaps in an attempt to understand his own. Writing stories was what propelled him out of bed each morning, kept his lungs pumping, and his heart beating steadily. The words he wrote were as essential to him as the blood running through his veins. They were the sum of his life now. But suddenly, all that was being threatened as he was being asked to love again, and a little shadow tiptoed back into his life, a small ghost awoke.

Why did he not simply tell Verity the truth?

He stood for what felt like a huge stretch of time, with the underside of one forearm resting on the window frame, staring blindly into the darkness outside. He was vaguely aware of his damaged foot throbbing as he battled the memories of the one loss in his life that had been far worse than all the others. At one point, he curled his fist and brought it down hard on the window sill. With a huge effort of will, he steered his attention to his work, as he always did, in an effort to steady himself. Work was his antidote, his anchor in life, and as he struggled with his buried emotions, he forced himself to envisage Burma where the sun hung like a giant yellow circle in the sky. Burma, with its vast complexity, rawness, and huge casket of untold stories. Burma, with its unfolding, unpredictable and often cruel drama. He imagined himself peddling a push bike or hiring a clapped-out motorcycle, the sun in his eyes forcing him to squint almost permanently, his own sweat a reminder that he was still alive. In Burma, he was simply a hunter-gatherer of stories with no painful past or certain future, a messenger who kept the civilised world in touch with a remote, chaotic place ripped up by war and hunger, brutality, corruption and laughter. In Burma, he lived in the moment, grabbing each day as it came and grateful for it, his heart acknowledging the truth of a place where so many laws lay like broken shells on a beach.

He pushed away from the window, and turned awkwardly to stare at the solitary flame from the candle on the desk. The air in the study had settled, and the candle lit a smooth circle on the desk's surface. He picked up a paperweight, and weighed it in his hand before carefully replacing it. Why did he deny himself Verity now? Was it simply because the feel of her dancing in his arms, the sight of the long dark lashes on her cheek when she closed her eyes, and the brilliance of her smile were too much? If he let Verity into his life, he would not be able to keep secrets anymore. To lie to her was unthinkable, and yet he could not tell her the truth.

He heard music come on in the main room and the soft shuffle of Verity's footstep as she approached the study door. There was a pause, a gentle knock, and then the doorknob turned.

13

When Edward retreated to the study to avoid her, Verity wanted to hurl her wine glass into the fire. She stifled a sob, and stalked to the kitchen to find her cardigan. With the garment tugged around her, she stretched out her hands toward the fire and stamped her feet in an attempt to get warm. She was almost fifty years old, for goodness' sake – what was she thinking? It was a fact which spoke for itself! Women her age were not desirable; she had humiliated herself! She shook her head, sadly. 'No fool like an old fool,' she muttered to herself, bitterly.

Another creaking groan from the back of the house brought her back to earth. She held her breath, sensing danger in the vulnerable state of the place, and not wanting to be alone. She reflected on Edward, shut in the small study, and on the moments they had recently shared – from the first shocking encounter when the plane had hit turbulence the day before to the tender way he had bathed her face, and his instinct to hold her hand in the full force of the wind. Her thoughts turned to Matt, and her self-absorption stalled. Was this how these things started and marriages were lost? Was the dance with Edward not so dissimilar from Matt touching that woman's knee?

She stirred. Caught somewhere between dreaming and waking, it seemed that she floated like a balloon cut loose in a dense night sky with the wind rushing around her. Her heart fluttered, and she moistened her lips as she slowly came to, blinking at the pale ceiling.

It was daylight outside but the light was still grey, and she wasn't sure she wanted to wake up. With some trepidation, she recalled the night before. She and Edward had muttered apologies to each other, sheepishly blaming the drink. It had been awkward making up the sofa beds and agreeing to "call it a day". As Verity lay quietly on the sofa, she heard rain splatter on the veranda roof, and the wind wail. Would this storm never stop? Quietly, so as not to disturb Edward, she got up and pulled on a sweatshirt to keep warm. In the kitchen, she closed the door, and set about making coffee. Checking the clock, she saw it was mid-morning. Her head pounded and her body ached as she moved around the kitchen; she really should not have drunk so much, and she was too old to be sleeping on a lumpy sofa, two nights in a row. Restored by coffee, she heated a pan of water on the stove, and carried it quietly through to the cloakroom where she washed at the small basin. She examined her face in the mirror – not a good sight at all; her skin appeared grey, her eyes shot with red.

As she tiptoed back into the salon, Edward awoke, and checked his watch. He flinched as he placed his injured foot on the floor. With his ruffled hair, crumpled t-shirt, and the curious flat daylight, he appeared like a modern subject in a Vermeer portrait, all muted tones and quiet isolation. He turned to look at her.

'Good morning.'

'Good morning.'

'How are you?'

'I've felt better.'

'Ha,' he nodded, sympathetically.

'Would you like a coffee?'

'Sure, if there's one made already.'

'I made a pot.'

She filled a mug and put it down in front of him. He pulled on his sweater and hobbled to the row of tall windows where squalls of rain tipped onto emerald grass.

'It's losing momentum,' he remarked.

'What shall we do today?'

'Not much we can do, I guess. Sit it out some more.'

As a makeshift breakfast, they ate the last of the drying bread with some butter and jam. Verity avoided eye contact with Edward, and did her best to pretend that the night before had not happened.

'I'm going to fetch some logs,' she announced, tidying away her plate.

'I'll help.'

'I can manage. You need to rest your foot. It's badly swollen.'

'Okay, but watch out for anything that might be unstable.'

'I will.'

While Edward went to wash, Verity wrapped up in her coat and ventured across the courtyard with the barrow. It was still raining but the storm had lost its edge and no longer felt dangerous. Tiles, ripped from the roofs of the house and outbuildings, lay smashed on the gravel. Branches were scattered everywhere, festooned with tattered leaves. The barn door remained wedged in the pine trees, and a metal bucket rolled noisily around the courtyard before Verity bent and stood it upright beside a wall. She filled the barrow and pushed it to the space beside the front door, unloading logs and making a small stack under the eaves. The exercise banished the fog from her brain. She fetched an armful of kindling from a separate pile in the barn, stacked it indoors beside the fireplace, and replenished the log basket in the house, before building a fresh fire. She positioned a couple of the well-seasoned logs in the grate over the flames, and feeling quite satisfied, went to wash her hands.

She insisted on examining Edward's foot. The wound was red raw and swollen and it had bled, although her rudimentary butterfly stitches still held. A mass of blue bruising distorted the shape of it. She cleaned around the site gently, holding a cool cloth against the swelling in an attempt to ease it. She rinsed out the bandage and hung it beside the fire to dry, piling cushions on the coffee table again for him to rest his foot on. He thanked her, and settled to read his book.

Smells of wood smoke and damp stone lingered in the salon, and conjured memories of Verity's childhood home in France. She remembered being trapped indoors during a mistral storm, only then there had been the promise of fresh croissants from the patisserie if she was good. Then, as now, the bad weather had seemed to go on forever, and she had found it hard to settle. Bringing her thoughts back to the present, she followed Edward's example, found a book on a shelf, and settled onto the sofa to read.

They ate a makeshift picnic of cheese, tomatoes and oat cakes for lunch. Verity opened some wine for Edward but stuck with water herself. He swallowed the wine like medicine, his face taut with pain. After eating, he fell asleep, and she turned and stared out of the long windows, letting her thoughts drift. She must have nodded off, because sometime later she was woken by the sound of yet more splintering wood and a loud crash that made her sit bolt upright on the sofa.

'What is it now?'

'It came from the little sitting room at the back.' He sat up.

A long groan followed by an awful rolling, rushing noise filled the air, and Verity instinctively urged Edward to his feet. 'We should get out now. This whole house is going to fall down around our ears.'

'It's not that bad.'

'What are you doing?' she demanded.

He pointed to a cloud of dust which puffed out from beneath the door. 'I think the ceiling has come down in there, that's all.' He limped to the doorway and ran his fingers over the thick stone wall, looking up and around, inspecting it.

She began to pace the floor. 'I just want to get out of here. I could take a walk, find phone reception, and call someone to come and get us.'

'But even if you did that, no vehicle would make it up to the house. The road will be blocked. I won't be able to walk very far. We need a better plan, and above all, we need to be sure the storm has passed.' He twisted the door handle to the small sitting room, and cautiously shoved the door open a little, looking around for more falling debris. Something blocked his access, and when Verity came forward to look through the slim crack, she could see that, as Edward had suspected, the ceiling of the room had come down.

'My God, what a mess,' she whispered and coughed as dust laced the air. The insipid smell of damp plaster leached from the room.

Edward pointed upwards. 'The rain's been coming in through the hole in the roof ever since the tree smashed through it.'

'What's going to happen next?' Verity wondered aloud as they sat at the kitchen table drinking tea.

Edward pushed his hand through his hair, leaving it standing up in peaks. 'I found a map we can take a look at. Hopefully we can leave in the morning. We need to make our own way out somehow.'

'Hey, look out there! I don't believe it! It's stopped raining.'

'I want to check the garage and outbuildings around the courtyard. Hopefully, we'll find a bicycle or two we can use to get down the hill.'

'There's a bunch of keys hanging in the cloakroom; we could try them.'

'Perfect.'

She wrapped the clean bandage back around Edward's foot and the rudimentary splint, and secured a plastic carrier bag around it, in an attempt to keep the wound dry. Edward took a swig of whisky straight from the bottle, before locating his walking sticks. The outdoor air was refreshing. An occasional squall of light rain still flew at them, and a breeze gusted through the trees beside the drive. Verity tried a selection of keys in the keyhole of the rickety garage door, eventually twisting one triumphantly in the lock, and turning to grin at Edward. He followed her into a dark garage.

'Well, look at that! I remember seeing these around when I was a child,' she said.

Edward squinted at an old Velosolex Triporteur which had one flat tyre, and murmured, 'I wonder if it has fuel.'

'It has been cared for. Look, someone has put this new wooden carrier on the back.'

'It's a classic. Let's push it out into the yard so I can see what I'm doing, and I'll try to get it going. Ouch!' Edward hobbled on his foot.

'I'll push it, and then I've had an idea about something to help your foot.' She left Edward examining the vehicle, and back inside the house, located her yoga mat. Taking Edward's damaged boot, she put it on the mat and drew around it with a biro. She found some scissors, and a trussing needle and some butcher's string in a kitchen drawer. After cutting out the shape of a sole and guessing at the size and shape of two upper pieces, she set about sewing together a soft boot with a wide opening and high bridge to cushion Edward's swollen foot. When she presented the results to him, he threw his head back and roared with laughter.

'Miraculous,' he declared, inspecting the bright blue creation.

'It will protect your foot better, I think. It's not waterproof but if it fits, I can hunt around and try to find some glue later.'

'You're a genius.' He perched on a stone bench beside the garage wall.

'Does it fit?'

'As good as.'

'Here, you can even lace it at the top.' She bent to help and their fingers touched. His face was so close that she could see beautiful flecks of light chestnut in his dark irises.

'Remind me to always take a yoga mat with me on my travels – they have so many uses,' he grinned.

'Hate to say I told you so! How are you getting on here?'

'The engine started okay, there's fuel in it, the tyres need air but there's a pump I'm about to try next. As it's going to be downhill much of the way, my only concern is the brakes.'

While he continued to work on the Triporteur, Verity fetched her camera and took shots of the damaged house and landslide, and more photographs of the landscape. As she explored, she wondered how she might capture such views on canvas. Bold, abstract sweeps of colour using oil paints laid thickly with a palette knife, she decided. Alone with her camera, she experienced a growing sense of belonging as she wandered around the extensive garden and out onto the hillside. The afternoon light had a yellow hue and sea salt hung in the air. Verity breathed slowly and the tension ebbed from her body. Through the zoom lens, she framed sections of the rugged landscape – a patch of sunshine piercing the forest canopy and lighting up a tree trunk and leaves, the sand-coloured cubes of a rocky outcrop, and the twisted form of a wind-bent pine. By the time she returned to the courtyard, Edward was attempting to push the Triporteur back into the garage, and she rushed over to help.

'How's it gone?'

He frowned at the eccentric-looking vehicle, the cut on his cheek appearing raw in the sunlight and the curve of his jawline tense with determination. 'I think the tyres will hold – I'll know more in the morning. I'm a bit concerned about the brakes. There are some steep downhill runs from here.'

'Do they work at all?'

'They're so-so, and I don't think it's ever been the safest vehicle on the road.'

Dusk fell, and the salon cooled a few degrees. Lit candles flickered and a fire crackled in the grate in what had now become a familiar setting. Verity fetched the boot she had made and some superglue from a kitchen drawer, and sat hunched over the coffee table, using what light she had. With neat precision, she sealed the boot as best she could. Edward sat huddled on the sofa with his foot propped up and a glass of whisky cradled in his hand. He claimed it was by far the best painkiller. In the kitchen, Verity found some more tinned tuna and a packet of pasta which she cooked for supper, and they opened another bottle of wine. After eating, they retreated to the fireside and Verity pulled on another jumper and fetched one for Edward. She asked him to tell her about Burma.

'What do you know?'

'Absolutely nothing, other than I once watched a film about Aung San Suu Kyi.'

'The majority of the people are among the kindest and friendliest in the world, and the country is littered with beautiful temples and beaches, but that said, it's a place that is emerging from five decades of military rule – a time when there was no freedom of speech and no freedom of the press. For a long time, it was considered one of the most isolated societies in the world and even today, in parts it can still feel like you're stepping back hundreds of years. In 2010, the first general election for twenty years was held and was hailed as a transition from military rule to democracy but in reality, many of the old laws still apply – and the media is still by no means free. The army is a law unto itself, and it can be a dangerous place for anyone who criticises or reports negatively on government officials or policies. Censorship laws were reformed very recently – literally, only a couple of months back – but the reforms are still very much in their infancy.'

As he told her stories of his adventures, Edward gazed into the fire and Verity was transported to a colourful place she could only imagine. She topped up their wine and asked him lots of questions which he answered with great insight and understanding of Burmese culture. She sensed his excitement and his longing to return, and thought sadly how much she would miss him after he was gone.

When it came time to sleep, they hugged each other, lingering for a moment as old friends sometimes do, before hastily separating. Within minutes of lying down, Edward's breathing deepened into sleep, but Verity lay wide awake and restless as a half-moon cast luminous light into the salon, and a series of hot flushes swept through her body. A host of unanswered questions and unspoken words had seemed to dance in the air around her and Edward all day, and she knew she did not want to say goodbye to him.

14

When she awoke, the first thing that Verity noticed was the silence. The wind had stopped and everything was still. She smelled coffee, and turned her head to find Edward limping towards her with a mug.

'Did you sleep well?' he asked, smiling.

'Eventually. You?'

'Not too bad.'

A little later, they ate a simple breakfast together. Food was scarce but after rummaging in a cupboard she had found tinned fruit and the remains of a packet of muesli. Edward checked the Triporteur while she tidied up the house which had begun to smell quite damp. Addressing the day ahead, she decided to take only the things she needed back with her; her coat, passport, money, camera, phone and a few small essentials that would fit into her handbag. Nothing else mattered, and too much luggage would just be a hassle. They would have to take the hand luggage belonging to the others in addition to Edward's case, and that would be more than enough. She packed away the remainder of her things, and left her suitcase in the cloakroom. Pausing for a moment to look at the clear cerulean sky, Verity suddenly understood what the weekend at Les Chênes had taught her. She knew now that if she did not make changes in her life when she got back to London, she never would. She realised that she had to start living her life for herself, and stop trying to please everyone else. Outside in the sunshine, she lifted her chin up to the salty air and closed her eyes for a moment. It was not going to be easy.

She cleared some fallen branches off the driveway so that she and Edward would be able to drive off the property, and then they prepared to leave. With the Triporteur loaded up, Edward stood with his hands on his hips, his weight favouring his good foot, grinning at her. His hair was ruffled, as ever. She smiled back at him. She wore her coat buttoned up, her handbag strapped across her chest with the house keys safely inside. He showed her the map, and they stood for a moment together while he traced his finger over the planned route, his glasses perched low on his nose.

'This way would be quicker – down to the coast – but my guess is the landslide over there will have covered the road here, and we don't want to find ourselves pushing all this lot back up the hill. Better we try to get across here – my guess is it's a fire track kept clear for emergencies and maybe used by hunters, and it will take us down to this small town.' He put his spectacles in his pocket, and fixed his dark eyes on her.

'I really don't want to leave. I love it here,' she admitted.

'I know. I can see why. I'll never forget this place either.'

'I hope this is not goodbye for us two, you know, when we get back to the "real" world.'

'I hope not too.'

'Okay.' She nodded and gave him a brief hug. Edward pushed a lock of hair from her face and held her for a moment. Neither of them spoke.

She climbed up and sat on the luggage facing backwards, while Edward took the driving seat, for as long as his foot would allow. He started the engine, and the eccentric vehicle shook and juddered to life, slowly gathering momentum as it rolled over the gravel drive and down onto the narrow hillside road. They made rickety progress, and Verity tightened her grip as they built up speed. Edward warned her before testing the brakes a couple of times, and each time the Triporteur jolted and slowed obediently, he let out a whoop of delight. Verity sat in silence and watched the beautiful house get smaller and smaller in the distance. The journey she was on now was a new beginning, she told herself. At the end of this French mountain road lay her future.

The town was surprisingly empty. Most of the restaurants they found were closed as the holiday season was over. Storm debris littered gardens and several fallen palm trees had been pushed to the side of the road. After stopping to ask advice from a pedestrian, they got directions to a little *relais* that stayed open all year round, and was tucked away on a narrow lane off one of the main roads through the town. As they drove up to it, they saw a few diners sitting out on a wide terrace and enjoying the gentle sun. Edward parked the Triporteur in the small parking area.

'Let's order some food straight away – I'm starving,' he suggested, his voice heavy with pain after the journey. They ordered the fish of the day and a beer each, and some bread and olives as a starter. Verity tried to call Matt while they waited for the meal but he didn't answer his phone. Edward got through to Jay, and reassured him they were both safe and well. He learnt that Jay, Caro and Matt had sat out the storm in a hotel in La Lavandou, further along the coast. It had not been too bad an experience for them; some interruptions to power and inconvenience from not having their own luggage, but they had managed.

'They'll be about three quarters of an hour,' he told Verity.

They had just finished eating their main course when a rude crunch of tyres on the stony lane announced their arrival. Several car doors slammed, and Jay's cheery voice boomed across the little car park, rippling the peace on the sunny terrace. Edward stood up, and limped towards his brother before embracing him.

'What have you done?' Jay examined the bruises on Edward's jaw and temple, and stared down at his foot.

'Silly accident.'

'Have you had that checked?'

'Someone is on their way here. The waiter told me the nearest emergency clinics are in Cannes or Nice but his sister is a nurse, and has offered to come and take a look.'

'Verity, come here!' Jay crushed her in a hug. 'You must tell us all about your big adventure!'

Matt greeted her with a dry peck on her cheek. 'All right? You survived then?'

'Fine, yes.'

'We were starving, we couldn't wait to eat,' Edward apologised, as they all sat down.

'We've been surviving off meals put together from oddments found in various cupboards,' Verity elaborated, running her fingers back through her hair.

'You poor things,' Caro commiserated.

'It wasn't so bad, but I certainly appreciated that lunch.'

Everyone sat down and the three who had just arrived ordered a main meal while Verity and Edward ordered dessert and more drinks. While they ate, Edward told the story of the power loss, the tree falling on Verity's bedroom, his stupid accident, and finally the discovery of the Triporteur in the garage and their journey down from the hills.

'We were frantic about you guys,' Jay said. 'We tried to call you a hundred times, and we tried to drive back, but the main road out of town was blocked and the emergency services were telling everyone to stay put. It was bedlam, loads of trees down, burst water mains, and flying roof tiles. The big clear-up has begun now but the main route up into the hills remains buried by a landslide. We had just managed to get a detailed map of the area to work out how to reach you by some other route when we got your call.'

'What a weekend.' Verity shook her head.

'I see you brought our bags though. Lifesaver!' Jay grinned. 'I left my passport in mine.'

After the meal was finished, Jay, Caro, Matt, and Verity decided to take a stroll along the beach to fill the time while Edward waited for the nurse and caught up on his emails. Caro and Jay walked ahead. Matt looked pale and seemed weary, and as Verity made no effort at conversation, they walked in silence past gardens that were littered with broken branches and damaged vegetation.

'What a crazy weekend,' she offered, finally. They walked past a garden where a woman hung washing on a line, and called out a greeting. Verity raised her hand and called 'Bonjour, Madame!' Matt frowned as if he did not understand the exchange.

'How's your father?' Verity asked.

'Back home already. Panic over.'

'Already? But he had a heart attack.'

'It was minor. They've given him a few pills, and the doctors are keeping an eye on him.'

'Well, I'm glad to hear it.'

At the bottom of the lane, before stepping out onto the beach, Verity sat down on a bench and took off her shoes and socks. As she bent down, she noticed a couple of cigarette butts squashed onto the dusty pavement beneath the bench. One had lipstick stains. She wondered who the smokers were, and what story they shared.

'Are you leaving your shoes there?'

'Yes.'

'Well I hope they're still there when you get back.'

'I'm sure they will be. The beach is practically deserted; and who would want my shoes?'

Down on the tiny, disappointing beach, Verity relished a warm breeze which blew off the sea and the rush of each wave as it curled onto the shore. The sand was cold but soft and golden, filtering up between her toes in much the way she had imagined it might when she had packed her case for the weekend, a lifetime ago. In places, the beach was littered with debris – driftwood, seaweed, and ugly plastic containers all tangled together. A man poked a stick around in the detritus while his dog ran in big circles, glad to be outdoors again.

Up ahead, Caro had linked her arm through Jay's, and the couple walked with their heads bent in close conversation, in vivid contrast to Verity and Matt. Folding her arms against the breeze, Verity strode down to the shore line, and allowed frothy little waves to run over her feet.

'Did you hear from the girls this weekend?'

'No.'

She suddenly wished she was travelling on with Edward, getting on a plane to colourful, exotic Burma like they did in romantic novels, her paints and brushes in her bag, not a care in the world. Conversations with Edward had been so spontaneous and light-hearted with none of the baggage that she and Matt carried. She sat down cross-legged on the cold sand, and drew circles in it with her finger while Matt stood beside her, his hands shoved into his trouser pockets, restless fingers jangling coins.

'You'll get a damp backside,' he remarked.

'Mm, never mind.'

'Are you all right?'

'Fine! This is all so beautiful.'

'Bloody waste of a weekend.'

'Was it?'

'Well, what d'you think? I was bored shitless.'

'Sorry to hear that.'

'Weren't you?'

'No, it was all a bit...dramatic. Not much chance to get bored.'

'I suppose it was. How was that Edward? Seems like a nice enough chap. Decent, if he's anything like his brother.'

'He is, yes. Decent.'

'That's all right then.' Matt jangled the coins some more.

Verity sat a moment longer, not knowing what to say.

'Look V, I'm sorry if you got the wrong impression of Ellie and I. It's not what you think.'

'I saw your hand on her knee.'

'I don't recall that.'

'So, I'm imagining things now, am I?'

'No, no. I'm sure you're right.'

After sitting a while, staring out at the flat expanse of the Mediterranean, Verity sighed, got up, and brushed the sand off the back of her trousers. By the time they got back to the *relais*, Edward was sitting with his foot wrapped in a fresh bandage with a proper splint.

'How is it?' Jay asked.

'She cleaned and dressed the wound, and advised an x-ray and antibiotics. Everywhere is shut today, but she's given me the name of a doctor I can visit in Nice in the morning. It's a damn nuisance but I need to get it sorted before I fly on to Yangon – you put your life in your hands with the medical care out there.'

The restaurant owner offered to keep the Triporteur in a shed around the back of the building until it could be collected at some later time. The waiter's sister returned with some crutches, and Edward paid her. They settled the bill for lunch, and loaded their luggage into the car. Verity put her coat back on.

'Where's your suitcase?' Matt asked.

'Back at the house. There was no room for it.'

'We can go fetch it now,' Jay said.

'The road is virtually impassable in places, you would never get a car around some of the rock falls.'

131

'Well, surely we can do something. Don't you need it?' Caro asked.

'No, it's fine. Honestly.'

'I will arrange to get it sent back to London for you,' Jay offered.

'No worries, really – it's just a few old clothes.'

'And a yoga mat,' Matt reminded her.

'I had to cut up the yoga mat to make that shoe for Edward.'

Jay guffawed. 'That bloody mat had its uses, then.'

At the airport, the others checked in while Edward sought advice on a hotel as he was not due to fly to Paris until the following morning. They stood in an awkward cluster to say their goodbyes. Edward and Jay clasped each other as if neither man wanted to let go. There was lots of verbal reassurance that they would meet again soon. Verity took a deep breath and smiled a bright farewell to Edward, allowing herself one brief glimpse of his magnetically dark eyes before tearing her attention away. Edward finally turned from the group, and with a waving hand held high above his head, headed for the airport exit.

'Well, that's that then.' Jay rubbed his hands together, his eyes rounded in sadness.

Verity's instinct awoke, extraordinarily, as it had so many years before, and a voice in her head urged her to run after Edward. But she took a deep breath, took a last glance at his receding figure, now a small silhouette in a doorway, and followed the others doggedly to the security gate.

15

Cold air curled around Verity's head as she exited the terminal at Heathrow, and crossed the pavement, clutching the collar of her coat. Clouds hung low over ugly sprawling buildings, a dirty dusk fell and diesel fumes soured the air. The taxi journey from Heathrow to Fulham depressed her. Fine rain drenched the suburbs, the taxi cab reeked of air freshener, and she and Matt sat wrapped in silence, some distance apart from each other on the back seat of the cab. Matt frowned and chewed his lip, and Verity's stomach churned with tension at the thought of all the work she had to catch up on.

Matt inserted a key forcefully into the lock of their front door, and shoved his shoulder against the wood. The door opened with the customary squeak. Verity recoiled at the brightness as he flicked on lights before bending to snatch a scattering of mail off the hall floor.

'Anything for me?' she asked.

He shuffled the letters. 'Nope.'

After the charm of Les Chênes, the Fulham house appeared small and soulless. 'Why are you clutching the mail like that?' she questioned.

'I'm not clutching the mail!'

'You did, and you grabbed at it.'

'Verity, what's wrong with you?'

'Oh, I don't know,' she relented. She could have sworn that Matt had glanced at the top letter and hastily held it to his chest, but maybe she was imagining things. 'I'm going out to get us some bread and milk,' she said.

'Good idea.'

She turned straight around, and headed back onto the dark street, trudging a pavement slippery with fallen leaves. Nothing in London ever changed, she realised, with a sinking heart. Mild depression and anxiety, the doctor had said. One in four people suffer, so common at your age, take these pills. Come back in a month's time if you don't feel better. The prescription was still crumpled in the bottom of her handbag. As if drugging herself would make anything better! In the shop, she queued to pay for her goods. Reaching into her bag for her purse, her fingers touched a smooth piece of ruby corundum that Edward had pressed into her hand during the meal at the *relais*, before the others had arrived. He had bought the crystal from a monk in Burma, he said. It had special properties, and was believed to banish nightmares.

'But I don't have nightmares,' she had denied.

'You cry out in your sleep,' he had told her, quietly.

Sensing her unease, he had explained he often lived in cultures where complete strangers gave each other generous gifts, if there was seen to be a need. Possessions were transient, and held lightly. She had not known what to say. While they ate, she had spotted a little shell in a dusty corner of the patio, picked it up and given it to him in exchange.

'In my culture, we reciprocate.' She had smiled. What did these things mean?

She scurried home through the empty lamplit street. Soaking in a bath later that evening, she soaped herself slowly, grateful for the deep warm water after several days without a proper wash at Les Chênes. Her naked body stretched out before her with its caesarean scar and various unwanted curves, all visible in harsh relief. She imagined what Edward might be doing, alone in his hotel in Nice. She pictured him showering and then lying alone in a wide, empty bed. Her stomach contracted with longing, catching her by surprise. So, there's life in me yet, she noted wistfully. She went downstairs in her dressing gown to say goodnight to Matt, and found him preoccupied and working at his desk. He barely looked up as she entered the tiny study.

'I rang Tills earlier,' she told him.

'Oh?' He closed his laptop and sat with his shoulders hunched, looking down at his hands.

'Are you all right?'

'Yes. Busy.'

'Tills had been drinking. She was slurring her words.'

'She's a student.'

'She's young and naïve. I'm worried about her.'

'You're always worrying about something.'

'Perhaps with reason. I had a nice chat with Livia too. She's settled into the new flat, sounds very happy with Josh.'

'Good, good.'

'I only came to say goodnight anyway.'

'Goodnight then.' He did not make eye contact.

She straightened the front of her dressing gown and pulled the belt tighter, and feeling she was being dismissed, frowned at her husband's bent head. Matt kept his gaze fixed on his own clasped, manicured hands. There was something wrong, she knew it. Quietly, she turned and left.

Monday morning dawned grey and wet, and Verity left the house early for her studio. There was a lot to be done; an ongoing workload of design jobs, stock deliveries to be chased in preparation for Christmas at the shop, and a long To Do list to prepare her business for sale, which she had to keep out of sight of her staff for a little longer.

After work, she drove to Teddington to fetch Charlie. The dog wagged his short tail so frantically that his little arthritic body swayed stiffly with the effort. Verity bent to fuss over him.

'You look tired,' Fiona remarked, head tilted on one side and shrewd eyes narrowed in Verity's direction.

Verity bent to pick up a carrier bag containing her dog's bowls and some leftover food, and ignored her mother's prying comment. She could not face staying for tea, citing the traffic and lots of catching-up of work to be done at home that evening.

Days unrolled, and Verity tried to fit back into her normal routine. She set up her easel in the tiny upstairs box room, and attempted to paint from a photograph she had taken at Les Chênes. There was barely room to breathe in the space, let alone work. Her technique was rusty and the results were all poor. Om Interiors exasperated her, and she snapped at a client. Mel witnessed the scene, and raised an eyebrow at Verity afterwards.

'Are you all right?'

'I'm fine. Sorry. The woman was really getting on my nerves, going on about her bloody drawing room. She's just told me that due to my attitude, she'll be going elsewhere.'

'Crikey.'

'I know. I've never had that happen before.'

'Anything I can do?'

'No, to be honest I didn't want the poxy job anyway. I'm sorry, Mel, I don't know what's wrong with me. I'm so tired I could sleep forever, and I just can't see the point in anything anymore.'

'That's not like you.'

'I couldn't care less about our clients or their stupid jobs.'

'I'll make us a coffee. Maybe you just need a holiday.'

'I've just had one.'

'No, a proper holiday. Two weeks in the sun. You know? The sort of thing normal people do – except you. You never do.'

'I know, I know. Maybe that's it. I feel like I've picked up some weird virus or something.'

Evenings stretched out emptily with Matt working late and Tills away – long snakes of time that left her agitated, unable to sit anywhere for more than a few moments, tidying cupboards that did not need tidying, drumming her fingers or rubbing her jawline, and frowning, always frowning. The fridge hummed noisily in the quiet kitchen while she ate alone. Planes droned overhead every minute or two. The emptiness of her home made her brood on the past. The TV bored her, no music was ever quite right. She found herself drinking the best part of a bottle of Pinot Grigio each evening. Her so-called friends in London were all manically busy with work or with children still at home, and too exhausted or frantic to do anything more than exchange the odd text. Verity wondered what the point of it all was. When she herself had been equally busy, she had not noticed how, as the years had crept by, the friends she had made when the girls were little now saw less and less of each other. She tried walking the streets of Fulham in the evenings so that, with any luck, she might sleep most of the night, and not keep waking up, sweating and agitated, but the sight of normal people eating shared suppers in restaurants, loving life and happy, made her feel ashamed and embarrassed by her own loneliness and apathy. She wondered if she needed further blood tests. It could not be normal to feel so bleak and drained and lifeless, could it?

Matt had a series of late finishes at work, and part of her was glad to have him out of her space. He seemed to be in a permanently bad mood and being in his company often made her own emotional state worse. She had spoken to him again about the scene in the pub and made it clear – now that his father was miraculously recovered from the small heart attack – that she would not tolerate deceit of any kind. He had again denied any inappropriate behaviour, and she had eventually decided to simply forget the incident and put some trust in her husband. As hard as she tried though, she was finding it difficult to get the doubts and suspicions out of her mind. Something was not right about Matt but at the same time, she could find nothing to suggest an affair. She did not like herself very much when her mind became filled with speculation and suspicion. She wanted to be able to believe him, and get on with her life. It was not easy though, as he rarely made eye contact, and rarely smiled either, and she had been spoiled by the attention she had had from Edward at Les Chênes.

After one restless night when she was besieged by a flurry of hot flushes, she got up early and headed out along the path that ran beside the wide brown Thames, taking deep breaths to loosen the tightness in her chest. A cold breeze made the tip of her nose sting. She pulled up her scarf to keep her neck warm, and dug her hands deeper into her pockets. That morning, she could not rid her mind of nagging thoughts about Matt. He was certainly hiding something. She still did not believe he was having an affair, but there was something she could not put her finger on. She paused to contemplate the muddy river water. The tide was high and the water smelled dank. She strode on to Bishops Park where she observed other people's lives; the mother who, half asleep, pushed her energetic toddler on a swing, a jogger with a ponytail which bounced as she ran with headphones clamped to her ears, and a man in a smart raincoat with a mobile phone tucked under his chin and a small dog on a lead. As she wandered, Verity carried her unhappiness, curled up inside her like the fronds of a young fern. She was no longer a part of this place, did not belong in Fulham, and wondered in that moment if she ever had.

In an Italian restaurant that evening, she noticed the way Matt and a waitress glanced at each other, and how a light in Matt's eyes lit up for the waitress and extinguished as his gaze returned to her.

'Do you still see her?' she asked, suddenly.

'Who?'

'That tart in the black top, whatever her name was.' As soon as the words were out, Verity hated herself.

'You are incredibly rude about someone you don't even know.'

'Do you still see her?'

'Of course, I do, every day. I work with her. And she's not a tart.'

'So now you're defending her?'

'It's not a case of that. We're not in the school playground. You're incredibly crabby and judgmental these days.'

'You really don't understand me.'

'Well, I'm trying but no, you're right, I don't,' Matt replied reasonably, and Verity felt fleetingly ashamed of herself.

Their respective work schedules had begun to dictate their lives completely. Without Tills to consider, they had become like the proverbial ships that passed in the night. Verity painted in the evenings, but ended up putting her canvases out for the dustbin men with sad regularity. Her life felt like one step forwards, and two steps back. On the occasions when they both finished work at a reasonable time, they often met like this, there being no real reason to buy in food or rush home to their empty nest.

After they had ordered their meals, Matt launched into an account of his day, his hand slicing through the air, his tone indignant at some business deal gone wrong. Who was he really, she wondered? His mouth had settled into a straight line over the years and his face had filled out, so that he was developing jowls. Lines were now etched from his nose to the corners of his mouth but the shine in his eyes still reflected his determined character. He paused and twisted his signet ring, an ancient habit.

'What are you smiling at? You think that's good?' he queried.

'Sorry, I was miles away.'

'You didn't hear what I said?'

'I drifted off for a moment.'

'I was saying that we're having to let people go.'

'Oh God, Matt, I'm sorry. How awful.'

'It's a nightmare. Everyone's on tenterhooks, wondering who'll be next.'

'Is your job safe?'

'You didn't hear a thing I said, did you?'

'Sorry, long day.'

'Yes, my job is safe for now, but that's not the point. As I was saying...' His explanation escaped Verity's grasp again, as his rabbling words, snapping and popping with stress, became lost in the fog of her own tired mind. She willed herself to concentrate on her husband's difficulties but failed. The meals arrived, and Matt began to eat quickly and silently, his head down. Verity picked at her food, appetite evading her. When his plate was almost empty, he spoke. 'How's business with you, anyway?' he muttered, reaching for his glass.

'Good.' She rallied. 'Order books are full, the shop is looking good for Christmas, and sales are steady.'

'Oh, that's very sensitive of you.' His lips pursed.

'What do you mean?'

'You could at least try to be more tactful.'

'Tactful? What do you mean?' She stared at her husband.

'I mean, not rub in how well you are doing.'

'I'm not rubbing it in, and you were the one who asked.'

He drained the dregs of wine, and looked at her thoughtfully. 'You're changing, you know. You never pay me any attention anymore.'

'From where I'm sitting, you get plenty of attention,' she retorted, suddenly exasperated. 'Everything is about you, even if you don't see it.'

'No, I don't see it – at all.'

'Well, perhaps you should look harder! I've spent over twenty years taking care of you, Matt, and now,' she went on, unable to stop herself, 'now, finally, when I actually want something for me and I ask you to compromise to help me fulfil my ambitions, you dig your heels in. And you have the gall to tell me you need some attention! What I want to know is, what I *really* want to know is, when do I ever get any?'

'You're being over-dramatic.'

'Ha. Is that what you think?'

'You're being emotional, always have been.' He dabbed the corner of his mouth with a linen napkin.

'So, you don't think there's any validity in what I say?'

'You're exaggerating.'

'In what respect am I exaggerating?'

'You're just irrational at the moment, V. You're brooding at your empty nest. You're tormenting yourself.'

'I miss our daughters, yes. But that has nothing to do with my desire to paint – or with what is going on between us. You think because I don't see things your way, I'm irrational?' A woman from the table opposite caught her eye. Verity glared back at her, and the woman looked away hastily.

'No, that wasn't what I said. You're entitled to think whatever you want.' Matt placed the napkin on the table beside his plate, and signalled to the waiter.

'Oh, thank you, Matt. Very nice of you. I'll bear in mind that I can think what I want.' Sarcasm (a quality she detested) had crept into her tone. 'Silly me, I never knew I could simply be myself – but wait a minute! The trouble is, when I try to be me, you lose interest because I'm no longer giving you my undivided attention! So, in truth, you don't want me to be me, at all! It's all so obvious. You can barely look at me these days, let alone be in the same room as me.' Her voice shook.

Matt rolled his eyes, and handed his card to a hovering waiter who avoided looking at Verity. 'I think it's time we went home.'

Verity stood up, embarrassed at herself, and grabbed her coat off a nearby stand, plunging her arms into the sleeves messily, and then having to take a moment to smooth the coat fabric. His car was parked in the street outside the restaurant. He jangled his keys in the cup of his hand as Verity insisted that she would walk home.

'You can't, don't be silly.'

'I want to. I need air. I've been stuck indoors all day.'

'I don't like to think of you walking the streets after dark.'

'I've been doing it for quarter of a century, Matt.'

'As you wish, then.'

She turned, and paced away down the street in the direction of home. A part of her wished that her husband would run after her, rain apologies down on her, and look lovingly into her eyes again, like he used to. She longed to hear him promise that he would support her artistic endeavour and declare that he admired her work and was proud of her, but he was never, ever going to do that, she realised desperately. She walked briskly along the glistening pavement, hearing the hiss of passing car tyres on the damp street as Matt drove off. She was so angry and frustrated and hurt that her chest tightened, making it hard to breathe as she paced out. Her phone rang in her handbag, and she paused beside a high stone wall to fumble for it. An unknown number glowed on her screen.

'Yes,' she answered, panting for breath.

There was a delay on the line and a gurgling noise as if someone were calling her from under water. 'Hi, is this a good time?' Edward asked with gentle hesitance.

'Edward!' She reached for the wall and her hand became smeared with city grime. 'How lovely to hear from you. I was hoping... I didn't know if you would ever call me!'

'I didn't know either.'

'You didn't?'

'No.'

'Well, I'm pleased you did. How are you? How are you getting on?'

'I'm fine. I'm in Yangon and it's very hot and dirty and noisy. I always forget how chaotic everything is.'

'I can't imagine heat – it's freezing here, and wet. I can see my own breath hanging in the air.'

'Where are you?'

'Out on the street, walking home from a restaurant. It must be really late for you?' She cradled the phone between her cheek and shoulder as she roughly wiped her hand with a tissue.

'It's half past three in the morning, if you can believe that. I can't sleep. My hotel room is opposite a sports bar and they get rowdier as the night goes on. How are things with you?'

'Oh, same old, same old. Very busy at work.'

'I'm coming to London in early December to stay with Jay and Caro.'

'That's great.'

'It seemed right to let you know. Given the friendship between your husband and Jay, I thought you might hear and I... I wanted you to know.'

'That's good, it's good you told me.' The line hissed. 'How is your foot?'

'Healing, slowly.'

'And your work?' Verity asked awkwardly, recalling Edward's concern about the safety of journalists.

'Disappointing.'

'Oh, I'm sorry to hear that. Is there nothing good?'

'I just need to persevere.' He chatted on, describing his life in Yangon. Verity stuck one finger in her ear and bowed her head as she strained to hear his voice over the faltering connection, and then she looked up at the orange-stained night sky over Hammersmith as she spoke her replies and relayed her frustration with city life and the slow progress on her business sale. She smudged a tear off her cheek, not sure if it was the cold air making her eyes run, or her erratic emotions.

'Do you have an email address? Can I write to you?' he asked. 'I guess that's okay?'

'Of course. Yes, that's okay. I'd love that.' She gave Edward the details, including her studio phone number and address. Was it right to receive emails from another man? She did not know, and at that moment, did not care. 'I'd love to hear all about what you're doing.'

'Me too. I want to know how it all goes for you.'

She sniffed.

'Are you crying?'

'No. Yes. A bit. I don't know. It's been a long day.'

'Are you okay?'

'Yes, I'm fine, really I am.'

'Don't cry.'

'I'm fine. I don't know. Maybe they're happy tears.'

'Do you need to talk?'

'No, it's okay. I'm fine.' She took a deep breath.

'I wish I could help you out a bit. It sounds like you have a lot on your plate.'

'That's really nice of you, thank you.'

'Send me some photos of your paintings.'

'I haven't done anything decent for ages. I keep throwing most of them away.'

'I'm sure you have. I want to see them. I've never seen what you do.'

'You want to see my work?'

'Yes, of course I do.'

After they had finished talking, Verity's spirits soared. She walked back to Rannoch Road with her head high. Back home, she shoved open the sticky front door and then slammed it behind her, leaning against it, for a moment, filled with a new determination.

'That walk did do you good, you look quite radiant,' Matt observed, steadily.

'Have you taken the dog out?'

'No.'

'I'll do it then.'

Matt regarded her curiously, and then turned back to the television.

'Can I show you my latest painting when I get back?' she tried.

'Maybe at the weekend, I'm tired now. I'm about to get in the bath.'

'I see.' She nodded, and left the house with Charlie, stepping out onto the quiet street. Unless she reminded him, Matt would not ask to look at her paintings at the weekend. The truth was that Matt was not interested in her painting, full stop. And Matt would continue to focus on what he wanted, and not see a problem with it because Verity had never objected or stood up for herself before. That was the truth of the matter. In all the long years of her marriage, she had done everything to please him while neglecting herself, or at least that was how it now seemed. He did not understand that she had changed and wanted to do something for herself. And also in some ways, she was reaping what she had sown. She had never asked for much from Matt, and he had got used to not giving her much.

As Charlie pottered along the street, sniffing a corner where the pavement met a brick wall and cocking his skinny, arthritic leg, Verity looked up at the sky. Even in the city, she still had the sky, she thought in an attempt to console herself – although the inky dark was saturated with reflections of silver and yellow from lit-up buildings, streetlights and cars, and she could not see the stars. She looked down and shook her head bitterly. An occasional glimpse of the sky was not enough! She needed the earth under her feet, clear air, raw untouched landscape, and the music of birdsong not sirens.

And she needed it soon, before it was too late for her, before she became too old to paint, too old to live the life she wanted.

The next morning, instead of taking her customary walk by the river, Verity decided to jog. Extra weight had recently appeared on her hips. A pair of trainers she had once bought but never used now cushioned her feet as she stepped into the street and began to stride out. After a warm-up period of five minutes brisk walking, she upped her pace to a slow jog. Her hair flopped over her eyes and her lungs protested almost immediately but she kept going, forcing her leaden legs to move. In no time, she was struggling to get enough air into her lungs. By the time she reached the riverside, she was gasping like a goldfish and a trickle of perspiration ran down the side of her face. She slowed down to a brisk walk again, pushing her hair back off her face. She would start out slowly, she reassured herself, as she walked with her hands on her hips and her chest heaving. She made a mental note of the lamppost where she had stopped, and vowed to go a little further the next day.

Matt left for a marketing conference in Manchester. Edward emailed Verity, a series of long eloquent paragraphs about a trip he had been on to a troubled region called Kachin in the far north of Burma, and although he was careful not to elucidate or make comment, describing only the landscape, abandoned temples, wildlife, the generosity of people he stayed with, and the food he ate, the email was nonetheless captivating. By reading between the lines and searching online for news of the region, Verity was able to visualise the change ripping through Burma as its people attempted to recover from years of military rule, as old ways clashed with new, and popular perception wavered. Edward also wrote of the regular problems with Yangon's electricity supply. He described the gaudy colour of the street vendors' stalls, and the traffic noises and street-food smells that were a feature of his daily life. He wrote from a busy email café, he explained, and it might take a day or two for him to read any reply she sent.

Was it right to receive an email from Edward that Matt knew nothing about, especially as it made her so happy? Verity did not know. Each day had become such a struggle, and her depression (or whatever it was) sapped her energy, making her feel flat and foggy, so that some days she did not know what was right or wrong anymore, and was not always sure she could trust her own

144

judgement. One thing was certain though; Edward's words brightened her day, and she decided there was no harm in that.

16

In Stella's kitchen, the air ponged of a dirty nappy.

'Hello!' Stella croaked.

Verity hugged her friend, and examined Stella's red eyes and pink, flaky-skinned nose. 'You're ill!' she declared, and fanned the air. 'Hello, baby Tom! Do we need to change you?' She made big eyes at the baby, who gurgled.

'Oh sorry, I can't smell a thing.' Stella opened a window behind her kitchen sink.

'Let me take him. You look really rough.' She took Tom, kissed him on the forehead, and carried him upstairs to change his nappy.

'Coffee or tea?' Stella called up the stairs.

'Tea, please. Why didn't you say you were sick? I could have come sooner. Where's Mandy?'

'Working. She's always working, bless her.'

'Right, you sit down.' Verity returned to the kitchen, and put Tom in his bouncy chair. She washed her hands. 'I'm going to take care of you.'

'You don't need to do that, Vet. I'll be fine just as soon as I shake off this damned cold.'

'I'm your best friend. Do as you're told!'

The two women chatted while Verity tackled a mountain of washing up in the sink, and wiped down all the kitchen surfaces. She made cheese on toast for lunch, and heated up a bottle for the baby. Stella fed and rocked him in his chair, and handed him a succession of toys, in between dabbing her nose, and updating

146

Verity on local gossip. After lunch, Verity insisted that Stella took a nap with the baby. She fetched wellies from her car, and took a walk through the village with Charlie. It was a route she had often taken as a child, and at the top of the hill on the other side of the village were splendid views. Halfway up the incline of the hill, Charlie stopped and refused to budge, stiffening his legs and using the full weight of his barrel-shaped body to express his exhaustion. Verity gave in and, mindful of the vet's instructions about Charlie's arthritis, picked him up and carried him to the top of the slope where she set him down again. There was a copse of beech trees at the crown of the hill. Charlie sniffed around, turning up leaves with his nose while Verity admired the view over the rolling Oxfordshire landscape. The air hung with droplets of autumnal white mist, and yellow leaves carpeted the earth beneath her boots. The landscape was beautiful, and her heart leapt at the sight of the huge sky and the sweep of the Chiltern Hills stretching into the distance, but something was missing from the scene, and whittled away at her peace of mind. What was it?

Matt had returned to Fulham the day before, distant and agitated after his conference in Manchester, and Verity wondered if it was her husband's mood that still bothered her. On arriving home, he had only given her cursory details of his trip. He kept pushing his hair back off his forehead as if he was agitated. She had asked him if he was all right, and he had snapped back that of course he was. His jaw had tightened with irritation at her question, and she had backed off, leaving him to his own bad mood. His continuing sulk had been the main reason she had chosen to escape to Stella's for the day. She had decided to start focusing more on her own needs and stop fretting about her husband's. While Matt had been away up north, she had made a list of houses for sale online that she had intended to show him on his return, but his bad mood had stopped her. Originally, she had imagined Matt coming to Oxfordshire with her, and them staying for a whole weekend in a country pub somewhere; but she had changed her mind about that too. Instead, she now planned to drive past the houses on her list with Stella, and if she found anywhere that looked promising, she would show Matt when he was in a better frame of mind.

Looking around her now, at scudding grey cloud and the brown November landscape, Verity experienced the tiniest seed of doubt about her plans. The scenery was beautiful in its own way but was it worthy of a painting, or many years' worth of paintings, as she proposed? Would she find inspiration here? It was convenient for Matt's commute but it was a long way from the sea, and many days' outdoor work would be lost to the weather. Such a location suited many artists, but would it work for her?

She wandered back down the hill, lost in thought, with Charlie cradled in her arms. Back in Stella's cottage, she fetched the dog a bowl of water before making herself a cup of tea. Despite the chilly air, she opened the back door wide in a bid to freshen up the cottage and blow out a few germs. Charlie tottered back out into Stella's garden, and Verity followed. The garden comprised a wonderfully wild slope where grass grew in rough tufts and dew-laden spider's webs laced the skeletal remains of a few perennials in a flower bed. Could Verity see herself working in a cottage like this? If she was living here, what would she paint on a day like today? A landscape of greys, muted purples and dusky yellows? The soothing curve of a hill? The freshly ploughed soil of a farmer's field? Would these features inspire her? She shivered and headed back indoors. The dog followed, and Verity noticed his nose was running.

'Aw Charlie, you need to see the vet,' she muttered and crouched down. 'You poor thing.' She cleaned the dog's nose as she would a child's before scratching him behind his ears and making a fuss of him. The little dog closed his eyes for a moment, and Verity smiled fondly as he tottered across the tiled floor to curl up on the rug beside Stella's Aga.

Stella and baby Tom slept on, and quietness seeped into Stella's cottage in a way that it never did to Verity's house in Fulham. Verity sensed the isolation of country life. It was beautiful but mildly disconcerting too. What would she do when she wasn't working? She shook her head at all the doubts that crept into her mind.

Stella eventually reappeared looking refreshed after her rest, and carrying a dewy-eyed Tom on her hip. She leant and pulled the kitchen window shut, and closed the door.

'Brrr, I'm freezing. Are you mad, woman, leaving the door open?' Stella shuddered before leaning against the rail of the ancient Aga to warm herself.

'Sorry, just getting some air in, and it's so beautiful out there. Does Mandy never come home?'

'She does a long day at the pub on a Sunday; it's a popular day for people to eat out and she'll likely not be back till late this evening.'

'Jeepers, I don't know how you do it, looking after a baby for hours on end.'

'I don't know how I do it either. I'm getting too old for all this. Still, it's only until she can get back on her feet.'

'What about Tom's father? Does he never help out?'

'He's bloody useless; he's still a kid himself. His mother will sometimes take Tom for a day but she gets stressed if Tom cries.' Stella rolled her eyes. 'But enough about me and my sad life. Did you have a nice walk? Here, hold Tom a sec, would you?'

Verity reached out her arms and took the warm baby. 'I went up the hill,' she replied, as she sat down on a kitchen chair and cuddled Tom on her knee. The infant chewed his fist and dribbled on her trouser leg. 'Shall we go for a drive, and look at those houses after Tom's had his bottle?'

'Of course, we can.' Stella scraped a chair across the floor before plonking herself down on it and catching a loose strand of hair into a clasp on the top of her head. She took Tom from Verity and the baby settled in her arms with his bottle.

'Go on then, spill the beans. What's that look in your eyes? I know you.'

'Oh, I don't know.'

'Where is your mystery man now?'

'Burma. He's working in Burma.'

'Has he been in touch then?'

'Yes, he's coming to London.'

'Are you're going to see him?'

'Yes, I am. But it's not like that. We're just friends.'

'Oh, so if you're *just friends*, you've told Matt about him, have you?'

'No, you know I haven't.'

'Everyone will think you're having an affair if you do see him, you know. It's the way people's minds work.'

'Well, I'm not having an affair or anything like it, and anyway no-one will know.'

'Don't you believe it.'

'I live in London. It's a big place.'

'Are you not in the least bit tempted?' Stella winked in an exaggerated fashion.

'No! I'm married – and even if he is being an arse, I still love my husband! And besides, Edward doesn't fancy me.'

'Pah! I don't believe that for one moment.'

'It's true.'

'Hmm. Well, time will tell, I guess.'

Baby Tom stopped sucking his bottle, and Stella sat him up and idly rubbed his back until he burped. 'Come on, let's go for that drive while the young man here is happy. Blow out the cobwebs. Just think, if you moved out here, we could see each other all the time.'

'That would be so nice. I haven't got any real friends in London any more – everyone I like has moved out or is too busy.'

'The sooner you get out of that city, the better.'

They took off in Verity's car with Tom in his seat in the back and Charlie on a rug beside him. Stella held a sheaf of property details which Verity had brought with her.

'I know exactly where this one is. Turn left at the bottom of the lane,' Stella instructed.

That evening after an early supper with her friend, Verity drove back to London. Despite the cheerful face she had put on for Stella, yet more feelings of uncertainty plagued her. They had driven past one property after another, none of them quite right, and Verity's latest impression of life in the country had depressed her. The light had dulled further as the cloudy November afternoon had advanced. The curves of the hills and the fertile fields she had beheld were lacking in the dramatic spirit she sought for her work. She could not help but compare the flat fields of the Oxford plain to the Massif des Maures and the glistening, shifting plateau of the Mediterranean Sea. Oxfordshire had been chosen partly because Verity had once loved the place, but had she spent so long fantasising about it that she had forgotten the reality? If they moved to Oxfordshire, would she really be making a huge mistake, as Matt implied?

Back home, alone again while Matt was out on his usual Sunday evening visit to the pub, Verity sat with her laptop on her knee and a cup of tea at her side. Edward had sent her another email, and a smile spread over her face as she read it.

Today I ate one of my favourite dishes. It is called tea leaf salad, and is a traditional Burmese dish made from fermented tea leaves, tomatoes, garlic, nuts and fried beans. It is slightly bitter and crunchy at the same time, mouth-watering, and a boost to a weary man's spirits. You would love it!

I have to confess I wish you were here to share some of these meals with me. As I sat in the street-side café earlier, enjoying the salad, it reminded me of the simple food we ate at that kitchen table in France, and how much I enjoyed our brief time together. It is no small thing, to enjoy good food and another person's presence!

Yangon is beautiful, noisy, dusty, enchanting and infuriating – all in the same breath. The city and the heat are making me cranky today as my foot is still playing up – but it is healing, and for all the negatives, there is a special magic about this place that still enchants me and keeps me here.

I have to get on with finishing an article now but do write back and tell me how you are, and how your plans are going.

Your friend always,

Edward.

That night, Verity woke and flung off her duvet as her body burned with sudden heat, her face and limbs became moist with sweat, and her mind raced with the half-remembered fears from a dream. Questions sprang into her head like little goblins. What if she tried to become an artist, and failed? What if she met up with Edward again and did not tell Matt, and then he found out? What if they moved house and became even more unhappy? She rolled onto her back, spread her hand on her chest and willed herself to be calm. The cool bedroom air soothed her hot skin. She reached into her bedside drawer for the small chunk of ruby corundum that was supposed to banish such night horrors, and it felt cool and smooth in the palm of her hand as she clutched it to her heart.

Matt was asleep upstairs, having returned early and disgruntled from the pub. He had moaned about his day, and not even asked her one question about her visit to Stella. The orange glow of a street lamp crept around the corners of the bedroom curtains, and beyond the window, life in Fulham lumbered on, half asleep, half eternally awake. Knowing that it was early morning in Yangon, and rather than write a reply to his email, Verity quietly picked up her phone, and called the number Edward had given her.

The sound of his voice made her smile in the darkness of her bedroom.

'I got your email, thank you. I thought you might be out already.'

'Verity, what a surprise! I'm just on my way to get a bowl of mohinga for breakfast.'

'What's that?'

'Fish stew.'

'Ew, for breakfast?'

'I like it these days.'

'Sorry, so have I caught you at a bad time?'

'Of course not.'

Talking softly, they exchanged news, and Verity ran her doubts about Oxfordshire past Edward.

'You have to work out what you need,' he replied thoughtfully. 'No-one can do that for you. Maybe contact other artists working in the same location?'

'Good idea!'

'Just take small steps, one at a time. You've waited this long, there's no rush.'

'I've been waiting for this moment for *so* long that I'm impatient, I suppose.'

'Just be gentle on yourself, go slowly.'

'I'm not sure I know how to go slowly.'

Edward chuckled. 'That's because of where you live. Believe me, life is a lot slower in other parts of the world.'

'London is hectic. But sorry, I'm moaning.'

'That's okay. You're having a bad night, and being short on sleep is miserable. Plus, you have a lot on your mind.'

'Tell me about you.'

'I've reached a hiatus myself and am feeling pretty restless. I've long wanted to write an anthropology book, focusing on life in the more remote cultures I've lived in. It's early days but I'm starting to gather ideas about what approach to take.'

'Sounds interesting. Would you write it on Burma, do you think?'

'Possibly, but I'm not sure. I have a few other ideas too.'

They chatted on for several minutes, with Verity talking in hushed tones. After they had said goodbye, she put down her phone and stared up at the ceiling, her mind alive with images of Burma. Sleep felt more impossible than ever.

On one of the last days of November, and after a long day at her studio, Verity drove to a house in Notting Hill where she had arranged to meet Jane Templeman, the owner of Les Chênes. Jane had brought Verity's suitcase back from Les Chênes after a recent trip to organise repairs to the house. When Verity saw the case standing on the tiled floor just inside Jane's doorway, the sight of it brought memories of the Côte d'Azur tumbling into her mind.

'Thank you so much for retrieving my things. I hope it wasn't too much bother,' she said, and could not help glancing beyond Jane at walls hung with paintings of all shapes and sizes. Aware that she might appear rude, she turned her attention quickly back to Jane, an elderly woman whose skin shone as if it had recently been scrubbed. Sharp blue eyes twinkled watchfully from her round face.

'It was no problem. Have you got time for a cup of tea? Or maybe even something stronger?'

'Oh, that'd be lovely, thanks.'

'Come in, come in. What would you prefer?'

'Whatever you're having.'

'I made some damson vodka.'

'Just a small one. I'm driving,' Verity laughed.

'You're surprised at me. Good. You like the paintings?'

'Yes. Wonderful to have so many.' She peered at another wall.

'Most of them are done by ex-students of mine. Before I retired, I used to teach fine art. Have you just finished work?'

'Yes.'

'What do you do?'

'I'm an interior designer.'

'Oh God, close your eyes! This place is falling apart. We got this house when we were first married and Notting Hill was cheap, long before they made that wretched film. We never found the need to change much over the years.'

'I like it, and it reminds me of Les Chênes in some ways.'

'Now you're being polite.'

'No, I'm not, honestly. I'm selling my interior design business anyway.'

'Oh?'

'I'm going to paint, actually. As in pictures.' Verity gestured at the walls.

'Well, how very interesting!' Jane pointed to a chair, and Verity sat down beside a circular table cluttered with a Telegraph newspaper open at the crossword, a pen, a poinsettia, a pair of crimson reading glasses on a red string, and a cat's flea collar.

'Tell me about your plans to paint.' Jane set a small liqueur glass full of dark liquid in front of Verity.

'I do landscapes mostly and the occasional portrait, but I need a lot more practice, and to be honest, I also need to find the guts to go through with my decision to start this new career. It's one thing having dreams but quite another trusting in them, I'm finding. I'm wavering – vacillating daily. I've spent my whole life playing it safe, and never really believing I could actually make a living from art. My father was an artist so I know how tough it can be. And I'm a bit scared, to be frank.'

'Oh? What was your father's name?'

'Ralph MacLeod.'

Jane's eyes widened. 'Good gracious, well, you will certainly have artistic genes, then. And he was successful. No reason why you shouldn't be too.'

'He struggled for a long time.'

'What is it they say? "Feel the fear and do it anyway!"'

'I'm trying,' Verity sighed.

'One piece of advice I'll give you for nothing, and that is – you don't want to get to my age and look back and regret. That would be the most awful thing. The only consolation of old age is reflecting on our small achievements – and our tempestuous love affairs, but that's another story! So, you go for it and paint while you still can. It might not turn out to be what you expect but you'll always be able to say you tried. And I can see a steely light in your eyes – that's good.'

'You can probably see my terror!'

'Don't you worry about that. Just begin. We only live once!'

Verity sipped the fragrant vodka. She relaxed into the cushioned wicker chair, and continued to chat, asking Jane lots of questions about Les Chênes. She learned that Jane and her late husband had bought the house as an escape from the pressures of London life in the late '70s when they had a young family.

'The population down there remains seasonal, sadly. The area is littered with second homes and only a tiny population are resident all year round. It's a shame really – such a strange, dislocated place in many ways, for all the hype. My youngest son still occasionally uses the house but his children are teenagers now and don't find it as exciting as they used to. I go down a couple of times a year. I avoid peak season as the traffic is infuriating and all the locals get overworked and grumpy. I keep meaning to rent the place out over the summer but never quite manage it. But changing the subject a bit, do you know my son Adam? Is that how you got to be at Les Chênes?'

'No, I haven't met him, but I think he knows Jay Farrell who works with my husband. That's how we came to be at your house – through Jay.'

'Ah Jay, yes, we all know Jay. Such a lovely man. And not well again, so bloody unfair.'

'Really?'

'You didn't know? I believe he's taken ill again. I'm sorry – me and my big mouth – I've shocked you now. Listen, why don't you stay for supper? I've got a shepherd's pie in the oven and there's far too much for one. You'd be doing me a favour.'

Verity felt overwhelmed with a sudden sadness. She looked around her at the whitewashed walls hung with all sorts of sketches and watercolours, and wondered why Edward had not said anything to her. Perhaps he did not know yet?

'I'd love to stay, thank you.' She recovered her poise. 'It was Jay's brother and I who were stuck in your house during the storm.'

'Ah, I don't know the brother at all, other than he got in touch with Adam after your visit, and very kindly offered to replenish my wine and whisky stock and pay for some phone calls he had made. He confessed to Adam that you had helped yourself to a few bottles while you were sitting out the storm – quite right too, I say.' Jane's eyes sparkled. 'There's no need, of course, for anyone to replace anything, and I'm really not bothered about a couple of phone calls – and I passed a message back to say as much.'

'We did drink quite a bit.'

'Nothing much else you could do, I suppose.' Jane raised an eyebrow.

'Not really,' Verity replied, vaguely.

Jane served out supper, having first put on the pair of magenta-framed reading glasses, and transferred the newspaper and flea collar to a Welsh dresser at the side of the room. She spooned shepherd's pie onto large white plates, setting one before Verity.

Soothing classical piano music played from a radio in the kitchen which adjoined the dining area.

'We have to have our greens,' Jane muttered, spooning sliced cabbage onto each plate. 'We also need something decent to wash down the bloody cabbage with,' she continued with a twinkle in her eye and sloshed some burgundy – "brought from France" – into large wine glasses. 'Just a tad for you, as you're driving later,' she added, with a wink.

With a full tummy, and after a long chat during which the two women exchanged stories and got to know each other a little, Verity relaxed. It was good to spend time with someone who understood the hurdles she faced, and was sympathetic.

'I want to be able to capture the spirit of a place,' Verity mused. 'And I love colour. I love that painting there, on your wall.'

'The Shona Barr?'

'Ah, is that who it is?' Verity stood up and studied the painting more closely, noting the navy and lilac line of a hill, the same colours echoed in a curve of beach, and patches of turquoise sea. 'How does she do it?'

'She painted that in Scotland, you know.'

'I wish I could produce something like that. My father worked in Scotland for a while, but couldn't hack the weather. That was before we moved to France.'

'Do you know the Scottish Colourists?'

'I love the Scottish Colourists! Peploe and Cadell, in particular.'

'You should go up there, take your easel. And if you ever want to go south to France, you can use Les Chênes whenever you like. You know, dear, you're at *that* age for a woman. It's a turning point – massive, in fact – and largely unrecognised in our rigid Western world. This is *the time for you*. You want to paint, you go and paint, my girl, because you don't want to reach my age and realise you've left it all too late. I really can't stress it enough, though of course you don't have to listen to an old bat like me.' Jane pushed her glasses up into her fine grey hair, making it stick out like a spiky halo around her head.

'You're not an old bat.'

'Compared to you I am, believe me. I expect you feel overwhelmed, not certain of your entitlement, hormones all over the place, nobody understanding you.'

156

'How do you know?' Verity giggled.

'Been there. But I was lucky with my husband – I had a good 'un. He understood me, encouraged me to unearth my creative soul and fly.'

'What happened to him, if you don't mind me asking?'

'Motor neurone disease. Brutal, and utterly, utterly unfair. I nursed him to the end.'

'I'm sorry.'

'Don't be. It's life. I adored him and I knew how lucky I'd been to share a life with him. D'you have a good one?'

'I'm beginning to wonder.'

'Sorry, too personal. When all's said and done, a husband is just another human being, and no human being has a right to ruin the life of another. That's the wonderful thing about growing older – you learn what real love is, and you're no longer led a merry dance by your oestrogen levels and the urge to procreate.'

Verity burst out laughing.

'Glad I made you laugh. It's really none of my business but a man who helps you at this stage of your life is a keeper. You just keep beggaring on and keep your spirits up, and let the rest of life be as it will. It's so important to have purpose, and I bet you have talent. I'd put money on it. There's some obligation which comes with talent, you know. You have to use it or else your life goes all out of kilter and you get sick, literally, mentally, whatever. We all owe it to ourselves to understand who we are and what we're here for, and then line our lives up so we can live honestly, with the truth. But I'm waffling and lecturing you. It's the wine. I do apologise.'

'No, no – you're not waffling at all. Or lecturing me. I think you might have helped a penny drop with me. I think I have a clearer picture of what I have to do now.'

'Just believe you can do it.'

'Believe?'

'Believe in yourself, that old cliché. Much easier said than done, of course, but you'll get there, I suspect. Now, coffee? We need to clear your head before you drive.'

Back at Rannoch Road later that evening, Verity opened the suitcase, and the smell of wood smoke on her clothes sent her senses reeling. That night she awoke again with her body burning and her heart thumping, the remnants of a nightmare hooked

157

around the edges of her mind. She flung off her duvet to cool down. In the nightmare that lingered ghoulishly in her mind, her parents had both been alive, and arguing. Her mother had screamed at her father that he never did the right thing, that he did not know how to behave, and that he did not care about her or Verity. Verity had cried a strong, silent cry in her sleep, and it had woken her. Where did these dreams come from? She had real tears caught in her eyelashes. She leaned out of bed, turned on her bedside light and found a tissue to blow her nose. The dream had brought back a memory of a time when her mother had *actually* screamed at her father, most uncharacteristically. Her father had disappeared for weeks afterwards, and Verity had fended for herself and her mother who had been quite ill with what Verity now suspected was depression. The illness had clung to Fiona like a heavy cloak, and bowed her frail body with its weight, often rendering her literally unable to move. In those days, mental illness brought a sense of shame, and it had been a chilling and confusing time for Verity. Stella had been her only ally, and Stella's Mum had helped where she could. Week after week, Verity had struggled to perform basic tasks around the house to keep herself and her mother fed and clean while Ralph MacLeod had stayed away, and Verity had not known where he was or if he would ever come back. Lying fanning herself on her bed, Verity recalled the quiet terror she had lived in. She had longed for her absent father, and to add to her fear, had walked through each day with the dread that if she was not very, very careful she might somehow lose her mother too. She had made up her mind during that time to always be good – very, very good – to make sure that nothing worse happened. What a legacy.

When the doctor had suggested that Verity might be suffering from depression too, she had wrapped up the idea tightly, and shoved it somewhere in the back of her head. She still had not even ordered the prescription which remained crumpled in the bottom of her handbag. She did not ever want to be drugged up like her mother had been. Ever.

When her father had eventually returned home, how had she ever forgiven him? She shook her head at the resilience of her younger self. As she recalled it, her father's return had taken such a weight off her young shoulders that after an indecently short period of mistrust and suspicion, she had forgiven him completely, and never asked where he had been in case it prompted him to go back there. Verity had lived like a shadow from then on, in case she inadvertently did something to make him go away again.

Her hot spell passed, and she shivered and pulled the duvet back over herself. She lay awake, listening to the sounds of the first planes circling overhead, queueing to land at Heathrow. A car door slammed, down in the street. It would soon be time to get up. It was strange; Verity had not thought about her parents' relationship for years. Sometimes, through these vivid dreams, it was as if all the unresolved issues of her past came back to haunt her.

'Are you growing your hair? At your age?' Fiona asked, from her favourite chair in the claustrophobic sitting room in Teddington. Verity had just arrived at her mother's house, and immediately sought out the tiny coal fire for warmth.

'I thought I might.'

'And is that a new lipstick?'

'Yes.'

'It suits you.'

'Thanks.'

Charlie whimpered, and got up from his spot in front of the fire before backing to the side of the room and squatting down urgently.

'Oh no!' Verity exclaimed. 'Charlie!'

The poor dog trotted out of the room with his ears back.

'He can't help it,' Fiona tutted. 'He's getting very old. I'll get some paper towels and disinfectant. Not to worry.'

'Charlie,' Verity whispered, and followed her dog, bending to stroke his small head as he cowered in the corridor. It was not the first time he had lost control of his bowels. 'I'll make another appointment with the vet. Poor Charlie had an infection in his nose the other day that he's been treated for, and now this,' Verity confided to her mother as she helped her to clean the floor.

'He's a very old dog.'

'Do you think he's happy?'

'Happy enough for now.'

Verity took a deep breath. After clearing up, mother and daughter washed their hands together at the kitchen sink.

'Mum, I have to tell you something. I'm planning to sell my business and move out to the country.'

'Are you?'

'I want to paint.'

'Ah.' Fiona's thin pink fingers stilled, suspended under a flow of cold water from the tap. 'I hope you're not going to run off and leave me here in my old age. You are my only child,' she replied tartly, and then thinking better of it added, 'but of course you must do what makes you happy. I'll survive. What does Matt think of this plan?'

'Not a lot,' Verity managed.

'Is he standing in your way?' Fiona went on.

'A bit, yes,' she confessed, wary of where the conversation was leading.

'Hmm.' Fiona nodded and gazed into the middle distance as she dried her hands furiously on a threadbare towel. 'It's a shame. The truly great marriages are the ones where each person sees inside the other's heart, and responds. A rare thing, sadly, but they do exist. I didn't get that myself, as you know. My advice to you, should you ask for it, would be that you can't let a less-than-perfect marriage clip your wings. You'll end up bitter like me. And I say that if painting is what you really want to do, don't let Matt stop you. And ignore my silly selfish comment earlier.'

'You are the least selfish person I know, Mum!' Verity cried. 'Do you really mean that about Matt?'

'What I mean is, that man has ruled the roost for far too long.'

'Mum?'

'At my age, you're allowed to speak your mind. And you've always been a worrier and far too concerned about what other people think of you. You get that from me, unfortunately. So, if you want to paint, paint – and bugger the rest of them.'

'Mum!' Verity laughed, astonished. 'I think I still have to consider my family.'

'You feel guilty and uncomfortable, I know – I can see it in your eyes. I'm just saying you've done your bit for your family. The girls are grown up, and it's about time Matthew Westwood learned a little give-and-take. Don't let any of them rule your life now. This is a time for you, before you get too old like me. The girls are more than capable of looking after themselves a bit, and it would do them good to see you fulfilling yourself. And Matt – well, it's about time,

160

frankly. Your family all have to learn to think about you for a change. Be brave.'

'I don't know what to say, Mum.'

'And I expect I've said more than enough. I'll make us some tea now.'

'I didn't think you approved of my painting?'

'Whatever made you think that?'

'You never seemed very pleased about it.'

'Oh, I was pleased. Possibly never showed it – but that's my way. I wasn't always a good mother, I fear.'

Verity's fingers brushed her mother's bony forearm. 'You were a great Mum.'

'We both know that's a fib. But it was what it was. Now, where was I with the tea?'

'Mum, never mind the tea. Something's bothering me. Was there anything I could have done, when you were ill? I was never sure, am never sure, that I helped you enough.'

'No, dear, there was nothing you could have done,' Fiona replied thoughtfully as she picked up the tea tray and led the way back down the bare corridor to her front room. 'You were a child. And a very good child at that time. But there was a lot I could have done. I let your father run me ragged, I never took enough rest, I lacked inner resolve. In this life, we have to put ourselves first and we have to give ourselves a break no matter what demands the world is making on us. I realised that in the end of course, but not before I'd made myself quite ill.'

As Verity watched her mother take the cosy off the pot and fill their tea cups, she had to blink back tears, but a curious thing happened too. In the light of her mother's encouragement, something suddenly blossomed inside her – a lost energy returned, and her willpower unfurled like a flower. Instinctively, Verity knew that her mother was right. She would find the strength to do what she needed to do, and she would not give up.

The air grew colder, the days shorter, and Christmas decorations appeared in every shop front and restaurant throughout the city. Charlie was given some more medication to settle his stomach but the vet told Verity that at Charlie's age, there was only so much she

161

could do. Verity prepared simple meals of chicken and rice for her dog each day, and only took him for gentle walks.

In the post at her studio, she received a beautiful hand-painted card depicting a gnarled, exotic tree, and a female figure walking with a sun shade towards a charming wooden house. It was a genuine watercolour, exquisitely painted using a very fine brush. Verity marvelled at the workmanship. Inside, Edward's handwriting was strong and clear, and he had written a short message in real black ink.

See what your fellow artists in Burma are up to?
Edward

She propped the card up on her desk.

The first bleak day of December arrived. Verity was now jogging daily, and in a short space of time had built up her fitness so she could slowly run the whole route she used to walk. The first time she managed it had felt like a triumph — and like a part of her life at least was under her control.

'You're never at home these days.' Matt stood in the tiny sitting room, accusing her, as soon as she arrived home one morning, sweaty and panting.

'I just went out for a run.'

'I know. You're always bloody running or working. It's Sunday, and I'm struggling with everything going on at work at the moment. I need someone to talk to.'

Verity considered her husband. There were shadows beneath the troubled blue eyes. 'I heard from Jane Templeman that Jay Farrell is ill again. Is that what's bothering you?'

'Partly, yes. But there's a lot of other stress too.'

'I've got to decorate the shop window today, as I told you. You can always come and help me if you like, and we can chat while I work, or perhaps we can have supper together.'

'I want to talk to you now, not later.'

'We can talk, but not right now. I'm also very busy.'

'I'm not asking you for much.'

'You mustn't worry about work so much. I'm sure everything will sort itself out in good time.'

'That's easy for you to say.'

'You're upset that I have to work today,' Verity finally snapped, 'despite the fact that it is you who so desperately wants me to keep my wretched business and do all this bloody boring work. Do you not see anything ironic in that?'

'I'm sure you don't have to work on a Sunday.'

'I do! We've been flat-out all week and as you know, I refuse to open the shop on a Sunday so today is the only chance we have to put up the Christmas display.'

'D'you know what? Do what you want! Go to work. I'm out of here. I can't stay in this bloody house by myself all day.'

Verity held up her hands, speechless, as Matt strode to the front door, wrenched it open and slammed it shut behind him. She bent to console Charlie who, terrified by the raised voices, cowered beside the sofa.

The following day, despite some fear and reservation, and in accordance with the schedule she had always planned before Matt had raised his numerous objections, Verity put Om Interiors up for sale through a company called Scorer Hardy who had a good reputation for selling well and fast. She did not tell Matt. Her business attracted two potential buyers within hours of being on the market, and Verity sat at her desk and chewed her lip, feeling only apprehension where she should feel excitement.

As she agreed the first appointment for a viewing, she realised that she could not continue to hide her plans from her staff. The pressure was too awful, her head throbbed and her back ached constantly. Taking a deep breath, she called a meeting and broke the news to everyone. The experience left her exhausted. As the week drew to a close, she was grateful it was Stella's birthday that Saturday, and she would be able to escape and leave some of her stresses behind for a weekend.

As she prepared to leave London, Edward messaged to say he had just arrived in the country and would love to see her. Bearing in mind what she knew about Jay, she agreed to a quick coffee, figuring Stella would understand if she was an hour late.

'So, you're okay to look after Charlie while I go down to Stella's? I think he'll be more comfortable here as baby Tom keeps grabbing at him and he's not well enough to cope,' Verity checked with Matt. 'I've cooked him some of his special doggie meals. They're in the fridge. And I bought you a ready-made lasagne for dinner tonight, and some salad.'

'The dog will be fine with me. When are you off?'

'Soon. Will you take Charlie for a short walk after I've gone?'

'Sure.' Matt disappeared into the front room, and Verity heard the news channel being turned on. 'I suppose Stella supports your mad plans to live in Oxfordshire?' he called back, raising his voice about the sound of the television.

Verity took a deep breath; not sure she could cope with another argument. 'She thinks that life in the country isn't all it's cracked up to be but she supports my desire to change career.'

'Hmm. Someone's talking some sense about rural life, anyway.' He glanced up from the television as Verity put on her coat.

'What are you doing over the weekend?' she asked.

'This and that. I might swing by and see my father.'

'Right, well. Send my love to your parents. I'm off.'

He nodded to her. 'Enjoy yourself. Get some rest. You look rough.'

Verity bent and kissed Matt's proffered cheek, and drove away with suspicion filling her mind. There was something in the air – perhaps an unusual note in his voice or the fact he had not made a fuss about looking after the dog? Verity frowned and drummed her fingers on the steering wheel as she sat in her car on the Fulham Palace Road, already trapped in the weekend traffic.

17

It was a bitter December morning, of the kind he had forgotten existed, and Edward was grateful to find a warm seat in the busy café in Hammersmith. His leather jacket remained zipped up and a scarf wrapped around his neck to keep out the hideous cold which seeped into his bones, even when he was indoors. It was impossible to keep warm anywhere in London at this time of year, and he shivered miserably. As he waited for Verity, he drummed his fingertips on the table top, unable to calm his anxieties. It had been a long trip back from Yangon, and he had been rightly worried about what he might find when he reached London. When Jay had initially called, saying he had found a swelling in his armpit which had subsequently been confirmed as the cancer returning, Edward had bent double, as if he had been punched. Later, in a separate phone call, Caro had sobbed to him, her voice shaking as she related more details of Jay's condition. The first time Jay was diagnosed, Caro had been calm and positive, a classic pillar of strength – and so her distress this time around concerned Edward, and all he could think to do was travel back to London at the earliest moment. Jay had told him there was no rush, but some note in his brother's voice had told him otherwise.

On his arrival in Putney, Caro had insisted he stay with them, and Jay had seemed to need him around too, so Edward had agreed, but he already knew that their neat terraced house was going to be too cramped for the three of them.

'Great to see you!' Verity interrupted his thoughts and smiled warmly as she approached, her well-cut curly hair momentarily dishevelled by the damp weather. She wore slim fitting trousers tucked into flat leather boots, and a polo neck in soft grey wool which suited her tall figure.

'Good to see you, too.' He stood up and kissed her cheek. 'I ordered us both a coffee as I know you're in a rush.'

'Thanks. I can't believe you're here already.'

'Me neither really.'

'How are you?'

'So, so... so, so... Jay's not well again. That's why I'm back here,' he confessed.

'I heard about his illness returning. I'm very sorry.'

'It's pretty awful.'

'Is he going to be okay?'

'I don't know. I think the outlook is pretty good. He's most likely just having a bit of a setback, but everyone is understandably on edge.'

'How is he in himself?'

'He's remarkable really, very stoical, though in bad moments he blames himself for the cancer recurring, thinks he must have done something wrong or wonders if he could have done more to prevent it. He's beating himself up a bit but the doctors have assured him it was nothing he did or didn't do. It's a tough time for him. He's had to stop work again as the treatment makes him so sick and exhausted but I admire his attitude – he's being really positive in the face of it all. Caro is a bit wobbly this time around but as always, she's very caring towards him.'

'It's so unfair. I really hope he recovers soon. Will the treatment take long?'

'A few months, I think.'

'Poor Jay,' Verity sympathised, shaking her head.

'Yeah, it's a bastard disease.'

'He'll get through it.'

'I hope he will, yes. I'm going to stick around for a bit, and help where I can. I'll need to rent a place as it's pretty cramped all staying together while he's so ill. But enough about me. Where are you going this weekend?'

'I'm going to stay with my friend in Oxfordshire. It's her birthday.'

She sipped from the mug a waitress had put down in front of her. Despite her well-groomed appearance, Edward noted that Verity still bit her lip when she wasn't speaking, and nervously fingered the silver bangles at her wrist. She was rarely completely still. He had little doubt that she needed to find a more peaceful approach to life, and possibly would if she was happier with her work, but he knew it was not his place to advise. All he could do was listen and support her where possible.

'So, what is it that's bothering you?' he asked quietly.

'Whether the English countryside is the sort of thing I want to paint,' she replied bluntly, eyes round with uncertainty.

'And?'

'And I'm not sure. I'm planning to turn my whole life upside down so that I can make a new career but I'm not sure I've thought it through very well, and it's all a bit scary. I decided to tell my staff about the business going on the market yesterday too, as I became uncomfortable making plans behind their backs, and I have a second viewing by a woman who seems genuinely interested. So, it's all feeling very real. Everyone is concerned about the security of their jobs, quite understandably, although nothing will change for months, and it's pretty stressful. I'll do everything I can to persuade the new owners to keep the staff on, but ultimately, it's out of my hands. It's all a bit horrible.'

'I guess it's not something you ever imagine having to do when you start out in a business and begin employing people.'

'Very true. Anyway, never mind. I'll cope. What about you? What will you do while you're here?'

'I'm going to accompany Jay to his chemo from now on, do some of the chores he would normally do at home – fix things, cook for him, help keep the place running – anything that helps, and means Caro can carry on going to work each day and doesn't get over-burdened. We haven't worked it all out yet, but we will. When Jay rests, I'll take the chance to go running and catch up on my own stuff.'

'You're a good brother.'

'He's all the family I have.'

'If there's anything I can do to help?'

'Thanks.'

'I guess I'd better get going shortly,' she said, draining her coffee. 'I don't want to be too late for the birthday girl.'

As they parted outside the café, Edward kissed her on the cheek, and caught a whiff of her warm, floral scent. He wondered what the story was behind her having to make so many decisions alone when she had a husband who could help. He did not ask. He never had asked, he realised as he walked down the street away from her. And in the same way that he never asked about her marriage, nor had he yet found the courage to be completely open about everything that was on his own mind, either. He had promised himself he would come clean and tell her everything, but somehow, when he was actually with her, his firm intentions flew away like birds.

18

Verity unlocked the wide door of her studio, and flipped on the lights. Before she had left for the weekend, she had asked Mel to tidy the pattern books and brochures, and to make sure the worktops were clean, the light fittings had working bulbs, and to leave instructions for the cleaner to dust and hoover in every corner. Normally, they were too busy to keep the place spotless but it would be these small details that would make such a difference to the second viewing, due to take place the next day.

She paced around her studio on the quiet Sunday evening, arms folded. She was agitated, having driven straight from Oxfordshire where the trip had involved drinking lots of wine with Stella and had raised more questions than it had answered about her future. She had made the journey back to London, tired and hungover, and was seriously beginning to doubt that moving back to her old childhood village would be a wise decision.

She began by checking Mel's and the cleaner's efforts before tidying her own work area. She heaved old sample books and notepads out to her car, wanting the studio to look busy and thriving but professional and organised too. Time ticked by as she noticed one small thing after another that needed her attention. She unwrapped a box of reed diffusers from the storeroom and placed them on a discreet shelf to release a gentle mimosa and lemon fragrance into the studio space, sorted out the contents of a cupboard she felt sure the potential buyers might open, and made a mental note to buy some fresh flowers for the reception desk, first thing in the morning. She went through to the shop, and was pleased to see that the shelves were clean and well stocked, and the till area was neat and tidy.

When she had finished, and everything was as good as she could make it, she realised how hungry she was, and decided it was finally time to head back to Rannoch Road. She pushed her hair back off her forehead and put her hands on her hips, assessing the studio space for one last time before she left. It was an exciting architectural space with its bare brick walls and wooden floor. One of her father's huge landscapes hung on the wall behind her desk, adding a creative flourish to the atmosphere, although Verity had made it very clear that the painting was not included in the sale. Just before she locked up, she paused again, looked around her, and took a deep breath. Whatever happened next would be out of her hands. Within a matter of months, if everything went to plan, she would no longer be coming to this place every day. What would that be like and how would she cope? She had yet to make any concrete plans about how she would begin her new career or what she would do first or where she would go to paint, but as she envisaged the freedom, a life with no more impossible-to-please clients, no more rushing from one place to the next and no more stress, a ripple of excitement ran through her. When the great day came, and she was free from it all, she would cherish every single moment.

Verity knocked, and nudged open the door to Matt's little study. He was working at his laptop and hastily closed the screen before turning to look at her. She glanced around at the tiny space, sliced from the end of their one reception room, and thought – as she always had – that the room was a mistake in terms of design, as it made a pokey study with no natural light.

'Would you like a bite to eat? I'm going to heat up a quick bowl of soup before I take a bath.'

'Didn't you have supper with Stella?'

'No, I told you. I was at the studio.'

'That's unusual for you on a Sunday.'

'You know what we get like at Christmas.' She fidgeted with the silver bangles on her wrist.

'I don't want to eat but I could murder a whisky. I'll fetch one myself. There's something different about you.'

'Really?'

'No need to look so guilty.' Matt followed her into the kitchen where he stood and trailed his fingers along the worktop. 'So, I suppose you went looking at houses?'

'No, I didn't, actually. Well, I drove past a few to check them out but I didn't go in.'

'It must be just the country air that's put a flush in your cheeks then.'

'Quite probably.'

'I've been doing some thinking. Sit down a minute, have a drink with me.'

'I don't want a drink. I'll have this soup. I'm starving.'

'Whatever… But listen, what I want to say is, before you go ahead with making any rash decisions, you need to be sure you've thought things through properly. I know you, V.'

Verity felt heat rise in her cheeks. 'I'm not a child.'

'Please don't get defensive. You're a good artist but we both know that's not enough, don't we? There's a lot of luck involved and you have to be marketable. I'm simply trying to be realistic here.'

'Well, I do know all that, and I won't get "marketable" unless I try.'

Matt's lips straightened into a thin line and he shook his head. He rubbed the pad of his forefinger over a blemish on the worktop.

'Have some faith in me!' she snapped, slamming a pan onto a hot plate.

'I do have faith in you, I do… But I have to be honest with you, darling, I'm just not convinced. It's terrible timing, there's a huge recession going on. And I'm probably the only person in your life who has the guts to tell it like it is. Stella's not going to tell you, nor is your mother. I'm just trying to do you a favour here before you start something you might regret.'

'Don't you trust me?'

'Of course I trust you.'

'You know what I think? What I think is… The one thing I *genuinely* regret is that I ever listened to you, twenty years ago, when you talked me out of doing this before, and I ended up being sucked into the world of interior design. I seriously regret it!'

'Oh, come on now, V. You can't blame me for choices you made twenty years ago.'

'No, I'm not *blaming* you, but you were very persuasive, and using a similar line of reasoning as I recall, twenty odd years ago – and back then I listened to you. And I'm not going to make the same mistake twice. But let's be clear here. Are you actually, seriously telling me you don't think I'm a good enough painter or savvy-enough businesswoman?' She fixed her blazing eyes on him, refusing to show the hurt that fizzed inside her. For one, long, stretched-out moment, he avoided her livid stare, pressed his lips together and tipped his head to one side, as if weighing up a decision. It was all she could do not to thump him. He had no faith in her! It was so obvious! He did not trust her judgement, did not believe in her. She turned away, bumping into a chair clumsily, and refusing to let him see her face as her confidence crumpled. Distractedly, she picked up the empty carton of chicken soup and stuffed it into the bin.

'I'm sorry, V,' he mumbled.

'D'you know what, just get out of my kitchen. And don't say another word.'

Tills arrived home for Christmas, and the Rannoch Road house sprang to life again. Abandoned shoes filled the space beside the front door, coats and sweatshirts hung askance on the backs of chairs, Tills' work files from university littered the kitchen table, and the bathroom was filled with shampoo smells that made Verity nostalgic. She had tried to overcome her hurt at Matt's hideous lack of faith in her by running each morning beside the river, attempting to sweat out the devastation and anger that regularly welled up inside her. She did not speak to anyone about what he had said, feeling too ashamed and afraid that he might be right, and that she might in some way be being foolish or suffering some embarrassing mid-life crisis.

Tills had made new friends at university who lived in London, and she was keen to be out with them the whole time, as well as seeing all her old friends. Her phone beeped constantly with incoming messages, and she was hardly ever home, apart from in the mornings when she slept until midday. Mixed with the joy of seeing her again, Verity felt increasing irritation and concern, as her daughter looked thin, and never ate properly or relaxed.

One evening, Tills came clattering down the stairs, chattering on her mobile phone. She breezed into the kitchen, finished her call, flung her phone down on the table, and turned on Verity's ancient radio, finding Capital Radio, and upping the volume.

'Turn it down,' Verity commanded, as she chopped vegetables quickly on a wooden board.

'I love it.'

'Turn it down. It's too loud.'

Tills folded her arms, and rounded her eyes at Verity, in challenge. Verity moved swiftly to the radio, and turned the volume down herself. 'Listen to your music on headphones if you want it that loud. But it won't be good for your ears.'

Tills pulled out a pan from a cupboard, filled it with water, and set it to boil.

'Dinner is in an hour,' Verity observed.

'I'm making some pasta. I'm going out.'

'Where are you going?'

'To a club up in town.'

'Isn't it a bit early to go to a club?'

'My friend has a free house.'

'What does that mean?'

'His parents are away. We're going to his place first.'

'Tills, you're not going to drink too much, are you?'

'No, Mother, of course I'm not.'

Verity washed her hands and dried them, leant on a worktop and studied her daughter. Tills boiled pasta and heated up sauce from a jar. She left a trail of mess around the kitchen, and Verity moved in her wake, folding and sticking down the top of the pasta packet and putting it back in the cupboard, rinsing out the sauce jar and placing it in the recycling bin, and when Tills had finished eating, Verity wrapped up the parmesan, put it back in the fridge and put the cheese grater in the dishwasher. She tried to chat with Tills as she did all this, but Tills only gave monosyllabic answers in between chewing and being fixated by more messages on her phone. When she had finished eating, Tills left her bowl on the table.

'Would you stack that in the dishwasher, please?'

Tills sighed and flashed her beautiful blue eyes – Matt's eyes – at Verity. Tills' skin had erupted in spots during the term she had been away, and Verity felt a flash of pity for her. Matt arrived home from work, dropped his laptop bag on a chair, and engulfed Tills in a hug. Tills squirmed from his grasp.

'How's my little girl?'

'Dad!'

'Not so little anymore,' Verity remarked.

Matt had undergone a transformation since Tills had arrived home. He was home each evening for dinner and joined in with conversations while they ate, unlike when it was just the two of them, and Verity had to initiate conversation or else eat in silence. Just the evening before, she had chewed her food and watched as Matt had animatedly dispensed advice to Tills about what to look for in a student rental property for the following academic year. Tills had shovelled down her food, and hardly listened to a word her dad had said, and Verity had almost felt sorry for Matt as his advice had fallen on such deaf ears. Matt, conversely, had not seemed to notice that Tills was not paying him any attention.

'I'm going to get ready to go out.' Tills grabbed her phone, and scurried out of the kitchen.

'She looks too thin and pale, and her skin is awful,' Verity murmured to Matt, once she was safely out of earshot.

'She's a teenager. Give her a break.'

'She's drinking too much. Did you notice how she knocked back wine over dinner last night? She never used to do that.'

'She's growing up.'

'Can you give me a lift in about half an hour, Dad?' Tills called down the stairs. 'It's raining. I don't want to get wet.'

'Of course, I can, sweetheart.'

'I'm making dinner for us.'

'Stick mine in the oven. It'll keep.'

'She wraps you around her little finger.'

'She's my little girl.'

'Hmm.' Verity switched off the irritating radio completely, and massaged her temples. 'I love her but she's driving me mad already.'

'You need to chill out.'

'Oh, do I?'

'Yes.'

Verity held her husband's gaze before looking away.

Her phone showed that it was twenty-three minutes past one. Verity lay in her bed, fretting and unable to sleep. She was aware of becoming angrier by the day, and overwhelmingly frustrated at Matt's continued lack of interest in anything she did or said. She often felt an urge to scream at him but knew from experience it would get her nowhere. Her mood was not helped by the nagging guilt she experienced, as she had still not found the courage to tell him about Om Interiors going on the market, let alone that the business might now sell. The second viewing had gone exceptionally well, and she expected to receive an offer any day. On top of these stresses, Tills had still not come home from another night out and she worried about her, out in the streets of London at night.

Verity sighed, flicked on her bedside light, and sent a message to Tills, asking when she would be home. She lay a while longer waiting for a reply, and must have drifted off to sleep because the next thing she knew it was quarter to four in the morning, and she had woken with a dry mouth and the bedside light glaring in her face. On checking her phone, there was still no reply from Tills. Worry made her stomach churn. She tried to call Tills, and there was no answer. Her fears raced on futilely until eventually, she fell into a shallow slumber, just as daylight broke.

'I know you've got used to living away from home but you need to tell me if you're not coming back, and you need to reply if I text you,' she told Tills, as calmly as she could, when Tills reappeared, late the following morning. Verity had put off going to work, unable to function until she knew that her daughter was safe.

'Sorry, Mum, everything was fine. We were just having fun and all crashed at Johnny's.'

'Who's Johnny?'

'My friend. I told you. He had a free house.'

Tills' skin looked chalky and her breath stank with a metallic, alcoholic odour.

'I'd like you to decorate the Christmas tree for me. I've got a lot of paperwork to do at my studio, and I'm really pushed for time now, you've made me late.'

'I need to grab some sleep, and then I'm going out.'

'What, again?'

'Yes. I've just come back to have a rest and a bath. I'll do the tree tomorrow.'

'I want it doing tonight.'

'Why?'

'Because that's what I planned.'

'Mum, it can wait until tomorrow.'

'I want it doing later.'

'Oh, okay, all right, I'll do the tree later!'

'Good. Have you eaten?'

'I'm going to grab a cheese sandwich.'

'When was the last time you had a proper meal?'

'I had a kebab last night. I'm not hungry, Mum.'

'You need to eat properly.'

'Don't fuss! I'll make a sandwich!'

'And what time will you be back tonight?'

'I dunno. We might all crash at Johnny's again.'

'I don't like this, Tills.'

'Chill out, Mum.'

'Don't tell me to "chill out"! It's extremely irritating! I want you to keep in touch. While you're in this house, you're still my responsibility.'

'I'm eighteen years old.'

'And I'm still your mother. Do me a favour.'

'Okay, Mum. Okay.'

'Now give me a hug.'

Tills briefly leaned in towards Verity, and she put her arms around her daughter's skinny frame, feeling her shoulder blades beneath the baggy top. 'You're getting thin.'

'Mother, don't fuss. I'm a student. Students eat badly, drink too much, and are constantly sleep-deprived and knackered. It's all perfectly normal. And I'm sorry if you worried about me but you really don't need to.'

Verity laughed despite herself. Till's mouth curled in a little smile too.

'You're right,' Verity relented. 'I do need to 'chill out' but you need to keep in touch with me too.'

'I will, Mum. I'm sorry.'

'Okay.'

Returning from work that evening, Verity stepped through her front door and tripped over a pair of Till's Converse boots. She hung up her coat and collected a towel from the back of the turquoise sofa, and a half-empty coffee mug from the mantelpiece. The Christmas tree stood bare in the corner of the room and the boxes of decorations were still unopened.

'Hello?' Verity called.

'Hi Mum!'

'You haven't done the tree.'

Tills skipped down the stairs. She had painted her eyelids with a thick line of kohl, clogged her lashes with layers of mascara, and wore a top that showed her ribs and stomach to the world despite freezing temperatures outside.

'You promised you'd decorate the tree.'

'I will, Mum, I will, but I crashed out after you went to work, and now I'm really, really late.'

'Are you going to Johnny's?'

'No, his parents are back. They went a bit ballistic and grounded him. We're all meeting in a bar that has a happy hour.'

'I need you to do two days in the shop for me this week. I'll pay you.'

'Okay, I'll think about it.'

'Tills, I'm very busy with Christmas, and Julie is off sick again. I need the girls from the shop to do the clients' home decorations because they know what to do, and I need you to help in the shop.'

'I said, I'll see, Mum.'

'Tills, you'll do it!'

'That's really unfair! You could have asked. I do have a life, you know.'

'Yes, and so do I. A very busy one!'

'Jesus.'

'Don't use language like that.'

'Okay, okay. Tell me the days and I'll do it.'

'And you are not going anywhere until you've decorated that tree *nicely* and put some decent clothes on.'

'I haven't got time now.'

'Make time!'

Tills glared at Verity, and Verity glared back at Tills. Tills begrudgingly flung half a box of decorations around the tree,

177

refused to change her clothes, and stalked out of the house for another meet up with her friends. Matt returned from Christmas shopping. Verity had rung him, and asked him to buy them a ready meal that she now put onto a tray in the oven.

'She still hasn't decorated the tree properly for me. I told her to do it before she went out and she snuck out anyway!' she complained.

'You always get stressed at this time of year,' he replied wearily. 'Just cut her some slack.'

'She's being utterly selfish!'

'She's being eighteen.'

'It would help if you actually stepped in and disciplined her instead of leaving me to be the bad guy all the time.'

'Okay I'll try, I'll try.'

After supper, Verity wiped down the kitchen surfaces, and Matt slid a document across the worktop and offered her a pen.

'Sign here, please,' he asked, a rare and beguiling smile lighting his face.

'What am I signing for today?' she asked, pushing her hair back off her face.

'House insurance.'

'There you go.'

19

Verity arrived at her studio early to find Mel already there. She made them both a coffee, while Mel updated her with the latest status of the ongoing jobs. She had stomach cramps, her head was foggy and she struggled at the thought of the day's massive workload and the tedious Christmas house-dressing she had booked. It was good money but her customer was always stressed and hounded her at this time of year, expecting her to meet impossible standards and deadlines.

'Scorer Hardy called,' Mel said. 'That man, the agent or whatever he is, has sent you an email. You need to look at it, he said.'

Verity sat at her desk, massaged her temple and scrolled through her emails, opening the one from Scorer Hardy. She quickly scanned the contents. *This offer to purchase said business is contingent upon the buyer's inspection of all the books and records of the business and the buyer's satisfaction with the information contained therein,'* she read aloud. 'Yes!' she squealed, clapping her hands. 'I did it!'

'Who are the buyers and what are they like?' Mel asked, lips pursed, hand on hip.

'When I know more, I promise you'll be the first to know. It's just an offer; I'm not there yet. There's some negotiating to be done. I'm going to do my very best to look after you and the others throughout this process, Mel. I promise.'

'I know you are. It's the other party I'm worried about.'

The offer was under her asking price and Verity knew she had to negotiate. Her immediate priority for the day changed. She delegated the house dressing to Mel, knocked back a couple of painkillers, and pulled out her last set of accounts to re-familiarise herself with the figures so that she could present a good case when it came to negotiations. She was not going to leave anything to chance.

That evening, she and Matt sat at their kitchen table, eating a salmon and rice dish that Verity had hastily thrown together after work. Her eyes felt dry and sore, and she was looking forward to a soak in a deep, warm bath. Matt, by contrast, appeared to glow with energy. He had taken to wearing cashmere polo necks to work, a change of style that made him look both hipper and younger.

'Can we talk? I've got something to tell you,' she asked, between mouthfuls.

'Why do I get the distinct impression I'm not going to want to hear this?'

'Well, that part is up to you.' Her eyes ached and her resistance was low but she had to tell him.

'Go on then, what is it?'

'I've had an offer for Om Interiors.'

'Great. Thanks for telling me you put it on the market.'

'Could you at least try to sound positive?' Verity put her cutlery down, pushed her hair back off her face, and massaged her temples as another hot flush consumed her.

'What d'you expect me to say – well done, darling, I'm thrilled for you?'

'Well, that would be nice.'

'Will you accept the offer?'

'It's not good enough.'

Matt nodded his head as if he had already anticipated her reply. 'Have you told your staff? How are they?'

'Okay for the most part. I'm taking us out for Christmas supper at that Italian in Hammersmith, my treat. I'm being honest with them.'

'That's generous of you. So, you went ahead, put it up for sale and told your staff first, before you told me – your husband – anything?'

'I did – because I've dreaded telling you and I decided there was no point in mentioning anything unless I actually got an offer. I now have an offer, so I'm telling you.'

'Big of you, V. Big of you.'

'Don't be like this, Matt, please.' She examined her husband, feeling little sympathy but managing to conjure some from somewhere. His eyes were lowered and he twisted his signet ring absent-mindedly. 'You're so tense these days,' she observed sadly, 'and yet you refuse to tell me what's wrong. I've thought about it, and I don't believe all that guff about you doubting that I'm good enough or worrying I haven't thought things through. You know me far too well not to know I'll be examining every detail and I'll work bloody hard. Perhaps if you explained exactly what it is you're so bothered about, we could work something out – together? Whatever it is, it can't be that bad.'

'I've told you – redundancies at work, recession biting – this is not a great time for me. And please, don't get over-emotional about my comments. I was just being realistic.'

'I'm not getting emotional! You have an opinion and you're entitled to it, even though I could have done without hearing it. But you have to understand, it's just your *opinion*! Neither of us has a crystal ball. Neither of us can read into the future. And I'm going to give the painting my best effort which is all I can do. I'll work hard, you know I will.'

'It's not all about *you*, I keep telling you. We're in the middle of the biggest financial crisis this country has ever known.'

'Yes, and you told me your company was safe.'

'For now.'

'Well then, there's never going to be a perfect time, is there?'

Matt levelled his gaze at her.

'We can work it all out together, Matt.'

'Maybe with more time, I'll get used to the idea.'

'Well, if this sale goes ahead, it will still take a while to process. I simply wanted to keep you in the loop.'

'And I can't stop you, or persuade you out of it,' he stated, turning the corners of his mouth down and nodding.

'So, is that some kind of agreement from you, then?'

'Sounds like it's already out of my hands.'

'I want more than that. I want your support.' She spread her fingers, pressing them down on the cool wooden surface of the table. 'I'm doing this for us, for our future – a house in the country! You'll be able to come home every evening to a house with more space, not a little box in a row. There'll be no mortgage, cash in the

181

bank. You can have a big study, not a little hovel. We can choose a peaceful location, with a golf course nearby if that's what you really want. We can make new friends. The girls can come and bring their friends and boyfriends for weekends in the country. It will be a new chapter for us, Matt,' she sighed, exasperated. Why *was* he being so stubborn? His reaction had changed from enthusiastic to angry to borderline apathy, all in the short space of a couple of months. He avoided making eye contact with her now, stared down at the table, and sucked in his cheeks in the usual irritating manner.

When he did eventually look up at her, his eyebrows were raised and defiance glittered in the startlingly blue eyes. 'This is boring. We've been over it a thousand times,' he shrugged.

'Well I'm sorry if I'm boring you! I thought I was building us a better, more exciting future,' she shouted, stalking out of the kitchen, stomping up the stairs, and retreating to her bedroom where she slammed the door, sat heavily down on her bed, and then fell back across the duvet, spread-eagled. She stared blindly at the ceiling. She needed energy. Despite her husband's negativity and despite her own mounting insecurities, somehow, she knew she had to find the courage and willpower to stick to what she wanted to do. If she did not, her future would look bleak – another fifteen years in a job she hated, all the while living in a place she hated, doing nothing but getting older every day. She had to try. She owed it to herself to try, no matter how exhausted she was. She was nearly fifty years old. It was now or never.

Verity approached the Georgian townhouse, and checked the number beside the door before locating the right apartment, and pressing a bell. The house stood in the middle of a row, and faced a tiny, black-railed park full of tall, leafless plane trees whose camouflage-patterned bark caught the pale afternoon light. The row made up one side of a square of similar terraces, tucked away in an area just south of the Euston Road. The square had an abandoned air about it, unusual in central London. Pavements were empty of pedestrians, and there was little through traffic. A plump grey sky hung overhead, a thin, mean wind whipped around her legs, and the tip of her nose stung with cold.

She pressed the doorbell again, wondering if she had the right house. As she waited for an answer, a nagging concern about how

Matt might react next, recurred. Matt could be bullish; he was the type who always came out of a disagreement fighting. He would be planning to negotiate with her before he agreed to go ahead with putting their house on the market, which should surely be their next move since the estate agent had given her such a promising valuation. Hopefully it would only be a small concession that Matt would ask her to make, but there would be something, some compromise on location or lifestyle – she knew it in the way that only a wife in a long marriage could know such a subtle thing about her husband. There was also still an air about him that she could not define. He walked differently. She knew it sounded stupid, but he did. He had more energy, a bit of a buzz about him. She knew him far too well, that was the problem.

'Ah, it is the right house!'

'Sorry, that buzzer is intermittent. Have you been waiting long?'

'No, don't worry.'

Edward's rented studio-apartment on the first floor was miniscule. A wide bed with a black-checked cover filled most of the space beyond a tiny kitchen area. Pillows and cushions on the bed were stacked, dented, against a wall, and his laptop and various books and papers littered the bedcover.

'You could do with a desk in here,' Verity remarked.

'I could.' He was barefoot and his hair stood on end as if he had just run his fingers through it. 'Sorry, I lost track of the time. Are you okay?'

'Yes, a little stressed, that's all.'

'We should go out. It's ridiculously cramped in here.'

'But it's warm – and it's freezing outside.'

'Okay, so long as you don't mind the mess. Coffee?' he offered.

'Thanks. So, this is your latest little home-that's-not-really-a-home.' She peered out of a tall Georgian window at two rows of neat, empty gardens. 'Were you working?'

'Yes, I'll tidy up.'

'It doesn't matter to me, you can leave it all there.' She slipped out of her coat, and folded it over the back of one of a pair of armchairs that were squashed beside the window. Edward's battered suitcase stood in the corner behind the chair, like an old friend. His trainers sat on a shelf, some headphones on a higher one. 'I wonder why they give you so many shelves in such an impermanent space?'

'Haven't a clue. It's a bit like living in a matchbox, but the location is great. I wanted somewhere affordable but close to the park so I can run, and here it's blissfully quiet and only one change on the tube to Jay's. It's been a good idea to give us all some space despite their continued insistence that I can stay at their home.'

Verity ran her fingers back through her hair, sat down in the armchair and crossed her long legs carefully in the confined space, leaving the opposite seat free for Edward. She stared through the window at a grey bank of cloud, noting variations in the cloud formations, and calculating how many shades of paint she might need to replicate them. He put a coffee down on the tiny table in front of her knees.

'I'm out of milk,' he apologised.

'Black is fine. How's Jay?'

'Losing his hair and feeling crap.' He stuck his hands in his jean pockets and did not sit down.

'How awful. Don't they miss you not staying with them?'

'I'm still there most days.'

'Is there anything I can do?'

'Not really, but thanks. It's great you've come to visit. You're working today, I presume? How long have you got?'

'I'm truanting and I'm the boss, so I can take as long as I want.'

'We could go out for something to eat if you like. I missed lunch and I'm starving.'

'Me too. Haven't eaten since breakfast time.'

Verity looked at the rumpled bed cover, and at the bed itself, looming large in the small room. What would Matt think of her being here? What would anyone think, come to that? Anyone would assume that she and Edward had met for sex. Or for the hope of it, at least. She took a sip of coffee, and it scalded her mouth.

'So, tell me how it's going,' he asked, his kind dark eyes meeting hers as he finally pulled back the chair, and sat down.

By the time Verity arrived home, Matt and Tills had already fetched an Indian takeaway.

'Yours is in the oven,' Matt informed her.

Tills said, 'Dad tells me you're selling your business, Mum.'

Verity glanced at Matt who paused and then resumed his chewing, but did not look up at her.

184

'Oh, he did? Well, I've had an offer on it, yes.'

'That's really good. You've wanted to do that for ages.'

'Yes, I have.'

'It's great, Mum. You can finally paint now.'

'Yes, I can, and I'm glad you think it's great, Tills. Nothing is certain yet, and there are quite a few things to sort out but it's positive news.'

'That's so cool.'

Matt let out a loud sigh, scraped his chair back and stood up. With lowered eyes, he strode out of the kitchen. Moments later, the front door squeaked and slammed as he left the house.

'What's wrong with him?' Tills asked, astonished.

'He doesn't want me to sell Om Interiors.'

'Oh, great. Well, how was I to know that? He didn't tell me. The atmosphere around here sucks at the moment.'

'Don't say that, Tills!'

'Well, it does. Everything's changed around here!' She stuffed the last forkful of food into her mouth, and shoved her chair back noisily too, before also stomping out of the kitchen. Verity tipped her takeaway into the bin, still full from the late lunch with Edward.

That night, she lay awake in her bed, waiting for the sound of the key in the door that would signal Matt was home. Tills had invited a friend to stay the night, and Verity could hear them laughing and watching a late night film in the next bedroom. Eventually, over-tired but still unable to sleep, she got up and made herself a hot chocolate. She sat at the kitchen counter with her mug, took out her laptop, and began to search online.

Edward had made a couple of good suggestions about how she might move forward. As she sipped the delectable hot drink, she found a forum of *plein air* artists from the South of England. The forum appeared to be thriving with lots of current threads and comments. She registered to join, soon losing track of time as she read through some of the comments the artists had left, and scrolled through paintings they had uploaded. She was touched by how supportive the group were towards each other's work, and toyed with the idea of uploading a picture of her own straight away, but did not feel confident enough. On another website, she found listings of upcoming workshops in locations like France, Germany, and even one in Alaska, and made a mental note that a workshop

185

might be a good investment to hone her skills and get her back into the swing of regular painting. On yet further investigation, she found the website of a small art school in South Oxfordshire which looked promising. She might be able to take a class there, even teach one to supplement her income, given time. She researched some of the recommended painting locations in the south of England, cautiously gathering knowledge for her future.

Eventually, she started to flag. Matt was still not home. His late nights were becoming a regular feature of their life. Change could not come fast enough.

On the day before Christmas Eve, Verity stood in Harrods with Matt, trying to choose a Christmas present for his mother, Marjorie. The dry heat of the department store made her eyes smart, and she peeled off her coat as another hot flush sent sweat dripping from her armpits and between her breasts. She ran her fingers back through her hair, and fanned herself, uncomfortable and exasperated. She needed to organise a staff list, a fixtures and fittings list, details of her lease, and a stock valuation – all that, and her shop was very busy too. She had at least managed to recruit Tills to help out, but she was still completely overloaded with last minute requests from her clients. In response to the first offer on the business, she had requested a higher one; her tension was increasing hour by hour as she waited to see what the response would be, and the last thing she needed was to be helping Matt choose his mother's present.

'Have you sent a card to Auntie Pat?' Matt asked her distractedly.

'I haven't sent any cards.'

'Christ, why not?'

'I've been a bit bloody busy, Matt. You send cards if you want to.'

'We've missed the last posting date.'

'You can still send them.'

'It's not my job.' He pointed at a bowl. 'This is the one. What do you think?'

'Cards are not my job either. And you're pandering to your mother's snobbery for brand names, Matt. We can't afford to get them that one. Let's just go to John Lewis and buy them an ordinary glass bowl.'

'My mother specifically asked for this one.'

186

'I'm sure she did, but tough. Look at the price. It's ridiculous!'

'You're very stingy, you know that? It's a nice bowl, isn't it? I mean, aren't you supposed to know about things like this?'

'Yes, it's a nice bowl, Matt. But your mother lives in a kind of financial la-la land. Actually, now I think of it, I have a similar one in my shop we can give her for cost. I object to us wasting our money in this hideous place.'

'It's the one mother wants.'

'Does she always have to get what she wants?'

'Well, I'll pay for this then.'

'Don't, Matt! Don't pander to her! It's ridiculous!' Her phone rang, and Verity rustled through the depths of her bag to find it. 'Yes?'

The agent from Scorer Hardy stated that the buyer would meet her half way between the asking price and the initial offer. 'No, I'm not falling for that. It's my price or no price,' she barked, and finished the call.

'Does the word 'compromise' never figure in your vocabulary?' Matt muttered, picking up the glass bowl.

'I'm not bloody compromising.'

'No, I think we're all getting that message, loud and clear.'

'Most husbands would be supporting their wives at this juncture.'

'Not if their wives were bringing the house of cards tumbling down, they wouldn't.'

'And what does that mean, exactly, Matt?'

'Figure it out.' He turned away from her and put on a charming smile for the sales assistant as he held out his credit card.

Tills eventually finished decorating the tree, and hung tinsel on the mirror over the fireplace and along the top of some paintings on the wall. There was tinsel everywhere, it seemed. She had bought it herself to 'brighten things up'. She had also crammed the mantelpiece and window ledge with Christmas cards, mostly from her own friends, and tied some baubles to Charlie's basket. Verity smiled at that last gesture.

Livia arrived from Manchester, her dark wavy hair, so like Verity's, grown a little longer, her olive skin glowing with youth, and her grey eyes sparkling with vitality. Verity hugged and admired her, so happy to see her.

'Where's Dad?' Livia asked, coming down the stairs, after changing to go out.

'He won't be back till later. Something to do with work.'

'On Christmas Eve?'

'I know.'

Tills appeared, face all made up and hair back-combed to look 'effortlessly' dishevelled.

'I might not see him until the morning then,' Livia said

'So, where are you two off to?'

'To meet Molly and Becky, and some of the others. Just for a drink — we won't be late.'

'Oh, okay.'

'Do you need a hand with anything before we go?'

'No, no. I've just got a few things to wrap.'

'I thought Dad would be here. I'd never have left you on your own on Christmas Eve otherwise,' Livia commiserated.

'He'll be back soon — don't you worry. And you know me, I quite like a bit of peace.'

'Are you sure? I can't wait to sit down and chat with you, but you know what it's like at this time of year, everything's such a rush!'

After her daughters had left, Verity poured herself a glass of wine, and ran her fingers back through her hair, not sure whether she was happy or sad to be left alone on Christmas Eve. The house had swollen claustrophobically as every available space was stuffed with Christmas paraphernalia. Cupboards were crammed with extra food, the fridge was packed to bursting, and even the cupboard under the stairs was rammed with bottles of soft drinks, half-used rolls of wrapping paper, and spare dog food. Verity sighed, and sat down to draw up a list of what she needed to do for Christmas lunch the next day, knowing that if she did not, the sprouts or red cabbage would still be in the fridge drawer on Boxing Day, forgotten. She wondered where Matt really was; it was not like him to be out on Christmas Eve. She finished writing her list, took her wine glass and wandered into his tiny office, and looked around. His grand old desk filled about a third of the room space. Three silver-framed photographs of old sailing boats hung on one wall, and a desk lamp, leather blotter and the ubiquitous Newton's cradle were the only items on his desk. She pulled open a drawer and found pens, paper clips, a stapler, and a pair of headphones. She

188

examined other drawers that held papers and files. There was nothing to tell her anything she did not already know about her husband. Why was she even doing this? She pulled herself together, and was leaving the study just as the front door squeaked open, catching her, like a rabbit in the headlights, in the full focus of Matt's piercing gaze.

'Looking for something?' he asked lightly, smiling.

'Just the Sellotape. I'm glad you're back. Would you help me wrap a few things while the girls are out?'

'Sure. Christ, what's with all the tinsel?'

'You'll have to ask Tills about that,' Verity laughed.

Christmas Day dawned, and Verity awoke, exhausted. With Livia home, she and Matt had to share a bed, and for much of the night, he had lain sprawled diagonally, snoring like a steam engine, and she had tried – and failed – to sleep curled up in a ball, clutching the edge of the mattress, head buried under the duvet to block out the sound of him. She lay still for a moment, blinking at the ceiling. Slowly, her mind moved to consider her day, and all the cooking she had to do, and she groaned inwardly. She loved Christmas in so many ways but right then she wanted nothing more than to roll over and go back to sleep.

When the girls had come home the night before, the family had all sat in the sitting room together for a while, Matt with a whisky, and Verity and the girls with a hot chocolate. For a moment, it had felt like the old days, but then Verity had been struck by the changes in her daughters. She had studied Livia, dark-haired and elegant, all grown up in so many ways, and Tills, the tousled student, and reflected that she used to know every detail of their lives – what they had eaten on any given day, which items of their clothing needed washing, when they had last had a tummy ache or where they had gone with their friends – so many minute details, and she had known them all. But now there were huge gaps in her knowledge. She barely knew who her daughters spent time with, certainly did not know what they did in their free time, or what new clothes they had bought. To the background music of carols playing, both young women had sat and exchanged news with their attentive parents, sketching in a few details of their daily routines, doling out little nuggets of information about their lives that she and Matt had lapped up. She had been struck by just how irrelevant she and Matt had become – their opinions and input, once precious, were no longer required, at least for most of the time – and it had made her feel detached and sad. Everything was changing so quickly. When the hot drinks were finished, Livia and Tills had gone upstairs, and Matt had sat quietly with Verity for a moment.

'We did a good job with them, didn't we?'

'Yes, though Tills...'

'I know – there's a bit further to go with her.'

Verity swung her legs out of the warmth of the bed, and sat a moment on the edge of the mattress; she was so exhausted. Christmas Day. She took a deep breath.

'Happy Christmas,' Matt muttered from beneath the duvet.

'Happy Christmas,' she mumbled. She stood up, found her dressing gown and headed for the shower. After a coffee by herself downstairs, she dressed the turkey with a lattice of bacon before shoving it in the oven, and then called up to Matt and the girls. They all sat sleepily around a fire which Matt lit, and opened their stockings. For a moment, it was again as if the girls had never left home, and Verity was assaulted by thoughts of all the years they had spent together. On this day each year, for so many years, the four of them had sat like this, extracting small, wrapped gifts, and laughing at the predictability of an orange in the toe of each stocking. This year, Charlie shuffled through discarded wrapping paper that littered the floor, sniffing it where at one time he would have nosed it in the air and chased it around, barking. It was both a moment ripe with nostalgia and a scene whose existence was threatened.

As soon as stockings were emptied, Livia excused herself to call Josh, and Tills sat on the sofa flicking through a new magazine and eating a bar of chocolate, looking pale, her spots particularly red and sore that morning, boredom already evident in her loud yawns. One day, they would not come home for Christmas, Verity realised. They would initiate their own traditions in their own homes. She folded up the empty stockings – she had made them when the girls were little, intending that they become a kind of family heirloom, and sure enough, everyone had exclaimed at their reappearance the evening before. With them tidied away, and in a short lull before the next phase of the day, she sat for a moment, cradling a second cup of coffee, trying to work out whether she had done a good enough job as a mother.

After a family breakfast, she left Fulham to drive to Teddington to collect her mother. The roads were almost empty, and she turned on some music and relished the simple joy of being out of the confines of the house. She felt as if Matt was being overly attentive – he had made her a stocking, thoughtfully filled with her favourite chocolates, some cashmere bed socks, and the latest detective novel by an author he knew she liked. He watched her much more than he normally did, and kept offering to help. It wasn't normal. His actions were disarming though, and had re-kindled a hope in Verity that everything might be all right between them, after all. She turned up her car heater a touch and took a mint from a tin, popping it into her mouth. With no traffic, the journey would take her about an hour, half of it blissfully alone.

As soon as she got back to Rannoch Road with her mother, she set to work in the kitchen, putting the potatoes in to roast, and enrolling the help of Fiona, Livia and Tills in the final preparations. She set her mother the task of laying the table while she and the girls peeled and chopped vegetables, and Matt sorted out wine to go with their meal. Matt's parents arrived from Highgate, shortly after noon.

'We had to park down the street!' Marjorie announced. She dangled her coat from her hand until Verity offered to take it from her. 'Oh, you've done such a good job with this little place, I always forget.'

'Come in, come in, mother. Take a seat and I'll get you a drink. Father, hello. Let me take those from you.' Matt took a couple of carrier bags from his father and placed them under the tree. The two men shook hands.

'Not like that dear, take them out of the bags,' Marjorie instructed Matt.

'Hello, Granny! Hello, Grandpa!' Tills hugged each in turn. 'I'll do it, Granny, don't worry. Are you better now, Grandpa?'

'Never felt fitter. My, you've grown up.'

'Right, what would everyone like to drink?' Matt rubbed his hands together.

Verity passed around some squares of smoked salmon on toast, and perched on a chair arm to talk with her mother-in-law.

191

'Lovely dress, Verity, it suits you. Is it cashmere?'

'Unfortunately not.'

'You see, you're tall, you can get away with shapeless clothing. Oh, look, here comes the little dog. He's still alive? What is his name again? Oh, he's walked straight past me. Well, I never.' Marjorie made the same remarks, year after year, and Verity stifled a yawn. From Marjorie's point of view, the house was small (she always forgot how small), Verity's dress was never quite right, and the dog was utterly confounding. After a polite interval, she escaped back to the kitchen, and Fiona followed.

'I've come to help you.'

'You've come to escape.' Verity winked.

'Some people never change.' Fiona rolled her eyes. 'Now give me something to do.'

A short time later, lunch was ready.

'I just need to pop to the little girl's room,' Marjorie announced, and pointed up the stairs. 'Is it still up there?'

'Yes, Granny. Let me show you,' Livia offered.

They all sat down around the table, and waited for Marjorie to reappear.

'Don't wait for me! Start serving, start serving! So quaint to eat in the kitchen, but you keep it very tidy, Verity.'

'There is nowhere else to eat, Granny,' Tills remarked.

'Where am I now?'

'Sit here, Mother. Allow me.'

Matt carved the turkey, crackers were pulled, and paper hats perched on heads. Verity handed around dishes, and spooned stuffing and red cabbage and sprouts with chestnuts and devils-on-horseback onto numerous plates, and felt a wave of relief when everyone was served, and they all finally raised their glasses in a toast.

'So, tell me, how's it hanging?' Jim asked his son.

'Business is good.' Matt pressed his lips together, and nodded seriously at his father.

'What are you working on?'

'You're not allowed to talk shop over Christmas lunch, Jim.'

'So, what are we supposed to discuss, Marjorie – shopping? Let's talk about shopping everyone.'

Marjorie blushed and looked down at her plate.

'Livia, how's life in Manchester?' Fiona came to the rescue, and the conversation softened for a few moments until Jim intervened again, and began to drill Livia about her prospects of a promotion. He then turned his attention to Tills and impressed upon her the need to study hard, from the outset, and to *succeed* at all costs. Urgency spilled out of his wide body, and Verity vaguely wondered if her father-in-law was not inviting another heart attack. She put down her knife and fork and rubbed her temples before taking a sip of the expensive wine Jim had brought with him, pointedly putting it on the table, and relegating Matt's choice to a kitchen counter.

Matt shrank in his father's presence. She noted the usual subtle signs; his shoulders stooped, and his eyes remained cast down. He drank frequently, so that his wine glass emptied quickly. She had seen it all before, many times. Whenever Jim was around, it was as if the strength leaked out of Matt. Jim was like a steam-roller, and none of them seemed powerful enough to stop him flattening every conversation with his opinions. Even though it was Christmas, he loudly aired his views on the stock market and various economic forecasts. The group's attention fractured, and Fiona, Marjorie, Livia and Tills broke away from the iron presence, and began their own conversation at one end of the table, leaving Matt to listen to his father, and Verity to sit and observe. Jim droned on about bonds and funds and investment companies that meant nothing to Verity, and as the conversation moved back to Matt's business, she saw his forehead knot.

'I've had to let people go, and re-structure,' he confessed.

Jim frowned disapprovingly at his son. Verity wanted to lean over and touch her husband's arm, and tell him that it did not matter what his father thought. She wanted to remind Matt not to play his father's game, that he would never win. Instead, she curled her fist against her chin, leant her elbow on the table and listened, knowing there was actually nothing she could do. On this subject, her husband would never heed her, and over the years she had learned this particular exchange was not her battle to fight.

'I have some great strategies in mind, good people who will listen. Verity, my father's plate is empty.' Matt rallied. Verity looked coolly at Matt, not wishing to play the game, but nonetheless handing over a plate of vegetables so that Jim could take seconds. She should not do it – she should not put herself in a service role to Matt and his father; Matt could easily have passed his father more food himself, but she kept the peace in Jim's presence, as they all did, and played her part. The difference between her and Matt, however, was that she knew she knew that the rituals were all a game, knew they would never be good enough for Jim – but Matt was still caught up in the fiction; he still had hope.

'You mustn't eat more roast potatoes! Think of your heart,' Marjorie fretted.

'It's bloody Christmas day. I'll eat what I want. And remember you're driving, Marjorie. I don't get to share a glass of good wine with my son very often.'

'You probably don't either, do you Marjorie?' Fiona suggested, eyes looking down at her plate.

'Oh, heavens, I don't matter.'

'Do you not?' Fiona persisted.

'No, no. They need their men's talk. It's important.'

Verity glanced at her mother, and Fiona raised her eyebrows but said no more.

Matt leant towards his father, and continued to explain his business strategy. 'I'm working on a notion of "implying the sacred" for a couple of our major accounts. It's what people today hunger for. If you can ally a product with something spiritual and essential, you get people's attention.'

Verity observed her husband's pitch to his father. It was an interesting idea, and one she had not heard of before, but she noted the light in Jim's eyes go dim. The concept was beyond him. 'Sounds like a load of hippy bollocks to me.'

Matt rubbed his chin, his face paled, and Verity was saddened to see her husband's vulnerability, and finally intervened in an attempt to rescue him. 'Has everyone finished?' she asked brightly. 'Girls, help me clear the plates.'

Matt sat on in silence and stared blindly at the table for a moment. He looked up and caught Verity's eye, his expression troubled by his father's sharp words yet again, as it had been so many times, over the years. For a flicker of a moment, Verity hated Jim Westwood. As she collected plates, she saw her husband's boyish gesture, echoed down over the years, in the way he raked his fingers through his pale hair and attempted to recover.

'Would you light the flame on the pudding in a moment, Matt?' she asked.

'Sure, sure.'

'Oh, do you remember when we always had a sixpence wrapped in paper, hidden in the pudding?' Marjorie recalled.

'My mother used to make a clootie dumpling. It's a Scottish tradition; you probably won't have heard of,' Fiona remarked.

'Well, don't the Scottish have curious names for things! You've done a beautiful job with this one, Verity.'

'It's Marks and Spencer's.'

'Oh, you are so funny. Whoever would have thought of that?'

'She's a working woman. It's born of necessity,' Fiona stated defensively.

'Poor thing. I don't know how she does it.' Marjorie shook her head.

As everyone ate and chattered, Verity looked around the lunch table at her family. Her family. This was it – this odd collection of people with their physical similarities and their peculiar tensions, their shared experiences and their long-standing small battles, all wearing colourful paper hats apart from Jim who had pointedly left his folded up on the table, as he always did – his refusal to wear the hat still unwittingly reinforcing a family tradition that was uniquely theirs. Verity had diligently built up their Christmas routines over time, repeating the same things year on year to give her children the love and security of repeated seasonal festivities. Where would they all be in one year, three years, five years? Would they all be sitting in some as-yet-unknown cottage kitchen or would Matt still be clinging on to this place? Her mother would be older, her daughters too. And Verity? What would Verity be doing? How would it all work out? If she got her way, this would be the last time they all sat around this particular table to eat a Christmas lunch. To her surprise, and despite all her earlier, somewhat maudlin nostalgia, she felt suddenly invigorated that this might genuinely be the last such meal in this house, and her mood soared at the prospect of beginning anew.

'A penny for them,' her mother remarked.

'Sorry, miles away.'

Verity cleared plates, and suggested Jim and Marjorie retire to the comfy sofa for tea or coffee. There was a scraping of chairs as her in-laws promptly did as they were told.

'You've done yourself proud, and you can relax and let your hair down now,' Fiona murmured quietly to her daughter.

'Almost, but not quite yet.' Verity subtly raised an eyebrow in the direction of Matt's parents, and shared a small smile with her mother. Fiona asked Verity if she was tired, and offered to leave for home whenever it suited.

'I'm fine, Mum. We still have the presents to do and you must enjoy your time with the girls now.'

'I'll make us all some tea and coffee then,' she offered. 'You go and sit down.'

'I'll get the girls back to help you.'

Tills came into the kitchen and muttered, 'Dad's drunk too much.'

'He's just trying to impress Grandpa, Tills. You know how competitive they get,' Livia followed. 'Go and sit with them, Mum. Get Dad to chill out a bit.'

Fiona brought in a tea tray and set it on the low table in the centre of the room. She poured tea and coffee and handed round cups. The girls sat on the floor and Verity perched on the arm of a chair.

'Well, this is cosy. I do want to watch the queen,' Marjorie said brightly. 'Where's the telly?'

'You've missed her, Marjorie. You'll have to watch the highlights later,' Jim intervened, gruffly.

'But I always watch the queen.'

'No, you always miss her and watch the highlights later, have done for years.'

'Where is the telly?'

'It's over there on the wall, Granny.' Tills pointed.

'How do you watch a telly that's up on the wall, Matthew?' Marjorie asked, frowning.

'Mummy and Daddy don't have much time for telly,' Tills said.

'Well, how very odd.' Marjorie shook her head again.

'You say the same things to them every bloody year, Marjorie. For Christ's sake, you're like a stuck record.'

'Right, let's open some presents.' Matt jumped up, rubbing his hands together. 'Tills darling, do the honours. Here we are. Here's one for you, Mother, and one for Fiona.'

196

Presents were exchanged and the atmosphere lightened a little as everyone became absorbed in the process of unwrapping paper and giving thanks. Verity gave Matt a new polo neck jumper – the style he had recently begun to wear. It was knitted from chunky wool and would be great for weekends in the country, she thought. He thanked her, but something in his tone signalled that the jumper was not quite right. Matt had bought Verity a new I-pad which Tills and Livia seemed thrilled about but Verity was at a loss to appreciate, having little idea what it did that might be different from her laptop.

'Thank you,' she said, as warmly as she could. 'I'm sure I'll learn to love it.'

'You can take better photographs with it,' Matt suggested.

'Ah, wonderful, very useful.'

Verity looked at her husband, her head tipped slightly on one side. Was he now encouraging her art? She felt thrown again, and unsure.

'I want to raise a toast to Mummy, even though we don't have any drinks left,' Livia announced. 'Mummy has just yesterday accepted an offer on her business. Next year she'll begin a new career as an artist. I'm so proud of her for following her dreams.'

Verity felt the warmth in her cheeks. 'Thank you, Livia darling,'

Her mother congratulated her. 'Well done, Verity. To your new venture!'

Matt looked at Verity in disbelief, and Verity was suddenly horrified, realising that with Matt having been out all day and most of the evening, and with everything else she had to think of for Christmas, she had this time, genuinely forgotten to tell her husband that she had accepted an offer on Om Interiors, of almost the full asking price. Marjorie's mouth fell open with confusion, and she silently turned to Jim as if expecting him to tell her what to say. Jim frowned. 'Why would you give up your little business? Have I missed something?' He barked, gruffly.

Fiona intervened swiftly. 'Verity is finally putting herself first, and following her long-held ambition to paint. She has talent, like her father.' The pride and firmness in her mother's voice centred Verity a little.

'Very nice too, I'm sure,' Jim responded flatly.

Matt remained silent but scraped back his chair to get up and pour his father another drink. Verity watched father and son exchange glances, finally allied in their opinion by her decision, or so it seemed. She felt guilty that Matt had had to learn the news this way.

'At least you've only got this small place to keep going. Not too many overheads,' Jim commiserated with his son. She felt a familiar surge of anger at the way Jim dismissed their house as somehow not being much, and Verity's contribution as irrelevant, and she glanced over at Matt who, despite his own feelings, shook his head subtly at her, the direct look in his eyes warning her not to react. Charlie came and sat by Verity's feet, and she took a deep breath and stroked his silky ears.

That evening, after Marjorie and Jim had left, and Verity had driven her mother home, and with Tills and Livia upstairs watching a movie together, Verity and Matt found themselves alone and staring into the fire, wiped out after the strain of the day, and in Matt's case, after an excess of whisky.

'When were you going to tell me?'

'I didn't hear until late on Christmas Eve afternoon, Matt. I'm sorry. I wasn't keeping anything from you, I just forgot. Livia was with me when I got the call. She didn't, doesn't, know how you feel about it.'

'My father wasn't happy today.'

'Your father is never happy, or impressed, by anything we ever do. You must surely know that by now.'

During the silence that ensued, she got up off the sofa, went upstairs and changed into her running clothes. The house was pressing in on her. The air indoors hung laden with heat and cooking smells, and Matt's brooding presence loomed large. She needed to get some space and fresh air.

'Where are you going?'

'For a run. Want to come?'

'Are you mad, woman? It's ten o'clock at night and it's Christmas Day. Of course, I don't want to go bloody running.'

'Suit yourself.'

As soon as she had tugged the door shut behind her, Verity's spirits lifted. She ran past rows of houses where lights burned and sparkling Christmas trees stood, proudly displayed. Her lungs pumped air in and out efficiently now that she was fitter, and the sensation made her feel strong – but the main reason she ran was so that, after the fog of a troubling day when her emotions had been pulled in all directions, she was able to remind herself who she really was.

20

On the day after Boxing Day, first thing in the morning before Verity had properly woken up, Livia said farewell to her parents, and left to catch the train back to Manchester to be reunited with Josh. As the family stood on the tiled garden path exchanging hugs, the taxi engine throbbed impatiently, a plane groaned overhead, and a light drizzle fell, dusting their shoulders with tiny, sparkling raindrops.

Back in her kitchen, nursing a mug of coffee, and with a fuggy head and un-brushed hair, Verity deemed her Christmas holiday over. Livia's visit had been far too short. She felt a lump in her throat – happy and proud that Livia was making a new life for herself, but missing her already.

Life at Rannoch Road quickly resumed its tense normality. Matt dressed and left for work, claiming irritably that he needed to 'get on top of things', Tills went back to bed, and Verity decided the sensible thing would be to go to Om Interiors and sort out the chaos that the first day of the sales would no doubt have left in its wake.

By mid-afternoon, restless and a little depressed, she arranged to meet Edward for a walk in Hyde Park, with a view to cheering them both up. It was the first time she had initiated contact with him, and she felt a little ambivalent about it, but told herself Edward was just a friend and she could not help it if he happened to be male.

Edward walked with his hands stuffed into the pockets of his leather jacket and a scarf wrapped around his chin and neck. She walked beside him, her winter coat tightly belted to keep out the cold.

'Are you pleased to be selling your business?'

'I can't tell you how pleased.'

'I think we should celebrate. We should find a little bar and drink some champagne and raise a toast to the next phase of your life.'

'Would you do that with me?' She was surprised, delighted.

'Of course, why not?'

'That's so nice of you.'

'This is a milestone for you, the shedding of a skin.'

A brisk wind blew across the Serpentine, rippling its grey surface. A swathe of bleak cloud hung above them and the naked branches of fastigiate trees saluted as they walked by. The light soon began to fade, and by the time they reached the main road again, vehicles had turned on their headlights.

Edward hailed a taxi. 'Do you have to go back to work?' he asked.

'Not really. The shop will be closing and design work is dead quiet at this time of year.'

'Great!'

A taxi pulled up, and Edward gave the driver instructions.

'Where are we going?' she asked.

'Surprise.' He grinned.

Verity had never imagined Edward as a champagne drinker but sitting opposite him and noting his sparkling eyes and raised glass, she realised how little she knew about him.

'Cheers! To your new life as an artist.'

'Cheers, and thank you.'

'You deserve to do well.'

'I hope so.'

'Of course you will! You're surely not having doubts?'

'It does feel like a leap in the dark.'

'Everything in its own time, you'll see,' Edward encouraged. 'Are you hungry?'

'Starving.'

'Great, this is just the place for you then. I discovered it the other evening. Classic English pub food.' His eyes shone; they were the same colour as the mahogany bar furniture.

'Sometimes you sound very American,' she teased.

'That's because I am very American.' He asked the barman for a couple of menus, and they huddled over their table and chatted until a waiter brought their supper – a steak and kidney pie for him and a massive plate of fish and chips for her. Later, when they had finished eating and drunk the whole bottle of champagne, they wandered out onto the street. The pavement shone up at Verity, a dazzling collage of black and silver with colours heightened by rain. Edward grabbed her hand and hailed another taxi. Verity felt much better for the food and light-headed from the champagne. She leant against Edward's warm body in the back of the cab.

Back at Cartwright Gardens, they hurried up the stairs to Edward's flat where he swept all his work off the bed and they fell onto it laughing at a joke he made, still with their coats on.

'There's nowhere proper to sit in this tiny place!'

He rolled onto his side, and looked at her. He put his hand on her coat, right where her belly was.

'Edward, I simply can't lie on a bed with you,' she muttered, sitting up, and removing herself to the one of the small armchairs.

'No?'

'No. I don't even know why I came back here. I need to get home. They'll be wondering where I am.'

'Sure. Of course. Coffee before you go?'

'It might sober me up a bit, yes.'

'Come here first.' He got up off the bed and stood in front of her, and Verity obediently rose. There were only inches between them, and he put his arms around her shoulders, and drew her to him. She was immediately cocooned in the subtle scent of vetiver and felt the soft leather of his jacket against her cheek. Her stomach flipped, and her knees weakened.

'Verity, Verity, what are we doing?' he murmured.

She softened and moved her arms around his waist. 'I don't know.'

'I'd love to kiss you,' he whispered and bent over her, and for a second, his warm, soft lips pressed fleetingly against hers. She leant away, and looked into his mahogany eyes, as her body ignited.

When Verity arrived home, the house was empty. Charlie's tail thumped against the side of his basket in a lazy welcome. She found a note on the table from Matt, saying he had gone to the pub, and another from Tills saying she was staying at a friend's house. As she was getting ready for bed, Matt returned, his cheeks flushed from the cold night air and his eyes a little red from drinking. She pulled her dressing gown around her and folded her arms.

'I was trying to call you. Jay and Caro want us to go to dinner tomorrow evening, just an early, casual thing,' he said, shrugging off his jacket and flinging it on a bedroom chair. 'I've told them we'll go. I know he'd appreciate some company. That brother of his is over on a visit. He'll be there too.'

Verity froze for a moment, and then recovered. 'That's nice. Did you ask if we can take anything?'

'I didn't ask. I'll ping you their number, and you can talk to Caro. Where were you earlier?'

'Out having a drink. Where were you?'

'The same. Long day.'

'It certainly was.'

'Matt, would you mind sleeping upstairs now Livia's gone back? I could really do with a good night's sleep.'

'Sure.' He bent over and pecked Verity on her cheek. 'You okay?'

'I'm fine.'

'Night then.'

'Good night.'

Verity sat down on the edge of her bed, her back bowed, forearms resting on her thighs. Guilt made her feel nauseous. Was this how affairs began? A friendship that toppled over some invisible boundary? She had not had any intention of kissing Edward, and yet when his lips had pressed softly against hers and his fingers had laced through her hair and cradled her head, it had felt like the most natural and heaven-sent moment she had experienced in years. And she had wanted more.

The warmth of Caro and Jay's house wrapped itself around Verity as soon as she stepped from the bitterly cold street into their welcoming hallway. A candle in a wide glass container, delicately scented and with several lit wicks, was placed on a chest beside the hall wall, and there was another on a low table in the reception room, filling the air with the sweet, calming fragrance of geranium. Verity's immediate impression was of sanctuary. Jay kissed her cheek and took her coat. Caro embraced her. Edward brushed her cheek with his lips briefly, and introduced Penny, Caro's sister, who shook her hand.

'I'm sorry we're late.' Verity handed Caro a bunch of flowers and a small gift.

'Oh, Madonna lilies, my favourite. And chocolates, how gorgeous. Thank you. What an evening you've had, you poor things,' Caro commiserated.

'My car simply wouldn't start. I'll call the AA in the morning.'

'Such a nuisance.'

'It was okay. We just had to wait a bit for a cab.'

'You didn't want to drive then, Matt?' Caro enquired.

'Are you kidding? No, I didn't. I wanted to enjoy a few drinks with my old friend here.' Matt slung his arm around Jay's shoulder and gripped his friend. 'Bald is in these days, mate. You're lucky, right on trend as always. You're looking good, you're looking good.'

Jay grinned sheepishly. 'Getting there.'

'It's just a setback, nothing more.' Caro smiled bravely.

'Who needs bloody setbacks though?' Matt released Jay, and grinned at the rest of the party. Verity touched the hair at the back of her head and looked around her at everything, anything, but Edward. She felt his presence acutely. He had combed his hair back off his face, shaved, and dressed in a pale linen shirt which draped softly over his broad shoulders.

Despite his suaveness now, the car refusing to start had prompted a highly volatile reaction in Matt, causing him to swear and yell and kick the car tyre – an outburst which had set Verity's nerves on edge. Her thoughts were still a bit scattered, and jumped like fleas inside her head. She had not wanted to come to the dinner in the first place, for obvious reasons, fearing perversely that Matt would turn into some kind of mind-reader, and know what Verity and Edward had done the evening before. After the car had failed to start, she had felt relieved, and had argued that they must cancel the dinner, but Matt had insisted they get a cab. On top of the car drama and the social awkwardness, Tills was out again that evening, and Verity's instincts were on alert. She had said as much to Matt, who had shouted again, calling her neurotic. She had stood in her kitchen nursing a mug of herb tea as they had waited for the taxi, and wondered if perhaps she *was* over-reacting about Tills. Maybe stress was affecting her judgement? It was quite feasible that Tills was behaving normally, and Verity was not. In addition to all this, the dog was not well again. Poor Charlie had staggered a couple of times, almost losing his balance, and he was withdrawn, lying in his basket, and not seeking Verity's company the way he usually did.

'We've kept you waiting. Would you like us to go straight through to the table?' Matt asked, taking charge.

'There's no hurry,' Caro replied.

'Come through – Caro's just being kind. I'm sure it would be much less bother for her if we sat now.' Jay extended his arm to indicate that they move through to the next room. Verity, keeping her eyes down to avoid Edward's gaze, noted a polished wooden floor overlaid with a vintage Moroccan kilim, and in the kitchen, a smart limestone floor with a gorgeous Persian rug in the dining area. Jay and Caro lived in comfort. She glanced up, and met Caro's sister's curious gaze.

'You can sit here,' Penny pointed to a chair. Verity had already forgotten her name, and felt embarrassed. Where Caro was slender and dressed modestly in a pale silk top and loose evening trousers, the sister wore a navy dress that clung to wide hips and plunged at the front to reveal large bronzed breasts. Verity sat obediently where she was told, put her clutch bag on the floor and tucked her chair in. Edward sat down beside her, as instructed, one hand resting casually in his lap. Caro took her seat at the far end of the table, and Jay at the end beside Verity. Matt and Penny sat opposite.

Jay poured Verity a glass of wine, and then one for Penny before passing the bottle to Edward whose forearm lightly brushed hers as he reached across her. A slice of homemade onion tart and a little garnish of salad sat on a plate in front of each person.

'Are you not having any wine?' Verity asked Jay.

'Water for me. Easier on the stomach at the moment.'

'What a shame. I'll have to drink for you, mate. Cheers!' Matt raised his glass. 'To Jay, and a full and prompt recovery!'

'To your good health,' Verity murmured, raising her glass and smiling at Jay's pale face. The side-effects of his treatment were shocking. His hair was gone and a light in his eyes was gone too. He was a different man from the one she had met on the trip to France, but she smiled positively, and Jay raised his glass of water to her.

She tried to savour the tasty starter but was rigid with tension and found it difficult to swallow, so washed the tart down with liberal amounts of wine. By contrast, Matt was the life of the party, and was making a very good job of getting Jay and Caro to laugh. Even Edward smiled. Penny seemed utterly entranced with him, her made-up face and large bosom were turned in his direction, and she sipped her drink slowly and listened to him in apparent wonder. Verity watched too, as her husband told some anecdotal tale of hijinks on a golf trip he had once taken with Jay. He smoothed his hair as he spoke, and looked younger than his years in his cashmere polo neck. He brimmed with confidence in the spotlight of everyone's attention.

Verity got up to help Caro clear the starter plates. Over in the kitchen area, Caro pulled a tray of roasted fish from the oven.

'That looks and smells wonderful. You've worked so hard,' Verity encouraged.

'I enjoy cooking.'

'What kind of fish is it?' She held the plates in turn so that Caro could serve each slice. 'Monkfish. It's Jay's favourite.'

'You know if you ever need any help with anything, you only need to call me,' Verity offered.

'Thank you, that's very sweet of you.'

'I mean it. It's not just words.'

'I sense that, and I appreciate it, really.'

Verity carried the plates to the table, placing one before each person.

'Thanks,' Edward murmured.

She glanced at the crown of his head. She had held it between her hands and kissed the parting of his thick dark and silver hair, only the evening before – a fact which seemed impossible now.

Caro put out bowls of pumpkin puree and mixed mushrooms, and a couple of ciabatta loaves on a board.

'This looks splendid, Caro,' Matt announced.

'I'm being spoilt by my wife, I must confess. These are all my favourite foods.' Jay smiled.

'Lucky you!' Matt responded, and fixed a look on Verity. The negative jibe was not lost on her, and she raised her eyebrows back, in her own defence.

'Believe me, you don't want to go through what I'm going through to get served your favourite dish, mate,' Jay remarked, having noted the unspoken exchange.

'Well, that is very true.'

Edward topped up Verity's wine glass. Jay spooned pumpkin on to her plate. Verity wanted to enjoy the meal but was terrified she might say something that would give away her long friendship with Edward or their recent meetings. It was so hard to remember what they should and should not know about each other, and the wine was not making it any easier.

'You look a little worn out too, if you don't mind me saying so,' Jay murmured. 'Busy Christmas?'

'Yes. Lots on at work too.'

'Ah, well tuck in. This will soon sort you out.'

'This dish reminds me of home,' Edward observed.

'Didn't our mother make one similar? I love it,' Jay agreed.

'She did. Just plain pumpkin mash with butter, right?'

'Yes,' Caro nodded.

'So good and simple.'

'You're so American sometimes!' Penny exclaimed.

Edward shrugged. 'Guilty as charged.'

'My brother has been reporting on the situation in Burma since we last saw him,' Jay informed Matt.

'I should imagine there's a lot of investment potential there, provided they can reassure the rest of the world of some political stability,' Matt declared, sounding uncannily like his father.

'Oh, there's potential all right, but at what cost to the people of Burma?' Edward responded cautiously.

'I expect they need the work. They need money. It all comes at a price but will be better for them in the long run.'

'If the Burmese people get the profits, and the investors and government don't simply exploit them, I agree with you. But how likely is that?'

'Not all business men are bastards, you know.'

'Hmmm, but most are focused on profit above all else. What Burma needs is some forward-thinking investors who are aware of human rights issues and will treat the indigenous population fairly, and not just as a means to an end. It's still a majorly rural, poor and uneducated population, and they're already being horribly abused in the name of progress. Added to that, digital technology is in its infancy there, and the manufacturing sector is still very small. There's lots to weigh up.'

'What's the best thing about Burma, Edward?' Caro asked. 'All I can think of is Aung San Suu Kyi and all her noble suffering.'

'The best thing is the ordinary person you meet in the street, without doubt. The majority are sweet and positive and incredibly friendly. And then there's the beauty of the landscape, the ancient temples and so on.'

Verity smiled. 'I'd love to visit there.'

'I'm sure you will one day.'

Verity made the briefest eye contact with Edward, and felt the heat rise in her cheeks. Penny narrowed her eyes fractionally, and tipped her head on one side, watching. Verity looked away, and reached for her wine glass.

'We five all went on holiday last October, Penny,' Matt leant over to her, 'and we were hit by a tremendous storm. Have you heard the story?'

Penny shook her head.

'Did I never tell you what happened?' Caro apologised to her sister.

'Those two were stuck in a farmhouse high up on a hillside, cut off from everything for three days while the rest of us were marooned down at the coast. The weather was unbelievable, and the road up to the farmhouse was blocked with fallen trees and the like, and so we couldn't reach them. They had to stay at the farmhouse with a tree fallen through the roof, no power, and not much food. A proper survival story.'

'Goodness!'

'Now my question to you, Penny, is – if you were stuck in an isolated house for three days with a handsome brute like Edward, what would you find to do?'

Verity's breath caught. Her plate of food swam out of focus.

'Oh!' Penny spread her hand over her ample chest, and laughed throatily. 'That would be telling!'

'Excuse me a moment,' Jay said suddenly.

Verity was aware of Jay's chair scraping across the rug as he left the table hurriedly. She blinked and gathered her thoughts.

'Don't worry. He doesn't like a fuss,' Caro murmured.

'Poor bugger.' Matt shook his head.

Verity noticed the muscle in Edward's jaw tense. 'All this will be over as soon as his chemo is finished.'

'Sure, sure it will.'

Verity put her knife and fork together on her plate, and downed the remainder of her glass of wine. Did Matt suspect? Did he know? A sense of shame ballooned in her head, and she felt her cheeks burn.

When Jay returned, his skin looked waxen. He dabbed the corner of his mouth with his napkin, and Verity smiled reassuringly at him, masking a feeling of dread that swelled inexplicably inside her.

Despite Caro's protests, after the main course was finished, Verity insisted on helping her again. Edward also helped clear the serving dishes while Penny rounded her eyes at Matt, put her hand on his arm, and told him a story about a recent cruise she had taken, and how she had lain in the sun in her bikini all day for ten glorious days, been invited to dine at the captain's table, and spent her nights dancing until the small hours.

'Ignore my sister. She's harmless really,' Caro whispered in the kitchen, rolling her eyes. 'Drinks when she's nervous and flirts too much.'

'Oh, I don't mind. The two of you are very different.'

'That's families for you. I've only made a plain almond and orange cake for pudding with a few raspberries. It's enough, isn't it?'

'Of course it is! It sounds lovely.'

'I've tried to stick to things Jay might manage. His mouth is sore. The chemo gives him ulcers.'

'I can't imagine what it must be like for him.'

'It's horrid, but most of his symptoms will pass when the treatment ends, and the prognosis is pretty good.'

'Is it?' Verity looked into Caro's eyes.

'Yes,' Caro smiled.

'I'm so relieved to hear that, and will be so happy for you both when this is over.'

Caro served out the desert, and the evening lumbered on with Matt and Penny in full flow, swapping stories and laughing loudly. Edward was quiet, as was Jay, and after a while, Jay turned pale, and excused himself again. 'Apologies, but I need to lie down for a while.'

'Here, let me help.' Edward got up, and offered his brother an arm.

After they had left, the room fell silent for a moment.

'May I use your loo?' Verity asked, and Caro told her where it was. In the toilet, Verity took a deep breath. Matt's flirting with Penny was getting on her nerves. As for him guessing about her and Edward, there was nothing to worry about, she reassured herself; Matt could not possibly know anything, and it had only been a kiss, really. She had fled the tiny apartment – flustered, aroused, and confused – with Edward making no move to stop her. What she needed now was a coffee. She washed her hands, smoothed her hair in the mirror and braced herself. She pulled open the cloakroom door, and bumped straight into Edward. He caught her by the elbow.

'Okay?' he whispered.

'Yes. How's Jay?'

'He'll be fine. He just has some nausea, and is feeling really tired. I tried to get out of this evening but Caro wouldn't hear of us not being all together again. I think we need to talk.'

'Yes, we do.'

Edward squeezed her arm, and then said, far too brightly, 'Come through. Let's get you a coffee.' Verity looked up, confused, and saw Penny, halted in the corridor, watching them with a little smirk on her face.

Edward helped Caro make coffee for them all while Penny stretched her arm along the back of Matt's chair, and flirted even more openly with him. To Verity's irritation, Matt did not move away from her encroaching bosom, and if anything, seemed to bask in the attention. She tried to ignore him, and chatted with Caro as they drank the coffee. Edward got up to change the music, and Penny tore herself away from Matt to organise a glass of brandy for him.

'Can you help me find the brandy glasses?' she called back to Caro from the living room. As she spoke, Verity's phone rang and she bent to retrieve it from her bag. Instinctively, she moved away from the table to take her call, and into the living room where Caro and Penny stood with their backs to her before an open cabinet, full of glassware.

'Isn't Matt the one who's having the affair?' Penny whispered loudly to her sister. Too late, Penny turned and saw Verity, hastily grabbed two brandy glasses from Caro, and scurried back to the dining room. Caro then turned, and paled with shock at seeing Verity so close. Verity gawped. Her phone, having stopped ringing, started again. She answered it, distractedly. As she stood and listened to the voice on the other end, she spread her hand over her chest, and asked in a shaky voice that the caller repeat himself.

21

'I'll drive you in Jay's car. Get your coats. Where does Jay keep his keys, Caro?' Edward demanded.

'Here.'

'What did the person say, exactly?' Matt asked.

'It was her friend Johnny. She's unconscious and in the ambulance now. Johnny knows her phone pin. That's how he managed to call me.'

'But what happened to her? I don't understand!' Matt's voice thundered.

'Alcohol, Matt. Bloody alcohol. I keep telling you she has a problem but you don't listen.'

'Okay, into the car. Your daughter is in the best hands.' Edward shepherded Verity and Matt towards the front door.

'She fell?'

'No, he said she passed out.'

'How did she end up in an ambulance?'

'I don't know, Matt.'

'Which hospital?' Edward asked.

'St Thomas's.'

'Do you know the route?' Edward touched Verity's arm, focusing her.

'Yes.'

'Go, go,' Caro ushered them out.

Verity climbed into the back seat, Matt sat in the front, and put his head in his hands. Edward started the car. 'Put your seatbelt on,' he ordered Matt.

'It'll be quicker to cross over the river and go along the Embankment,' Verity said. 'Do you know how to get to the bridge, Edward?'

'Yes.'

'I'm sure they're over-reacting, and it's nothing a few mugs of coffee won't sort out.' Matt snapped his seatbelt into place.

'She was completely unconscious.'

'Jesus,' Matt cursed.

'She is receiving professional care. That's the most important thing,' Edward stated firmly, as he manoeuvred the car deftly along the sleepy Putney street.

'If she gets through this, I'll do anything,' Verity prayed. She was grateful for Edward's presence as he would get them to the hospital quickly. Sitting in the back of the car, she hugged herself, feeling very alone.

'She will get through it,' Edward insisted.

'How can she be unconscious?' Her voice wobbled. She leant back against the car seat.

'Breathe deeply.' Edward glanced at her through the rear-view mirror.

Verity's thoughts log-jammed in her head.

'If Tills wasn't used to drinking much and she went on a bit of a binge, this can happen,' he explained.

She lost track of time. Lights flashed past outside the window. The car swerved, stopped, accelerated again. She felt sick. Silently, she plea-bargained with a God she did not believe in, promising that she would be good, better, even change her whole life around, anything, if only Tills would be okay.

'Bloody hell!' Matt muttered.

'You keep swearing. How much have *you* drunk tonight, Matt?' she snapped.

'Not as much as my daughter, obviously.'

'There's a procedure,' Edward began, his voice calm and reassuring. 'They'll test her alcohol levels, top up her fluids and blood sugar, monitor her heart rate, and ensure her airways are kept clear.'

213

'You seem to know a lot about this,' Matt remarked, tersely.

'My ex-wife was an alcoholic.'

'Jeepers, sorry mate. So, all this is just routine treatment after a bender, then?'

'It can be, yes.'

'But she's eighteen years old. Why would she do this to herself? I feel responsible,' Verity raked her fingers through her hair. 'I knew we should have kept her in tonight. I had a gut feeling.'

'You didn't cause this.' Edward was firm.

Verity leant her head back again and closed her eyes.

'Straight on,' Matt instructed.

'The embankment would be quicker,' she insisted.

'Not at this time of night. We'll go over Westminster Bridge.'

'That's not the fastest way!'

'It's the way we're going. Edward, please, take the route I suggest.' Verity groaned.

'What about drugs? I'll bet some bastard gave her drugs. I'll kill them. She's such an innocent,' Matt muttered.

'No, she isn't, Matt. Not anymore. I keep telling you. She's gone off the rails. We should have grounded her.'

'You can't ground an eighteen-year-old,' Edward remarked steadily, checking his mirror before overtaking a bus.

'He's right, V.'

Tears welled in Verity's eyes, and she felt around in her coat pocket for a tissue.

'Not far now,' Edward reassured. He steered the car into the hospital entrance, and dropped them off outside the main doors.

'Go! I'll park and come and find you.'

Verity found she was strangely calm. She glided down the corridor that led to the emergency department, oddly insulated against all the sights and sounds of the hospital, her senses and emotions numb. She prayed continually that Tills would be okay. They were told to sit in a waiting area, and wait for a nurse to come. A hotchpotch of characters sat around on plastic chairs, absorbed with their phones or staring glumly into space. The lights were bright, the floor worn but spotless. The reception staff sat in a glass cage, insulated from danger and drama. Verity's hand trembled as she dabbed her nose with a tissue.

When the nurse came out to talk to them, she looked not much older than Tills, and was quietly spoken and professional, explaining that on arrival, Tills had been unconscious and her breathing irregular. They were treating her now. The nurse asked Verity questions about any medication Tills might be taking, whether Tills was allergic to anything, and whether she might be pregnant. 'We've done a toxicity test and she's getting a little help with her breathing. We've put her on a drip to help with her fluids,' the nurse explained.

'Is she going to be all right?'

'She's being monitored carefully. The tox screen showed no drugs, but your daughter's blood alcohol levels are 0.34.'

'What does that mean?'

'It's quite a high level and we need to give her extra support while her body metabolises the alcohol.'

'Is there nothing else you can do?'

'We're doing everything we can.'

'But – but she will recover?'

'We'll continue to monitor her. Your daughter is in good hands.'

'Can I see her?'

'She's with the doctors now. We'll let you know as soon as you can go in.'

Verity put her hands to her face. This was not happening. She wanted to wind the clock back and re-live the day, keep her daughter at home safe with her. She felt sick with fear.

'She's going to be fine,' Matt stated. He stood up and paced the waiting area.

'Hold me.' Verity stood.

Matt squeezed her roughly for a second, and then let her go, swivelling away from her. 'What a bloody mess!'

Verity stood alone, not knowing what to do, and feeling utterly helpless.

Edward appeared. 'Well?'

'They're doing everything they can,' Matt stated.

At the sight of Edward, Verity's emotions un-stopped. Heat rose in her cheeks and tears poured down her face. 'Poor Tills! I just want to be with her!' She rubbed the tears from her cheek with the palm of her hand. Edward put his arm around her shoulder, and Verity leant her head against his chest for one blind moment and rested her hand his stomach. Edward's hand cradled her head fleetingly.

When she opened her eyes, Verity saw Matt's blue eyes drilling into hers. 'You two.' It was not a question, it was a statement. 'France. The bloody weekend in France. Of course. I knew it.'

Verity froze. Edward drew away. A woman who cradled her injured arm looked up from the chair opposite, and watched them silently. 'No, Matt. You're wrong.'

'Of course, it crossed my mind. It would cross anyone's mind, but I… You bastard.'

Edward glanced at the floor, and then raised his eyes to meet Matt's livid stare. 'It's not what you think.'

'Jesus.' Matt shook his head and laughed bitterly.

Verity's stomach turned. 'Matt, he's telling the truth. We're both telling the truth about France.'

'Oh, really?'

'Edward and I – we met before, years ago. We're old friends, that's all. I should have told you before.'

'Well, how very cosy for you both. D'you know, I always had a hunch I'd seen you somewhere. Remind me, where was that exactly?'

'I think we need to remember why we're here,' Edward replied slowly.

'Well, I know why I'm here. The question is, Edward: why are you here?'

'Matt, don't! You're drunk. Just calm down.'

Edward held up his hands.

'Edward, I think you'd better leave. Thank you for driving us here,' Verity stammered. He hesitated. 'Please,' she insisted.

'You have my number. Anything you need – and I mean anything.'

'How very sweet.' Matt's sarcasm dirtied the air.

Edward paused, still uncertain.

'I'll be okay,' she mouthed.

He turned, and Verity watched as he walked away, stiff-shouldered and with a determined stride. She glared at the woman with the injured arm who gawped with fascination.

'Well, this is just brilliant! So, when did you meet him before?'

'This is not the time, Matt.'

216

'Oh, I think it is.'

'At a party, years ago. It really doesn't matter!'

'Were you lovers?'

'No! And Matt, stop shouting. Have you forgotten where we are?'

'Of course not! I just want to know what I'm dealing with here.'

Verity pressed her fingertips into the side of her head. 'Okay, so if we're setting the record straight, *you* are dealing with a friendship, nothing more. I, on the other hand, have just overheard a conversation about the fact that you are, apparently, having an affair. Yes, you may well look shocked. And actually, d'you know what? Don't even bother to deny it. Because I'm not interested. This is *not* the time! I'm just warning you: don't take the moral high ground with me right now because I haven't done anything wrong, and I'm in no mood to take any crap from you. I really don't care about us and our stupid lives right now. I just want Tills to be all right. You should have listened to me about her!'

'So now I'm to blame for Tills' behaviour?'

'I didn't say that! But we're not helping her. She told me before Christmas that the atmosphere in our house was unbearable.'

'And whose bloody fault is that? You're the one causing all the stress!'

'While you never listen to me, and are never at home anymore, because you're too busy shagging your secretary!'

'She is not my secretary.'

'So, you don't deny it then?'

'I can't talk with you when you're like this.'

'She looks like a secretary.'

'That's a very bitchy thing to say.'

There was by now a ripple of interest in the hospital waiting room, and a couple more heads had turned to see who was making such a fuss.

'Okay,' Verity hissed, suddenly self-conscious. She raised her hands in frustration, and then let them fall down by her sides. 'I think we both need to calm down.'

'Where's the bloody doctor? Why aren't they telling us anything? I'm going to find someone. This is unbearable!' Matt shouted.

'We have to wait.'

He ignored her and paced away towards the locked door to the emergency ward. He pressed the buzzer there. Verity slumped

217

down on a plastic chair, and had strict words with herself. The fact was that she and Matt had both drunk too much that evening, and were now having an argument worthy of an episode of EastEnders in an A & E waiting room. What sort of an example were they for Tills, when it came down to it? No wonder Tills thought it was normal to drink when her own parents regularly over-indulged, and lived such messy lives. Guilt thickened her throat and trickled into her mind, thick as tar.

An elderly man in a tatty overcoat came to sit on one of the plastic chairs beside her, as Verity tried to get a grip on her emotions. She sat up straight and took a few deep breaths.

Matt reappeared. 'Still busy with her.'

'Can we see her?'

'Not yet.'

'Do you think she's got in with the wrong crowd at university?'

'How should I know? This is such a bloody mess. And d'you know what? I do blame you for this – you and your bloody ambition. You are her mother, after all, and if you weren't so bloody wrapped up in yourself all the time, this wouldn't have happened.'

Verity jumped up and moved so close to Matt that her nose almost touched his chin. She was so angry that her head felt like it might explode. She poked Matt in the chest with her finger. 'I've had enough of your stinking male attitude. Don't. Say. Another. Word.'

'And you *have* been having an affair with that American, haven't you? Admit it!' Matt flung his hands in the air, pivoted away, and sat down with his head in his hands.

'I have *not*. More fool me, it seems.' The old man got up and moved to another chair. 'I suppose you think it's one rule for me and another for you?' Verity persisted.

'Give it a rest, V.'

Verity felt for a chair, and sat down. She had not had an affair, it was true. But neither had she been entirely honest or well-behaved either, and while she could not answer for Matt and whatever he had been up to, she liked to think of herself as a decent person. And if she had not been so preoccupied with selling her business or – it was true – meeting up with Edward, would she have spent more time with Tills? Could she have prevented tonight? Was Tills being here in this hospital actually her fault? She stood up again, feeling overwhelmingly restless, and paced around hugging herself, rubbing her arms with her hands. A male nurse approached them. 'Everything all right in here?'

'What's happening with our daughter?' Verity asked.

'She is being stabilised and monitored.'

'This is your fault!' Matt repeated, jabbing his finger at Verity, and ignoring the nurse.

'This is not helping anyone,' the nurse addressed Matt.

'I'm out of here!' Matt stood up abruptly.

'Where are you going?' Verity exclaimed.

'Anywhere but here!'

'You can't... you can't leave Tills! Matt, let's get you a coffee. You need to sober up.'

'There's nothing I can do for Tills here.'

'When she wakes up, she'll want to see you.'

'Well, she'll have to bloody wait. Maybe it will give her time to reflect on her own stupidity.'

'Matt?'

'She has to be taught a lesson. You've said so yourself.'

'But not now! Tills needs our support now. We need to pull together.'

'Steady on, steady on. Why don't we all take a moment, have some time out now.' The nurse held his arms out. 'How's about that coffee?'

'Well, I'm glad you can be so rational about it!' Matt completely ignored the nurse, and glared at Verity.

'Let's just focus on doing what's best for Tills.'

Matt walked over and pounded a wall with his fist.

'If you don't calm down, sir, I'm going to call security,' the nurse stated calmly.

'I'll spare you the effort, mate,' Matt spat, and strode out of the waiting area.

'Matt?' Verity stared at her husband's receding figure.

'Are you all right?' The nurse asked her.

'Yes, yes.' She was breathing heavily. She shook her head. 'I'm so sorry about that. We were out to dinner. He's had a bit too much to drink. It's not been the best night. I'd just like to see my daughter now if I can, please.'

'I'll go and find out what the situation is.'

Verity blew her nose on a tissue, and swiped a tear from the corner of her eye. The only thing that mattered right now was Tills getting better. Her world shrank to that one thought.

'You can come through and see your daughter now.' The nurse smiled reassuringly.

Tills lay on her back on a trolley bed in a cubicle with her eyes closed, a tube coming from her mouth, and another running from a cannula in the back of her hand. Verity registered the quiet, busy atmosphere, and approached her cautiously, bending over her pale shut face, stroking her hair, and pressing her lips to her smooth forehead. A young doctor explained the blood and urine tests they had taken. He asked her whether Tills might have intended to harm herself.

'No, no,' she rejected the idea hastily. 'She's just started university. She has lots of friends. She's bright and happy, loves dogs, wants to travel in the summer and write a blog.' She stroked Till's limp hand. 'When will she wake up?'

'It's not possible to tell. We have to wait and see, and continue to give her body the help it needs. The alcohol levels in her bloodstream have stabilised. Is your daughter a regular drinker?'

'No, she's never had a problem. All through her teenage years she's been a good girl – quiet and sensible. But I did notice a bit of a change in her when she came home from university this Christmas. She's been going to lots of parties and so on. I just thought it was normal for someone her age.'

'It's possible that if she's not used to much alcohol, and then suddenly drank to excess, this could be the outcome.'

'I feel so helpless. What can I do for her?'

'There's nothing you can do right now. We're taking care of her.'

The doctor left. Verity stayed at Tills' side, stroked her hair and whispered, 'I love you,' over and over. Overwhelmed with heat, she tugged off her coat and flung it on a chair. Time slowed, each moment stretched to snapping point. Verity felt utterly helpless and besieged with memories of Tills as a little girl, with her fair wavy hair and gap-toothed smile. She remembered the way Tills was always singing around the house, and her special relationship with Charlie – the mutual love between animal and child. All that could not end, surely? Was it really like Matt insisted? Had she not cared for her well enough this holiday, had she made her unhappy in some way? Was what she was trying to do with her life really that de-stabilising for her family? Was it utterly selfish?

Verity's phone rang from her bag, and she found it and answered. It was Tills' friend, Johnny, the boy who had called her earlier.

'How is she?' Johnny sounded nervous.

'How the hell do you think she is? What happened, Johnny?'

'I'm so sorry. I really don't know. One minute she was fine, drinking with all the others, and the next, she collapsed.'

'What were they drinking?'

'I don't know. They were sitting around a table. I wasn't part of it.'

'Where was this?'

'In our friend's house.'

'Do you realise that Tills is unconscious with tubes coming out of her everywhere? Do you know how serious this is?'

'I know, I'm sorry. I should have taken better care of her. She's my friend. I wanted to let you know I have her bag here, and her phone.'

Verity relented a little. Even though she was angry, she had enough sense to realise the situation was probably not Johnny's fault. 'I'm sorry, I didn't mean to yell,' she apologised. 'It was you who called the ambulance, wasn't it?'

'Yeah.'

'Well, that was very sensible of you, and I'm grateful.'

'My Mum's a doctor. She's warned me for years that if anyone ever passed out drinking, it was serious. You can thank her. I wouldn't have had a clue.'

'You did the right thing.'

'So, when she wakes up, would you tell Tills I have her stuff?'

Johnny's sweet optimism touched Verity. 'Of course.'

'Tell her I'll come and see her when she's feeling a bit better.'

Verity ended the call and put away her phone, feeling suddenly drained. A nurse checked the machines at Tills' bedside. All around, Verity heard the quiet chatter of staff and patients, and the beeping of monitors in the busy unit. Another tear rolled down her cheek, and she took a deep breath.

'Why don't you go and get a hot drink?' the nurse suggested. 'Your daughter is going to feel pretty rough when she comes round. It won't hurt if you take a moment for yourself. This must be a shock for you.'

'She will come round?'

'They usually do. Is there no-one you can call to be with you?'

She thought of Matt, and shook her head. 'I'll sit a moment longer, and then maybe get a coffee.'

The nurse left, only to return a few moments later. 'Here she is. Someone to see you.'

Verity looked up. Edward stood at the foot of Tills' bed. 'Do you mind?' he asked.

'No, of course not.' Verity stood. 'She's still unconscious.'

'I don't want to cause any further complications. When Tills wakes up, I'll leave straight away. But I saw your husband get into a taxi, and I couldn't bear the thought of you being alone here.' He put his arms around her, and she responded, leaning against him, needing his warmth and reassurance. 'She'll be fine. I just know it. Don't be hard on yourself.' He wiped a tear from her cheek with his thumb.

'You went through this with your wife?'

'Oh yes, more than once.'

'And she recovered? She was okay?'

'She did, although it's not a pretty business. As to being okay, well, you know the story. I think this is a bit different – a case of youth and inexperience – and Tills is paying a heavy price for it.' He looked fondly at Tills' pale face. 'I'm sure she'll be back to her normal self in no time. A couple of days and this will all feel like a bad dream.'

'Really?'

'Yes. The young ones bounce back.'

'I can't help thinking I'm to blame for this. If I hadn't been so absorbed by my own life, maybe this wouldn't have happened. Maybe I'd have noticed the signs. Maybe I could have stopped it happening.'

'Oh, Verity.' Edward shook his head, and held the top of her arms softly but firmly. 'This is not your fault. You must understand that. Nothing you did or didn't do caused this.'

'But how do you know?'

'I just know, take it from me. It's easy to blame yourself for someone else's behaviour. You feel horribly guilty in some way. But the truth? The truth is this was Tills' shout, no-one else's. And given her age, I expect it was just naivety on her part and she'll learn from it.'

'Matt keeps saying it was my fault. He has a point.'

Edward looked at the ground, and shook his head.

'What? Say it! Tell me what you're thinking,' she demanded.

He shook his head again.

'Please.'

'What I don't understand is why you would believe him? It's so obviously not true. And excuse me for pointing this out, but his daughter is seriously sick and he leaves the hospital? The man's being an idiot tonight. I'm talking out of turn, I know. He's probably just sick with worry and this is his own method of coping.' Edward exhaled loudly. 'Listen, we're getting way off point here. What's important for now is this young woman.' He gently squeezed Tills' foot.

'One thing at a time,' Verity whispered.

'Exactly.'

'I'm so grateful for everything you've done tonight.'

'Oh, it's nothing.' Edward rubbed her arm a little, and she was calmed by his solid presence in her newly-shifted world.

'You know we can never be close, Edward. I want to be clear about that. What happened last night was just too much champagne. I don't want you to get the wrong impression.'

'Let's not talk about that now.'

'I need you to understand.'

'I do. I understand.'

'And another thing. Did you hear what Caro and her sister said about my husband?'

'I did.'

'Is it true?'

'I have no idea.'

'Well, now is not the time but I know you've heard something, haven't you? You know and you aren't telling me.' A monitor connected to Tills began to beep loudly. Verity swung around to her daughter. 'Someone, come!' she called out.

'Step aside.' Edward took Verity gently by the arm as a group of doctors and nurses swarmed around Tills.

'What's happening?'

'Her heart rate has dropped. We need to give her some drugs to prevent her falling into a coma.'

Edward grasped her hand. She heard sounds, his words of comfort, gentle by her ear, but her attention remained transfixed by her daughter. She was asked to move further away as doctors and nurses buzzed around the bed, speaking in urgent voices, mentioning drugs and bodily conditions she had never heard of. She registered tension in the atmosphere; even Edward was rigid beside her, which made her more afraid. She glimpsed Tills' face between the bodies of the doctors. It looked strangely still and blue. The doctors tried one drug after another, checking and monitoring Tills' reactions. Nothing, nothing, nothing was working, but still they tried. Sometime later in a moment of clarity, Verity looked at the clock, and twenty minutes had passed since the machine had started beeping – an eternity. She focused on her own breathing, and prayed and prayed that Tills would survive. The world closed in around her, and narrowed to the one spot on the floor where her gaze stayed fixed. Edward had his arm around her but she was frozen, her breath like lead in her lungs. The machines beeped on, incessantly, signalling that nothing was right, nothing was working.

And then, suddenly, the machines fell silent, and the atmosphere in the small cubicle expanded back to normal. A doctor puffed out his cheeks and exhaled. A nurse, her eyes still wide with alarm, managed to catch Verity's eye, and smile. Verity looked at her child; her colour was returning.

'Your daughter has been lucky this time,' a doctor said.

Verity squeezed Edward's hand.

'Thank you, God!' Edward murmured, surprising her.

'You were worried, weren't you?' she realised.

'Yes, I... Oh, it's nothing, doesn't matter.'

One nurse remained but the other medics went, and Verity approached Tills cautiously, picked up her slender hand, and pressed it to her cheek. Her skin felt soft and warm. 'Please wake up, Tills,' she whispered.

Another hour passed. Verity could not speak; words eluded her. Edward was there the whole time, a gentle expression on his face, his body exuding reassurance. He knew when to murmur encouragement, and when to step away and give her space. It was as if she was suspended in a bubble of time where everything that was normal and familiar had blown away, out of sight and only she, Tills and Edward remained.

And then, with no warning, Tills moved and groaned.

'Help, someone!' Verity called, and a team was there in seconds, removing tubes and other bits of medical equipment from Tills' head and mouth, and checking monitors, and talking to Tills in calm voices. Tills was moved to a more upright position, and groaned and muttered.

'I feel sick,' she whined.

Even though the words were not great, Verity had never felt so glad to hear her daughter speak. She looked around for Edward, but he had disappeared.

'She's going to feel pretty rough,' a doctor said.

'Mum?' Tills voice was faint with hope.

'I'm here.'

'Mum, I'm sorry.'

'That's okay, don't worry. I'm just glad you're safe.'

'Mum, I don't know what happened.'

'You passed out. You drank too much and you passed out. Don't worry about it now.'

'I feel terrible. My head.'

'Is there something wrong with her head?'

'That's the alcohol,' a doctor said. 'Everything is fine. But she's going to feel very hungover for a day or two. After we've run a few more tests we'll transfer her to another ward, and keep her in overnight for observations.' While the doctors attended to Tills, Verity moved out of her line of sight and sobbed with relief. She fumbled for her phone to call Matt and tell him the good news. His phone rang on unanswered, and she stammered out a brief message.

'Mum!' Tills called out.

Verity reached for Tills' hand, and squeezed it. 'I'm here, love.'

'Okay, we're just going to check you over and remove the catheter. Mrs Westwood, would you like to wait outside?'

'Mum, I feel horrible.'

'Aw, sweetie...'

'You'll feel a bit rough for a day or two,' a nurse said.

'My head hurts.'

'Once we're sure you're stable, we'll give you something for the pain.'

'I'm going to wait outside, Tills, like the doctor says. I'm not going anywhere. I'll be right back.'

'Okay, Mum. I'm so sorry.' Tills still sounded drunk; her s's were slurred.

'That's okay. Don't worry about that now; you just concentrate on getting better. I love you.'

'Love you too, Mum,' Tills whimpered.

Verity left the cubicle, and walked down a corridor. She did not know where she was going; all she was aware of was a huge wave of relief washing through her. Now that Tills was awake and talking, she knew the worst was over. She wanted to fall to her knees in thanks.

'Verity,' Edward's voice called softly. He was waiting down the corridor, his dark eyes serious and shadowed with exhaustion, his expression questioning.

'She's feeling rough but she's conscious and talking to me.'

Edward placed his hands gently either side of her face, and kissed her forehead.

'I can't tell you how relieved I am,' she whispered.

'I'm so happy for you. And for Tills. Let's get you a coffee. There's a machine just along here.'

'I don't want to go far.'

'It's just here. You look exhausted. You need a hot drink.'

'Did I tell you that earlier, the boy who called the ambulance rang again? He sounded really sweet and concerned. I think the whole thing was just a horrid accident, like you said – naivety.'

'Well, it's not the first time this has happened to a college kid.'

'I know, but I thought – hoped – she knew better. I'm relieved but I'm pretty angry with her too.'

'You can have that chat with her in a couple of days when she's more likely to listen.'

'Edward, thank you again, for everything.'

'It's okay.' He took her hand and squeezed it. 'You've been great all through tonight.'

'I don't know about that.'

'You were. Believe me. Here we are. Let's grab you a coffee and take it back.'

'I don't have change for the machine.'

'Here.'

They walked back to the waiting area. Verity sank down wearily, and sipped the scalding coffee. 'I'm sorry Matt was so awful earlier.'

Edward shrugged. 'You don't have to apologise for him.'

'He's not great with hospitals.'

'I expect I have as good a reason as anyone not to be great with hospitals but I'm here. It's no excuse.'

'We had an argument after you left. He accused me of having an affair with you. A nurse threatened to call security.'

'I figured as much. I'm sorry.'

'Hey, never mind.' She gathered Edward's hand, and held it in her lap. 'Not now. Let's not talk about it. Right now, I'm so happy that Tills is okay.' A nurse appeared and told Verity she could see her. 'Listen, go home now, Edward. I'll be fine now.'

'I wouldn't dream of it.'

'But it's really late.'

'I don't mind. I'm staying – out of sight for sure; Tills does not need to see me right now – but I'm here, and whenever you want, I'll take you home.'

'But I might be here for hours.'

'It doesn't matter to me. You can be here all night.'

'You don't need to do that.'

'I do.'

She squeezed his hand, and hurried away to re-join Tills.

'I'm scared, Mum. What happened to me?'

'I told you. You passed out.'

'Oh God!'

'You're okay now. Try not to worry. The worst is over.'

'Where's Dad? Does he know I'm here? Don't tell him, will you Mum?' Tills' words were still slurred, and Verity winced at her daughter's inebriation. She felt a sudden snappy irritation mixed in with her relief.

'Dad's not here right now but he's been to see you.'

'He's cross, isn't he?'

'We're both trying to understand what happened.'

'My head is killing me.'

'They'll give you some painkillers soon, I'm sure.'

'Mum, I still feel woozy.'

'I'll call someone.' Verity stepped out of the cubicle and called a nurse who checked Tills.

'You're going to have one helluva hangover in the morning,' the nurse warned. 'But these fluids will help. You've been lucky tonight, you know.'

'Don't feel lucky.'

'No, well, maybe when you've had a bit more time to think about it, you'll realise.' The nurse's voice was gentle and kind but Verity heard her implied message loud and clear. She felt embarrassed.

'I'm sorry. She's never done anything like this before.'

'No, well, we all make mistakes. It's usually kids younger than your daughter, believe it or not.'

'We'll be having words, sorting this out.'

'There's lots of help available. I'll give you some information before you leave.'

Tills dozed. Verity looked at a clock. It was the small hours of a new day. As she sat on a hard, plastic chair, peripherally aware of background voices, beeping machines and busy activity elsewhere on the ward, anger and hurt grew inside her, making her chest tight and a knot harden around her heart. Now that Tills was out of danger, the other truth hit her like a balled fist: what Caro's sister had said. Was it true Matt was really having an affair, and everyone knew about it? Had Matt as good as admitted it earlier? Her forehead crumpled into a deep frown. In the drama, she could not remember exactly what Matt had said. But she knew what she had seen – his hand on that woman's knee in the Blue Anchor. And she was not a fool. Sometimes you did not need words to know the truth; it was there, a vibration which struck straight to the heart, if only you cared to notice. Matt running from the hospital earlier was so weak, it was almost unforgiveable. To choose his own wellbeing when Tills was lying unconscious on a hospital bed was pure cowardice. She hunched her shoulders, trying to come to terms with everything. Edward must have known about the gossip too, from Caro and her sister, and probably Jay as well. He had denied that he knew anything but he was no doubt protecting her. Humiliation welled inside her, and hurt turned to anger. She picked her fingernails as a stream of darkening thoughts ran through her head.

After a series of checks on Tills, a doctor told her they would be moving her to a different ward for the night.

'You really should go home and get some rest. She's stable now, and we don't foresee any further problems. We'll call you if there's anything to be concerned about.'

'I'm not sure.'

'Mum, go, I'll be fine. I just want to go to sleep,' Tills insisted, dozily.

A nurse handed Verity her coat. Verity allowed Edward to drive her back through inky London streets. A fine rain fell and the windscreen wipers swept from side to side in a hypnotic rhythm as they drove in silence. She shivered repeatedly. Edward pulled up outside the house in Rannoch Road.

'You knew, didn't you, about Matt and that woman?' she asked, her hand on the car door handle.

'No, I didn't know. The first I heard was this evening when you did.'

'Forgive me when I say I don't believe you.'

'I can't make you believe me.'

'I feel betrayed.'

'I'm sure you do.'

Inside the house was empty. Matt's attic bed was untouched. Verity ran a bath and soaked in it for a while in an attempt to warm herself before crawling into her own bed. She slept for four hours with her phone beside her. In the morning, she rang the hospital, and they confirmed that Tills could come home. Recalling the state of her car, she rang the AA, and a man came and fitted a new battery within an hour. She left a message for Matt to say she was going to collect Tills. The message was her duty done with him, as far as she was concerned. His empty bed was speaking more honestly than his words ever did.

Tills grumbled all the way home. Verity made her some soup, watched her eat a little, and then sent her up to bed.

One storm had passed, Verity thought grittily. But another was brewing.

22

It was still dark. The bedroom radiator creaked as it began to warm up, and the first aeroplane droned overhead. Verity awoke, filled with the urge to run and clear her head of emotion and stress. Her mind was tangled with imaginings of Matt in bed with that woman, her lost trust in Edward, and echoes of the scare Tills had given her. Her life had degenerated into an overwhelming mess. She flung her duvet to one side, pulled on her tracksuit, and checked on Tills, who slept peacefully. After trudging downstairs, she hastily ate a banana, and laced up her running shoes. Her hips were stiff, and she circled them, and stretched her calf and thigh muscles, before heading out of the door.

Outside, a grey light turned houses sepia, and white mist lingered in the street. She wanted to elbow the buildings aside, and rip up the concrete that smothered the earth beneath her feet; but she determinedly focused her attention on the rhythm of her footfall on the empty pavement.

She and Tills had chatted the day before. Tills had cried and Verity had hugged her, eventually. Tills had apologised repeatedly, explaining that she had been 'nominated' by some people at the party to drink certain alcoholic drinks in a game. Verity had stressed how stupid drinking games were but knew that Tills had already learned her lesson. Her daughter's clouded, haunted eyes had spoken volumes, as had her translucent skin, and continuing nausea. Verity was convinced she would not make the same mistake twice. She would talk to Tills some more when she was feeling better, but for now Verity accepted the whole chain of events for what they were – stupid and naive.

As she jogged on down the street, her thoughts inevitably turned to Matt. She had remained furious with him but had stifled her anger, for Tills' sake. Now that she was out of the house and alone for the first time, she wanted to yell at the sky. Matt must have got her messages about Tills but still had not returned her calls. There had been *nothing* from him but silence, for almost forty-eight hours, and his phone remained switched off. She had considered phoning his work or his parents, but something had told her he would not be there, and she could not face the humiliation. She had contemplated calling Caro but pride and a sense of dignity had prevented her. As a result, she was powerless, waiting and not knowing where her husband was, or who he was with.

Many, many years before, Matt had swept into Verity's life with his confidence, good manners, and charm, and had filled some primeval need in Verity for a steady relationship, marriage, and security. She had loved him, and she still did, but at the same time, as she ran on down a neighbouring street towards the riverside, she now saw her marriage in a much sharper light. She visualised the long trail of all her and Matt's shared years together, where good times had also been littered with hurt and disappointment, dishonesty and lies, and now perhaps even betrayal. She wondered what it all meant. Her trainers beat a steady rhythm on the footpath, and she could hear her breath, coming steadily in and out, but no answers came to her. Seeing Tills hover on the brink of life two nights before had terrified her to her core. Tills' existence, which Verity normally took for granted, had become so fragile and temporary, vulnerable and uncertain, like a flame that could be extinguished at any moment with one careless puff of fate. Since Tills' recovery, Verity had emerged from ignorance, and now saw life more clearly than she ever had before. It really did not last for ever. You had to savour every moment. All the clichés were so true. That night's events in the hospital had put her petty worries about work and money in their place, and made her appreciate more than ever that what mattered – the only things that mattered – were the people she loved.

As her muscles warmed up and she lengthened her stride, taking in the wide expanse of river at her side, it dawned on her that in many ways she was stronger than her husband. When the going had got tough, he had been unable to cope. Whatever excuse he made, he had basically bailed out. He had not only abandoned Tills in that hospital, but he had abandoned her too, and she was not sure how she would ever forgive him – she would certainly never forget. She shook her head in fury and, caught off guard, tripped on an uneven paving stone, only just catching hold of a wall in time to stop herself from falling. She paused for a moment beside the wall, bent over, hands clasping her knees and her chest heaving, before standing up tall again and running on.

She did not like to blame others for her own predicament and as she ran on beside the wide swirling Thames, Verity saw how in her marriage to Matt, she had allowed a bad situation to develop – one in which Matt held all the cards. Over the years, she had not made her own voice sufficiently loud, she had bent to her husband's will, lived the life he wanted, in the place he wanted. This could not go on. She was a strong person, worth more than this, and it was time to stand up for herself. A small knot of resolve hardened inside her.

Back home, she stood at her kitchen sink and drank a full glass of water. She went upstairs and checked on Tills, still not completely trusting that she had recovered, but reassured by the pale face resting on the pillow, lips softly parted, and chest swelling with each precious breath. Downstairs again, the grey light of an end-of-year day filtered in through the windows of the Rannoch Road house. Following a hunch that she had been ignoring for months, Verity walked into Matt's study, determined to be thorough this time. She began with the top left-hand drawer. Her nerves rippled. Systematically, she went through every single drawer and its contents, skipping nothing. Part-way through the process, dread and disbelief spread through her as she read a mortgage statement. She put the document down, stepped away, and made herself a coffee before returning, and diligently making neat piles from a mess of bills, overdue demands, and loan agreements taken from the back of a drawer. The fact that Matt was hiding this mess from her was more fuel for her anger and mistrust but it was not what she looked for. What she expected to find was proof of his infidelity, and in that respect, her hunch had been wrong, and she stood baffled, looking around her. There was nothing at all to suggest an affair.

She finished her coffee and made a rough attempt to assess the impact of the bills, loans, credit card statements, mortgages, and bank overdrafts which lay piled on the desk before her, but she could not begin to get the measure of them and felt hugely impatient. She rang Francesca, who on hearing of Verity's plight, and knowing that it might have repercussions for the business sale, told Verity to courier the documents over for her to look at straight away. Verity bagged up the paperwork and sent it off a short while later; then she went upstairs and took a long, hot shower.

When she came downstairs again, she found Tills sitting in the kitchen, tentatively nibbling a piece of toast.

'How are you feeling?'

'Bit better, thanks.'

'Aw, let me give you a hug. We all make mistakes, Tills. The trick in life is to try not to make the same one twice, but even that can be hard.'

'I'm never touching alcohol again. I never knew it was so dangerous.'

'Well, for now that's probably sensible. But you will have another drink one day, and it will be fine. Are you going to get your stuff from Johnny today?'

'Yeah, we thought we'd go to the cinema, chill out a bit. Where's Dad?'

'I'm not sure.'

'You know, I've wanted to say for ages, Mum, but he's being really unfair to you. About you wanting to move and change your job. He should be supporting you.'

'Yes, I agree, but it's complicated. And that's for me and Dad to sort out, not something you need to worry about. As far as you're concerned, you just need to explain to Dad, like you did to me yesterday, that what happened was the result of a silly drinking game. He won't be pleased, but eventually he'll understand.'

'Yeah. I need to face up to my friends too. I'm so embarrassed that they could all take it, and I ended up in a hospital. I'm such a lightweight.'

'You're not, Tills. You're really not a lightweight. And it's in this kind of situation that you get to know who your real friends are. Anyone who doesn't support you and show one hundred percent concern for you isn't worth wasting your time with. D'you understand that?'

'Yes,' Tills sighed. 'I think so.'

'Look, here, buy yourself and Johnny a nice healthy lunch before the cinema, yes? A fresh start?'

After Tills had left, Verity was alone in the house once more, and sat at her kitchen table taking deep breaths. She picked up her phone, prepared to leave another message for Matt, and was surprised when he answered the call.

'Yes.'

'We need to talk.'

'I don't want a bollocking, V.'

'I'd like you to come home now.'

'How's Tills?'

'Out with her friend.'

'What, again? Jesus Christ.'

'If you'd been here, you'd realise it's the best thing for her right now.'

'Okay. I'll be back in a bit.'

'Good.'

She went out into her tiny garden with Charlie, and stared up at the blanket of cloud overhead and the backs of the neighbouring houses, always so much messier than the fronts. She was not looking forward to the confrontation, and back inside, fumbled with the kettle and made herself a strong cup of tea, wondering where to begin. She prayed for courage, not sure why she did so. Her hand shook as she lifted the mug to her mouth, and her tummy rumbled with nerves. A little while later, her phone rang again with a number she did not recognise.

'Is that Verity?'

'Yes, it is.'

'Verity, it's Caro. I hope I haven't called at a bad time.'

'Caro, it's not a great time.'

'How's your daughter?'

'She's much better, thank you. On the mend, no harm done.'

'I'm very happy to hear that. Listen, I'd like to meet you, to discuss what you overheard the other evening. And to apologise. I feel awful about it.'

Verity's shoulders stiffened. 'You don't need to do that.'

234

'I do. I'd really like to, and I think it's important to clear the air. Please would you meet me for coffee somewhere?'

'I don't know, Caro. I'm not sure I can stand any more gossip right now.'

'I know, but please consider it.'

'Okay, I will, but I have to go now.'

As Verity stood, reflecting on Caro's offer, she heard the key in the door. Matt walked straight to the fridge, grabbed a beer, ripped off the ring-pull, and flung it on the kitchen table. Charlie let out a short bark from his blanket in the corner. Matt was unshaven, and his eyes were clouded with exhaustion.

'Tills is much better today.'

'Glad to hear it.' He gazed at Verity steadily, as if assessing her.

'Sit down, we need to talk.'

'I'm all right where I am, thanks.'

'I don't know where to begin with you. Part of me wants to ask you to pack your bags and leave right now. Where have you been?'

'At a mate's place. And I don't want a hard time from you.'

'From where I stand, you don't get to dictate my mood or what I say to you, Matt. You left me when I needed you, when Tills needed you – and seeing Tills in a hospital bed, unconscious and with tubes coming out of her, and with no-one able to tell me if she would survive or not, has changed me. I am seeing our marriage and our life together in a very stark light, I'm warning you, and I'm in no mood to beat around the bush. I want some answers. Where have you been?'

'Keep your hair on.' He shuffled his feet, and leant uncertainly against the worktop but kept his eyes glued to her.

'I'll ask again, where have you been?'

'Don't you ever believe me? I just told you, I've been at a mate's place.'

'What mate?'

'None of your business.'

'Why did you leave us at the hospital like that?'

'I was pissed, and angry at the sight of you and that smarmy Edward Farrell, all cosied up. What man wouldn't be, seeing his wife behave that way? And I couldn't cope. I got your messages so I knew Tills was okay, but I went on a bit of a bender.'

She narrowed her eyes at him.

235

'I know. I put my hands up. Not very clever, not very brave. But it's the truth. I've never been good with hospitals – just the smell of them makes me want to heave. And I was all churned up.'

'But our daughter – you left our daughter. And you left me to cope on my own. And if you don't like hospitals, you could have just come home. It's not good enough!'

'What can I say? I was angry at seeing you and that American.'

'But there was nothing to see! For heaven's sake, he was just being kind. I told you at the time, we're friends. Anyway, he has nothing to do with any of this.'

'Strikes me there's more to it than that. What am I supposed to think?'

'You're supposed to trust your wife.'

'I'm trying.'

'Look, it's a harmless friendship, nothing else. As I told you in the hospital, Edward is someone I met years ago, an old friend. There's nothing going on but I didn't think you'd understand.'

'You're right about that.'

'I'm sorry, I should have told you. That was a mistake.'

'And France. You knew him before France but you never said?'

'Yes, I knew him before France.'

'So, when we all met up for that weekend away, you – what? Just pretended you didn't know each other? You can see how fucking weird this is!'

'We didn't recognise each other straight away, and there was so much else going on.'

'Likely story.'

'It's true. And I wanted to tell you later, but I didn't think you'd understand. And it didn't really matter because I had no idea Edward would be coming back to England. Besides, you're twisting everything around. This is actually not about me! You walked out on our daughter when she was critically ill, and you haven't been home for two nights. And I still don't know where you've been!'

'It's not always all about you, V.'

'No, it isn't. This isn't about me at all. Tills almost died in that hospital.'

'I'm sure that's an exaggeration.'

'No, actually.'

'Seriously?'

236

'Her heart began to fail. They spent nearly an hour pumping her full of drugs to keep her going.'

'Well, I didn't know that.'

Verity stayed silent, and let the facts sink into her husband's thick, stubborn skull.

'Christ. I can't believe that. Seriously?'

'Yes.'

'I love Tills, you know I do. You know I'll make it up to her – I'll explain. Where is she now?'

'Out with her friend for the day, I told you. She's feeling pretty rough and repentant.'

'Well, you know, in some ways I'm glad to hear that.'

'It still doesn't change the fact that you left her, you left us both, when we really needed you.'

'Is she upset?' He pulled up a chair, sat down, and tapped the ring-pull repeatedly on the table top.

'She hasn't put two and two together – and maybe she never will, she was in such a bad way. She was scared you were going to yell at her too – which I warn you now, won't help anyone.'

Matt took a long drink of beer. He stared at her and Verity met his gaze until he finally looked away.

'Which friend did you stay with?'

'One of the guys from work.'

'Do I know him?'

'I doubt it. Look, what is this – some kind of inquisition?'

'I think I'm entitled to an explanation.'

'Well, you've got one. As much of one as you've given me.'

'I'm finding it very hard to believe you, let alone forgive you. Not much makes me angry, Matt, but I'm pretty bloody furious at you right now.'

He pressed his lips together, and stared hard at the table top.

'What happened to Tills has made me understand, finally, how fragile life is,' Verity went on. 'I see, more clearly than ever now, how I want to live my life. And that's not the way I have been.' Sweat gathered in her armpits, she pushed a strand of hair off her face, and kept her eyes fixed on the top of her husband's bent head. 'I don't want to fight,' she continued, firmly. 'I just want the truth. Are you having an affair?'

Matt's face blanched. 'I am *not* having an affair. Jesus!'

237

'So, tell me how I'm supposed to believe you when you clear off for two days and don't even answer your phone. You have plenty of opportunities; you're always working late these days. And I saw what I saw with my own eyes in the pub – your hand on that woman's knee.'

'This is just such bollocks. I knew you'd give me a hard time as soon as I got through the door.'

'Okay, you explain then. You explain the hand on the knee, and Caro's sister gossiping. You owe me that at least. I haven't seen you for two days and your friends are gossiping. You've completely dug your heels in about us moving to the countryside. You surely can't expect me to pretend everything is all right?'

'Okay, okay, hands up. I'll admit there were a couple of lunches that weren't strictly business, yes. A bit of stupid flirtation maybe – but nothing more, I swear – and all totally light-hearted. Ellie and I bumped into Caro and Penny in a restaurant, a bit the worse for wear after securing a new client. God knows why Penny should deduce anything from that. I dine out with business associates all the time, and I can't help it if they happen to have tits.'

'Ah.' Verity pressed her lips together, and nodded to herself. She stared hard at the table surface.

'Come here,' he mumbled, and stood up and edged around the table, putting his arms clumsily around her before kissing the back of her neck. 'You are silly to get so upset.'

'Don't do that.' She wrenched herself free. 'There's another thing. I went through your papers.'

He looked at her, eyes rounded in surprise. 'You had no right!'

'Oh, I had every right, especially after the past couple of days. We've got loans and all sorts I didn't even know we had, and my name is on everything, it seems. I had no idea. I was unaware of any of it.'

'I'll take care of it. But this snooping is way out of line, V!'

'No, Matt, it isn't. And if you hadn't cleared off with no explanation, I never would have looked. Anyway, I've already taken care of it. I've sent all the papers to Francesca for her to sort out so I can understand what's going on.'

'Already? You've done that already?' he bellowed, and wiped some spittle from the corner of his mouth.

'I couriered the papers to her. She's been doing a lot of extra work for me recently, so she didn't mind. And I need to know where we stand, financially. It's a crucial time for me.'

'You can't do that!'

Charlie staggered off his blanket, and barked furiously.

'Stop!' Verity exclaimed. 'Stop shouting! You're frightening the dog. And I can, actually. My name was on every paper I looked at. It's okay, Charlie.' She stooped and patted the dog.

'Damn you!' Matt pounded the kitchen table with his fist.

Verity took a deep breath to steady her voice. 'I'm sick of living like this, Matt. I'm sick of tiptoeing around and trying to be nice and apologising for the fact I want to live my life the way I want to live it. I'm tired of living in this stupid city where you constantly spend too much money and hide stuff from me. I want more from life than this! Can't you see that?'

'You've really changed. I'm not sure I know you anymore, V.'

'Yes, I have changed, Matt. I've woken up.'

23

Edward stood in his studio apartment, and rubbed the back of his head. He had received a message from Verity informing him that Tills had recovered, and thanking him for his help, and then immediately after that, a second message had appeared like an impulsive afterthought. He sensed desperation in its two short words: 'Meet me?' After their last conversation, when she had accused him of knowing about her husband's rumoured affair, he had assumed it would be a while before she wanted to see him again as she had been so upset. He sighed and flung his cell phone onto the bed before stripping off his running clothes and heading into the shower. As hot water washed over his body, he considered his options. He had returned to England for two reasons: the first was to help his brother, and the second was to tell Verity the truth about his life, once and for all. So far, events had conspired against him making any progress with his confession, but he knew that the time had come. He stepped out of the shower, wrapped a towel around his waist, and messaged her back, agreeing to a meeting.

She was agitated. He could tell by the way she stamped her feet to keep warm. A chill wind whipped curls of hair around her face, and she fidgeted with the strap of her handbag. After greeting each other with a peck on the cheek, they queued at the counter of a crowded café.

'I'm sorry about the other night when I accused you of not being straight with me about Matt. I was tired and I wasn't thinking clearly. I know you would never lie.' She reached for napkins from the counter, automatically taking two and handing him one, a gesture which touched him as he was so used to looking after himself.

'No worries,' he murmured.

They found a tiny table, hemmed in by other tiny tables where diners sat crammed together, talking at the top of their voices.

'I know what you're going to say,' he offered, having registered her troubled frown and inability to look him in the eye.

'You do?'

'Yes, but go ahead.'

He listened respectfully as she quietly expressed her deep shock on realising that Tills had so nearly died, her subsequent reaffirmation of what her family really meant to her, and the indisputably 'grey area' of her relationship with him.

'You don't have to explain.' He touched her hand which rested in a tight fist on the little table. 'I don't want our friendship to become a problem, and you have to put your family first.'

'I do need to explain. I want to be your friend. I will always be your friend but I can't continue to meet you at the moment.' She turned her hand so that her palm was open, and cradled his fingers. 'Don't you see? We kissed...and then that thing happened to Tills. It feels like some kind of punishment. And it's not just that. There are many ways to deceive a person, and I've certainly deceived Matt.'

'Yes. I get that, totally. What a mess.'

'I'm so sorry, so very sorry.'

'There's no need to apologise. Listen, I must be honest too – I came here to say more or less the same thing, although for different reasons. We can't go on like this.'

'You did? You agree?'

'Hey, hey, don't cry.'

The tip of her nose had turned pink, and her eyes reddened. 'Sorry. I'm a wreck today. I don't know what's wrong with me. I think it's all too much. I never intended to do anything wrong but I've made such a pig's ear of everything. I'm going to go away for a couple of weeks when Tills goes back to university, sort my head out.'

'Where will you go?'

'I thought I'd go back to my childhood home on the Isle of Skye. I want to revisit places from my past and try to make some kind of peace with it.'

'You'll go alone?'

'Yes. I need time to think. I'm not exactly great to be around these days, for all sorts of reasons. My assistant Mel is always reprimanding me because I never take a holiday, and it's true – I don't; and Matt, well, Matt is not much interested in my company at the moment, and all things considered, I can't say I blame him.'

'Don't be so hard on yourself. You've had a lot going on.'

She had barely touched the quiche and salad on her plate, and he had lost his appetite too. He felt the urge to get out of the stridently noisy café, and into the open air. She had never promised him anything; he understood why she needed not to see him. What she was saying was basically right and he had intended to say much the same to her, and yet...and yet... Why then, did it feel as if he were being ripped in two?

They agreed to abandon lunch, and left the café. Outside in the biting air, Edward offered her his arm. 'One last walk together, for old times' sake?' he suggested. Hesitantly, she slipped her arm through his, and they set off toward Hyde Park, side by side, in a walk which was an echo of days gone by. He took a deep breath, and looked up at clouds scudding across a wintry sky. In the park, they wandered over the pale grass and between bare trees, meandering aimlessly, both lost in thought. It had always been the same between them, he realised. The time was never right.

'Why does it have to be so hard?' she cried.

'It doesn't. We both have to accept our situation, that's all.'

'I find that so difficult. It's not right. Look, here.' She pulled the piece of ruby corundum from her coat pocket. 'I carry it everywhere. And I carry our friendship here.' She spread a hand over the front of her coat, where her heart lay. 'But I'm not free to see you, in any way. I made a big mistake, misjudging our friendship, and not understanding the impact it would have.'

He was lost for words.

She went on. 'What did you mean, in the hospital the other night, when you said you have "as good a reason as anyone not to be great with hospitals"? It has bothered me ever since.'

He stopped walking, and took a deep breath. Confronted with such a direct question, he knew the time had finally come to speak. 'It's one of the reasons I came back to London,' he began quietly. 'To tell you something I need you to know.'

'Go on.' She looked at him, uncertainty clouding her grey eyes.

'I had a son,' he sighed and paused. 'I had a son. His name was Theo. He lived with his mother, a woman I met travelling many years ago, who came from Sweden. She was another journalist like me, and we had been seeing each other on and off as our work would allow, for a year or two. Sanna didn't discover she was pregnant until after our relationship ended, and she had gone back home to Stockholm to take up a post as a news presenter for a Swedish television company. She went ahead with the pregnancy, and only after Theo was born did she tell me about him when she fell ill for several months and needed my help. From then on, I supported them, and visited regularly. She recovered and married another Swede around two years after Theo was born. She went on to have two more children, and we were both happy to have things turn out that way.

'In May 2006, I was in Sweden, visiting Theo in the village just outside Flen where they all lived, and I was teaching him to ride a bike in the quiet road outside their home. I pushed the bike gently off, and proudly watched my son ride slowly down the quiet road, making his first attempt on a two-wheeler, his hair lifting in the breeze, his little shoulders rigid with concentration as he gripped the handlebars. But then... The bike began to wobble. It was like watching a slow-motion movie. Theo fell sideways, still gripping the bicycle handles, and hitting his head on the tarmac road, knocking himself unconscious. I ran to catch him as soon as I saw the bike tilt, but I was too late, I was too far behind him.'

Edward could not speak for a moment, and shook his head. Verity stopped walking, sensing what he was about to say.

'He was in hospital for less than twenty-four hours. It would have been his seventh birthday, two days after the accident. He would be fourteen now.'

'Oh, Edward.' She took both his hands.

'I want you to understand, to know why I, too, am stepping back from our relationship. Losing Theo is why I won't settle, why I will no longer commit myself. I have many wonderful things in my life for which I am grateful but since losing Theo, I'm afraid. I'm afraid of how easily beautiful things can be destroyed. What happened to Tills the other night felt like a warning sign to me too.

'I don't... I don't normally talk about Theo or the accident at all, but while I was away in Burma this last time, something changed, and I realised I wanted to explain myself to you. I wanted you to know, to understand who I *really* am.'

He struggled, unable to go on. She watched him, her pale face pinched and pink with the cold, her lovely eyes reflecting concern. 'I'm so very sorry,' she said quietly, and circled her arms around his waist, squeezing him to her. 'I had no idea – and to think what I put you through the other night. It must have been like déjà vu for you. I'm really, really sorry.'

'It's okay, you weren't to know, and I volunteered to be there. It was difficult but it was also completely different, and I wanted to help you.'

'But your boy? Your beautiful little boy. Oh, Edward.' She shook her head, speechless.

He found the strength to continue, and clumsily went on. 'Sometimes I'm desperate to put the past behind me, sometimes I never want to let the memory of Theo go. I have to live with my negligence every day.'

'It was an accident!' she cried. 'Life is never just about us. We have to understand that sometimes we are simply a part of another person's story and they have their own destiny, their own path, that we don't get to influence.'

He shook his head, and they walked on in silence for a while. The wind ate into his skin. He barely registered her at his side, as he struggled with a sudden, familiar, surge of dark emotion.

'Theo. And what was he like, your little Theo?' she probed, gently.

He was silent for a moment, unable to find words. And then slowly, a memory returned. 'Oh, he was boisterous and loud, and spoke mostly Swedish, which made things a little difficult for me sometimes. He was learning English though so it was getting easier. He loved dinosaurs and Lego and boats, and fishing for crayfish with traps or for lake fish, using his little rod. When he was very young, his favourite toy was a wooden train with carriages and sections of track he could build into all sorts of designs, and painted wooden buildings that he could use to build imaginary worlds. He loved that train track. We mostly communicated by doing things together – walking in the forest, playing ball in the little park close to his house, taking a boat out on the lake near his village to fish, that type of thing. He was the sweetest kid. Huge chocolate-coloured eyes.' He had to stop.

'I'm sorry. Don't say any more.'

'No, I want to, I need to. He was born on June 1st, 1999 in Stockholm. I wasn't there, as I said. I wish I had been now. Sanna always said she found it hard to believe she was actually having our baby, almost did not believe it until he was born. She was fiercely independent, but then not long after the birth she was quite ill, and realised the child needed his father. Of course, I went to her, although I was quite shocked to learn I had a child, and I stayed and helped to look after Theo for a couple of months with her, until she recovered. I thought perhaps that Sanna and I might start again at that point, but when it came to it, neither of us wanted it. We got on fine as friends but there was nothing more, and those few months finally proved that. Shortly after she recovered, and I moved out and began travelling again for work, she met her future husband.

'She was there when the accident happened; she witnessed it too. She blames herself for not having insisted Theo wear his cycling helmet. I'm ashamed to say I never even thought of a helmet. I was used to kids in the Far East and Africa – no safety equipment there – and a helmet never crossed my mind. I still can't believe I was so ignorant and stupid. And poor Theo paid the price.'

'Edward, you can't say that! It wasn't your fault.' She stopped, put a hand on his chest and looked up at him. 'I'm so sorry you lost Theo, and had to go through that much pain. It was a tragedy but you must not blame yourself.'

'I think of him every day. The anniversaries – his birth, his passing – are still tough but I can think about him now without breaking down, which is an improvement. Make no mistake though, I should have thought, I should have run faster to catch the bike, maybe even jogged beside him instead of standing and watching him.'

'You are being too hard on yourself. We all make mistakes in life – none of us are perfect.'

'Yes, and some mistakes are bigger than others.'

245

'I know, I know. I can see why you think the way you do, and I would probably feel exactly the same way, but it's not right. You couldn't have known what was going to happen. Your intentions were good – to have fun with Theo and teach him to ride a bike. You were being a really good father, and you could not have anticipated whatever it was that made that bike wobble and Theo fall so badly.'

'I should have. I should have seen it coming.'

'But don't you see how easy it is to say that after the event? Hindsight is a wonderful thing. We can all look back at mistakes we made and imagine how we might have done things differently.'

'My *mistake* cost my son his life.'

'Sanna was there too. She didn't see any danger either. She didn't remember the bike helmet either.'

'And she says that not a day goes by when she doesn't feel guilt.'

'So, maybe you both made a mistake. Or maybe the chance of danger was so miniscule that it was not reasonable to predict it. The thing is, you both loved your son and you were both doing the best you could to make a good life for him.'

'But we failed him.'

'No, you didn't! The road failed him. The bike failed him. It was his time, there was nothing you could have done. It could have been a little wobble, rectified just like that. What happened was way beyond your influence.'

'Well, it is kind of you to say it, but that's not how I see it.'

'Oh Edward, I'm so sorry.'

'That's what I wanted to tell you, anyway. I needed you to know.'

She stopped and pulled him towards her again, wrapping her arms around him, and holding him tight so that warmth from her body eventually reached him. 'You are one of the best men I know.' She looked up, and her eyes searched his. 'Allow yourself to heal from losing Theo. You'll never forget him, of course, and nor would you ever want to. But you must believe me when I say, these things are beyond us. That whole chain of events with Theo, not all of them were in your control, by any means. Something much bigger and more powerful than us mere humans was at work there. You have to trust me on this.'

He took a deep breath. Her words were lit with truth but he rejected any option of self-forgiveness. Her eyes appealed to him to

246

see reason. He brushed her hair gently back from her face, and put his arms carefully around her too. 'I will consider what you say,' he began. 'Of all the people I know in the world, you are the person I trust most to be honest with me. But I can't promise that I'll ever change my feelings about this.'

'Fair enough. But lose the harsh words you tell yourself. Begin with that. There's no need for them, honestly.'

'I'll see.'

'Oh Edward. Is this why you keep moving, and have never made a home for yourself?'

'Perhaps, but I was restless long before Theo's accident.'

'Your lifestyle should be a positive choice, not a negative one, driven by loss and sadness.'

'I know.'

'You're not alone with this.'

'Not now, perhaps. I will think on what you have said, if you promise me something too. It's important to me that you understand what I'm trying to tell you. It's not that I don't want to be with you. That evening when we were dancing at Les Chênes, I wanted you too but I had made a vow to keep my distance and not get involved again, especially with someone as precious as you. Losing Theo was the very last straw, and it's much better this way. I want you to know. To understand this. I don't want you to go on through your life thinking I don't care about you because I do, more than any woman I have ever known, despite our circumstances. If you ever need my help, I'm here for you. If you ever fall, I will catch you. But the reason I agreed to meet you today was so that I could tell you about Theo, finally, so you can understand, and never doubt me. I was guilty of not saying anything at Les Chênes or at any time since then, and of perhaps making you feel unattractive and unwanted. Nothing could be further from the truth. You say you are not free to see me, and I accept that, but I also add this: I am not free to see you either. If we had got together the first time we met, perhaps everything might have been different. But we can't turn back time, and whatever either of us feel, it is too late – for both of us – now.'

24

After finally crossing Loch Alsh via the Skye Bridge and negotiating winding island roads, Verity arrived at the holiday cottage where she would stay for two weeks. She stepped out of her car, inhaled the sharp clean air, stretched her stiff body, and was almost blown off her feet by a sudden gust of chilly wind. Darkness had fallen already, and a three-quarter moon in a starry night sky illuminated the cottage where it sat tucked neatly into the rocky hillside on the Sleat peninsula. She took a moment to survey the quiet, monochrome, windswept landscape.

The Isle of Skye, with its rugged hills and wide sweeps of deserted coastline, huge skies and billowing wind had often been recalled by her parents, and not always fondly. Her father had produced many landscape paintings of the Scottish island which had been much admired. He had sold most of them, but Verity had kept two, and her mother still possessed photographs of all the paintings he had produced in this place. She had looked through them with her, before leaving London.

While clearing out clutter in the days before she came away, Verity had found her father's Leica camera, and his *plein air* painting stool and easel in an attic cupboard. She had rescued them years before from her mother's rubbish pile, along with an eccentric clamp which had an old but serviceable umbrella attached, that her father had often used to protect himself from sun or rain when he was painting. Verity was not convinced the umbrella would stand up to the high winds of wintry Scotland but having these cherished objects in the boot of her car was a comfort. Her father's equipment lay nestled alongside her own boxes of paints and brushes, and a number of bare canvases in different sizes were stacked on the back seat. Despite the time of year and inclement weather, she hoped she might produce some *plein air* work of her own during her stay.

When she had told her mother that she was leaving for the Isle of Skye, Fiona had looked astonished.

'At this time of year?' she had queried, her voice riddled with disbelief.

'Yes.'

'You must be mad.'

'That's exactly what Matt said.'

'Are you going alone then?'

'Yes.'

'I see.'

'I've never been anywhere on my own before and I'm almost fifty years old. Doesn't that strike you as odd?'

'Many people would not want to go on a trip alone.'

'I know. But I want to. I think it will be good for me.'

'I see.'

'What did Dad think of Skye?'

'Well, we only lived there for a year or two, when you were a wee bairn, but he hated the midges and the isolation, not to mention the foul winters. More the midges than anything else though – they put him off the place for life. He could never seem to find peace on that island, if I'm frank. But why on earth are you going there? And why now?' Fiona had persisted.

'I want to revisit the places I lived in as a child.'

'But why?'

'I need to get to know myself. I think of all the millions of things my young eyes must have seen that I have forgotten, and I can only think to return to some of the places I have lived, the landscapes I have known. It will help me to understand myself, and to decide what and where I want to paint in future.'

'Well, if it were me, I'd be waiting for the weather to improve. Be sure to pack your woollies and your rain gear.'

The cottage was in fact a wood-clad bungalow with a new slate roof. Inside, it had wooden floors throughout and white-painted walls that gave a stark light to the interior. The accommodation consisted of one large room with a vaulted ceiling, and a tiny kitchen, bedroom and bathroom. Vast glass sliding doors in the main room revealed a view of inky, scudding clouds now swept in over the star-studded sky, the dome of a barren hill in the distance, and further shadowy hills beyond. Verity had expected to feel nervous at the prospect of staying in such a remote place on her own, but in fact she felt surprisingly safe and excited.

The owners of the bungalow were obviously organised. It was sparkling clean, they had left the keys exactly where they had said they would, and on the kitchen worktop was a welcome basket containing a few essential foodstuffs, an information sheet about the cottage, and some brochures about local attractions, shops and restaurants. She put the kettle on, found a teabag, and made herself a mug of tea before turning off the lamp in the main room to see more clearly out of the windows and take in the night-time landscape.

One thing now seemed undeniable, after the past week or two in London – she had to give Matt the benefit of the doubt about the rumours of his so-called affair. He had continued to deny it, and she had eventually conceded, deciding that to take a snippet of tawdry gossip as gospel truth would be a mistake. She had reasoned that most gossips would assume she had been having an affair with Edward when she had not been, and so who was she to accuse her husband who could easily have made the same mistakes, the same errors of judgement. He had repeatedly explained that he only met Ellie as a friend and colleague, and Verity had eventually concluded that she and Matt had both been guilty of overstepping the same invisible boundary in their marriage. Now it was time to stay positive, and get their marriage back on track. They had been overly-polite to each other since their confrontation in the kitchen. Matt had come home straight after work each day, and they had cooked proper meals together in the evenings. It was not going to be easy to move forward but she was certain they would manage somehow, and grow to trust each other again.

Verity finished her mug of tea, switched the light back on, and made herself a couple of slices of toast. The wind howled around the cottage, and she shivered. She went into the bedroom and changed into her pyjamas, pulling on thick socks and a jumper for extra warmth. It was at bedtime each night that she felt Charlie's absence the most. At the beginning of January, the little dog had been sick. He had run out of the kitchen, and she had eventually found him, cowering behind the sofa. He had been shaking, and it had taken Verity a few minutes to coax him out from his hiding place. His little body had felt rigid in her arms. Later that morning at the vet's, and while Verity had stroked her precious and beloved little dog and whispered into his silky ears to reassure him, Charlie had been put to sleep. After leaving the surgery, she had sobbed all the way home, swiping tears from her eyes as she drove. On returning to the empty house, she had hurriedly tidied away his food and water bowl, bundled his lead and little winter jacket into a bag, and tucked them in a cupboard out of sight. That weekend, she had driven out to Stella's and buried Charlie's ashes in a quiet, sunny corner of her garden.

As she cleaned her teeth and got ready for bed in the bungalow, she recalled Charlie's trusting brown eyes, his grey whiskered nose and stocky little body, his loyalty, his love of a walk outdoors or a warm spot beside a fire, and began to sob. She gave up trying to clean her teeth, and blew her nose loudly on a piece of toilet paper. Life could be so hard, and was at best so fragile, that sometimes it terrified her.

In the days after losing Charlie, Verity had worked at Om Interiors, and in the lonely evenings after she and Matt had eaten, she had undertaken a frantic clear out of the Rannoch Road house, beginning with a row of built-in cupboards which lined two walls of Matt's attic bedroom. Even though she had got rid of lots of their possessions to prepare for the house to go on the market, she still had too much clutter stuffed out of sight, and had decided to get rid of all of it, and live free of the junk she had housed for years. In one cupboard, she had come across a stack of unsold canvases, small still lifes which she had painted during the years of her marriage. There were many pictures of flowers in vases, and one larger canvas depicting an empty fireplace, caught in slanting sunlight. On all the canvases, her subject matter was unrelentingly domestic and claustrophobic. They were not what she had ever wanted to paint, and she had felt exasperated just looking at them, and put them all out for the bin men.

After climbing into bed in the bungalow and snuggling under a plump duvet, she fell straight into a deep sleep and slept soundly for an astonishing ten hours – the longest stretch of time she had slept in years. The next morning, she sat up in the bed, sipped tea and stared through rain-streaked windows, realising that her mother had been right, that she was ill-equipped for the cold wet weather, and also that she needed food. After eating toast spread with another little pack of butter and tiny jar of jam from the welcome pack, she headed out, taking one of the main roads. She was keen to get a sense of the island, and to see if she recognised any places, or could spot anywhere she might want to paint. In the town of Portree, she bought a knee-length waterproof coat and trousers, a warm beanie hat and walking boots, and stocked up on provisions at a grocer's shop. On the return journey, the spectacular island landscape was a tonic. The rain had stopped and patches of watery sunlight blotched the landscape, lightening swathes of hillside and sea. Low sunlight added drama, making the atmosphere almost surreal. A double rainbow arced across an entire valley, and snow dusted the mountain tops like icing sugar.

Verity had always been interested in land and seascapes – in particular, places where land gave way to sea, the transition, the meeting point of the elements. The fact that everyone lived "life on the edge" in one way or another had preoccupied her a lot recently. She knew it was a cliché but also recognised deep truth in the observation that life was precarious, and that no matter how much some people liked to believe they were in control, or the orchestrators of their own fate, life was utterly unpredictable. She longed to capture something of this uncertain drama, balance, and fragility through landscape paintings, and to celebrate life's temporal beauty. There were plenty of places on Skye which echoed this human predicament, and so much magnificence too. It was as if the island clung to the edge of the world, and every swerve of the road offered a feast for the eyes.

Verity's phone only worked on the high ground behind the bungalow, and there was no wi-fi, although internet was still available via her phone in certain places on the island. At first, she felt unnervingly cut off from her life in London, and worried in case something happened at work or Tills needed her and could not get through, but there was nothing she could do about it. She had tried to call Matt but he had not answered.

She settled into life at the bungalow, and got the hang of the wood burner, the unpredictable weather, and the shortness of the days. She also learned to keep her hair tied back and her new beanie hat wedged down on her head whenever she went out. She began to understand what had attracted her father and so many other artists to the magical island. At one point, a dramatic hailstorm transformed the landscape, darkening and deepening the colours of the hills and flattening the dove grey loch; and the previous afternoon there had been a deep, salmon-pink sunset which had taken her breath away. Even in winter, there was an abundance of subject matter for painting, right outside the window. It was certainly a place to gather thoughts and restore energy. Knowing him as she did though, she could also appreciate why her father had eventually longed for human company and warmer climes. Unused to long stretches of silence, she too made a decision that she would get out and sit in a café or pub every other day, just to have some human contact.

One morning she got up and dressed warmly, and drove out across the island to a small cove. After parking her car on a grassy verge, she wandered around a little hamlet in search of the stone and slate cottage where they had once lived when she was very young. There was not a soul in sight as the cluster of cottages appeared empty, and there was only the sound of gulls and a bustling wind for company. Her mother had described the cottage as white-painted and beside the shore. Verity had no real memory of it but found a place which matched her mother's description – a solitary house beside a rutted single track, overlooking a bay. She studied the cottage with interest, and took a photo on her phone to show her mother. A vigorous wind careened off the sea, and cold nipped at her ears and fingers as she walked on past the cottage, and down to the shoreline. Apart from a few similar stone cottages tucked into the grassy hillside behind the bay, the location was majestically free of human influence, and about as wild a place as any she had ever visited. She identified the Cuillin Mountains beyond the loch – jagged shapes of purple and grey between flat sea in the foreground and blue cloud-studded sky beyond. The wind filled the air with its rushing sound, and on the hill behind her, a sheep baaed. Verity's mind stilled in the wild landscape. The fact that she had lived here, in this remote place, in her earliest formative years, would certainly explain her constant yearning to be out in nature. Standing on the shoreline, listening to the lapping waves and crying gulls answered some obscure longing, deep within her, one that had niggled away inside her for as long as she could remember. Tears sprang to her eyes. Now she could see that her strong desire to leave the city made absolute sense. It was a desire to return to her roots.

The lack of daylight hours on the island was a big disappointment that she had not anticipated. Working outdoors, direct from nature, would involve a different approach from that which she had always used at Om Interiors, she realised. Rather than being proactive and deciding what she would do each day, as an artist she would have to work with the weather and the light, and work more responsively. It would be a challenge. On the island, occasionally and without warning, a thick fog rolled in, and visibility was reduced to a few feet. Many more hours were lost on a murky day when the clouds hung low and rain drenched the landscape but the compensations were some stunning sunrises and sunsets which completely took her breath away. She began to anticipate the sudden and spectacular displays in the sky, and loaded her father's old Leica with film, in preparation. She headed out before dawn, wrapped up in her new outdoor gear, and found a place to watch the sun rise, with a flask of hot tea and the old camera. She set up her easel and paints at one end of the bungalow's large living space, spread a huge sheet on the floor, and managed to complete one canvas and begin another, painting what she could see through the vast windows. The experience felt like a dress rehearsal for her dream life.

She managed to contact Mel and learned that business was steady and sale items were flying off the shelves of the shop. She spoke with Francesca, who told her she might need to take legal advice over the loans Matt had taken out, which did not bode well. Standing out on a windy hillside, she called Livia and then Tills, and left another message for Matt. He had so far only called her back once while her phone was out of range, and while he obviously could not predict when she would have good reception, his message had only been about how busy and tired he was, and he had not asked about her at all.

She got in touch with a local photographer, and paid him to take her out around the island for half a day to places where the

254

landscape was most dramatic and suitable for painting. Through Martin, the photographer, she discovered a few sheltered spots with appealing views, and subsequently ventured out with her easel and managed to work outdoors for a short period before her fingers became so cold and stiff that she could no longer grip her brush. Martin developed her camera rolls, made large prints of her favourite images, and supplied her with fresh film. She took to sitting and chatting with him in the late afternoons when the sun had set, and the weather was bad, and she felt the need of human company.

Nursing a mug of lapsang souchong tea one particular afternoon in the back room of his tiny shop while he talked to a customer out front, Verity recalled the first time she had tasted the tea, at home with her father. They had been at the cottage in Oxfordshire, just her and him. It was his favourite tea and he had wanted her to try it, had put lots of sugar in to tempt her, and she recalled feeling bewitched by her father's presence and full of love for her parent, but a little afraid too. Something had been wrong between her parents that day. Her mother's absence was unusual, and her father had been especially attentive to her. She had been right to feel unsettled, she could see now, as her father had left them, disappearing to Portugal, the very day after that quiet afternoon spent drinking tea together. Emotion welled in Verity at the force of the memory, and the mug she held cupped in her hand, wobbled as she forced back tears.

'Are you all right?' Martin asked, returning to his messy back room, and slumping in the chair opposite hers, which was also pulled close to the wood burning stove.

'The smell of the tea reminds me of my father.'

'Ah, funny, how smells can do that to us.'

Martin, who was bearded and probably in his sixties, was a man of few words – a fact that Verity appreciated – and as they sat for a few moments longer in silence, her emotion passed. Martin turned the conversation, and told her of another location at the top of the island she might like to visit the following day while the weather forecast remained good.

'With the sun so low, when the skies are clear, you get some beautiful light here,' he remarked wistfully.

255

Later, on the slow drive back down to the bungalow, with the road stretching emptily before her, and the black sky throwing down streaks of silver rain against the windscreen, Verity examined her reaction to the smoky tea, and tried to face up to her uncomfortable memories. That afternoon years before, drinking lapsang souchong with her father, was the first time she had known something was terribly wrong with her parents' marriage. Of course, there had always been rows and disagreements; but that day, something different had been going on. It was nothing her father said, it was the way he had not looked her in the eye when she had innocently asked where they would go on their summer holiday, and the fact he had been looking for things, and putting them in a leather holdall, and when she had asked what he was doing, he said he was tidying up. Her father never tidied up. Looking back on it, that afternoon marked the death of something beyond just her parent's marriage; it had signalled the end of her childhood. No wonder she had felt so emotional at Martin's.

When it came to it, her father had never said goodbye to her. He had left it to her mother to explain his departure. Driving back across Skye, Verity's heart pounded as she recalled this awful lack, and she was astonished to realise that she was still angry about it, almost four decades later. How was it possible to carry resentment for so long? Her father would be in his eighties now, if he were still alive. Her life had moved on, and yet the past still haunted her.

Back at the bungalow, she peeled off her coat, and set about reigniting the wood burner, and as she selected logs for the fire and adjusted the flue, she vowed to try to forgive her father, and leave her past where it belonged. She poured a glass of wine, pulled a chair close to the warmth, and began writing a letter to him, balancing her sketchbook – the only paper she had – on her knee, and scribbling down her feelings and all the things she had ever wanted to say to him. She told him how angry she had been when he left, how hurt, how much she had missed him, her handwriting untidy and punctuation erratic as she poured out her emotions onto the paper. After several pages of outpouring, she wrote more slowly, and the tone of her words gradually changed, as she moved on to say how much she had always admired his work, in some ways and with hindsight could understood his point of view, and finally, with her wrist aching from the effort of writing so much, she

256

confessed that she had never stopped loving him, no matter how indifferent she had pretended to be sometimes. She paused, re-filled her wine glass, ate some wedges of strong cheddar on oatcakes, and put another log on the fire. She had filled pages of her sketchbook with scrawled handwriting, and felt exhausted, but at the same time as if a huge weight had lifted off her shoulders. Crouching beside the fire, she slowly tore out each page, and without reviewing what she had written, opened the wood burner doors and fed each sheet into the fire. She sat back on her heels, and watched as the word-laden pages curled and scorched brown. Flames danced briefly as her outpourings were transformed into sudden flares of light and heat, before turning, finally, into charcoal black ashes. It was an ending, but also a fresh beginning.

Later the same evening, after grabbing a bread roll and heating up a tin of tomato soup to assuage her endless, new-found appetite, she knelt on the rug in front of the wood burner, and studied some photographs she had taken in France, bringing them up on her laptop screen, and examining them, one by one. There were pictures taken after the storm at Les Chênes and during the journey down from the hills – not many, fewer than thirty in total – but precious all the same. She took her time and compared images of the Massif des Maures with photographs of the island landscape that Martin had developed for her, intending to learn something more about the subject matter for her future paintings. Her attention was constantly drawn back to one particular photograph of Edward, his hair blown by the wind, his gaze piercing straight through the camera lens at her. At the sight of him, her chest ached and she felt torn by a huge sense of loss. From a distance, she could see how their friendship had shifted, slowly and inevitably, towards something more intimate. Had they always been in denial about their feelings?

During her second week on the island, Verity grew to love the solitude of the tiny little bungalow on the hillside, and her mind flew free as she painted, not caring whether the final product would have value, only needing to get to know the feel of a brush in her hand again, the touch of it dabbing canvas, charcoal scratching on paper, and pencil rushing over the surface of a sketch book. She rediscovered the way to make paint lie thick on a canvas in order to recreate what she saw and express what her heart knew.

257

Occasionally, she wondered if her father would approve of her ambition, and whether, if he had still been alive, he would offer any advice. She would never know. Sometimes she sensed that he was looking out for her, drawing her eye to the way the sun hung behind a bank of trembling purple cloud, or light bounced harshly off a choppy sea. It was a fanciful notion, born from the spirit of the empty hills, the stillness of her focused mind, and the whisper of her paintbrush flicking repeatedly against a canvas.

One night, she woke up sweltering and terrified after a bad dream where her paintings had hung unsold in an ugly dark space, unvisited by anyone, and looking all wrong. Her daughters had been far away somewhere out of touch, and Matt no longer recognised her, and asked her who she was. She was getting used to the vivid nightmares and burning hot flushes, all symptoms of how much her body was changing, but even so, this one was disconcerting. She lay and listened to the howl of the wind outside the bungalow, clutching the piece of ruby corundum, and reassuring herself that the dreams were not reality. Unable to get back to sleep, she got up, pulled on a sweater, and made herself a hot chocolate, taking it back to bed and opening the curtains to watch the night outside while she sat up with the duvet tucked around her. The wind roared, and rain lashed noisily on the roof and windowpane, reminding her of the storm in France. Eventually, a weak sun crept over the brow of the hill outside the window, and she watched the day's watery sunrise. The light was too flat, too short, and too bleak, she thought grumpily. It was not what she wanted for her work, she knew with a sudden certainty, and the realisation chilled her. While the landscapes of Oxfordshire were five hundred miles south, would they also not give her what she needed, what she craved, as the subject matter for her paintings? If she based herself in Oxfordshire, even with a view to painting all around the British Isles, would she be rushing into something without thinking it through properly? Should she be widening her horizons? She reflected on her father's decisions, so closely allied to her own, all those decades before. If she had learned anything from him, it was that her next move had to be well-researched, and certain to give her what she needed for her work, or else there was no point in it.

She frowned, placing her empty mug on the bedside table before snuggling down under the bedcovers again. As an artist, she wanted to be able to sit outdoors for hours, all day if necessary, time and time again, and she wanted to be warm, not freezing cold. She was searching for a different palette of colours in a landscape too, for fewer of the blues, greys and purples she had found here in Scotland, beautiful though they were. She yearned to use turquoise, orange, lemon and vivid green. She knew that some would argue she had all of these things and more, right outside the window, but for her something was still missing. Something did not feel right. Perhaps it was simply the wrong time of year? Perhaps when summer came she would find what she was looking for – but summer was only one season, and she suspected it would not sustain her, it would not be enough. She sighed. Would she never find what she was looking for?

On a visit to Martin's shop later that same day, a little Jack Russell trotted past the photographer's window, and tears began to run down Verity's cheeks before she had a chance to stop them. She hastily brushed them away. Martin scratched his beard, and then patted her shoulder before offering her a whisky.

'It's none of my business, but you're not having a very good time of it here, are you?'

'I'm sorry, I'm being ridiculous. I lost my dog a couple of weeks back. I mourn for him as if he were human.'

'You're not being ridiculous at all. You've lost a friendly soul from your life. Anyone who ever loved a dog knows that. Look, drink this, and then come and look at these now. Your photographs are good, you know, very good. I don't say it lightly. You have an eye. If you've gained nothing else here on Skye, you can take that compliment on with you.'

By the time that she left the island, the days were starting to draw out a little longer but the wind remained as bitter as ever, and rain and hail storms were a regular feature of life. Verity had bought and painted even more canvases. She had slept soundly, night after night, for the first time in years, and felt thoroughly refreshed as a result. She had survived for two weeks, mostly happily, on her own. She was now ready to return to London, mend her marriage, and plan her future.

25

She sat in her accountant Francesca's small home-office in what used to be an upstairs bedroom, blinking slowly, having had very little sleep, and finding it hard to absorb what the woman was telling her. When asked, she had said she wanted the bad news first, but she had not expected it to be quite so bad.

'As the mortgage is in joint names, you are liable for the default too,' Francesca explained.

'When was it last paid?'

'June. You'll probably still be able to negotiate with them. As for the banks where you have signed guarantees and charges relating to the matrimonial home in order to support loans to your husband's business, my advice would be to take legal advice.'

'I never knew.' Verity shook her head, disbelief trickling through her body like ice-cold water. She folded her arms and hunched her shoulders, a frown etched on her face. 'But surely, this can't be right?'

Francesca, a neat plump young woman, paused and gave Verity a sympathetic smile. 'But you signed the documents.'

'I signed but I never asked. I trusted my husband.'

Francesca looked down at her tidy desk, and straightened her pen. 'And the banks didn't contact you or advise you directly about any of this?'

'No, I never went to a bank. I simply signed the stuff that Matt asked me to sign.'

'You could have a case against the bank, then. You really do need to speak to a solicitor.'

The overheated office, which had a window overlooking several neglected ribbons of suburban lawn, smelt of cheap furniture polish.

'And the good news?' Francesca prompted, sliding the neat pile of Matt's papers to one side.

'Please,' Verity nodded stoically.

'The documentation for Om Interiors is ready. Everything's in order. It's looking good.'

'Well, that is good news,' Verity remarked brusquely. 'But given this new set circumstances, I don't know what to do with Om Interiors now. My situation, it seems, is not at all as I had thought it was.'

She left soon after, and strode down the street as quickly as a sea of commuters walking in the opposite direction would allow. Dense rain flattened her hair, and made her head throb with cold. All these years, Verity had been carefully saving up to make her dream come true, and now it seemed there was no money! No money equalled no dream come true; it was that simple. She squashed down her welling emotion until she reached the sanctuary of her studio where her staff had already left. She picked up a discarded coffee mug and hurled it against the studio wall, letting out a scream of rage, before calming herself and setting about clearing up the mess. Anger made her breath jagged, and she sobbed loudly in the empty space as she crouched over a dustpan and brush. Having cleared up, she sat down at her desk and inhaled deeply. Plenty of people made their dreams come true without a bean in the bank, she told herself firmly – but then, what had she worked for all these years, if not for some kind of security? She was no longer a twenty-something with boundless energy. She needed some basic creature comforts. What, oh what, was she going to do?

Verity had always prided herself on remaining calm when a crisis hit, but this time she struggled to keep her thoughts collected. Back home again, and preparing to confront Matt, she chewed a fingernail as she waited for him to come downstairs to the kitchen to talk. Her head throbbed even though she had knocked back two paracetamol. Fury, frustration and disappointment formed a tight corset around her chest which prevented her from breathing

261

properly. As she opened the discussion with Matt, she somehow managed to bottle up her anger, despair, and the crushing sense of loss, fearing that if she let her emotions loose, she might explode into a thousand tiny pieces.

'Do you know what you have done?' she asked, her voice shaking.

'Of course, I bloody know what I have done,' he snapped back. 'I'm not stupid. I did the only sensible and logical thing, and that was to use my capital to support my business through what is globally acknowledged to be the biggest financial crisis since The Depression.'

'But?'

'You obviously don't understand, so please don't interrupt me. My decisions were the best, given the cards I was dealt. The political climate, the crash of 2008, forced me to make some very difficult choices, and while you have been smugly raking in the profits, thanks to the rich bitches who shop at Om Interiors, the real world, myself included, has faced disaster.' Matt raked his hand through his hair, the cerulean eyes glimmering with defiance. 'And I strongly resent your implication.'

'What implication?'

'That I have been foolish.'

'I haven't said that.'

'No, but you're thinking it. You have disapproval written all over your face. Don't judge me when you know nothing of the real world, and live in a little bubble surrounded by rich women who dream of fucking wallpapers and sofas all day long.'

'For your information, I took measures to respond to the downturn, stocked a host of cheaper goods in the shop to ensure day-to-day turnover, made sure my prices were competitive, and targeted my interior decorating advertising to the wealthy, mainly immigrant and second homes community, who still have money to spend.'

'Oh, what bollocks.'

'It is not bollocks, it's fact – and I can prove it! But it's not me and my business we're discussing here, it's you, so let's stick to the point, shall we? I'm not judging you, I'm bloody livid, and this is why.' Verity shook the list she held in her hand, and with a trembling voice began to read out each financial transaction, as outlined by Francesca. Matt listened and remained defiantly silent, his arms folded across his chest, as he sat facing her across their kitchen table. As she concluded the list, which made clear his extravagance, and looked up at her husband for an explanation, her hand shook. Somehow, hearing herself read it all out loud, made the situation even worse. The loss of money was one thing, but it was not the main thing, she realised. It was the fact her husband did not respect her, did not share his financial difficulties, had not involved her – worse in fact, had tricked her into signing papers knowing full well that she did not know what she was signing. He had borrowed money behind her back using their joint assets, and had so obviously lied about the provenance of the new car, the smart wardrobe, and the meals out, that practically everything they had done in recent years, or everything they "owned", was now tainted by his duplicity and weakness, and not his – or her – success. It made her feel sick.

'It's the deceit that's killing me,' she remarked, quietly.

'Oh, don't be so emotional. It's only money. House prices will rise, everything will be fine.'

'You really have no idea, do you?'

'Well, that's an arrogant assumption, coming from you.'

'What do you mean?'

'You want to chuck everything in and sit on a hillside, dabbing paint on a canvas all day, for fuck's sake. It's all you ever talk about.'

'Well, there's not much likelihood of that happening now, is there?' She stood up suddenly, fearing the emotion inside her might combust if she did not do something, and stumbled out of the claustrophobic kitchen before her stupid husband could say another word. She darted upstairs, roughly pulled off her clothes and changed hurriedly into leggings and a fleece, her breathing ragged and fingers fumbling as she tied up her hair before rushing down the stairs again, and out into the dark, wintry street, barely aware of what she was doing. Her trust in Matt was shattered, and her intention to repair her marriage waivered. How would they recover from this? What should she do now? And why, oh why, when this was not the first time he had almost ruined them, had she not seen this disaster coming?

That night, when she returned, cold and shaking from her run, Matt had taken to his room, the attic door firmly shut in her face. It was probably for the best, because as soon as she stopped running, her body shook and tears ran down her face. No longer trusting him, she did not want him to see her so weak and afraid. She soaked in a warm bath, ducking her head beneath the water before sitting up and taking deep breaths to try to regain some sense of calm and balance. After drying her hair and pulling on her warmest pyjamas, she drank a hot chocolate downstairs and then got into bed and lay there, rigid and unable to sleep as one worry after another shot through her mind like bullets. She finally managed to fall asleep after checking her clock for the last time, just after five a.m..

When she awoke, she noted with dismay that her skin looked blotchy, and the whites of her eyes were threaded with tiny red blood vessels. Her head ached, and she swallowed another painkiller. Matt had already left, she could tell by the deep silence in the house, although for once she had not heard him go. She had guessed he would avoid her. It was what he always did at times of conflict. She knew him well in some ways, at least. She could not face breakfast, and changed into a neat trouser suit, preparing herself, like a robot, to face another day.

Verity sat back in her studio chair, and gazed out at an empty parking space and the brick wall beyond. Realising that all the years she had spent working away in this building, dreaming of a different future, a future where she was happily occupied, doing what she wanted to do, were now wasted years, her profits spent by her foolish husband, made her heart thump erratically and her chest tighten with anger. Why had Matt hidden the debts and told so many lies? Was he really so weak? Did he really not trust her? Or was it simply because he was stubborn, wanting his own way as always, not caring about her at all? Matt was, quite simply, very different from Verity, she realised – too different. He was a man hopelessly addicted to a lifestyle she had no desire to share, where people worked on blindly, earning money and spending money, round and round in an endless, mindless cycle, with no thought about what they were doing with their lives. She rested her hands on her desk and took a deep breath. Her fingers trembled.

She made herself a strong coffee. Design work had begun to come in again, as her clients had recovered from the effort of Christmas, and were suitably restored by their January beach holidays in the Caribbean, heli-skiing experiences in Canada or spa breaks in

Indonesia. Verity's normal cynicism about her clients' privileged lives was held in check by the fact that she needed their custom, especially during this delicate stage of the sale process. It would soon be time to call a meeting to update her staff on developments, an event she had been dreading even though she had worked in the background to make a case for everyone's continued employment. What bothered her most now was how to proceed and what to tell everyone. Should she still sell her business? She could easily back out and continue to work. They would need the money. What should she do?

She sighed and ran her fingers through her hair. What she really wanted to do was take the day off, drive out to the country somewhere and sit on a hill by herself. The phone rang and she dealt with a new enquiry. After that, she took a deep breath and opened her laptop. Think. She needed to think.

By the time she got home that evening, Verity was exhausted and seething. Matt was already home and had taken a shower. His hair was combed back off his face and still damp, and he had changed into his jeans and a casual shirt. His well-manicured feet were bare. Verity was struck by how well he looked. It seemed as if their financial disaster made no difference to him whatsoever.

After she had dropped her bag and coat on the sofa, Matt leant forward to peck her on the cheek. She ducked, avoiding contact with him, and he stepped back and pursed his lips.

'You look tired,' he declared.

'I am.'

'We need to talk, get a few things straightened out.'

'Oh, you think so?'

'Sarcasm doesn't suit you.'

'Losing all my money doesn't suit me.'

'I've had time to think about everything you want.'

'This I must hear.' She massaged her forehead with her fingertips, and made her way to the kitchen.

'Are you all right?'

'No, but go ahead. I'm fascinated to hear what you have to say.'

'Have you eaten?'

'I'm not hungry.'

'I'm going to cook something while we chat.'

'Go ahead, but just cook for you, I don't want anything.'

'Are you sure you're all right? You look pale.'

'Headache.'

'Take a pill.'

'I already did.'

Matt put four lamb chops under the grill, and took out some ready-made tubs of potato salad and coleslaw from a supermarket carrier bag on the kitchen table. Verity watched and listened as her husband began to outline their future, as he saw it. They would stay in London, he declared, as he spooned out the ready-made salads onto two plates. She knew it was best, really, it was the only sensible way. They could take some advice on debt management, and set about recovering some of the losses. Many people were in the same boat after 2008. There was no shame in it. When they retired, they would get a house in the country.

'Won't that be brilliant?' His smile was dazzling.

She could not reply.

It was up to her what she did with her business, of course. Matt could not stop her selling it – although he thought it would be a 'grave error' if she did now, given the circumstances.

'You knew all along, didn't you?' she interrupted. 'Right from the autumn, from long before the autumn in fact, you knew that I would never be able to leave work. You knew but you didn't tell me. You let me carry on hoping, carry on dreaming.'

'I tried to tell you.'

'No, not really. Not at all, in fact. You never gave me a reason. In fact, you hid the truth from me. You hid your loans and your reckless spending habit from me very well – so well that I had no idea at all.' She stood up and began to tidy up after him automatically, dropping the empty salad tubs into the recycling bin and wiping a splodge of mayonnaise off the table top. He either ignored or did not register her accusation, and responded with his back to her, while attending to the chops, reassuring her that he had not spent unnecessarily – it was important to appear successful in order to be successful, to "fake it until you make it" – and he blithely repeated that everything would be all right, especially since she had managed, he did not know how, to retain such a successful business.

He transferred two cooked chops to each plate, rapping the serving tongs onto the china as the meat stuck to the utensil, so that Verity's nerves jarred. He pushed one plate towards her normal place at the table, having seemingly forgotten that she did not want to eat, sat down in his own place, and shovelled a forkful of potato salad into his mouth, chewing and nodding as he went on, elaborating about the life they would have, talking while his mouth was crammed with food. She continued to stand and watch him, her plate of food left untouched. Her husband had everything worked out, it seemed. Everything would carry on as it had for the past twenty years, nothing would change. She poured herself a glass of tap water, and knocked it back before refilling the glass from the kitchen tap. He did not appear to notice that she had not sat down with him, not touched her food.

'Do you still love me?' she interrupted.

Matt exhaled. 'Good grief. What's that got to do with anything?'

'Everything. It has everything to do with our future.'

'Of course I do. But we're past the days of silly romance, V.'

'I see. And you're basically telling me that I must live in the city and not work as an artist.'

'Oh V, it's not so black and white. Of course, you can still paint – we just have to be realistic.'

'And being realistic means I give up my entire sense of vocation because it is somehow "not real"?'

'We all have to make sacrifices.'

'And your sacrifice is what, exactly?'

'I work my guts out every day for us. Don't you think I have dreams too? Difference is I have a grip on mine!'

'If you tell me you love me, I'll do it all.'

'Now you're behaving like a teenager.'

Her fizzing anger abated for one long, eerie moment, and she became strangely calm. Maybe it was simply the painkillers kicking in, or maybe it was something deeper, but a shard of strength rose inside her.

'Paying off the loans will absorb most of the equity in this place, unless some miracle occurs at Windsor Westwood Marketing and you suddenly make a large amount of money, which from everything you've said recently, seems highly unlikely,' she began. 'So, even if I gave up my ambitions, and continued to slave away at my business at great personal unhappiness to myself for the sake of our non-marriage, we still could not afford to live here.'

'That is a gross exaggeration.' He looked down at the birch table, and shook his head.

'No, it isn't. A professional accountant has studied the figures. But the point is really, the *actual* point is: why would I do what you want, Matt, why would I do any of these things – give up my hopes, live in a house I don't like, in a place I don't want to be – for a man who has lied to me, spent all our money – and can't even tell me he loves me?'

'Now hold on, V.'

'No, you hold on, Matt! You know, I wouldn't care about any of it – or at least, I would cope somehow – if I felt you still loved me. I have heard you out, and waited and hoped that you might just say something that I could hold onto. I'm not saying I'd do exactly what you want but I'd learn to forgive, I'd muck in and do my best, work a way through all of this with you – if you'd just give me one nugget of love or affection to hold onto – but you can't do it! You've said nothing to show you care, and really that's because you don't – you don't love me – and without that, without our love for each other, what would be the point, Matt? What *is* the point of any of it?'

'All right, so you – you love me, do you?' Matt fired back.

Her fingers tightened around the glass of water. 'Yes,' she faltered, and nodded fiercely. 'Unbelievably. Despite everything. A part of me still does.'

'Well, how come you never show it then? You show that Edward Farrell more affection in a fucking hospital waiting room than you have shown me for years!'

'That is not true!'

'It bloody well is, and you know it.'

'No, it is not!'

She had to get out, get away before she broke something. She slammed down the glass of water, and stormed up to her bedroom, where she hurled a cushion at the wall. After ripping off her clothes, she turned the shower on full, and stood beneath its pummelling force. Her shoulders shook as she sobbed, and her tears mixed with the shower water. In her mind, she blamed Matt for everything – for his lack of love, his cowardice, his carelessness and his complete lack of any compassion. The way she saw it, she had no choice but to withdraw from the business sale, and keep on working. She was completely and utterly trapped, and her dreams lay in tatters. She hammered the shower cubicle in rage, and let out a massive scream of frustration.

On the morning that Verity finally agreed to meet Caro for lunch, London was experiencing the worst weather of the winter. Fat snowflakes whirled aimlessly over monochrome buildings, dying as they landed on glistening rooftops and damp pavements or forming little mounds of brown slush in hidden corners and gutters. A bitter wind blew from the north east, chilling Verity's shins and turning her feet to blocks of ice.

Inside the café, Caro sat neatly at a table, her face breaking into a concerned smile when she saw Verity approach. Caro stood and briefly embraced her before sitting down again, tucking her smooth hair behind her ears, and frowning. The café was quiet. Old wooden floors absorbed sound, bricks walls were painted soft white, and the lighting gave a gentle yellow glow that was a welcome relief from the hostile outdoors. On the counter top behind glass, an array of earthenware bowls offered appetising vegetarian salads.

'I've never been here before,' Verity enthused, as she wriggled out of her coat. 'It's lovely. Peaceful.'

'How are you? You look frozen through, you poor thing.'

Verity rubbed her hands together, and ordered a warming ginger tea from the waiter who placed a menu in front of her. The two women caught up with each other's news – Verity's trip to Scotland, and Jay's gradual recovery. They ordered their food, and Caro told Verity that, as a result of the improvement in Jay's health, and at Jay's insistence, Edward had returned to Burma. Caro paused after she had delivered this latest piece of news.

'I know you two are old friends,' she began. 'He told me. He likes you very much, Verity.'

'I like him too, but it became awkward – with Matt. I expect he told you that too.'

'Not really, no. He's a very private man. But I knew something had happened, reading between the lines.'

Verity explained to Caro that she and Edward had met many years before. She apologised for not telling her sooner, explaining that she and Edward had discussed it but decided to leave the past where it belonged. She confessed that she had not exactly been honest with Matt either, and related Matt's reaction to the moment in the

269

hospital waiting room when Edward had consoled her, saying how awkward it had been. As she apologised, she also made it clear that her friendship with Edward was just that – a friendship, nothing more. If this was not strictly the truth, Verity chose to keep the more intimate details to herself.

'About that evening at the hospital,' Caro responded cautiously, tracing her finger in circles on the table before sitting back as the waiter placed bowls of Moroccan salad in front of them both. 'Your daughter has recovered, I hear?'

Verity reassured Caro that she had, and began to tuck into her food, spooning the delicious couscous into her mouth, suddenly ravenous.

'I must apologise for my sister's behaviour on that night,' Caro offered, hesitantly.

'Oh, please don't.' Verity reassured, between mouthfuls. 'Matt explained about meeting you both one lunchtime. It was a misunderstanding.'

'Well, perhaps. But my sister is the most terrible gossip. She means no harm but she's forever putting her foot in it. I hope you can excuse that.'

Verity privately had her doubts, but she appreciated Caro's defence of her own sibling, and so nodded a response.

'But the thing is,' Caro began, and something about her tone, made Verity look up from her lunch. It was then she noticed that Caro's plate remained untouched.

'What?' Verity pressed.

'The thing is,' Caro repeated, 'something else has come to light. Very recently. While you were away in Scotland, in fact. And it is something I think you should know. I mean, if it were Jay, I would want to know. And I know you'll probably never want to speak to me again but I like you, Verity. And someone has to tell you.'

When the moment came, it was the smallest thing that actually gave him away. When she confronted him, loud and furious, and for once not holding back at all, Matt's beautiful blue eyes flickered from side to side, calculating rapidly, and then he looked away into the distance. And in that moment, she knew. She knew that what she accused him of was indisputably true. In that split second, she finally saw her marriage for what it was: a sham, a body with no heart, a polished emptiness.

When he finally spoke some moments later, he did not deny the affair. He did not argue against the fact that a colleague had disturbed him and the woman in a hotel room in York during a conference, recently, while Verity was away in the Isle of Skye, or dispute that the colleague might then have gossiped to Jay, who had then reluctantly passed on the information to Caro, who in the light of the sister's gossiping, had chosen to be loyal to her new friend, and brave enough to become the unwanted and unwilling messenger. Matt did not deny that the woman in question was indeed the woman in the black top who had left lipstick and sandwich wrappers in his car. Instead of attempting to deny anything, he twisted his signet ring, and continued to stand silently, staring at the floor, cornered and desperate to work out his next best move, but failing.

'What's good for the goose is good for the gander,' he tried clumsily, the china blue eyes flashing fearfully in her direction.

'Well, it would be, if that were the case,' she retorted hysterically. 'The difference being, of course, that I have never had an affair!' Something inside Verity broke in that moment, and she quietly turned and left the house. The gossip and rumours were true. What an utter fool she was. Struck by the deepest and most absolute feeling of exhaustion she had ever known, halfway down Rannoch Road, her knees turned to jelly, and she leant against a painted garden wall in the quiet street where all the curtains were drawn. Pain tore straight through her. She had never felt so cold or alone, and hugged herself while leaning against the wall, willing herself to breathe, to survive.

26

She received an email (an email!) from Matt, defending what he had done and accusing her of "never paying him any attention" and "not living in the real world". Everybody had affairs, he wrote, and whilst he would honour her request to stay out of the house, it would only be for a night or two, and then he would be back because they needed to talk. Verity deleted the email. She ate a bite of banana, and went out for a run beside the river. Arriving home, sweaty and red-cheeked, she caught sight of herself in a mirror, and realised how dreadful she looked. She made an appointment for later that same morning, got her hair cut and low lights to cover the grey, and on the way home, bought herself a ready-made meal from the local deli which she consumed, suddenly ravenous, mid-afternoon. Blindly, she managed to wade through some work.

The next day, she awoke before dawn, and wandered from room to room in her dressing gown, robotically tidying as she went. She avoided Matt's attic room, refusing to listen to the petty voice in her head which whined at her to go up there, tear his possessions apart and examine them forensically for further clues of his betrayal. What was the point in digging out more information? What new horror might she find? What painful illustration of what she already knew? No, she would not do that to herself. Matt could keep his tacky secret, and rot in it. Hastily pulling on a winter coat over tracksuit bottoms, stuffing a twenty-pound note into her pocket, and leaving her phone and bag behind on the kitchen table, she took off through the streets of Fulham, walking up the long Kings Road and further into the maze of the city, losing track of where she was, and only walking, walking, walking. Eventually, bone-tired, and sensing dusk approaching, she found a tube station, and sat in a rattling underground train which took her back to Hammersmith. Home again, she finally rang Stella, and poured out the jumbled, incoherent story of what had happened.

On the Monday, following an agonising weekend in which Verity had cried, run, tried to eat sensibly but failed, ranted at her empty house, left the television on just for company, and felt more miserable and alone than she had ever felt in her life, she returned to work, relieved to be going back to a routine that she understood, and to people she knew she could trust.

At work, she found Mel, and suggested they take a quiet lunch together. Over a bowl of spaghetti which she hardly touched, she made a proposition which Mel accepted on the spot. In the days that followed, Verity held meetings with Scorer Hardy, her solicitor and her accountant. She asked her staff to stay late for a meeting on the Thursday, and with everyone gathered, she ordered in takeaway pizza and wine, and put forward her revised proposals for the future of her business.

She came home to discover that Matt had been to the house, and collected some of his things. Furiously, she chanced on missing shaving soap, an open cupboard in his bedroom, and socks and underwear gone from his bedside drawer – sights which hurt her so much they made her cry out loud. Removing his personal possessions, small everyday things that were so familiar, to some other place that she did not know, was brutal, and felt horribly final. He had not asked her permission to come into the house, and his sneaky visit felt like an invasion of her private space. She phoned him, and ranted, telling him to keep out of the house and threatening to change the locks. He argued back, urging her to be reasonable, and they eventually agreed to meet in neutral space, at a café, the following Saturday afternoon.

In an attempt to be strong and to cheer herself up, Verity invited Jane Templeman to supper, the evening before she was due to meet Matt. Although she hardly knew Jane, a part of her felt like she had known her forever, and the sight of her reassuring, bulky body at the front door, so colourfully dressed in orange and grey, and her sparkling eyes that reflected so much pleasure simply from looking around, were almost too much for Verity, such was the contrast to her own frame of mind.

'My goodness, what's wrong?' Jane asked with concern, stepping into the house.

A tear rolled down Verity's cheek; she fumbled up her sleeve for a tissue, invited Jane through to her kitchen, poured them each a large glass of wine, and despite all her best intentions, sobbed out the details of Matt's betrayal.

'You must speak with him. The sooner the better,' Jane urged.

'We're supposed to be meeting tomorrow afternoon but I'm not convinced I have the strength yet.'

'You have to focus on *you*. On *your needs*. I'll help you. We'll make a list. Whatever you do, don't give him the pleasure of letting him tell you about his tacky little affair. You don't want to know. Not one detail. Not one sorry explanation. Let him stew in it. You have to go to that meeting with a plan, a list, if needs be.'

'You're very good at this.'

'One of the few benefits of age, my dear. These matters are seen more clearly. You could always get a counsellor or use someone as a mediator later, if that's what you want. This is just the first move, and you must play to your strengths.'

'I don't know. I don't have any strength right now.'

'Well, if you don't feel strong, just act it. It all amounts to the same thing. I'll give you some tips. You'll be going to that meeting looking bright, purposeful and tough, even if your knees are knocking under your skirt.'

Verity laughed.

During supper, Verity barely touched her food while Jane demolished two platefuls. Together they agreed a plan of the best way to approach Matt. Verity had sought the advice of a solicitor earlier that week, and had learned how she stood, and the extent of her involvement in Matt's financial catastrophe. She had hoped that having some solid facts to grasp would help to anchor all her anger and hurt, but in reality, the knowledge she had gained had only confused her further. Verity's trust in Jane had grown, and so she shared the details of the financial chaos with her, along with the solicitor's cautious optimism that, as she had received no advice from the bank involved, she might be absolved from some of the debts.

'He is a bit of a cunning fox, your fella, isn't he?' Jane commiserated.

'I can't believe how naïve I've been.'

'You trusted him.'

'I did.'

'Incredibly common for a wife to trust her husband, I'd say.'

'Yes, but I still feel like a fool.'

'I am so very sorry,' Jane shook her head. 'You must be finding it hard to forgive him.'

'You could say that. And do I have the energy to enter into a legal battle with Matt about it? I'm not sure I do.'

'Not now, perhaps. But if it comes to it, you must fight to protect your interests.'

After they had finished the meal, Jane asked to see the art work that Verity had produced in Scotland. She studied each canvas in silence, occasionally nodding and rubbing her chin, before politely making a couple of small suggestions which, rather than putting Verity off, fired her enthusiasm. She saw right away how she could improve the work – a bit of shading in one place, a light patch elsewhere.

'They are very nearly there. You can be proud. And I think you'll find a market,' Jane encouraged. 'You have such an eye, so much talent.'

The next morning, Verity went back to the hairdresser, and got her hair washed and blow-dried before she was due to meet Matt. She had run first thing, determined to look after herself and stay strong. For the meeting, she wore a new soft grey polo neck and her most flattering jeans with leather ankle boots. She wanted to feel good about herself, and present a bold front. Her wedding ring remained where she had put it the week before – in her jewellery box in the bedroom drawer. Instead she wore her silver bangles, and simple stud earrings. She had her list – the one she had made over supper with Jane – in her bag, outlining her requirements, and the way she intended to proceed.

As soon as Matt sat down opposite her in the busy café, her mind went blank, and her resolve faltered. He was wearing a tracksuit with a hooded top which she did not recognise. It looked new, and was an expensive designer brand. He had not bothered to shave, and the stubble on his chin made him appear younger, more masculine, and fashionable. He grinned at her as if he did not have a care in the world, much less feel any remorse. Grinned! Genuinely smiled, with sparkling eyes! It occurred to Verity that her husband might be happy for the first time in a long while. Appalled and upset by these first impressions, her careful composure abandoned her, and she lashed out at him straight away, accusing him of deception and lies, of hurting her, splitting their family, and behaving in a totally selfish, spineless manner. A couple of heads turned in the café, but the room was huge and noisy, and mercifully anonymous, and her vicious words went mostly unnoticed.

'Did you ever bring her to the house?' Verity heard herself hiss, and then before waiting for an answer, knowing simply from the look in her husband's eyes, she continued rapidly, 'You did, didn't you? Oh Christ. Are you in love with her?'

He was quietly defiant at first, his strength on a par with his apparently exuberant mood. He suggested that she was over-reacting, that men did not stray for no reason and she could not put all the blame for the affair on him. If he had been happy at home, he explained in a reasoning tone which made Verity's pulse throb in her temples, there would have been no cause for him to look elsewhere. He accused her of trying to make him feel guilty, and would not be drawn on whether he had been staying with Ellie since he had left the Fulham house.

'I can't win, can I?' he declared, smoothly. 'If I say I haven't seen her, you won't believe me. If I say I have, no matter what the circumstances, you're going to go ballistic and try to punish me even more.'

'Just tell me the truth!'

'No, I'm not saying anything, not when you're like this, and when I'm still kicked out of my own home.'

She pressed her lips together, exasperated, bereft. 'You have hurt me so much.'

'I haven't done anything *to you* except keep out of your way ever since you asked me to.'

'How can you even say that?'

'You have gall, d'you know that? Before you go accusing me, you need to look at your own behaviour with that seedy American.'

She glared at him, refusing to be drawn, and he at least had the decency to look away. 'I think we both know nothing happened there,' she stated quietly. He remained silent, and sensing her advantage, she remembered her list, and fumbled in her handbag.

'Right. This is what the solicitor says. You might as well know what you're up against.' She began to read, slowly and clearly. She reiterated facts and laws, and Matt's face turned pale. Eventually, as their drinks turned cold, and after some argument during which Matt fervently denied that he had tried to trick her into signing anything, and that she was an idiot with her head in the clouds if she thought for one moment she had a case against the bank, he capitulated and shouted at her to "put the house on the sodding market as she was so hell bent on it", adding that he would agree and not make a bother with the agent, as he was so sick to death of her "harping on". Their marriage, he declared, was "obviously dead in the water". Then he stormed out of the café, leaving Verity speechless, drained, and having to pay for his cup of tea.

As her life fell apart, the rest of the world did not seem to notice. There were small exceptions. Neither Livia nor Tills were surprised to hear the news that their home was to be sold and their parents were separating, but there were tears. The Friday night following the meeting in the café, with Matt fully recovered and again looking abysmally healthy, the four of them sat and ate supper together around the birch table in the spotless kitchen at Rannoch Road. Matt stayed at the house for the entire weekend, like a guest. Verity's nerves rattled, her head throbbed, and she fought back a frequent urge to cry. She and Matt managed to keep to an agreed script for a full two days, and there were no arguments, no mention of Ellie Stansbury or the mountainous debts, just the oft-repeated storyline that neither of them was happy, and both of them wanted to move on. It was utterly exhausting, and after waving good-bye to her daughters on Sunday afternoon, and after Matt had swept out of the house, wearing an expression of grim fury, and carrying yet another bag of his possessions, Verity collapsed alone in an armchair, and wondered how her life had become so broken.

After that weekend, the house went straight on the market. Her spirits lifted a little at this development but Matt became even more bitter, still unprepared to accept his part in the situation, and pointing the finger of blame directly at Verity for everything.

'So, you finally got what you wanted all along,' he accused after another foray to the house, this time with her consent. She blinked,

277

unable to find words to argue or express what she felt, and studied the face of the man she had known and loved for almost quarter of a century, searching his expression for any signs of humility or apology, any faint glimmers of compassion. There were none. As always, the cerulean eyes blazed. His lips, now thinner with age, formed a tight straight line. He obviously still absolved himself of any responsibility, was still adamant that his (presumably ongoing) affair was in some way her fault, and yet at the same time, none of her business.

Her voice shook, as she mustered the energy to reply quietly to his accusation. 'No, Matt. You're wrong. I haven't got what I want,' she asserted. 'What I want, what I have always wanted, is a loving and honest relationship with someone I can trust. And what I want is a sense of purpose in my life, something to help me get out of bed in the mornings. Debt, divorce and deceit were never on my list.' It was a gesture at defiance, a small attempt to stand her ground.

Not long afterwards, she worked her last day at Om Interiors, running a hand over the soft grey paintwork of the door frame after she pulled the studio door closed for the final time. She would be back, of course, but not for a while. She took her staff out for dinner – all of them, including the book keeper, Francesca her accountant, various sub-contractors who made tapestry cushion covers or sewed curtains for her, and the cleaner. It was a strange affair. The Italian food was fantastic, plentiful, and seemingly enjoyed by everyone except Verity, who already felt like an outsider in the small company she had created. Nobody, not even Mel, really understood why she no longer enjoyed what was a glamorous job and a successful business, and while everybody was polite and wished her well, she could see discomfort in eyes that only fleetingly met hers, and the murmured conversations around the long table where a tell-tale glance was shot her way. As everyone gradually left the restaurant, saying they would see her soon and thanking her for the dinner and wishing her luck, Verity realised that she did not care what people thought. As she settled the bill, she felt relief flood over her. She had done it. She had finally broken free of her old role, not in the way that she had expected, but in the only way she could. Now she could begin to re-structure her life. Walking home down the chilly London streets alone, she pulled back her shoulders, raised her chin, and took a series of liberating deep breaths.

Of course, there was lots of interest in the Rannoch Road house, but it was a bittersweet experience. Matt officially moved out and rented a flat. Verity had no idea where he got the money from. On her solicitor's advice, she instigated divorce proceedings straight away to sever herself from his debts as quickly as possible, and send a serious message to the banks who had loaned Matt the money. She filled out the divorce petition, and paid the court fee, swiping a tear from her face as she did so. A perverse part of her still wanted to look out for Matt despite his hideous betrayals and the damage he had caused – she guessed it was entrenched habit, and tried to let the feelings go. Sentiment would get her nowhere, and it was time to take on board her new reality, bit by bit.

She spent the best part of a week clearing out more of the house, retrieving the furniture and bits and pieces she had originally stored when she had first prepared it for sale the previous summer, putting most things up for sale, and re-packing the remainder to return to storage, including her father's painting which she had removed from her studio. In between bouts of organisation, she made sure she went running each morning to keep sane, and kept researching what she would do next. Winter was ending, and blossom and daffodils appeared in parks and gardens around the city, filling her with a sense of hope. One morning, she sat in her local café, at the same table she had chosen six months before when she had been hovering on the brink of depression, and desperate to make changes to her life. So much had changed between then and now. She observed the busy street where a steady flow of people walked past. It was a windy day. Women's and children's hair flew around their heads, and noses and cheeks turned pink. It was still early, and there was something comforting about the routine being played out in the café. Salt and pepper pots were filled. A waitress ran a cloth over the windowsill. Fresh croissants were brought out from the kitchen, and displayed. Cheerful music played quietly. The last time Verity had sat at this table had been just before the weekend in France, before her reunion with Edward, and when she had still been ignorant of her husband's debts and infidelity. Another time, another world.

She tucked a lock of hair behind her ear, and sipped her coffee. She was still dressed in her running gear but had peeled off her fleece, and flung it over the back of her chair. Her cheeks were flushed from exercise. She felt emotionally ragged but, she had to concede, already a little stronger each day. She bit into an almond croissant hungrily, her lost appetite having returned. In her heart, she was no longer that shaky woman of six months previously. Somehow, in the midst of all her troubles, she had found a small reserve of strength she had never known was there.

Over another shared supper, this time at Jane's Notting Hill home, Verity asked her friend for some guidance about her future career.

'She told me to find my heart, and follow it,' Verity reported to Stella later. 'I was expecting her to tell me where to paint, what medium to use, what size canvas to work on, that kind of thing. But all she said was to follow my heart, and everything else will take care of itself.'

'Oh, right, that's very helpful then,' Stella replied, sceptically.

'But the funny thing is, I think I know what she means.'

'You do?'

'Yes, I think I just need to listen to what my heart is telling me.'

'Mm. Right.'

'Oh, Stella, stop it!' Verity laughed.

'You've gone all hippy on me, Vet. You know I can't relate to that stuff. But whatever, if you know what you're doing and it makes you happy, I'm right with you. So, just to be clear, what is your, er, *heart* telling you to do, do you think? Apart from eat fewer doughnuts and get more exercise?'

Verity smiled. 'I'm not telling you,' she teased. 'You'll have to wait and see.'

An offer came through on the house. Verity and Matt rejected it as not good enough; they agreed on that much, at least. The girls came home for a weekend, and Verity helped them to pack up their things into storage boxes. Tills announced that she and three friends had found a student house for the second year at university which they could rent over the summer months too. She planned to find a waitressing job, go travelling with the same friends that summer and write her blog. Verity reassured Tills that she would eventually find somewhere good for both of them to share, a place that Tills could still call home, but of course Tills had not been over-concerned.

'Where *are* you going to go, Mum?' she asked lightly.

'I've a few ideas, but I'm not sure yet. I'll keep you posted, I promise.'

'It will be okay, Mum, really, don't worry,' Livia reassured.

'Dad introduced us to his new girlfriend already,' Tills admitted.

'Did he?' Verity's eyes widened with shock.

'It's okay, Mum. Honestly.' Livia put a hand on her mother's arm, and glared fiercely at her younger sister.

'She wears Ted Baker and her handbag was Mulberry,' Tills enthused, making a face back at Livia. 'Mum is cool about this sort of thing, aren't you Mum?'

'Tills, Mum is not interested in that.'

'It's all right,' Verity intervened, shaking her head. 'Let's be clear. You don't need to walk on eggshells around me. I'd rather we were open and honest with each other.'

'The point is, she's okay,' Livia acknowledged tactfully. 'The girlfriend, I mean. It's all okay. Tills and I, we just want you both to be happy. You knew about Ellie, didn't you?'

'I did, yes. But I'm surprised that Dad has introduced you to her so quickly.'

'We're not kids anymore, Mum. We know these things happen. Half my friends have been through the same or worse,' Tills shrugged. 'I'm just glad there'll be some peace now,' she added, getting up off the bed, and continuing to sort through a huge, tangled pile of clothes.

The potential buyers came back with an offer of the asking price, and as they were cash buyers, the situation was the best that Verity and Matt could have hoped for. Matt's baffling response was to visit Rannoch Road, and to plead with her, and insist they had both made a terrible mistake. He stood in the kitchen, already emptied of decorative jugs and vases, and whose walls were now completely bare, appealing to her to reconsider, and for one moment, despite everything, including the fact that he had admitted he was now living with Ellie, Verity faltered. He begged her, arguing vehemently that it was not too late, that he still wanted them to keep the house, and to try again. Verity reeled, but she noticed that Matt still did not say he wanted her or loved her. He cited their years together and their children but omitted the three small words that might have swayed her. She managed to gather her resolve, and sensing his deep fear of the unknown, suggested they step out into the little back garden. She stared up at the watery blue sky overhead, criss-crossed with the vapour trails of aeroplanes, silent for a moment or two. She knew Matt did not really want to keep the house any more, or stay married to her – he was just afraid of an uncertain future, much like she was. After a while, she managed to reassure him, and they went back inside where he called the agent and accepted the offer. Immediately after the call was made, he left, and Verity felt deep sorrow at the sight of his departing figure.

As she had predicted, the estate agent announced that the buyers were also interested in much of the furniture, and many of the fixtures and fittings in the house – the kitchen table, her bed, the sofas and curtains – all of which had been part of Verity's re-design months before. She was well-prepared, and in fighting spirit managed to negotiate a significant price for the extras. The rest of her personal belongings and the girls' things, she put into storage. When it came down to it, the only possessions she really cared about were several photo albums, some sentimental things her girls had made when they were little – and of course, her art equipment and her collection of paintings, many of them her father's. She wrapped the latter carefully in bubble wrap and brown paper. They were valuable items, and she had chosen the storage facility with this in mind. In a final gesture of care towards her old home, she got a handyman to plane the excess wood from the front door, so that it opened and closed without a squeak.

On her last evening at Rannoch Road, she sat on her bed in her empty bedroom, her suitcase packed. She rang Stella.

'I'm leaving you a load of stuff at Mum's. There's some good bed linen and towels, and lots of kitchen things Mandy might like when she leaves home.'

'*If she ever* leaves home, you mean.'

'Exactly. Livia says she's got everything, and Tills isn't interested, so you can just give anything you don't want to charity as I don't want to clutter up Mum's space indefinitely. I'm spending tomorrow night with Mum.'

'Won't you tell me where you're going now?'

'No. I'll call you when I'm there.'

'Spoilsport. You do know where you're going, I take it?'

'Roughly.'

'You've always been a dark horse.'

Verity laughed, and then just as quickly, began to cry. 'Sorry, I don't know if they're sad tears or happy tears.'

'Probably a bit of both. You'll be fine, Vet, I promise. You're really strong and you've got through worse than this before.'

In the morning, Verity said goodbye to her old home, leaving it part-furnished and sparkling – the brilliant show home she had created. Contracts had been exchanged, and she would return to sign the documents on their completion in a few weeks' time, but she did not want to stay there a moment longer. She would leave her car parked outside her mother's house for the time being, and spend her last night in England there, before heading to the airport the following morning.

When Verity had told her mother about the separation, Fiona had been surprisingly accepting. In the same way that her daughters had not seemed surprised or yet had any dramatic reaction, Fiona had merely raised her head and gazed out of her kitchen window for a long moment before turning and giving her daughter a brief and unexpected hug.

'Well, I'm not really surprised. You'll be fine, dear,' was all she had said.

It had made Verity wonder if she was the only one who had not seen how wrong things had been between herself and Matt. She had not met Matt's parents since the separation but had spoken to them on the phone.

'No reason why you shouldn't both be perfectly happy in your new lives,' Jim Westwood had declared staunchly, but he had omitted to ask Verity what her plans were, or where, or how she would live. She had felt an odd mixture of gratitude and indignation for her parents-in-law's complete absence of curiosity.

As she approached her mother's front door via the familiar chequered tiled path, she heard a little yapping noise and a scuffle. Fiona greeted Verity while just about managing to hold on to a wriggling Jack Russell puppy.

'Mum?'

'Come in, let me close the door so he doesn't run out.'

283

'He's adorable!' Verity bent to pat the excitable puppy who circled around and around, wagging his tale, and trying to lick her hand. 'Is he yours?'

'Yes, I made the mistake of visiting the dog's home to volunteer to walk the dogs, and of course I fell in love with this little chap.'

'How could you not?'

'Indeed.'

'What's his name?'

'Alfie.' At the sound of his own name, the puppy barked, and scarpered off up the hallway. 'I always missed Charlie so much after he'd been to stay. And Alfie here is an excellent little guard dog already. He eats the mail though. I've had to put a cage around the letterbox.'

Verity laughed. Over supper at the small kitchen table, she outlined her plans, and Fiona tilted her head on one side and asked, 'Why are you going so far? It's very sudden.'

'I want to paint. It's a good place to paint.'

'Well, it is that.'

The puppy lay on his back in his new basket, fast asleep, his tummy round with puppy fat. Verity smiled at the sight of such an adorable dog. Knowing that her mother had Alfie made it that bit easier for her to leave. As she turned out the bedside lamp in her mother's back bedroom and snuggled under the heavy eiderdown, she felt jumpy about the flight the next morning, but told herself it was excitement, not fright. She reasoned that in the same way she had somehow learned to become frightened of planes, she could now *unlearn* that fear. Her new life was beginning – and she was going to embrace it.

27

Verity steered the rented Peugeot up the single-track mountain road, driving cautiously with one hand on the wheel while she ate a croissant from the patisserie in the town at the bottom of the hill. There were no other cars on the isolated route, and she relished the sight of the rocky, forested landscape while savouring the fresh buttery pastry. She drove past the remains of the rock fall that she and Edward had clambered over with the Triporteur, the previous autumn. Debris – a mix of broken tarmac, unearthed shrubs, and fallen rock – was still piled at the site. The road itself had been repaired with a defiant, irregular patch of *gravillons*.

In the end, it had not taken Verity long to know where she really wanted to go next. Provence had beckoned her with its seductive promise, and the chance to revisit her childhood home and practice the language she knew so well. Jane had suggested the idea, and had been generous in her support, offering Verity free accommodation while the builders were still on site at Les Chênes. Verity was not sure how long she would stay – she was aware of it being a safe and clichéd choice for an artist – but the truth was, it really suited her as a first step in her new life. She did not feel like a stranger in these hills, and that mattered, in her sensitive and unsettled state. Here, where the Massif des Maures plunged into the Mediterranean Sea, she felt secure.

On arriving a little earlier at the seaside town at the bottom of the hill, the place where she and Edward had reunited with the others after the storm, her spirits had immediately risen. Many places in the town were shut as the tourist season had not yet begun, and it was just as she had remembered it – sleepy, and nestled into a small bay on a craggy coastline. She had stopped at a traffic light, and noticed an out-of-date poster for an art exhibition still stuck on a lamp post from the previous summer, and had taken it as a good omen.

When she pulled up on the gravelled drive in front of Les Chênes, it appeared deserted. She got out and stood for a moment, looking around at green sloping hills resting lazily in the spring sunshine, the weight of the house keys in her hand. She could hardly believe where she was, and what she had done. A breeze danced across the front lawn and swirled around her as she walked around the outside of the house, inspecting it. Great progress had been made. The roof was intact once more. The fallen tree had been cleared away, and all that remained was a recently cut stump and a stack of logs, drying under the repaired veranda.

Inside, the house was still and quiet, and smelled of wet cement. It was still a mess – the piano and all the furniture had been cleared to one side of the big central salon and covered in dust sheets, and bags of cement and pieces of sawn-off timber were strewn on the floor. Verity found it hard to reconcile the building site she saw with the peaceful, romantic space she had first encountered. She navigated between building materials to open the French windows at the far end of the room, and let in some fresh air. The door to the small sitting room which had been so badly damaged was open, and through it, Verity saw that the wrecked ceiling had been cleared away, and scaffolding had been erected in the centre of the space.

There was a note on the kitchen table from the maid who had been keeping an eye on the house for Jane, wishing Verity a happy occupancy, and giving instructions about the hot water and the new internet connection. She had left Verity her phone number and a stem of fragrant citrus flowers from the garden, placed in a small vase on the table. It was a nice welcome.

Verity collected her case, a carrier bag with a few food essentials, and one or two other bits from her car, and set about organising herself. Jane had told her to take the main bedroom upstairs which overlooked the lawn and the hills, as it was spacious and there would be room for her to sleep and work, should she need to, away from the building works. After hanging her few clothes in a

286

wardrobe, and arranging the contents of her wash bag on the bathroom shelf, she went downstairs and made herself a coffee. Taking a pencil and notepad from her handbag, she began a list of things she needed, including a large dust sheet to protect the wooden floor upstairs from her paints, and some washing powder and basic foodstuffs. There was quite a lot to do, and Verity relished the idea of being busy. For all her joy at arriving in this place, she sensed despair lurking too, and wanted to hold it at a distance. She took a call from her solicitor, and agreed a date to complete the sale of the house. Her divorce, which was being dealt with separately, might rumble on for years, the solicitor had warned, as there would be legal proceedings against the bank regarding the loans, and progress on some matters would also depend on Matt. The monies from the house sale would not be available until all matters relating to the divorce had been settled, and Verity had resolved not to let any of it bother her, and to get on with her life. It was a simple enough decision, but she knew that in practice, there would be times when the reality would be frustrating and distressing.

In most respects, London soon began to feel like another world. Each morning, she rose early and ate breakfast on a bench in the garden. Bees buzzed lazily, collecting nectar from flowering shrubs. The builders usually arrived shortly afterwards, and begin sawing and hammering noisily in the small sitting room. The maid, Claudine, occasionally popped by to say hello, and to try to keep down some of the dust from the building work.

In the early days, Verity drove the hire car down to the coast, and passed most of the morning walking – firstly to each end of the short curve of beach which lay beside the local town, and then around the streets, where she often stopped at a little café for an Orangina to quench her thirst, and a pastry which she devoured. Unaccustomed to the gentle warmth of the sun, she often found she became hot and sticky, and bought a couple of cheap T-shirts with 'Côte d'Azur' and 'I Love St Tropez' plastered across the front, and a pair of inexpensive sunglasses.

She had told Matt where she was coming before she had left, out of some vague sense of being sensible and responsible. He had feigned disinterest, waving a hand through the air and instructing her to send him contact details. One morning, standing overlooking the sea, and watching it change colour as some clouds came in, she reflected on her lost marriage. A sense of just how alone she was welled up in her, bringing tears to her eyes. The old anxieties that she had carried with her in London had vanished, but in their place was a sense of devastation that Matt had dismissed her so swiftly, so easily. Had their marriage meant nothing to him? How had he been able to change, like the weather, in an instant? To swap allegiances, just like that? Or had the change been coming for years, and had she simply not seen it? One thing had become strikingly clear in recent weeks – when it came to Matt, she had lost all her power. He no longer cared what she said or did. His attention was gone elsewhere, and it was shocking. For most of her life, he had always been there, for better or for worse, and now he was quite simply gone. There was no-one to share the minutiae of daily life with any more. It was like experiencing a small death.

At Les Chênes, the builders had left for the day, and Verity kicked off her sandals and fell on the bed, her arms and legs spread like a starfish. She dozed for a while, and when she awoke it was dusk so she went down to the kitchen, and made herself a meal of freshly-caught fish, before returning to her room, and crashing out asleep on the bed again. She awoke in the middle of the night, and lay listening to the occasional rustle of the trees, the croaking of a chorus of frogs in the garden, and beyond, the profound silence of the hills.

In the morning, she called Stella, and said, 'Guess where I am?'

'Go on, shock me.'

'South of France.'

'Don't tell me, you're lying in the arms of a man called Pierre or Jacques.'

'No, I wouldn't be calling you if I were in the arms of a Frenchman.'

'He might be asleep, recuperating.'

'Ha! You're so funny. No, I'm sitting outside on a wooden bench with the sun tanning my legs.'

'I'm so jealous. When can I come, and stay?'

'Whenever you want.'

'I'll be taking you up on that.'

'I can't believe I'm here,' Verity murmured. 'What am I doing, Stell?'

'Getting a life – unlike the rest of us.'

Verity chuckled. 'I'll email you and send you some photos, very soon!'

'And I'll come and see you, just as soon as I can get some time off from babysitting and everything here, I promise.'

The weather changed. Unseasonably, it rained, and temperatures plummeted. Verity stayed huddled in bed, feeling exhausted, and fighting back tears which seemed to come at her out of nowhere. After a day of feeling sorry for herself, and embarrassed around the builders, she pulled herself together and took a drive. The Mediterranean swelled and heaved at the shoreline, moodily, like an animal with grey skin pockmarked by rain. She drove on to a big shopping centre just outside Toulon. She did not understand much about technology but needed a new laptop, and made her choice based on price (not the cheapest, but not far off) and colour – a nice shade of blue. With the laptop, she bought a printer, ink cartridges, and packets of photograph and standard A4 paper, recruiting a sales assistant to make sure she got items that were all compatible with each other. The experience was tiring, and on the way back, she stopped at a café, ate comforting onion soup, and treated herself to a crêpe with apricots for desert.

Back at the house, she set up the new laptop on the kitchen table where it was relatively safe from builders' dust, and felt chuffed when she managed to install the software and virus protection, and connect to the house broadband. Having had enough of staring at a screen, she changed into her running gear and took a run up the forestry track and back. As evening fell, she ate a simple baguette stuffed with pungent Roquefort and crunchy endive. It felt as if her life was starting to take some kind of shape.

She had taken photographs of the sea and mountains in the days since her arrival, and her first job was to transfer them to the new laptop, and print some of the images. She intended to use the photographs to practice painting upstairs when the weather was not right for her to paint outdoors, or during the long, lonely evenings. She also wanted to print some photographs from home, and watched as the new printer spat out a picture of Livia and Tills, taken just before they had left Rannoch Road, and one of her old ally, Charlie. Without Verity knowing how it happened, the printer spilled out a picture of Edward, from the autumn before. He was bent over the Triporteur, and sunlight cast shadows on his smiling face. Next came another photograph of him beside the fireplace in the next room, and another taken outside when Verity had set the camera on a ledge with the self-timer. In this last one, they were both laughing and her hair had fallen over part of her face. Verity hastily pressed the cancel button on the printer before it churned out any more. She took the photographs upstairs, and propped the ones of her daughters along the mantelpiece in her bedroom. She fixed others of the Côte d'Azur onto a large cork board she had bought, and left the pictures of Edward beside the bed, anchored under the piece of ruby corundum, not sure what to do with them.

Prompted by the photographs, she sat and composed an email to Edward, asking him how he was, and telling him briefly what had happened since their last meeting. Then she drank the best part of a bottle of the local rosé, and fell into bed.

The next day, it was raining again. Clouds were slung low over the sea but the air was fresh with ozone and scented by thyme that grew wild on the hillside around the house. She decided to return to Toulon for more provisions, determined to get organised and prevent herself from stagnating. The wipers swept rhythmically from side to side across the windscreen of the car, and Verity hummed along to a song playing on the car radio. The rain stopped, and she walked around a harbour, taking photographs of boats, whose rigging clunked as the vessels rocked in the shifting water. Around her, gulls squawked. Verity admired the pale stone architecture and broad streets of Toulon where ironwork balconies adorned rows of tall, elegant windows. On the advice of Jane, she drove on to an artists' supplier in La Valette-du-Var. She needed an easel, and chose a solid wooden one, deeming it a sensible investment. In addition, she selected canvases, brushes, oil paints, a palette and palette knives, paper, bulldog clips and plastic sheeting to supplement the few supplies she had brought from England. A man passed her as she stood deliberating beside a rack displaying tubes of oil paint. The dark stubble on the man's face, and the loose coat that hung cockeyed off his shoulders, reminded Verity of her father. It seemed like a good omen.

In the days that followed, the weather improved and Verity spent many hours outdoors painting. She took long walks through the hillside forest or along empty beaches where damp sand chilled her bare toes, and the sea breeze gave her skin a healthy glow. She revisited the *relais* where she and Edward had lunched after their ordeal, and introduced herself. She liked the owner, Catherine, immediately, and asked her advice about where she might buy a car, as she had extended the lease on the hire car for too long. Catherine had a friend in a nearby village who had one for sale, and offered to take Verity to visit her. Verity was nervous about the purchase, which was part of the reason she had put it off; but bolstered by Catherine's enthusiasm, she felt encouraged, and after a test-drive, agreed to buy the Renault, basing her decision on the non-mechanical observations that the car was clean and well cared for, the engine sounded healthy, and she instinctively trusted Catherine and her friend.

Verity bought Catherine and her husband Didier, a nice bottle of wine from their cellar to thank Catherine for her help, and as the restaurant was very quiet, the three of them sat out on the sheltered terrace in the early evening sunshine, and enjoyed the wine with some chunks of bread and fresh olives. They chatted about life in the village, and the places to go – and to avoid – for food and other provisions. Didier laughed as he told the story of the builder's son coming to collect the Triporteur earlier in the year, and the alarmed expression on the young man's face when he realised what he was expected to drive back up the hill.

Part of the deal with Jane Templeman was that Verity mowed the grass at Les Chênes, and so each week, she filled the lawnmower with fuel, and while the builders laboured on inside, she worked outdoors. In the evenings, she often sat on the veranda step in the sunshine, toasting her new life with a mug of tisane and honey. It was a quiet life, and she often felt lonely. One evening, checking her emails before bed, she saw a message from Edward.

Dear Verity,

I read your email with some surprise and concern for you. I am so sorry things went the way they did as I, of all people, know how devoted you were to your marriage. I hope that you do not suffer, and are finding strength, courage, and some peace.

My news, if you can call it that, is that I have decided to stay in one place for a while. I have been working on the anthropology book I mentioned, and have a publisher who is interested in reading an outline of my proposals.

Jay is in remission again, thankfully, and his prognosis looks good. He talks of early retirement and a place in the sun. Caro is, as ever, supportive.

With my warmest wishes,
Edward

Edward's email struck her as brief, and uncharacteristically formal. She sensed he was keeping his distance, as he had said he would, and in some ways, it was a relief. What Verity needed, more than anything else, was to keep her life simple. It was all she could do to get out of bed some mornings, and what little energy she had, she wanted to save for her work.

After a month in France, she returned to London for an overnight trip to sign the contracts for the house sale, do some necessary banking, and check on her business. What funds were made on the house sale were to be held in the solicitor's bank account, pending an agreement on the division of the equity. The mammoth task of proving that the bank was at fault for not ensuring that Verity knew what she had signed, coupled with Matt's continual objections about every detail, meant the legal process would take time, and Verity would need to rely on her own small income and savings to survive. She stayed with Mel for the night, and slept on the sofa at her flat. The decision she had eventually made was to keep Om Interiors but to make Mel manager. Chatting with her over dinner, Verity learned that the transition was going as well as it could, but she found herself not much interested in the ups and downs of the business; the thought of it exhausted her, and she felt enormous gratitude that Mel was embracing her responsibilities.

She had a hurried coffee with Matt who was obviously eager to be elsewhere, checking his watch twice, and twisting his signet ring, distractedly. He asked her nothing about what she was doing, but repeated several times how busy he was. As she left him, she blinked back tears, shocked that his affection for her had so completely and utterly vanished. Aged nearly fifty, she felt horribly alone, and on the aeroplane back to Nice, she sat with her face turned to the cabin wall, feeling utterly miserable.

Jane made an unexpected visit to Les Chênes, and caught Verity at work painting outside on the wide front lawn, with her hair tied up and wearing her paint-splattered 'I love St Tropez' t-shirt. Verity held one paintbrush in her hand and another between her teeth, as she put the finishing touches to a landscape she had begun that day, at dawn. Jane called out a greeting, appearing unmistakably English in her loose linen shirt, full skirt and sensible flat loafers. She immediately examined Verity's canvas where it sat, propped on an easel.

'I knew you'd do it!' she exclaimed. 'You have talent, my dear! On the basis of this canvas alone, I'm going to introduce you to my friend who's a local gallery owner. I'm also planning on holding an exhibition here at Les Chênes later this summer after the builders have left. I do it every year, and have quite a few contacts who come down here to buy. I'd certainly hang this, and we can take a look at any others you've done. I can think of a few expat friends who might be interested, right away.' Verity smiled, and looked modestly at the emerald grass at her feet, pleased beyond belief. 'But don't let me interrupt you.'

'I was just finishing. Let me get you a drink.'

'Tell me, I'm curious. How are you finding it?' Jane asked, as the two women wandered back towards the house. Verity stalled. 'I'm okay,' she said. 'I take one day at a time.'

'Is it all right here or is the place crawling with builders and noise and dirt?'

'It's fine, and the builders are sweet. The old boy and his son are conscientious, and pretty tidy really.'

'Ah, that's good. I've come to take a look at progress, and sort out some payments. It's much easier for me, knowing you're here, you know. Although they are very good, it doesn't hurt to have someone around, keeping an eye out.'

'What can I get you to drink?' Verity offered, as they reached the house.

'I'm fine, dear, I'll get myself a glass of water. I'm sorry I didn't give notice but I plan to stay a night in the little bedroom. My original plan to return to Nice and stay with an old friend fell through, just an hour ago.'

'Oh, don't worry. The morning light has left and I was about to pack up for lunch. Just let me tidy up my stuff, and then I'll get us some bread and cheese, and we can sit out on the lawn. You can tell me what you've been up to in London.'

While Verity put away her art equipment, Jane rustled about with keys and got the builders to carry out a pair of Adirondack chairs from one of the little sheds in the courtyard, and she fetched seat cushions from a cupboard in the back hall. When Verity joined her outside with a tray of fresh bread, cheese and tomatoes, the chairs had been positioned at the edge of the lawn, facing the spectacular view.

'That landslide,' Verity murmured. 'It disturbs me.'

'Paint it, then.' Jane chuckled.

'It has scarred the landscape quite brutally.'

'The hillside will recover in time, it always does. Now tell me about you.'

Verity relayed details of her progress so far, and Jane nodded, a satisfied expression on her face.

'When all this work is done, like I said, I'm going to have a big party and an exhibition. I'm inviting my local artist friends to hang paintings, and that will include you. It'll be late August time, probably, or very early September, and I expect there will be space for three or four canvases, maybe five. Are you interested?'

'Oh yes!'

'I'm meeting up with some of my friends later, at a little restaurant in the hills. I'd love you to come, and you can start to get to know some people. Would you join us?'

'I'd be delighted.'

Spring rolled into summer, and Verity spent hours each day, working on her paintings. She developed a habit of getting up before sunrise, packing the Renault with her art provisions, a flask of hot tea, a bottle of water, and a baguette stuffed with tomatoes and ham or cheese, and then driving to a vantage point, setting up her easel, and capturing the myriad variations of sunrise – over the sea, in the forest, on the hill tops. Monet had reputedly painted one of his most famous sunrises in forty-five minutes, and Verity set herself the same task. She learned to work quickly out in the fresh air, mindful of weather and changes in light, and to understand the colour mixes that worked, to paint what she saw in front of her eyes, and not what she thought a sunrise 'should' be. There were good days and bad. Some canvases shimmered, others remained lifeless, no matter how hard she tried. In the heat, hot flushes besieged her and she envisaged sweating out all her baggage from the past in a bid to stay positive. From time to time a storm blew in off the sea, and then she would be confined indoors, and would work upstairs in the large bedroom, to the accompaniment of saws and hammers and the builders' radio, painting from photographs, including some from Skye, and even attempting a portrait of herself with her mother and father, from a photograph taken many years before.

Her confidence, while growing, still waivered regularly, and fighting with self-doubt became a habit. No matter how hard she tried to ignore it, her insecurity often cast a shadow over her days. She questioned all the decisions that had brought her to Les Chênes – the fact she had not taken Matt back when he had pleaded with her that last time in the garden at Rannoch Road, the fact she had abandoned her daughters and fled to a foreign country, whether she was going through some mid-life crisis that would pass and leave her feeling foolish and regretful, her selfishness at leaving her mother behind, and so on, and on. As she had nobody to talk to, sometimes in the long evenings, negativity triumphed. There were nights when she went to bed with a tear-stained face, having drunk too much wine, and simply curled up in a ball, hugging herself and sobbing, longing for Matt and their life in London, appalled and unable to comprehend what had gone wrong.

One early summer's morning, as a blistering began its ascent on what promised to be a hot day with clear blue skies, she decided to take a break from work, and drive out to the village of Rians, where she had lived as a child. As she approached the village, set on a hill above farmland, the familiar sight of the ancient church reassured her that she had found the right place, and her spirits soared in recognition. The imposing church of Notre Dame de Nazareth with its row of circular windows, like multiple watching eyes, had gazed down on Verity many a time when she was a girl. The clutter of pale terracotta roofs of the village, a hotchpotch of different planes and angles, echoed the shapes and facets of limestone boulders in the uninhabited landscape. It was no wonder that Cezanne had painted in this region, she thought. There were cubes and triangles, and patches of light and dark, in abundance.

Wandering the quiet, dusty streets of the medieval village, and enjoying the sight of the ochre and lemon painted house walls with their equally colourful shutters and doors, Verity paused and listened as the familiar sound of the church bell struck. The fragrance of warm stone filled the air, and she cast her gaze past the domed crowns of a group of stone pine trees to the façade of the little house where she had once lived with her parents. It still looked the same apart from a satellite dish attached to the stonework.

Something inside Verity shifted as she remembered her past in this tranquil place, her father heading out to paint in the spectacular landscape, shopping with her mother in the village, the strangeness of being the only English girl in school, and the dark and shuttered interior of their home, a home where her mother had rarely been happy. Looking beyond the village to the hills, Verity fancied the spirit of her father was alive and well in the bewitching landscape, even though she knew the idea was fanciful. For a moment, she closed her eyes, and allowed a feeling of peace to wash over her. Seeing this tiny town and these hills again, feeling the sun on her back, as she had so many times as a child, she felt as if the troubles of her past were finally behind her, and she was ready to move on. The process that had begun by writing the letter to her dead father on the Isle of Skye now felt complete. In all his imperfection, Ralph MacLeod had only been human, and had done his best. Sensing that he was here, drifting through this landscape, however whimsical a notion, set Verity free. She need not compare her art with his – they were different people leading different lives at different times. She took a deep breath of fragrant air, and smelt coffee and tobacco from a café a few paces ahead. More signs from her father. Unlikely as it seemed, she sensed that his spirit sent her these things, to let her know all was well.

She bought a new yoga mat, installed a yoga app on her phone, and began to practise at Les Chênes in the evenings. She resumed her regular jogging, enjoying the forest track so much more than the streets of London. She was invited to supper with Catherine and Didier and some of their friends. One of Jane's artist friends invited her to lunch at her home in the hills. It was the start of a social life, and she enjoyed dressing up a bit, and chatting with people. Her painting began to fill her with a strong sense of purpose, and she was pleasantly surprised to find that her new friends took her art seriously, and showed her respect and genuine interest when she explained what she was doing. These small things made her feel more at home than she had for years.

A rainy spell cleared, and the weather slipped into a series of intensely hot days, typical of the Côte d'Azur. Tourists and second-home owners arrived, and brought a buzz to the region. Verity loved the sense of space in her house on the hill, and the sensation of being out in nature every day. She would have dearly loved a dog, but knew it was not practical – yet. The colours of the place, she loved more each day, and the sense of peace, and the freshness in the air. That she had chosen these simple things was proving to be a good decision. It was true that as a woman of almost fifty years of age, she remained largely irrelevant and invisible, even in the South of France, but as time passed she was not sure this was entirely a cause for sadness. It gave her a sense of liberation too. Nobody cared what she did, so she could do whatever she wanted. She could get up at dawn or lie in bed all morning. She left the silver hairs to weave between the darker ones on her head. She bared her limbs, imperfect as they were, to the sun. She read poetry, attempted to read Flaubert in French, chose the music she wanted to listen to, ate the food she wanted to eat. In so many ways, she was freer than she had ever been in her life.

As she had always intended, she finally found the right moment to write a postcard to Caro, bringing to a close the awkwardness and tension after their last lunch together, and inviting Caro to contact her, and to visit if she liked. The summer progressed, the roads and towns became clogged with tourists, and Verity kept to the hills as much as she could. She regularly spoke with Tills who was happy in Bristol having returned from a month's Interrail trip, and was working as a waitress and enjoying a string of music festivals. Livia was taking a two-week trip to Vancouver with Josh. The builders had finished repairing the house, and the exhibition and party were being planned. Verity worked night and day to produce more canvases, so that Jane would have several to choose from. Painting well was not always easy. Often Verity would finish a canvas and know the result was not good enough. At such times, she could understand why her father had been so moody.

She barely noticed her 50th birthday in August. She was so absorbed in her work, and in the new life that she was forging for herself that her "big birthday" seemed irrelevant although it was nice to receive messages from family and friends.

Just before the exhibition at Les Chênes, Fiona, Livia and Tills made a surprise visit to see her, staying in the *relais* in town for a long weekend. Everyone was delighted at the prospect of spending time together. Fiona insisted that they would not intrude on Verity just before her first exhibition, declaring that she remembered what her father had been like at this stage of things, and would not dream of getting in the way. Instead, Verity went to the *relais* for evening meals, and afterwards they walked the beaches or the cool forest tracks in the hills; and while Verity worked during the daytimes, Fiona and her granddaughters went sightseeing.

At the exhibition, Jane hung eight of Verity's paintings, including the portrait of Verity and her parents, insisting that it was good and showed her scope. Verity agreed to this, on the condition that the portrait was marked as 'sold', as she had decided to make it a gift to her mother. With the smell of fresh white paint from the walls still lingering in the vast central salon, Les Chênes played graceful host to the exhibition and party. Furniture was cleared to the side rooms with the exception of the piano, which held a huge vase of flowers and foliage from the garden. Chilled wine and canapes were handed around, and the French windows flung open to the fragrant air. Around thirty of Jane's friends attended, along with Verity's family, and friends and associates of the other artists who exhibited. Five of Verity's paintings sold, and she could barely conceal her delight.

Fiona, Livia and Tills returned to London, having promised they would be back to visit soon. The remnants of the exhibition were tidied away, and the sofas and other pieces of furniture returned to their rightful places. Before Jane left for London again, Verity arranged to stay on at Les Chênes until the following spring, at which point the house would need to be let out to paying visitors for a season to recoup the cost of repairs, and the rent would be beyond her means. In London, the legal proceedings rumbled along slowly but Verity managed to stay detached from the process for most of the time, as it all felt a world away.

Les Chênes was back to normal again, and with her family returned home, and many of the visitors to the region heading north again for the winter, Verity was left alone for much of the time. She continued to work, often reflecting on the modest success of the past six months, and strengthening her determination to persevere.

She was out in the forest, walking and enjoying glimpses between the trees of yellow evening light on an indigo sea, when she heard the motorbike coming up the hill. Curious to know who it was, and aware that she had left the house open, she turned and headed back down the rutted track.

A dusty motorbike stood on the gravel at the front of the house. A helmet and gloves were left on the seat. Verity felt a frisson of anxiety about who was visiting, and what they wanted. She walked quickly onto the lawn and around the corner of the house, and there he was, dressed in old motorbike leathers, his back to her, looking out at the hills. She would know his figure anywhere.

He turned, and smiled, his face ruddy from the sun, his greying hair ruffled and flattened by the discarded helmet. Her shoulders dropped with relief and joy.

'Edward!' she murmured, shaking her head and moving towards him.

Edward opened his arms and engulfed her in a hug, and the smell and texture of old leather and vetiver sent Verity spiralling back through the years.

Inside the house, he peeled off the leather jacket, and accepted a tall glass of water. His pale t-shirt stretched across broad shoulders, and a bicep swelled as he raised the glass to his lips.

'I'm sorry. I'm filthy. I've driven up from Spain.'

'Spain?'

'Yes, long story.'

'I'm so sorry about the way we parted. After everything you had told me.'

'I'm sorry too, about everything that happened to you.'

'Don't be. It's the right thing. Matt and I – in the end, we never had quite enough to make it work, you know? Something vital was missing.'

'You look well. Much better. Relaxed.'

'Yes, I am. It's no more cities for me. I belong living out in nature now. Out here, I feel connected, and I know what I'm doing. I'm painting, at last.'

'That's good.' He nodded. 'Really good. I can see the change in you. There's a new light in your eyes.'

'Really?'

'Yes. You look determined. The old Verity is back.' He chuckled.

'I am. And what about you? We parted with so much unsaid. I think of your little Theo every day, you know, and I often wonder how you are coping.'

'It was good for me, telling you. It closed a page. Talking made it better in some way. I won't ever forget Theo. I carry him with me, and sometimes I still feel the enormous pain of losing him, but I can move forward now. I have to move forward.'

'It's good to hear that; you look well too. So, what else is new? Come and sit outside a while. I'll fetch us some more cold drinks.'

Glasses in hand, the two of them walked through open French doors, down the veranda steps and out onto the lawn where the evening air smelled of grass and earth.

'What have you been doing? Writing a book, you said.'

'I have a publisher who wants me to produce an anthropology book on threatened indigenous peoples. And I've always wanted to write a novel about a nomadic journalist who travels the world telling other peoples' stories. Sounds familiar, right?' He laughed. 'So, I have two projects on the go.'

'That's brilliant!'

'I have options, and plenty to do, but at the same time, I'm changing. I don't feel the urge to be constantly on the move anymore, although I will always travel from time to time.'

'Where will you settle?'

'I don't know, that's why I'm here. I decided to go wherever it feels right, here.' He spread his hand on the centre of his chest.

Verity led them towards the two Adirondack chairs which had stood at the edge of the lawn all summer. Before they sat, he touched her hand.

'Put your drink down, here.' He took her glass, and placed it with his on the low table beside the chairs. His dark eyes met hers, a warm autumn breeze played at their feet, and in the far distance, the sea sparkled. 'You know, it's only ever been you.'

She saw the gentleness and love in his eyes, and an unfamiliar mixture of excitement and deep peace rose inside her. She hesitated though, aware that she was no longer young or impetuous, and feeling naturally cautious. Would a future with Edward, no matter how delightful, compromise the work she loved so much? If she accepted him into her life, would she lose the things she had fought so hard for? She frowned.

'What?' he asked softly.

'When I rise before dawn, and disappear in my car to paint the hills at sunrise, or lose track of time while I'm working and don't come back all day, or fly to London suddenly to be with one of my daughters, how will you react?' She watched carefully for his response.

He looked at her, steadily. 'You must do whatever you want or need to do, and we'll support each other. We'll work it out, one day at a time. I can show you nature and wild places to paint all around the globe, if that's what you want, or we can stay in one place. It won't always be a smooth road with me either, but my heart is yours.' He pulled her gently towards him, smoothed the hair back off her face with tenderness, and bent to brush his soft lips against hers.

'So, how does it end, this novel of yours about the nomadic journalist?' she murmured.

'Ah, time will tell.'

The azure sky grew stripes and splashes of apricot and lemon. The forest canopy on the hillside and the grass at their feet shimmered in shades of emerald green, and a spritely, scented breeze danced around the couple on the lawn.

She was home, at last, for now.

ACKNOWLEDGEMENTS

I'm hugely grateful to the following people who have helped me during the drafting and numerous edits of this novel:

My editor, Lorraine Swoboda, for wielding her red pen with such insight, skill and kindness.

My cover designer, the very talented Jane Dixon-Smith.

Katherine Heath, for her proof-reading and enduring encouragement.

Kathleen Mackenzie for driving me along rough tracks through the Massif des Maures, welcoming me to her Rannoch Road home all those years ago, and being such a loyal and brilliant friend.

Mary Tomlinson for her edit of an early draft and wise guidance

The women on the forum for encouraging my writing over the years, in alphabetical order – Debs, Dell, Denise, Donna, Helen, Janet, Lorraine, Maeve, Nette, Pammie, Ros, Sandra and Shirley, and all those who went before!

And for Alfie, my canine companion, who listens.

A NOTE ON THE AUTHOR

Jenny Loudon is a debut novelist who has worked as an editor, researcher and proof-reader. She read English and American Literature at the University of Kent at Canterbury, and gained a Masters in The Modern Movement. She currently lives with her family near Oxford, England.

www.ingramcontent.com/pod-product-compliance
Lightning Source LLC
Chambersburg PA
CBHW031658170626
46808CB00005B/1507